Don't miss the

MW00938967

Vickie McKeehan

The Pelican Pointe Series
PROMISE COVE
HIDDEN MOON BAY
DANCING TIDES
LIGHTHOUSE REEF
STARLIGHT DUNES
LAST CHANCE HARBOR
SEA GLASS COTTAGE
LAVENDER BEACH
SANDCASTLES UNDER THE CHRISTMAS
MOON
BENEATH WINTER SAND
KEEPING CAPE SUMMER (2018)

The Evil Secrets Trilogy
JUST EVIL Book One
DEEPER EVIL Book Two
ENDING EVIL Book Three
EVIL SECRETS TRILOGY BOXED SET

The Skye Cree Novels
THE BONES OF OTHERS
THE BONES WILL TELL
THE BOX OF BONES
HIS GARDEN OF BONES
TRUTH IN THE BONES
SEA OF BONES (2018)

Beneath Winter Sand

by

VICKIE McKEEHAN

beachdevils
PRESS

beachdevils
PRESS

ISBN-10: 1544244983
ISBN-13: 978-1544244983
Published by Beachdevils Press
Titles Available at Amazon

Cover design by Vanessa Mendozzi
Pelican Pointe map designed by Jess Johnson

You can visit the author at:
www.vickiemckeehan.com
www.facebook.com/VickieMcKeehan
http://vickiemckeehan.wordpress.com/
www.twitter.com/VickieMcKeehan

For my best bud, Wendy, your warm heart
and generous spirit go beyond best friend,
especially knowing I can call you, day or night,
and know, without fail, you'll be
up for our latest adventure.

"Winter must be cold for those with no warm memories."

~ Terry McKay, *An Affair To Remember*

Beneath Winter Sand

by

VICKIE McKEEHAN

beachdevils PRESS

Welcome to Pelican Pointe

To see the complete **Cast of Characters** list go to my website:
www.vickiemckeehan.com
under the **Pelican Pointe Series** tab

Prologue

Twenty years earlier
Turlock, California

The March afternoon had turned warm and golden by the time little Hannah Lambert ran across the playground to make her way home from school. She waved goodbye to a few of her classmates while scrambling to catch up to others like her best friend, Melody Mathis.

Melody lived on the same street as Hannah, in a blue-collar section of the city where hardworking people either labored for someone else or ran their own small businesses to survive. Woodworking shops were prevalent and produced a fair amount of cabinetry used by area homebuilders. Sheet metal shops kicked out truckloads of shipments earmarked for Detroit to be used in the auto industry.

It wasn't unusual for mechanics and locksmiths and factory workers who made up the neighborhoods to buy modest, cookie-cutter homes, have families, mow their lawns on Saturdays, have cookouts and barbecues, go to church Sunday mornings, and by afternoon spend the rest of the day rooting for their favorite sports teams.

Long before Hannah Lambert's family made Turlock their home, the city's dark past consisted mostly of the internment camp set up on the county fairgrounds where thousands of Japanese Americans were detained for the duration of World War II.

Gone were the barbed wire fences and the rows of barracks, replaced by carnival rides and crowds that came to watch monster truck rallies and listen to the Country and Western bands that frequently filled up the arena. The fairgrounds were where eager high school students competed for coveted 4-H scholarships and cherished the blue ribbons they took home. Hannah had even been there once to ride the Ferris wheel last year with her parents.

Hardworking principles went hand in hand with facing hardships. But despite the struggles, the Lamberts did their best to provide fun outings. Like many families in the neighborhood, sometimes Hannah's mom and dad found themselves short of cash before payday. If they ran out of milk or cereal, they might be down to eating peanut butter and crackers for supper. An occasion that could bring out her father's temper. Robert Lambert often railed at the low pay he received. He didn't like the idea of not being able to provide for his wife and kids the way he wanted. When things got tight, he'd often rant that he'd never be caught asking for a handout from the county, no matter how dire the circumstances got. He and his wife, Laura, often had disagreements about his stubbornness on the matter.

But Hannah was used to the squabbles. Generally a happy girl, on this sunny afternoon she chatted up Melody as they took their regular route home, meandering along the sidewalk in front of a string of modest houses with well-tended front yards.

"I got a gold star on my math worksheet today. How about you?"

Melody wrinkled up her nose. "I don't like math. It's my least favorite subject."

Hannah skipped along the footpath, readjusting the weight of the backpack she carried. "I do. I like counting things up. I can count to one hundred now by fives."

"Everybody can do that."

Hannah ignored the dig and went on with her cheery banter. "My mom says I might get a Barbie doll for my birthday."

"It'll probably come from the thrift store, used," Melody pointed out. "That's where mine came from."

Hannah had coveted Melody's secondhand doll for months now and Melody knew it. "I don't care where it comes from as long as I get one. Momma says if I'm good, I might get a new dress, too."

The back and forth continued like that until the girls reached the corner of El Capitan Drive. Melody lived to the right of the stop sign while Hannah lived in the middle of the block to the left.

The first grader knew something bad had happened the minute she stopped skipping and peered down the street toward her house, the one painted a light blue-green with white trim. She spotted a line of police cars in front. To Hannah, it looked as though half the town milled about in the yard or on the sidewalk or stood in the middle of the street.

Melody's eyes grew wide. "What do you suppose happened? Did your dad get loud again?"

"I don't know," Hannah answered, a lump forming in her throat along with the sinking feeling in the pit of her stomach that something was very wrong. She knew her father could sometimes let loose his temper in a bad way. Robert would sometimes drink too much and think he could solve his problems with a fist or a threat. Afterward though, he'd usually settle down to say he was sorry and they'd all move past the big blow-up as if nothing had happened.

But even to a six-year-old this looked way more serious than a simple fight or an argument. Instead of one patrol car sitting in front of her house there were more like a dozen. She stared at the ambulance parked at the curb and the other vehicle, an official-looking station wagon with a county logo on the side.

Since her father worked the night shift at an almond-packing plant operating a front-end loader, Hannah rarely saw him during the daylight hours when she was at school because that's when he caught up on his sleep.

He didn't drink much during the week. She could vouch for that. Her daddy rarely touched a can of beer, especially when he didn't have the cash to splurge on a six-pack.

Hannah stood there, glued to the sidewalk, remembering how her father had looked that very morning—overworked and tired, she'd thought. He'd picked up a few extra hours of overtime for the week and had been late getting home. By the time Hannah darted out the door heading for school, her father was just coming in. Because she'd been in a hurry to get to class, father and daughter had simply passed each other on the porch where he'd grunted a hello and she'd waved a quick goodbye.

But as the little girl stood there on the corner now, remembering the last time she'd seen him, she also knew he had a temper. To deny his outbursts at times when life didn't quite go Robert Lambert's way would be a lie. Maybe that's what had happened this time, thought Hannah, as she left Melody standing on the corner and ran the rest of the way toward the throng of people.

Her backpack weighing heavy by that time, Hannah was out of breath. Her lungs hurt as she pushed and shoved her way through the neighbors who lined the sidewalk. Some were too intent on catching a glimpse of what was happening inside the house to notice the little girl.

When she felt a hand wrap around her arm and pull her to the side, she saw the friendly face of Mrs. Carmichael from across the street. The lady who always let her help bake sugar cookies on Saturday afternoons had been crying.

"What's happening? What's wrong?" Hannah bellowed.

The plump Mrs. Carmichael's hand flew to her mouth. "Oh sweetie, there's been a tragic accident. Your father…your mother…they're gone, honey."

A shiver ran through Hannah. Suddenly she was very cold, cold enough that her shoulders started to shake and tremble. Tears trickled out of her amber eyes and ran down her cheeks. If she listened hard enough to the adults, she could catch horrible words drifting past their lips, words like gunshot, murder, suicide…death…funeral.

It was hard for Hannah to comprehend most of it.

But when Mrs. Carmichael began to cry again, it hit Hannah hard. Six years old or not, she wanted some answers.

Wiping away her own tears, Hannah tried to search Mrs. Carmichael's warm brown eyes for more information. But she had trouble getting the words out. "What about…Micah? What happened to…my baby brother? Is he dead, too?"

"Don't you worry none about the baby," Mrs. Carmichael assured her. "A social worker already swooped in about an hour ago and took little Micah to the hospital to get him checked out just in case."

That sounded reasonable enough to Hannah, especially when another social worker, an older, stern-looking woman with dark hair named Alice, came walking up to take charge of her.

Alice led Hannah to the back of the nearest police cruiser with instructions to stay put. "Don't budge from this spot. You stay here while I go inside and pack up your clothes and personal belongings. You move, you'll be in the way. Understand?"

"Don't forget to bring Mr. Peng," Hannah shouted at Alice's back. "I want Mr. Peng." But the woman never even turned around. With nowhere else to go, Hannah stayed put. It seemed like a long time before Alice came out of the house carrying a well-worn suitcase that had belonged to her mother, and the ragged stuffed penguin Hannah had nicknamed Mr. Peng.

Alice waved the stuffed animal toward Hannah. "I'm assuming this must be yours. It was next to your pillow."

"Yes. Yes. Thank you."

"You're welcome. I need you to understand that your family's gone, Hannah. You won't be coming back here.

At all. Now get out of the police car and come with me."
Alice started walking toward a brown hatchback parked
way down at the other end of the corner. Maybe that's why
Alice was in such a foul mood because with each step, the
social worker kept grumbling about the walk. "I couldn't
park any closer to your house because so many police cars
had already answered the call."

Hannah stopped walking. "Where are you taking me?
I'm not leaving here until I see my mom and dad. I bet
they're just sleeping. I want to stay here."

Alice whirled on the child. "Now you listen to me.
They aren't asleep, they're dead. Stop whining and move
those little feet."

But Hannah didn't hear the rest. Even though words
came out of the woman's mouth they made no sense to
Hannah.

"This old suitcase is the only thing I could find to hold
what few clothes you had, other than a paper grocery sack.
I packed a few changes of clothes for school and your
pajamas and whatever I found on your bed. You can take
everything here with you to the temporary shelter. It
should last you for a couple of days at least." Alice
glanced at her watch. "If I hurry though I should be able to
track down a foster family that will take you in for the
night. That'll have to do for now. It won't be permanent
but at least you'll have a roof over your head for the next
twenty-four to forty-eight hours."

"Where's Micah?" Hannah stubbornly wanted to know.
"Where's my baby brother? Before I go anywhere I want
to see Micah."

But Alice seemed not to hear her. The woman dragged
her every step of the way to that crappy brown hatchback
and stuffed her in the cramped back seat.

It seemed like hours later before the social worker
would even speak to her again. By then, Alice seemed
almost reluctant to answer a single question whenever
Hannah brought up Micah.

Being ignored unsettled the little girl. It caused a fear to creep up her back, an uneasy feeling that something sinister had taken place. The panic gripped her harder, and grew stronger, the further the woman drove away from El Capitan Drive.

Alice took her to an office where Hannah sat in a hallway and was told not to run around. An hour went by, then two. All that time Hannah sat there clutching Mr. Peng next to her chest in a death grip, afraid to move.

It wasn't until her stomach started to rumble—she'd missed her after-school snack of peanut butter, crackers, and milk—that Hannah got truly scared.

But eventually, Alice reappeared from behind closed doors. "You're a lucky girl. You won't have to spend the night in the temporary shelter. It's really a state-subsidized home for children like you. I'm driving you myself up to Modesto to drop you off at the Tollersons. They've agreed to take you for in at least a week."

"Will Micah be there? I want to see Micah!" Hannah pleaded.

"Micah is a baby, Hannah. He requires another kind of care other than the kind you require. You're six years old, a big girl. I'm sure Micah will end up with another family just as good as the Tollersons until we can get this all worked out."

But soon after arriving at the Tollerson house, Hannah's fear turned to something else. Quiet determination took over.

It happened after supper when Hannah realized Alice had come back. And she wasn't alone. The social worker had brought a supervisor. There were rumblings from the adults. These people who'd taken her away from her home didn't seem to have any idea which hospital had checked out six-month-old Micah.

Even after Alice's supervisor barked into the phone a couple of times, the adults seemed even more confused and agitated. They were all wringing their hands and muttering something about baby Micah that Hannah didn't understand.

Since no one would tell her anything about her brother, she assumed he'd died right along with her mom and dad. But an older girl staying with the Tollersons whom she shared a room with, named Tina Montgomery, set her straight. Tina told her that wasn't the case at all. The information gave Hannah hope and a reason to try harder to eavesdrop on the adults. So, whenever she could she tried to overhear their conversations. That grew tiresome after a while, especially when everyone—including Alice and Mrs. Tollerson—talked in a low voice, keeping their discussions muffled and hard to hear. It was impossible for Hannah to make out what the adults were saying.

Over the next few days, Hannah did poorly at her new school. Each time she brought up Micah, she was ignored. No one wanted to talk about her little brother. All her questions went unanswered. Every time she cried she was told to stop. She began to suspect these adults were in trouble for some reason, she just didn't know what it was.

But one night after supper, the answer came from Tina, who was packing up her suitcase to leave the Tollerson home for another more permanent foster family elsewhere.

"You keep asking about your brother, Micah. It's been all over the television—something about a baby going missing. The cops think Micah Lambert was abducted...kidnapped."

"It's not true," Hannah proclaimed. "He's in the hospital, maybe even dead. That's why they won't talk about him or tell me anything."

"You're wrong. They won't tell you because they screwed up. They let this lady take him out of the house and then disappear. They thought she was the social worker. These guys don't ever like admitting they made a mistake, otherwise you'd have reason to sue their asses off. They'd have a big, fat lawsuit on their hands. They don't want that."

Hannah began to cry. And after Tina walked out of her life there was no one to talk to that she could trust. She began to have trouble sleeping. The nightmares came and wouldn't leave for a long time. Whenever she asked about her baby brother someone would always change the subject. The secrecy she felt were lies that kept her angry and made her feel like she needed to do something to find him herself.

A month went by without knowing anything. One day a detective showed up to ask her questions. It soon became clear that law enforcement couldn't locate the "social worker" who'd showed up that chaotic afternoon at the Lambert house and whisked Micah off for his hospital checkup. The police and other authorities seemed embarrassed about relinquishing a baby to a total stranger without having seen proper credentials, a woman who had no affiliation to Child Services at all. And if the people in charge couldn't locate the lady who'd taken the baby, it finally dawned on Hannah that they couldn't very well tell her or anyone else where Micah had ended up.

As the weeks turned into months and the months turned into years, Hannah made a pact with herself. She'd never stop looking until she found her little brother. Not ever.

Because for Hannah, one thing was forever. After that one hideous day, she would never again get to cuddle little Micah in her arms, or put him to bed, or play with him in his crib.

It wasn't enough that she'd lost her parents that awful day. It didn't matter that her father had gone crazy and done something stupid. That was the official story. Robert Lambert had killed his wife and then himself. And afterward, some horrible woman had stolen Micah, taken him in broad daylight while the police watched her drive away. Even a young girl knew that was bold and daring, maybe even desperate. And it didn't make sense.

Hannah's world had turned upside down in a way that could never be fixed. And as Hannah fought the fear she felt over the years, she vowed she wouldn't rest until she found out the reason why. It was the only thing that kept her going through the turmoil.

Micah Lambert was out there somewhere. And she intended to find him or die trying.

One

Present Day
Pelican Pointe, California

New Year's Eve at The Shipwreck brought in the
biggest crowd since its grand opening two weeks earlier.
The pub was elbow to elbow, three deep, at the long
mahogany bar, and people were waiting to place their
orders. From one end to the other, the main room
reverberated with a lively mood that went along with the
loud music. The classic rock mingled with country tunes,
was courtesy of the local band, Blue Skies, who'd been on
stage now going on three hours.

People sat or hovered around the small tables toe-
tapping and listening, or watching the fast and furious
game of darts play out between Zach Dennison and Archer
Gates. Others hung out near the back room, a small area
with two pool tables, looking on while Fischer Robbins
and Cooper Richmond squared off in a not-so-affable
game of cutthroat. Losing a few bucks between friends, it
seemed, was a good way to cap off the old year.

Across the room, Hannah Summers was one of two
waitresses covering the entire bar, and she had her hands
full. The other server was Jill Campbell's little sister,

Geniece Darrow, down from Portland, who'd decided to stay on in town permanently. Both women had been slinging drinks for eight straight hours and didn't have much time to socialize with the customers other than keeping a steady flow of drinks coming.

It wasn't even midnight yet and Hannah's aching dogs were beginning to cry foul. She'd been busy from the minute the doors opened around three and hadn't even sat down for longer than five minutes, let alone taken her mandatory break because of the crowds and the demand.

Three hours ago, she'd formulated a simple strategy to get her to closing. To keep the tips coming in, she plastered a smile on her face, ignoring the pain in her feet, and made the most of the packed house. As long as the drinks flowed, her tips were on a record track to put a huge dent in her expenses and she didn't intend to let them slip away because her feet hurt.

Thank goodness the place had a no smoking policy nowadays. If not, her sinuses would be on fire after hours breathing in the secondhand smoke. She understood the new rule was a departure from what the previous owner had allowed. Some of the customers let her know about the change by grumbling loud and long whenever she got within ten feet of their table, giving her an earful about how much they didn't appreciate the directive.

But the new proprietor, Durke Pedasco, held firm. If people wanted a smoke now, they had to partake in the habit by stepping outside in the alleyway or linger along the front entrance. No exceptions.

That was fine by Hannah. She liked being able to breathe clean air and encouraged Durke to stick to the law, which the other owner had obviously chosen to ignore.

Hannah's eyes scanned the room, looking for anyone who needed a refill. Not for the first time tonight, they landed on Caleb Jennings, sitting at one of the tables with his family. The two had been eyeing each other all night. She in her short black skirt and white blouse, and he, wearing a brown wool pullover and a pair of tight, light-colored jeans that made his ass look firm and hard. No doubt from all that physical labor he did at The Plant Habitat, she mused.

In case he needed another beer, she walked over to where the group sat near the fireplace, huddling around a table. They'd been there for most of the evening, politely ordering, and not once all night had they harped about the new smoking policy. That went a long way in Hannah's book.

"You guys need anything?" she asked.

Landon Jennings called out over the din, "I'll try an order of those wings. They look fantastic, much better than the crap McCready used to serve in here."

"They seem to be very popular tonight. How many? You can get a half order or the full dozen."

"Give me the twelve-piece variety, the hotter the sauce, the better. Add some fries to that. We can all share. I think that should hold us until we ring in the New Year."

"I'll take another beer," Cooper said as he came up with Fischer in tow.

Drea drained her glass. "I'll have more of the chardonnay. That has a lovely flavor and nothing like that house wine Flynn used to serve."

"I'll be sure to mention it to Durke," Hannah said, reaching to pick up Caleb's empty bottle of beer and finding it still half full. She swirled the liquid contents around. "Looks like you've been nursing this one for several hours. It's bound to have gone flat. Want me to bring you another?"

Just to keep her at the table a little longer, Caleb nodded in agreement. "Sure. That'd be great. I think maybe this time I'll try one of the local craft beers."

"Which one?"

Caleb made her go through the list until she got almost to the end. "I'll take that one."

"No problem. While I'm in the kitchen, I'll bring you guys out a fresh order of chips and salsa. By the way, any drinks you order from this moment forward are on the house until after midnight. Thane Delacourt just phoned Durke to let everybody know Isabella went into labor this afternoon."

Fischer held up his phone. "Oh jeez, thank goodness. She was two weeks overdue and Thane's been driving everyone nuts. That man's been on edge every one of those extra fourteen days. I haven't even checked my messages for hours. Maybe I should see what's going on."

Hannah lightly elbowed Fischer in the ribs. "What's going on is simple. Pelican Pointe's population increases by one. The Delacourt family gets a new baby to ring in the New Year. Anyway, Thane wanted to buy everyone a drink. So…"

Caleb could only stare at the waitress. He didn't hear the last part of her spiel. He had to concede this might be the most boring way he'd ever spent New Year's Eve. For most of the evening he'd felt like the biggest third wheel horning in on date night. Sitting with his brother Cooper and Cooper's wife Eastlyn, Caleb could tell the newlyweds weren't out of their honeymoon phase yet. His sister Drea and her boyfriend Tucker Ferguson, were almost as kissy-feely. If that wasn't bad enough, he had to watch Shelby and Landon—his parents and his employers—go at each other like a couple of teenagers who couldn't keep their hands to themselves.

He wouldn't have minded it so much if not for the fact that he was flying solo, had been for months now. He hadn't gone out on a date since he broke up with Kara Bergstrom. The breakup had happened last spring. In his mind, eight months was too long to go without a female.

The only bright spot to this entire night had been the interesting and lovely Hannah Summers. Watching the pretty waitress zip from table to table had been pure pleasure. In fact, watching her do most anything provided him the best entertainment of the evening.

She had long legs that went with her graceful, five-nine height. Her model-good looks came with Rita Hayworth hair that tumbled down to her shoulders. She walked with a seductive saunter that he was convinced could lure men to their fates if she put her mind to it. She had a way of sashaying through the throng, hips swaying, taking drink orders and delivering a brew with a smile and a flirty attitude. But it was those sexy eyes of hers, a wild shade somewhere between amber and bronze, that just sucked him right in every time she looked at him.

He'd first bumped into the auburn-haired beauty in the grocery store. He'd never thought of the produce section at Murphy's Market as a great place to meet women. But that day she'd been filling a bag with cotton candy grapes and testing the fruit's sweetness. She'd looked sexy that day in a pair of little shorts and a cropped top, and every other day since.

To Caleb, they'd exchanged more than pleasantries, more than attraction. There'd been a connection of sorts. Some type of deep, down soul-searing appeal that dug in and wouldn't let him go. He couldn't explain more than that. That's why near checkout he'd asked her out for coffee. It wasn't like a date or anything, but rather a simple "welcome to town" sort of thing among neighbors, a friendly gesture that clearly showed having a cup of coffee together was the first step to appreciating and accepting newcomers.

It had hardly been his best pick-up moment, albeit successful enough.

That day, they'd spent thirty enjoyable minutes drinking lattes before he'd been called into work. Disappointed didn't cover how he'd felt leaving her sitting alone in the booth at the diner. One thing he was sure of—during their brief encounter he'd been able to pick up on—something that didn't quite mesh.

Even though the woman seemed to exude an outward bubbly personality, he got the feeling it masked something else. In that half-hour window, he'd had no problem spotting the guarded demeanor that usually went up around the same time he asked about her past. A simple get-to-know-you approach had a way of putting Hannah on edge. The cautious way she answered questions about herself only intrigued him more. Which made him want to dig deeper into that mystery she wore like a shroud.

When she brought back his beer and the chips and salsa, he forced himself to bite back his interest. It wouldn't do to come off too eager or too aggressive, not with a woman like this.

"They've been keeping you busy tonight," he heard himself say.

"And then some," she said with a polite smile. "The wings will be out soon. Because there's such a huge crowd here tonight, the kitchen's backed up with orders. Kirby has his hands full in there, so you may have to wait longer." She held up the chips and salsa. "These should keep you from starving though. And with Thane's offer, Durke's having trouble keeping up now, too. But I promise to get everything out to you as soon as it's ready."

"Take your time," Caleb called out over the noisy chatter. "We aren't going anywhere anytime soon."

"She likes you," Drea whispered to her brother once Hannah had gone on to the next table.

Caleb rolled his eyes toward his sister. "She has a job that depends on tips which generally equates to friendliness and good service."

"BS," Cooper chimed in. "You've been eyeing that woman all night. There's interest in your eyes, brother."

"In case you haven't noticed, she's nice to look at," Caleb returned, refusing to let Cooper get under his skin tonight. "I'm single and unattached. I can look all I want."

Cooper wrapped an arm around his wife. "Although I'm married I still know a hot body when I see one."

Eastlyn tugged on her hubby's hair. "Just don't go acting on that hot body," she cautioned in a mock warning.

Coop grinned and whispered something suggestive in his wife's ear. But not low enough that Caleb couldn't hear the evocative phrase.

"Jeez, guys," Caleb groaned. "Give me a break, get a room. The sooner the better. That goes for all of you. You're all making me—"

"Jealous?" Drea piped up.

"No. More like sick to my stomach. I'd've been better off staying at home and watching one of the bowl games on TV."

"No, you wouldn't have," Landon chided. "Drea's right. That woman likes you. You'd be crazy not to see it for yourself. You stay home on a night like tonight and you'd miss her checking you out."

"She's not checking me out," Caleb protested. Best not to admit he thought otherwise. And the idea made him almost giddy. He couldn't blame it on the beer as he hadn't had that much alcohol.

As the night wore on, he simply ignored the gentle jibes from his family, waiting out the hour when he could leave and get home to some peace and quiet.

Just before midnight Durke brought out the champagne and started popping corks. Hannah dutifully handed out little plastic flutes, circling the room with a tray laden down with glasses filled with bubbly.

As the clock approached the midnight hour, the countdown began, and with it, Blue Skies tried out several rousing renditions of *Auld Lang Syne*, much to the delight of the crowd. Around the room, the choruses were boisterous as cheery toasts went up, hailing in the New Year with more cocktails, which thrilled Hannah. More booze meant more tips.

After the festivities began to wind down and the last drink had been poured, the throng began to thin out. By the one o'clock curfew there were only a handful of hearty souls left to shove out the door and send on their way. Durke wisely herded them out with instructions to depend on their designated drivers for a safe ride home. But many had already thought ahead. They'd walked there on foot and would get home the same way, under their own power.

Durke turned the lock on the door and leaned back, letting out a loud sigh. "What a night. I thought closing time would never get here."

Along with Geniece, Hannah dutifully began to bus tables, collecting the empties and clearing away glasses, piling her tray to the brim to cut down on trips back and forth to the kitchen.

Hannah unloaded everything on the pass-through ledge leading into the kitchen near the bar sink. She turned to watch Durke near the cash register as he began counting out the day's take.

"Did you think it'd be this busy tonight?" she asked as she tossed paper napkins and other trash into the garbage bin.

"Nobody warned me, that's for sure. For such a small town, they showed up in hordes."

"Lucky you, lucky me. I must've made close to four hundred in tips tonight."

"Same here," Geniece piped up with a grin. "A day at the spa, here I come."

Hannah sighed in ecstasy. "A spa sounds great. But right now, all I want is to get off my feet. That means tallying up what I owe to the house and get out of here. If my math is correct, that's forty bucks to the house."

A tired Durke smiled. "You girls keep that. Both of you worked your tails off for it tonight. Besides, I decided when I bought this place that my waitresses wouldn't have to pony up a share of their tips. Manning the bar allows people to leave me a few extra bucks in the tip jar. That's enough for me."

Hannah grinned back at the affable boss. "And a break from the norm that I could learn to love. Although I don't much care for the little short skirts you make us wear."

"Thank the short skirt for the wad of cash in your hand," Durke pointed out. "The fish net stockings are almost as effective."

Hannah didn't want to get into a snit about the uncomfortable high heels that went with the nylons. "No doubt that's probably true, but I'm too tired to debate the issue. Thanks for letting me keep it all. You're a good soul, Durke. I'm happy to work for you any time you need me."

"You were a lifesaver, Hannah. Thanks for filling in for Darla. I know you weren't scheduled tonight. I appreciate you dropping whatever you had planned and coming in here like you did at the last minute."

"Not a problem. My plan was to heat up a frozen entrée in my little microwave and watch reruns of *Frasier* until I fell asleep."

Geniece shook her head. "That is just sad, girl. I wanted to kick up my heels tonight and got stuck here instead."

Hannah tried to remember the last time she'd "kicked up her heels" and couldn't. "Doesn't matter to me. You let me know whenever Darla calls in with a sick baby. I can usually sub on any given night." She held up her wad of cash before pocketing the roll. "And I can always use the money. Any time you need an extra pair of hands around here, give me a call. Want me to stay and help you clean up?"

"Nah, I've got this. You girls get out of here. Go."

Hannah didn't have to be told twice. But she did stop in mid-stride on her way to retrieve her jacket. "Did you get an update from Thane yet? About the baby…?"

"Sure did. The new doc delivered a baby boy a few minutes after midnight."

"They pick out a name yet?"

Durke scratched the side of his face where a stubble grew dark. "Jace, I think. It seems they had to scramble for a name because they were expecting it to be a girl. You go on home now, Hannah. Get off your feet."

"Will do." She didn't hang around to argue but grabbed her jacket off the peg and headed out the back door.

Stepping out into the dark parking lot, she heard firecrackers going off in the distance. She stopped to watch a few red, white, and blue Roman candles spear the night sky and sail out over Smuggler's Bay in a blast of light and cheer.

She exhaled into the chilly night air. While others might be willing to stay up and party longer, Hannah was ready to crawl into bed. But she still had to walk several blocks to the little guest cottage she'd rented, a bite-sized bungalow next door to the Bennett Animal Clinic at the corner of Tradewinds and Crescent.

On her way to reach Ocean Street, she lifted her head to the night sky and breathed in the salty sea air. After being cooped up inside all day with so much stale air and raucous noise, she briefly closed her eyes to suck in the peace and quiet—and bumped squarely into a male chest. It knocked her back a step.

"Caleb Jennings, I thought you'd be home by now."

"It's such a pretty night. How about a walk along the pier? We could watch Tandy Gilliam's personal fireworks display, such as it is. He takes to the water every year about now in his twenty-two-footer and rings in the New Year, lighting up the night sky in his own way."

"As great as that sounds, any other time…maybe. But I'm beat. I think my feet have swollen to twice their normal size after my shoes pinched my toes all evening. I'll be lucky if I can get these heels to slip off."

Caleb grinned. "Then I should at least give you a ride home."

"Thanks. But there's no need. I can use the walk."

"At least let me join you and protect you from our infamous ghost." He lowered his voice, making it sound scary and menacing. "The entity that haunts the alleyways and lurks around dark corners here at night. We have to protect the womenfolk from his…"

Hannah cracked up with laughter. "Word is that Scott Phillips is a lot of things. Malevolent isn't one of them. Besides, he doesn't scare me none." Although he had scared her the first time she'd witnessed his disappearing act. But she wasn't going to bring that up to Caleb. After all, she was a pro at putting up a brave front. "I've had to deal with all manner of ghosts long before I ever arrived in town."

Caleb stuck his hands in his pockets as they began to walk in step down the street. "Now see, that kind of statement just intrigues me more. Even if some of us deal with our own set of ghosts from the past it makes me wonder what yours are like."

"Ghosts in this little place? As in plural? Hmm. That's surprising since I've only heard of the one. But I'll take your word for it. You sound so ominous though. Might as well explain what you mean."

"Happy to. Over dinner."

She smiled again. "There's always a catch, huh? I like your idyllic little town. It has charm and the natives seem friendly enough. You've lived here all your life, I bet."

"Yep. I was born in the hospital over in San Sebastian, the next town over. I've been here ever since, except for the time I went away to college."

"That sounds so wonderful to grow up along the coast."

Was it wonderful? Caleb asked himself. Parts of those early years certainly couldn't be described as easy or perfect. Nothing about them was. Or so he'd been told by his older siblings. Maybe it was the nostalgia of a new year that brought an image of his dad into his head. He forced himself to conjure up Layne Richmond from pictures he'd seen. It frustrated him that he couldn't bring anything real to mind. Putting old photographs to memory wasn't the same thing. He'd last laid eyes on his father as a four-year-old. And most everyone agreed that such a young age rarely provided a true recollection of anything. It made him sad to think he couldn't capture a single real thing about when his dad had been alive. Brief as the wistfulness lingered, it stuck long enough to make him sigh.

"Where'd you go just now?" Hannah asked. "You spaced out for a minute."

"I guess I did. Sorry. My mind drifted back to a few of those ghosts. There's no such thing as an idyllic place or life…not anywhere. You'd be setting yourself up for a major letdown to think that way about here. If you're looking for perfect, that is."

She tilted her head to see his eyes. "Are you a little sad tonight, Caleb?"

"Maybe I am. New Year and all. I'm glad you like our little town. You've been here a whole three months, long enough to form some sort of opinion about the natives?"

"My initial reaction was positive since I found work here right away. Plus, I managed to locate a reasonably priced, fully furnished rental. How rare is that? It's tiny though, but it works for me. You don't really have to walk me home, you know."

It didn't escape Caleb how she'd neatly changed the subject, without saying too much. "Sure I do. It's a rule around here. You aren't allowed to let a pretty woman walk home at night by herself."

Hannah bumped his shoulder. "Such a gentleman. I'm not sure I've had the fortune to come across many."

"Maybe that's what sets us apart from the big city."

"I wouldn't exactly say San Mateo counts as the big city. But I get your point."

"You grew up in San Mateo. That's what? A hundred thousand people maybe. That's a thriving metropolis compared to here."

She studied him like a scientist might study an alien life form, a certain degree of skepticism on her face. "So…you remembered where I'm from. Are you usually this curious about all newcomers?"

"Not a big deal really. San Mateo isn't exactly the moon. And there's not much to talk about in a small town, except maybe the new person."

She stifled a laugh. "Somehow, it's hard to picture you hanging over the fence, gossiping with the old ladies about me."

"You? No way. But I often help those same little old ladies pick out their spring tulips. In exchange for the best growing tips, they always let me in on the juiciest buzz coming out of the rumor mill. You're a helluva lot more interesting than who's been coloring their hair purple. Or who bought two cases of booze at Murphy's Market. Right now, you'll be glad to know you bumped off Nellie Simpkins from the top spot after she took up smokeless tobacco again. Shame on her."

"Yuck. Smokeless tobacco. Not exactly me."

"I thought not. No, for you the rumor mill's been on overdrive about what brought you south. The smart money says you went through a disastrous breakup and you're looking for a fresh start. I'm not buying that one."

"Why not? That sounds downright fascinating, almost Hollywood-like."

"Because you have a determined look on your face that says, 'I'm on a mission.' I'd recognize that resolute attitude anywhere."

"You're mistaking that for tired feet." An awkward silence descended while she chewed her lip and wondered how he so easily saw through her hard-fought demeanor.

Sensing that he'd hit on a touchy subject, he backed off and went another way. "As a newcomer, I doubt you know the full backstory about Tandy Gilliam's love of fireworks. Some years back, that boy was banned from doing his celebratory display on shore after he burned down Ruthie May Porter's tool shed."

This time Hannah cracked up. Her laugh came from the gut and roared its way out like a freight train. "You made that up."

"No, ma'am. Tandy is Ruthie May's next door neighbor, has been for years. Brent banned him from lighting so much as a firecracker on land. He figured out the only way Tandy could be trusted with fireworks is to have as much water around him as possible. So, the chief of police relegated Tandy to his boat. Now, every Fourth of July, every New Year's Eve, every Christmas morning, Tandy stocks his little sloop with enough Roman candles to last about an hour and sets off his own fireworks celebration in the middle of Smuggler's Bay. Brent figures that if Tandy catches anything on fire out there, it won't last long."

"Ah. No need for the fire station to go on alert and the town gets a cheap fireworks display out of the deal."

"That's true. There's the official one put on by the city every Fourth of July. But since Tandy figures you can't have too many fireworks, he waits until the town's celebration is over and done with, and then lights up the night sky with his own creations immediately afterward. People stand along the pier and wait to see what he's come up with that's new, see if he can outdo what he did the year before."

"And to think you're walking me home and missing Tandy's spectacular display."

"We could watch the finale from your front porch. He usually doesn't wrap it all up until around one-thirty."

"Sure. Why not? I guess I won't be getting any sleep until he gets to the big finish anyway. You love living here, don't you?"

"I guess I do."

"And you like your job well enough?"

"I love my job."

"I can tell whenever I see you at the nursery hovering over a sick geranium."

His eyes twinkled with amusement. "My geraniums are never sick, a result of loving my work so much. Did you ever get that old car of yours running?"

"Old car? I take exception to that. Surely you mean my *classic* sought-after, 1970 Chevy Suburban with the distinctive grill and the double headlights. In case you haven't noticed, that make and model is a rare find, just ask any vintage car dealer."

She let out a low sigh. "Okay, maybe it is a tad old, but Wally's still working on getting me a great deal on a new engine. First, he had a tough time locating one until he found a guy in the Bay Area who collects classic Chevys and the parts to keep them running. I guess making the drive down here was more than the poor old girl could handle. The engine had almost two hundred thousand miles on it. I feel bad about pushing her like that. The motor gave out practically at the city limits sign. I hadn't been in town two minutes before it stalled out. I feel guilty that the poor thing gave me her last mile."

"How are you getting back and forth to work?"

"Wally loaned me a Chevy he fixed up until he gets mine running. Another example of how friendly the folks are here."

"Ever thought about getting a new one? We have a used car lot now."

"Run by Brad Radcliff. Yeah, I know. He came by to see me, left his business card. But I'm not in the market for a new car. My Suburban will be just fine once Wally gets done with it. Those cars are hard to come by, even harder to replace. I can wait. I've learned over the years to be a very patient person." She didn't mention the vehicle's sentimental value or how hard she'd fought to locate it.

"Just as well. I like your Suburban. You get major points for being able to drive a stick. Not too many people want to make the effort anymore."

"I had to learn the ins and outs of using the clutch on a hill early on." She chewed her lip, wondering how much she could trust him. She finally blew out a breath. "Look, can I tell you something sort of strange?"

"Sure."

One of Tandy's rockets lit up the sky behind them.

"That day we had coffee together at the diner, I got this sense about you there was a sadness lurking around from your past. Your aura is very cloudy, very murky. I think you're troubled about something."

He lifted a brow. "You believe in that sort of stuff? Murky auras?"

"I very much do." She stared into his eyes. "You don't like to talk about the past."

"Neither do you."

She could still hear fireworks spearing into the night sky when they reached the end of the driveway that led up to the little bungalow. From the popping sound one right after the other, it appeared that Tandy's finale was slightly ahead of schedule.

She pivoted where she could see the red, white, and blue streaks and felt Caleb's arm come around her shoulders. They stood there watching the last of Tandy's fireworks burn out.

The air calmed. A stillness blanketed the neighborhood.

She turned back to gaze up at the mint-green painted cottage with its white and brown trim. Behind that dark chocolate front door, she'd set up house. For how long, she couldn't say. But she'd signed a yearlong lease and was here until she got the answers she wanted.

She realized Caleb was talking to her, so she leaned on him to hear better.

Caleb gave her a strange look. "I'm not the only one who zoned out."

"Sorry. Like you, my mind wandered. What were you saying?"

"It's super strange you got the sense that I'm sad, considering I got the same kind of vibe about you. There's something in your past you're reluctant to discuss."

She angled her head so she could read his face in the light from the street lamp. "Hmm. I could say how odd that is, but then who really wants to talk about their dark past? Not me. And it seems, not you. Not anyone who's lived through a bad time. So, I think we're pretty much even on that score."

Caleb lifted a shoulder and stared into her amber eyes again. "Makes sense. But what exactly brought you to Pelican Pointe, Hannah?"

She patted him on the cheek and stood on her tiptoes to give him a light kiss, a barely-brush of lips. "I don't really know for certain. Not yet anyway, that's what I'm here to find out."

"Now who's being evasive and mysterious?"

She headed down the walkway but when she reached the little stoop, she turned back. "Not me. Happy New

Year, Caleb. And thanks for taking the time to see me home."

"Hannah?"

"What?"

"Will you have dinner with me next week?"

"I'd love to. What night?"

"Tuesday. I promise I won't get called in to work."

She gave him a wide smile. "Okay, it's a date. But you have to bring your A-game and prepare to answer some questions."

"I will if you will."

"It's a deal. See you Tuesday."

Inside her main room, the five hundred square foot space closed in around her. She kicked her shoes off at the door and plopped down on the little love seat near the window. She moved back the curtains to watch Caleb walk away.

She couldn't explain her attraction to him. Oh, sure, the man was good-looking, all that brown hair and those gorgeous blue eyes would never rouse the upchuck reflex from any female under the age of ninety. No question the guy was eye candy. He also seemed nice enough on the surface. But it was the aura surrounding him that intrigued her. It held the most questions. Something sad there that needed his attention. She felt he might be a kindred soul. His aura might even hold the deep-seated answers she was looking for.

Of course, he wasn't the right age; of that she was certain. She'd already hinted around that with his florist sister just to be on the safe side. Drea had provided her with Caleb's birth date. Amazingly, she and the landscaper had been born a scant two months apart. So, Mr. Jennings was definitely too old to be her brother, Micah.

But he might hold information without even knowing it, info that would lead her to Micah's whereabouts.

"You're barking up the wrong tree," said a voice from the corner of the room.

Hannah studied her ghostly guidance counselor and let out a frustrated breath. The man she'd come to accept for popping up at weird times could no doubt test the patience of a nun. Like tonight. She knew he wasn't real, yet she'd relied on him for the past three months and refused to give up now. She was in too deep. "Why don't you just tell me what you want me to know and cut this clue-driven mysterious crap? It's been a long damn day and I'm tired of your BS."

"Tsk, tsk, tsk. Is that any way to talk to me when I'm trying to help you?"

"Some help you are. You got me to move here. Why get me here and then stall? Oh. Wait. It doesn't work like that," she mimicked in unison with the words he so often used as an excuse for not telling her anything.

"Stop it," Scott lamented. "You think this is easy? It takes time for all this to come together."

"So you keep telling me. You're beginning to sound like a broken record. Same excuses over and over again. It must be tough being the big know-it-all in town and have everyone at the mercy of your beck and call."

"Tougher than you think."

"Oh boo-hoo."

"Are you this bitchy because you're tired, or what?"

"I'm like this because I'm losing my patience with you. I want to find Micah and you aren't helping. You said you'd help. That promise is what brought me here. So don't act like you're stumped at why I'm upset."

When he started to open his mouth, she leveled her finger at him and added, "And stop saying this takes time. I've been here three months already and...nothing. How much time does it take? Longer than three months? Three years? What? You need to be a lot more specific."

"And with that attitude you might be here a year before you figure it out," Scott said flatly. He pointed a finger right back at her. "I can only set your feet on the right path. It's up to you to find out the rest yourself. And just so you know, I'm not on a timetable to suit your emotions or your moods. You upset the apple cart and you'll have to deal with the consequences. Think about whether you're truly prepared to find Micah and then we'll talk."

Before she could get out her response, right in front of her, the image of the man vanished.

Left alone, she muttered, "I was afraid you were going to do that. Your shtick never changes. When the conversation gets tough, you always disappear."

Two

After walking Hannah home, he headed back to where he'd left his truck parked at the bar. The early hours of a brand-new year seemed like the perfect time to reflect about what might have been.

Funny how life was like a fierce game of poker. The dealer could make you weep with a losing hand one minute, and jump for joy at a full house the next. That's the way Caleb thought about his life. There were two parts to it—two polar opposites. A bad start had morphed into a win-win after his mother pulled her little vanishing act. Left abandoned, he'd gone to live with Shelby and Landon. The couple, who'd started out life as his aunt and uncle, had ended up Mommy and Daddy. He'd hit the lottery there. They'd raised him right since the night his mother disappeared into the waters of Smuggler's Bay.

He'd grown up knowing that the cunning Eleanor had discarded her kids without a glance backward. It was probably a good thing that he hadn't known the true depths of his mother's madness until he'd reached adulthood.

Growing up in the family landscaping business, Landon and Shelby had taught him the rewards of making things grow. Putting a seed in the ground and watching it take root became his salvation. It was the cornerstone of the family life he came to love. Even though, sometimes their close-knit relationship could be just a little too tight. And like most families, that closeness could often lean toward being a pain in the butt. Like tonight. He'd felt obligated to spend an evening out with the whole clan when what he'd rather have been doing was to plop down in front of the TV with a beer that didn't cost three bucks a pop.

Truth was, he couldn't blame his family. It wasn't their fault he hadn't mustered up the energy to find a date. Not when he had his eye on Hannah Summers.

Once he reached his truck and started the engine, he headed down Ocean Street. Halfway to the pier, he realized it wasn't like him to be this moody. Hadn't Cooper always been the sullen one in the family? Although that had changed for Coop this past year since he'd hooked up with Eastlyn.

Drea usually played peacemaker between the two of them. Brothers too much alike, he supposed. Drea could roll with the tide enough that nothing much seemed to bother her. Sometimes he found himself envying his sister's easy-going temperament.

Undeniably Caleb adored his family. But feeling like the third wheel, the odd-man-out thing tonight, had been a bit too much.

That's why when it came to his downtime away from work, he valued his privacy like an old man of eighty. The place he called home reflected that.

He'd bought a piece of property dirt cheap on a hill as far away from The Plant Habitat as he could get. It was on the opposite side of town, and yet the address was still considered to be within the city limits.

Once he reached Cape May, he took a left and drove along the street until it dead-ended into a half circle. He pushed the remote on the gate opener and followed the circular driveway around to the garage.

Each time he came home, he couldn't believe he'd taken the old abandoned radio station and reworked the dynamics of the place to make it livable. The building hadn't seen a DJ since Lyndon Johnson declared victory in a landslide back in 1964.

It had taken three painstakingly difficult years to convert the one-story building into livable quarters more in line with ranch-style architecture. He'd used the ramshackle building as his blank canvas, creating the one-of-a-kind home he'd always wanted, something unique and different, something no one else could lay claim to.

What had once been a rundown catch-all for storing trash and harboring field mice was now his pride and joy.

He couldn't do much about the rectangular boxy structure he had to work with, but he improved on the design by adding a garage to the side. That extra element with a slanted roof, broke up the oblong framework and gave him the space to add a much-needed laundry room and mudroom to the house.

The front of the building needed help to look like a residence. His solution was to build a front porch that stretched the length of the house. To spruce up the main entrance, he landscaped the perimeter with a mix of magnolia and blooming jacaranda, creating an arboretum of sorts using fragrant hyacinth and lavender along with a host of native California plants.

His aim was to have vivid green spring-to-summer foliage that would provide him with his own personal forest, his own flower garden, and a place where birds could make their nests and call home. He liked the idea of waking up to the sounds of thrush and robin and other bird life living in the clusters of greenery he'd created with his own two hands.

Inside, he'd ripped out the low ceilings to let in more light. He'd designed the layout himself, making sure that each room now came with nine-foot ceilings and huge windows. He wanted each room to have its own unique look and style. The living room was a step-down from the entryway. He'd built a skylight over the island in the wide-open kitchen along with a huge walk-in pantry. His master bathroom had an enormous walk-in shower complete with thermostatic controls for those end-of-the-day therapeutic body massages.

But his favorite room in the house was the sunroom off the kitchen. A bank of windows facing west allowed him to take in the stunning sunsets over the ocean. With a cold beer at the end of a long, work week, there was nothing more relaxing than having your own little spot to welcome paradise.

One thing he kept intact was the gates at each end of the property to dissuade strangers from driving up without an invitation. It might be overkill, but with a mother locked up in prison for murdering two people, one her own husband, he didn't take his security lightly or his safety for granted.

Even though it was well after two in the morning, he couldn't seem to settle. He went into his den where his desk was, and poured himself a shot of bourbon. Now that he was home he could relax in his own private sanctum.

To shore up his mood, he walked to his wall of shelves and thumbed through his massive collection of vinyl albums. He had Cooper to thank for introducing him to the likes of Mozart, Beethoven, Bach, and Chopin. But tonight, it would be Schubert's turn with all the man's musical genius to take his mind off the beautiful and intriguing Hannah Summers. Maybe he could count on the dynamic melody and the symphony of trombones to master putting his thoughts toward other things.

He sat back at his desk chair, swirling the whiskey in his glass. The movement to his right made him reach toward his desk drawer for the Beretta pistol he kept there.

"Whoa, that won't be necessary tonight," Scott said from across the room.

"I wish you wouldn't do that," Caleb groaned.

"What are you gonna do, shoot me again? I'm already dead. Why are you so jumpy anyway?"

"That's what I've been trying to figure out for the last three days. You'd tell me if Eleanor was planning a jailbreak, wouldn't you?"

"I'd warn you. Sure. But she isn't. You do, however, need to keep in mind that Eleanor Jennings Richmond does make friends easily, maybe too easily. Those friends of hers are the ones you should worry about."

"Preaching to the choir here. Are any of these so-called friends due for parole any time soon?"

"Brent could answer that question better than I could. You should get him to check with the prison system."

"Good idea. I've talked to Coop and Drea and they're as worried about her doing something crazy as I am. We all know she's fond of using her alias, Loretta Eikenberry. She still uses that name to write letters to me. She's crazy, Scott. All the way crazy. I no longer think she's pretending, although I used to. Dad says she's been mentally unstable for decades, as long as he's known her. And he should know. Were you aware that Landon thinks she might've killed their father?"

Scott made a face. "Yeah. I remember the rumors about your grandfather's purported suicide. It didn't make sense that the man I knew could do anything like that. After shooting Layne and Brooke, Eleanor's proved she's more than capable of executing her own father."

Caleb let out a sigh. "You realize that would qualify her as a serial killer, don't you?"

"I can count as well as anyone else."

"It's troubling. She's troubling." Caleb sat up straighter and stared at Scott. "It occurs to me that you could simply tell me what you want me to know about Hannah."

"What would be the point of that? Getting to know a person is the fun part of any relationship. I'm not giving you a cheat sheet to make things easier."

"Why not? It could avoid pitfalls."

Scott rolled his eyes. "What is it with young people these days? Why are they so weird about forming a close bond with the opposite sex?"

"I don't know. Maybe they don't want to get their heart ripped out. How do you know that Hannah and I won't end up hating each other at some point?"

"That's up to you guys. But having a partner in life whom you can depend on is a gift. Trust me on that one thing. Unless of course you figure out a way to piss it away or screw it up."

"I'm not looking to get tied down."

"No man's ever looking to get tied down. Somehow, some way, it just happens. You take one look at the right woman and…bam! Before you know what's happening, a string of words come flowing out of your mouth that suggest you should make a life together."

"That's a scary thought."

"You're attracted to Hannah, right?"

"Yeah."

"Then quit whining and see where the attraction takes you. For once in your life try enjoying the journey. You might be surprised where it takes you."

Three

The beginning of the new year brought Caleb a new project. Or at least he hoped it did. Quentin and Sydney had called The Plant Habitat and asked him to do the landscaping, front and back, at Bradford House.

Since the couple had bought the place, they'd decided to spruce it up, give it more curb appeal. The plan was to bring the yard back to life in such a way that it made a bold statement you could see from the roadway.

And that was right up Caleb's alley.

Quentin, the new doctor in town, stood in the middle of the overgrown front yard looking bewildered, trying to convince himself this was a good idea. "Sydney can't grow a tomato, and yet, my grandmother has talked her into planting a flower garden, both here and around back."

Sydney twirled in place, picturing the idea of it, trying to visualize the layout. "I want roses, daisies, anything that blooms. And then I want to put several benches along the walkway so that people can sit and enjoy the garden."

"You want to add a walkway?" Caleb asked, taking out the iPad he used for mapping his designs and began to key in notes.

"That won't be a problem, will it?" Sydney asked, angling toward Quentin. She slipped an arm through his. "A garden needs a winding pathway through all those cypress trees. Picture the walkway leading right up to the front door with all kinds of different flowering plants and greenery bordering each side."

Quentin cracked a grin. "I knew you'd find a way to spend more money. But I agree, it would look classier if the grounds got a makeover."

Caleb had long ago given up arguing with a client. But he did feel strongly about honesty. "The soil around here grows just about anything fairly well. We'll pick out plants that are relatively drought resistant and hardy to the area. That way, you don't have to spend a lot of time on maintenance. I just want to bring up one point. Haven't you guys recently acquired a dog for Beckham? Do you think Buckley will be able to restrain himself from digging up whatever we choose to put in the ground?"

Sydney grimaced at the thought. "That concerns me, too. Beckham promised he'd keep Buckley from digging up the yard, but I can't help wondering what happens while he's at school and Buckley's left out here all day."

Caleb nodded. "Exactly. That might get dog ownership off to a really bad start. You could bring the dog with you to the clinic. Or I could work with Buckley while I'm here on the premises during the day to try and keep him from digging."

Quentin considered that a workable solution. "Maybe we could do a little of both, coordinate our efforts. As you can see, you have your work cut out for you. When we moved in, no one had lived here for eight months. Apparently, my uncle let the place go downhill before he died. In order to whip this overgrown weed lot into anything that resembles a garden, it'd take me and Beckham most of the spring and summer to do it by ourselves. That's why we need the expertise of a pro."

"That's me and my backhoe. Or in this case my little Bobcat with a digger attachment. It'll take equipment to carve out the kind of space you want. You realize this is gonna cost you some major bucks, right?"

"Ballpark it for me," Quentin said.

Caleb tossed out a figure. "I'll discount that by twenty percent because January is customarily a slow time for us at the nursery and we could use the work."

Quentin grinned. "I'm liking this small-town mindset more and more the longer I'm here."

Caleb chuckled. "We try to do business locally and it benefits all of us. By the way, if you're looking to keep that boy of yours busy, it would go faster if Beckham gave me a hand after school. He's a hard worker. He proved that working at the tree lot during the holidays. I'd pay him the same going rate as before."

Quentin slapped Caleb on the back and the men shook hands. "I suppose a few hours after school wouldn't hurt him. As long as he gets his homework done and keeps his grades up and doesn't get behind at school, you can think of him as your right-hand man."

"When do you want me to get started?"

Sydney turned in a circle again, surveying the plot of land. She eyed the overgrown weeds in the yard, and the general state of disrepair that several years of neglect had brought on. "I want that old trellis to come down first. It's a safety hazard. Beckham tried to climb the thing and it almost snapped in two. And that rock pile of a flower bed over there makes me wonder why anyone would bother to stack all those boulders on top of each other like that. Is it possible for you to start today? Is that too soon?"

Caleb grinned and rubbed his hands together. "I was hoping you'd say that. I'm anxious to get to it. I can have a contract drawn up by the end of the day."

"Then bring it by the clinic and we'll get this thing started," Quentin concluded.

Caleb went back to the nursery to meet with Shelby and Landon. "This project could be our best advertising. Make Bradford House a showplace using native California plants and we promote our line of drought resistant products. The flowers and shrubs we've propagated save water and what better way to show people it can be done than to showcase what we can do there."

"That's a great way to look at it," Landon said, scratching his jaw. "What if we started at the end of the driveway by cutting down that god-awful overgrown hedge that's bothered me for decades?"

Shelby nodded. "We could replace it with wax myrtle and blue pearl sedum. Both are easy to grow and maintain, something that should appeal to Sydney and Quentin since they're so busy at the clinic."

"I was thinking more along the lines of manzanita. It's a colorful shrub that takes up a lot of room and its flowers attract hummingbirds. I thought I'd mix in a little shadbush, too. Here along the coast, shadbush should produce a ton of white flowers in no time. By spring it'll double in size."

"Oh, even better," Shelby crooned, turning to Landon. "I forget he has such a talent for putting together a landscaping package that fits the client down to the precise detail."

Caleb pressed a kiss lightly on the cheek of the woman he thought of as his mom. "I'm glad you approve. Let's hope the client agrees. I'll suggest manzanita and shadbush in the contract and throw in some carpenteria or anything else that will give them a nice bird garden in the spring and summer. And since Sydney wants greenery, I thought I'd use a variegated chlorophytum comosum. We've cultivated resilient variations right here that thrive in temperatures as low as twenty-five degrees. That's more than tough enough to grow outdoors."

When they were all in agreement, he headed to the office he rarely used to draw up the paperwork and closed himself off without distractions. For the next several hours, he got to work building his vision for the Bradford House makeover, at least for the yard. Using his software program designed to lay out the acreage plot by plot, he put that vision to the test, starting at the curb and working his way up the long driveway.

Hours later, he pushed his chair back and looked over his work. The sketches of the layout came to life as he pictured the game plan. If done right, the yard could become his masterpiece. After downloading the design to his iPad, he printed out hard copies of the contract for his file and one for the client to sign. He gathered everything he needed to show Quentin and Sydney his conceptual ideas and headed over to the clinic. If all went well, this time tomorrow, he'd be hard at work on what would be his winter project.

Four

For Hannah, Monday morning arrived too quickly to suit her. She went back to work at her regular job—the cleaning service she'd started. When she wasn't waitressing for tips at The Shipwreck, she scrubbed out houses Monday through Friday. After three months, she'd scrambled to get seven semi-regular clients on board her new enterprise, enough to pay the bills and keep her bank account in the black.

Her customers included the new doctor in town. Bradford House was big and usually took an entire day to clean. But she'd also talked the mayor, Patrick Murphy, into tidying his smaller house once a week that could be finished in four hours.

She'd done the same with the renowned sculptor and artist, Logan Donnelly and his lawyer wife, Kinsey. Thane and Isabella Delacourt, who now had a new baby, had signed her up for twice a week. And the former New York chef, Fischer Robbins, brought her in on a regular basis to vacuum, dust, do laundry and change sheets.

Aside from that list, her bread-and-butter client was the B&B, north of town. That job took up most of her week but it paid well. Mondays, Wednesdays, and Fridays she showed up at Promise Cove and spent six hours from eight to two giving the place a thorough dusting and polishing. The work included vacuuming from top to bottom and scrubbing out toilets.

Hannah didn't mind the chores. As she gunned the loaner Chevy in the direction of the B&B, she thought about it as honest work. Especially since the job allowed her to get to know some of her clients in a way other newcomers might not be able to connect on a intimate level. After all, cleaning a person's house gave you certain insight into their personal space, their personal habits. She knew, for example, that the mayor and the social worker Carla Vargas were all but living together. Patrick Murphy had admitted as much one morning when he'd insisted on fixing her an omelet before getting down to her tasks. Over a shared breakfast with him, he'd caught her up to speed on all the gossip.

A similar thing happened at each of her other stops. Her clients had a laidback approach to the help, which she most certainly was. Most of them applied that relaxed work environment to an often easy-going, friendly conversational tone that came off as chitchat between neighbors. Hannah found it refreshing that she worked for people who viewed her as an equal.

The talk this morning with Jordan Harris started out over a cup of coffee. "I don't know how Doc Prescott could've missed the fact that Thane and Isabella were having a boy instead of a girl," Jordan muttered as she put the finishing touches on a chocolate cake. "Six weeks ago we had a baby shower for Isabella based on her third ultrasound—the one Jack gave her—and bought everything in girly colors, pinks and purples, soft yellows. Maybe we should surprise her with another shower for little Jace."

"What does the new mom say about that?" Hannah asked.

Jordan waved a hand through the air. "Isabella is fine with what she has. She'd never one to complain about anything. That's just the way she is. You know she started that vegetable co-op near the lighthouse. It's been such a success I don't know why anyone didn't think of it before she got here. But Isabella is the one who got it all up and running without a hitch, got the volunteers to show up, and gives most of what grows there to the people who need it."

Hannah spritzed the top of the countertops to a shine while she talked and drank the bold, rich-tasting brew Jordan favored. "Right after I came to town, Isabella asked me to take it over, see to it that the co-op kept running after the baby got here. That was back when Eastlyn was still helping. But she's had to cut way back, too busy with her patrol duties and the Search and Rescue operation."

"What did you say to Isabella?"

"I don't see how I'd have the time to take care of it properly, either. Although I do love a beautiful garden and watching things grow."

"Maybe you should consider dropping the work at The Shipwreck."

"But I pick up solid money there in tips. I don't think I'm the right person for the co-op."

"If you ask Isabella, she might pay you a salary."

"Hmm. I don't know, Jordan. I'd have to think long and hard before giving up my extra income from the weekend. And Isabella did offer me a salary."

Jordan let out a sigh. "Okay. Think about it though. It's gonna be tough to find a dependable manager to replace Isabella. And just look how long I had to wait for such a reliable person like you to show up and help me out here. These days, not everyone likes to get their hands anywhere near a toilet."

Hannah laughed. She went over and laid a hand on Jordan's shoulder. "I'm not opposed to hard work, even cleaning toilets. I get your point about helping Isabella though. I'll talk to her about it and see if the two of us are able to work out a solution. You realize if I go, I won't be coming out here."

"That's the downside. But the town needs the co-op to continue." Jordan leveled her gaze on Hannah and added, "I like you. How'd you get to be such an agreeable sort?"

Hannah shrugged. "I'm not usually. But I'm beginning to really fall in love with the town and the people. Are you all so…down to earth all the time…or is that just my imagination?"

"I remember a time not so long ago the people here were downright rude. They weren't exactly accepting of strangers. In fact, you could say, they didn't take to outsiders. I ought to know. I was considered the town outcast."

"You? What changed?"

Jordan thought back to that horrible time in her life right after Scott had brought her here, and soon after, left her after his unit was deployed to Iraq. "It's a very long story. I guess you could say that somewhere along the way we realized if we didn't start taking care of each other, if we didn't change our ways, the town as we knew it would soon cease to exist."

"So you're suggesting that the people here haven't always been flying the friendship flag?"

"Oh yeah. No place is perfect. But when I got here Pelican Pointe was as far from friendly as you could get. These days, most of us do our best to make sure help is just a phone call away whenever anyone needs a hand getting through a rough patch. It wasn't always like that. New people have come into the mix that changed the dynamics. You know what they say about small towns, right? You're never truly accepted in one unless you grew up there. That mindset had to change here, otherwise no one would want to stay."

"How far back did this hostility go, that you know of?"

"Years. Decades. Scott thought he could change it. And, in a way, I suppose he has. Although he did have to die and come back to get it done."

Because she'd discovered Jordan's link to Scott weeks earlier, Hannah took the comment in stride. "That's just plain sad. I'm not sure how you'll take this, but, Scott's the reason I'm here."

"I figured as much." Jordan held up a hand. "You don't have to tell me the reason. I've long ago given up trying to figure out the mysterious ways of my first husband's ghost."

"It doesn't bother you that he's still so much a part of your life?"

"Nope. He's Hutton's father. That fact doesn't change. Besides, I have better things to do than to spend my time figuring out what Scott's up to. You know, for the longest time, I couldn't even see him like everyone else claimed to do. His own wife wasn't in on the whole ghostly encounter thing. It pissed me off. But then one day, I looked up and there he was, standing off to the side watching me."

"It didn't freak you out?"

"How could it, when everyone else had no problem seeing him? I thought, finally I'm included in the club."

"I'm not so sure it's a club I want to be part of though. I am grateful he showed up when he did to point me in this direction. I'm hoping it'll pay off."

"You're here on a mission. It sounds like a scavenger hunt."

Hannah bristled. It sounded too much like how Caleb had described her. Although they both might be right. If you could call looking for what was now a grown man a "mission" she should just accept that as her quest and be done with it.

Instead of getting into specifics, Hannah decided to keep it simple. "Something like that. There's no point in my going into greater detail because, who knows? Pelican Pointe could be just another dead end and Scott could be full of…you know what." She stopped short from calling it shit.

Since Jordan had heard similar stories before, she merely laughed and reached out to grab hold of Hannah's arm. "One thing you need to keep in mind is if Scott brought you here he usually knows what he's talking about. If you trust nothing else, you should trust that one thing. It's uncanny the way he guides a person once they're here in town."

"But I look around and see this idyllic place and wonder how it all fits with what I'm looking for. I am curious to know more about the colder side to Pelican Pointe, that time you mentioned when people were so rude."

"Downright unsociable. No community spirit whatsoever, not much connection to each other either."

"That's just it. That description doesn't sound like the town I've come to know."

While she scrubbed down the kitchen, Hannah listened as Jordan filled her in on those bad months that dragged into a year and how Nick had helped turn everything around.

For the rest of the day, Hannah went about her cleaning and thought about Jordan's experience in town. She mulled over the conversation until one thing about it stood out. Just how imperfect had Pelican Pointe been during its unfriendly past? Had it been a haven for a kidnapper? Had that kidnapper sold her baby brother to an unsuspecting pawn right here in town?

Right this second, she didn't know enough about the situation to make an assessment. That's why she needed to dig a lot deeper. She'd never gotten this close before. She wasn't sure exactly how to go forward. But she'd have to figure it out…and fast…before things changed and she lost her advantage.

Once Hannah finished up her work for the day, she headed back to town and dropped by Wally's Pump N Go to check on her car.

As soon as she parked the Chevy and got out, she heard the unmistakable high-powered whirring sound of an air compressor. She spotted the mechanic and owner standing underneath an older model SUV, impact wrench in hand, securing lug nuts in place.

"Hey, Mr. Pierce," Hannah called out. "How's it going this afternoon?"

"I told you to call me Wally. Mr. Pierce sounds like an old man."

Hannah tilted her head, studied the mechanic with his long brown hair tied back in a neat ponytail. "How long have you lived here?"

"All my life. Wouldn't live anyplace else. Pretty girl like you ought to think about settling down in a small town like ours."

They'd had a similar conversation the very first time she'd come to him about her car. "Any updates yet? Any hope you can give me would be appreciated."

He thumbed a hand toward the office. "See Lilly for the bill. The engine got here Saturday. Finished putting it in this morning. Even took her for a spin. For a rebuilt she runs great."

Hannah bounced on her toes before throwing her arms around the man's body. "Thank you! Thank you! You have no idea how grateful I am."

"I think you just showed me. That's what I do, honey. I fix cars, the older, the better. She gives you any trouble from here on out, you let me know right off. Even though I went over it from bumper to tail end and she's in good shape. Everything else checks out."

"Thank you again," she said before making her way into the office where Wally's wife, Lilly, sat behind a counter.

"I was just about to call you," Lilly declared. "I bet you're excited to get your Suburban back."

"Oh, I am. That old truck has great sentimental value."

"Funny how we get attached to our vehicles," Lilly said, reaching for the bill.

Hannah watched as Lilly rang up the amount and sucked in a breath when she saw the total come up in the readout. Digging in her purse, she handed over her Visa card and was surprised when Lilly knocked off twenty percent of the amount. "Why'd you do that?"

Lilly sent her a wily smile. "The engine guy in San Francisco knows Wally and gives us a discount so we decided to pass it on to you."

"What a nice thing for you guys to do. Thank you." Hannah waited for Lilly to run her credit card and then turned to leave. But a thought occurred to her and she turned back. "Lilly, how long have you lived here?"

"Years."

"I was talking to Jordan earlier about this one odd thing that keeps bugging me about the town. Do you remember a time when Pelican Pointe wasn't all that friendly?"

Lilly sat back down on the stool behind the counter. "You bet I do. That's a time in my life I don't like to think about. My kids were just babies back then. When my ex was sent to prison, I ended up moving to a rundown trailer south of town that belonged to my stepfather. It was such a mistake because Derek was a real asshole. At the time, I didn't have anywhere else to go and very few options. What I remember most is that whenever I came in to town to shop, everyone seemed to steer clear of me. I kept wondering how anyone could feel that way when they didn't even know me. I figured it was because they thought I wasn't good enough to be around them. Jordan was the exception to that. She befriended me, gave me a job, and then encouraged me to start my own sign business, even do artwork on the side. Then I met Wally and here I am. Happy as a clam at high tide. Why do you ask?"

"No reason. It's just that it's such a sweet little coastal town, it's hard to imagine it ever had a dark side."

"Then prepare for the worst. We even had a serial killer a few years back who had been killing for years. They even found a couple of bodies buried up at the lighthouse."

Hannah's hand flew to her mouth. She couldn't seem to comprehend that or think of a response until she finally uttered, "I don't believe it."

"It's true." Lilly waved a hand in the air. "Don't worry. He's long ago locked up. Carl Knudsen will never get out of San Quentin. Never. He got four life sentences without the possibility of parole and that's only because he took a plea deal to avoid the death penalty."

Lilly took one look at Hannah's horror-stricken face and reached a hand across the counter. "I'm sorry. I didn't mean to scare you."

"That's okay. I asked. I'm glad he's locked up. Although we all know California's death penalty hasn't been active in years."

"2006 is the last time," Lilly said. "Wally looked it up."

"I didn't know that. I should get going. I have a few errands still to run now that I have my own wheels again."

But the knowledge Lilly spilled took some of the joy out of getting her Suburban back. When she spotted her gray and white Chevy Suburban looking so forlorn in the corner of the lot, she should've broken out in a little dance. But as she crawled behind the wheel, a dread hit her. The car should've made her feel like she had a little piece of home in the palm of her hand. Instead, Hannah cranked the engine and put it in gear with her mind on Lilly's description of the town.

On the drive home, she began to seriously wonder if she'd landed in a Stephen King novel where his fictional Salem's Lot, Maine, might just mirror a few of Pelican Pointe's secrets.

Instead of heading to the cottage, she decided to drive through the streets and take a real look at where she lived. She went up and down Ocean Street several times and did the same thing along Main. She took her time perusing the side streets but still had a hard time picturing it as the evil killing ground for a serial killer.

As idyllic as the town seemed, she was beginning to believe she had indeed found where Micah might've ended up, stolen by some evil bitch who had an ulterior motive. It didn't mean her little brother might still be here. But if he had ever been around, she needed to dig up a few secrets, even if she had to stir the pot to do it. If she lucked out, something might come floating to the surface.

Five

Hannah had a schedule to keep. Tuesdays she cleaned the Delacourts' place and Fischer's little dormer-style house on Breakwater. She routinely did Fischer's Cape Cod first because she was usually done by eleven o'clock.

His bungalow had seven rooms total. Since Fischer worked as a chef, he kept his kitchen in immaculate order without her ever doing much to his sanctum, except unloading the dishwasher and cleaning around the sink. That left six rooms, one of which was a guest room that no one used. Each week, she did little more than simply tidying up and was beginning to wonder why the man had hired her in the first place.

But whatever the reason, Hannah was grateful for the work.

It usually took her no more than fifteen minutes to scour his one bathroom. From there, she stripped the sheets off his king bed, put on a fresh set, started a load of laundry, and began the task of going room to room to dust his furniture to a shine.

She had the routine down to the minute. Her precision allowed her to grab a quick bite to eat in between stops before getting to the Delacourt house a few minutes before noon.

But as she rang the doorbell, it occurred to her that maybe she should have called first. The family had a newborn now, maybe she should have checked to make sure they needed a clean house this soon after the birth.

But when Thane pulled back the door he looked so harried, so frazzled that she quickly went into apology mode. "I'm sorry, I completely forgot about the baby until I rang the doorbell. By that time, it was too late. I hope I didn't wake him up. If this is a bad time I can certainly come back next week."

"No, no. It's okay," he said as he pulled her through the doorway. "I could use a hand in the kitchen. There's a bit of a mess in there from three days ago when Isabella went into labor. Things have been happening around here so fast I haven't been able to keep up."

"No problem, I'm happy to start in there, anywhere in fact that you need me today."

Thane ran a hand through his thick blondish hair and led the way down an entrance hall into the living room. Hannah got a good look at the den's clutter, littered mostly with baby items that hadn't been put away in the nursery yet.

"We brought Jace home yesterday," Thane explained as he made his way into the dining room. "Neither one of us slept much last night. I have to leave for work in a few minutes to help Fischer get through the lunch rush. He's shorthanded. If you could lend a hand here until I get back, maybe tidy up some, I'd double your pay."

Hannah patted his arm. "You don't have to do that. I'm more than willing to help any way I can. I don't want to be in the way of the new mom though."

"Trust me. You won't. Jace and Isabella are asleep down the hall. When she wakes up, tell her I have dinner handled. I'll just bring home food from the restaurant."

Hannah had a better idea. "If you want, I could throw a chicken casserole together. I love pizza but it must get old even if you do own the business."

Thane's eyes lit up. "It does. Even Jonah's tired of pepperoni and sausage. If you could throw something else together that doesn't include those two ingredients, that would be great. Jonah loves chicken. I think there's some in the freezer. He'll be home from school in about three hours."

"Don't worry. You go on to work. I'll take care of everything."

She got busy in the kitchen, starting with digging out the frozen poultry. Solid as a rock, it needed a cold-water bath if she had any hope of getting it defrosted any time soon. She filled one side of the sink with water and submerged the frozen meat down under before turning to the countertops. She cleared away the mess and dirty dishes, filling up the dishwasher to the max. She went in search of the casserole dish and began to set out all the ingredients she'd need for dinner prep.

Isabella walked in carrying little Jace.

"Hey, should you be up?"

Isabella sent her a wave and laughed. "I had a baby, doesn't make me an invalid who needs a nursemaid. But if it were up to Thane I'd be strapped to the bed. That man thinks I'll break if I go to the bathroom."

"Aww, that's kinda sweet. So, your labor and delivery wasn't that bad?"

"I didn't say that. It hurt like hell, but once I held Jace in my arms, I totally forgot about the pain. Want to see him?"

Hannah held out her arms. "Of course. I love the name you picked out." She rocked the sleeping infant to her chest. "I wish he was awake so I could see his eyes."

"They're deep blue just like his daddy's. We had to scramble because Doc Prescott gave me several ultrasounds during my pregnancy and claimed we were having a girl. Imagine our surprise when Jace popped out. It was so funny, too. Quentin is sitting on this stool and tells me to push. I push and he goes, 'Uh, guys, I have seven pounds of baby here, but…surprise…it's not a girl.' I thought Thane might faint right there on the spot. For seven months Jonah had us convinced that he was getting a little brother. As it turns out, Jonah knew more than Doc Prescott did."

"Want me to fix you a sandwich? I was just about to start on the casserole for dinner."

"Bless you. I wouldn't turn down a glass of milk and a peanut butter sandwich. Here let me have Jace back."

Hannah relinquished the baby and watched as Isabella put him down in his infant carrier and took a seat at the table. "Have you thought any more about managing the co-op? I'm not rushing you, but since Eastlyn's become a cop, she's just too busy. I've been fortunate enough to get some help from the guys out at Taggert Farms. But with spring coming, they won't have that much time to devote to the fields at the lighthouse. If money's the issue I'll double what I offered you before. I'm desperate for someone to take over before spring gets here and the planting season comes and goes."

When Isabella tossed out a salary that topped anything she expected, Hannah blurted out, "That much? Wow. Really?"

"Yes. Because you're worth it. Listen to me, I sound like a commercial. But with the degree you have, you're a perfect match for the job. Your background is more than I could ever dream of getting from any outsider who simply answered my ad."

"Okay, I tell you what. Let me ease out of my cleaning business, ease out of waiting tables at The Shipwreck and it's a deal. Can you make do another three weeks with the extra hands from Taggert Farms?"

"Do what you have to do. I'll make it work. I'm just glad to finally get someone of your caliber that I can feel comfortable with, knowing your standards will be equal to mine."

The next few hours Hannah tidied up the house, dusting, changing sheets on the beds, and putting the finishing touches on dinner. She even had cookies and milk waiting for Jonah when he stormed through the door after school. For one brief flash of memory, the scene took her back to another time and place. She managed to shake off the image of that day so long ago and bring her tasks to a conclusion. When she began to gather up her things, she felt pride in the fact that she'd gotten so much done.

At four o'clock a text came in from Caleb. *We're still on for tonight, right?*

You bet. Looking forward to it.

Rain's forecast.

I know. You want to cancel?

No way. See you soon.

But by the time she loaded up her car with supplies, dark clouds promised to ruin their first real date. By seven, the coastal storm arrived with hail and rain that dumped an inch of water within an hour.

Despite the downpour, Caleb picked her up on time and held an umbrella while she climbed into his truck. He glanced over to see the vintage Chevy Suburban parked in the driveway.

"When did you get your wheels back?"

"Yesterday. You mind telling me what you have planned on a rainy night like tonight?"

He put the pickup into gear and headed down the street. "I'm taking you to my house. I wanted a place where we could talk and wouldn't be interrupted by wait staff or the other people in the restaurant."

"You sound so serious."

"I am. Because I intend to find out about your mysterious side tonight."

"I hate to break it to you, but I'm not that mysterious."

"Ah, but you are. You have this beautiful face that breaks out into the most amazing smile. But that smile hides an unhappiness that's evident in your eyes. There's no denying it, Hannah."

When they turned onto Cape May, Hannah was surprised to see that the street eventually gave way to rolling hills. With gently slops, she spotted a house surrounded by pretty landscape. All it needed was a babbling brook to be in the middle of the countryside. "I didn't know this place was out here. This is where you live?"

"It used to be the old radio station. Because of that it sat on the highest point in town. Not many people realize we ever had one of our own. When I set eyes on it for the first time I was in high school. It intrigued me even then. I came up here one night with a bunch of jerks to drink beer. They ended up throwing rocks and busting out all the windows. You know, like that scene out of *It's a Wonderful Life*."

"The old Granville house," Hannah furnished.

"Yeah, well, at the time, I didn't have the guts to make the assholes stop chucking rocks. Anyway, once I got serious about moving out of my parents' house and buying a place of my own, I thought of the old radio station. By that time, the building had sat empty for more than fifty years. I thought, what the heck, why not?"

She watched as the gate swung open. "I'm still trying to wrap my mind around the fact that you renovated a radio station. This…is…so…awesome. I expect the grand tour."

"And you'll get it," he promised as he unlocked one of the double doors and they stepped into a unique entryway. "It no longer looks like a lobby with concrete floors."

She took in the transformation. Caleb had renovated the space into a homey treasure, beginning with the chestnut-stained flooring. The shiplap midway up on the walls had been painted a creamy white.

She ran her hand along the narrow trestle table against the wall. "This is beautiful wood."

"Let me take your coat," he said, helping her shimmy out of her jacket. "I made that table myself with Cooper's sweat and labor. I should probably back up and start from the beginning. There was this old guy named Cleef Atkins who owned a farmhouse south of town. A while back, Cleef was murdered by this demented guy who came through town trying to get to Isabella. The fact is the psycho kidnapped her and took her out to Cleef's place to hide for a few days."

"Oh, my God. Jordan was right. Not such an idyllic town, after all."

"I told you, we aren't perfect. After Cleef's death, Nick and Murphy discovered a will. It seems the old rancher had gone and left everything he owned to the town. The property came with a barn and several outlying buildings filled to the rafters with old junk. At least on the surface that's what we all thought, it was just rusted-out old metal…and scrap. The city council decided to put everything in the barn up for sale and let the townspeople go out there and browse through what Cleef had collected over the years. That's where it turns amazing. People found treasures they wanted to fix up or recycle. Stuff like old fans and old motors. That's where Eastlyn found the helicopter she restored. Almost everyone in town found something they could repurpose from what Cleef had left behind. That's where I picked up the wood to make this table." He pointed to the transom over the front doors. "And I discovered that beautiful piece of stained glass hiding underneath a stack of old lumber."

"Still intact?"

"Other than some scratches around the edges, it was in perfect condition."

"What a wonderful way to remember Mr. Atkins. Every time you look at that piece you'll know where it came from and recall the day you found it. Do you realize spreading around his treasures like that he's already become a part of so many homes well after he's gone? I can't think of a better way to put all the junk he saved from going to the landfill to good use, can you? How many years do you suppose he hoarded this stuff?"

"Probably six decades."

"Is everything picked over?"

Caleb cocked a brow. "There's acres of finds left. If you want, I could take you out there to see for yourself sometime."

"If there's anything left, sure. I'd love to spend the day browsing through the place."

"Want something to drink?"

"Sure. A beer would be fine. But I want to see the rest of the house first."

She trailed after him into the kitchen and stopped to admire a room that would make any chef proud. "Don't tell me this island and countertop were repurposed stuff, too?"

"Absolutely. Much of the materials I used in this house came from Cleef's barn. And you know that Chevy you were driving? Wally found that in Cleef's old shed. All Wally did to get it up and running was to put in new spark plugs and replace the carburetor. He got all the rust off, put on a coat of primer, and painted the outside, getting it almost to the original shade of blue."

"I'm amazed there are people out there who can do that sort of thing. I wish I had that kind of talent." She sniffed the air. "What's that wonderful smell?"

"Dinner. Roast chicken with rosemary potatoes."

"You make a house out of an old abandoned building *and* you cook? Why hasn't some sharp-eyed Pelican Pointe female snapped you up by now?"

"I'm not in the market to be snapped up."

"Aww, that's a shame. Did you send out a bulletin stating that?"

He grabbed her hand. "Come on, smartass. Do you want to see the rest of the house or not?"

"Definitely."

He showed her his study, his bedroom, and the former executive offices he'd stripped down to the bare walls and converted the space into his video game room.

"But I saved the best for last." He led her through a passageway and to a staircase that went down to a secret room that at one time had been used as a bomb shelter. It was located directly underneath what was now his guest room. "I use it for storing emergency water and other supplies in the event of an earthquake."

Hannah surveyed the eight-by-ten-foot chamber with its shelves full of paper towels and toilet paper and canned goods. "That's the tiniest supply room I've ever seen, but it makes for a good catch-all, I suppose. It looks like you're ready for anything Armageddon-like."

"Hey, the Zombie apocalypse could happen."

She hooted with laughter. "I like the way you think. But I want to see the backyard. It looks like you have a lot of land here."

"It's pouring rain," Caleb pointed out as they made their way back upstairs.

"Oh. Right."

"How about if I show you the deck from the kitchen instead? I put more of the reclaimed wood to use that I found at Cleef's place. There was enough to stretch twenty feet across using the largest planked lumber he had."

"Weathered with sunlight and age. I like it."

"I usually drink my coffee out there…when it's not pouring rain, that is."

"It's a perfect spot. I bet the view of the rolling hills is amazing. How far back does your property go?"

"There's a drainage ditch back there. That's where the property line ends."

"Does it ever flood?"

"Nope, the runoff from the rain goes directly down to the ocean."

When he heard her stomach growl, he snatched her hand and led her back into the kitchen. "Will you set the table while I take out the chicken? I hope it's okay. I've kept it on warm for more than an hour now."

"It smells delicious. It'll be fine. I'm not that picky. I'll eat just about anything."

She got out dishes and silverware and took them into the dining room while he unloaded the oven.

He opened a bottle of merlot and lit candles before they sat down to eat. "I still can't get over this overwhelming feeling that we're connected in some way."

She took a sip of the red. "I hope you aren't suggesting that we're long lost brother and sister because…that would be…weird."

He laughed. "Don't even go there. I couldn't handle that." But then he caught the look on her face. "Are you saying you have a brother out there somewhere?"

"Who knows? Maybe. I'm adopted so anything's possible. You wouldn't understand."

"Why's that?"

"Look at your perfect family."

Caleb set his wine glass down on the table determined to set her straight. "My perfect family? Which one? The one I had before I was adopted was…" He laughed again. "Not perfect. The one after…pretty damn close. I'm adopted, just like you. Maybe that's our connection."

"That's kind of an eerie coincidence. Maybe we are brother and sister and just don't know it yet." She knew Caleb was too old to be Micah, but joking around with him about it seemed to push a whole series of buttons.

He frowned into his glass. "Nope. Not possible. I know who my real Mom and Dad are. Were. They had three kids they managed to screw up. Royally. Well, at least my mother did, anyway. If you count the half-brother my mother had at the age of fifteen, I believe all her children are accounted for, even if Jonathan Matthews is locked up in jail now." He sipped his wine again. "Maybe I should check and see when he's up for parole. How's that for your perfect family?"

His attitude explained the dark aura around him. "No doubt your mother is part of those ghosts you mentioned. Is she still living?"

"Absolutely. Locked up in Chowchilla. And yours?"

"It's a long, ugly story."

Caleb chuckled. "However ugly your story is I bet I can top it."

Her eyes narrowed before cracking a grin. "A challenge, huh? Then you go first."

"Let's see. I'm not sure this is suitable dinner conversation, but here goes. My mother killed my father and his girlfriend when I was around four years old, shot them with a .38 while they were sitting beneath the pier in town. According to my older brother, Cooper, it was a long, brutal night, especially when she woke him up, being her oldest boy—to help her dig a grave so she could get rid of the bodies. Are you with me so far?"

Chills went up Hannah's arms. "Oh. My. God. I'm so sorry."

"You might want to save your sympathy for my siblings and the dead. Because later, the crazy bitch—her name's Eleanor, by the way—Eleanor decided to fake her own death, and, in the process, put her own kids in jeopardy. She didn't give a shit about what might happen to us."

"How terribly sad."

"I don't even remember the incident. But Cooper and Drea do. They said Eleanor loaded all of us in a boat that didn't even belong to her. She rowed her three little kids out into the middle of Smuggler's Bay, and proceeded to jump overboard right there in front of us, making us all believe she'd drowned herself."

Hannah swallowed hard. "Trust me, it's a good thing you have no memory of something like that."

He stared at her from across the table. "Please don't tell me you can top that."

"Uh, well, here's the deal. Maybe that connection you feel, we both feel, is because we came from the same type of monsters."

"Oh no, not you, too. I'm sensing we may need an impartial judge here to determine who gets the prize."

"Maybe. I was six when it happened. And remember every detail about that day. I was at school when my father took his gun and shot my mother in the head and then turned it on himself. The strange thing is I had a little brother in that house at the time it happened. His name was Micah and he was only six months old. Some neighbor heard the shots and called the cops. It took them only a few minutes to get there. But somehow, after it happened, some strange woman showed up pretending to be from Social Services. She flashed a phony badge—that part's unclear by the way—and took Micah out of the house. She told anyone curious enough to ask that she planned to take him to the hospital to get checked out."

"And they believed her?"

"Apparently." Hannah picked up her glass of wine. "But here's the twist. No woman ever showed up at any of the area hospitals. Not in the state. Not anywhere. The authorities checked every clinic, every hospital, even every doctor's office within five hundred miles and found nothing. Even before I turned eighteen I was obsessed with finding him. I started searching myself. I've been looking for my kid brother Micah, ever since, without any luck."

Caleb rubbed his chin. "That's disturbing…and eerie. So how long after that were you adopted?"

"The summer I turned nine. I spent a little more than three years in the system, moving from foster family to foster family, a total of eight over something like forty months."

"Rough way to grow up. I was lucky. My mother's brother took us in. Who adopted you?"

"A nice couple from the 'burbs. Goodhearted people. Denton and Christine Summers were in their thirties, didn't think they could have kids so they adopted. Lucky me. No really, I hit the lotto with them. I thought at the time it was an omen. You know, a good one. It was, after all, summertime and I was going to live with a family named Summers in a trendy neighborhood in San Mateo. In my nine-year-old mind, I'd get to hang out at the beach, or rollerblade along the boardwalk. Life was finally looking up for me. Then about six months after I joined their little family, Christine discovered she was pregnant. We were all thrilled. One night she went into labor. Denton took her to the hospital. I got a call that she'd had the baby, nothing out of the ordinary, everything was fine.

And then, something went horribly wrong after delivery. The doctors told Denton that Christine had suffered a massive brain aneurysm that caused her to have a stroke. Those first few weeks afterward, Denton put her in a long-term care facility." Hannah looked away, bit her lip to keep from crying.

"And?"

She shook her head. "Christine didn't make it. She lasted another month and that was it. She was gone. I thought her death was my fault, that I must have some kind of curse hanging over me. Two mothers dying had to be more than a coincidence. The curse must've followed me into these people's lives. I was convinced it was true."

He reached across the table and laid his hand over hers. "Oh, Hannah. You know better than that. There was never any curse involved. It's called life."

"Sure. I'm just a good luck charm waiting for the luck to kick in. But there wasn't a whole lot of time for blame. Denton and I had a baby to take care of. That was the reality." Her face changed from lines of despair to the beginnings of a smile. "I have the cutest sixteen-year-old little sister this side of the fault line, named Cassie."

She chewed her lip again, a habit he noticed that reminded him of a sad little girl.

"The thing is, Denton kept me when he didn't really have to. There were times he probably wanted to send me packing back into the system or send me off to some boarding school and be done with me for good."

"But he didn't."

"No, he didn't. He stuck with the single fatherhood thing and made it work. He went to a string of lousy dance recitals, a few very bad piano performances, countless Saturday softball games, and burned supper more times than I could ever count. But through it all he gave me everything he gave to Cassie, everything he could afford for both of us. He made sure his girls were clean and well fed, made sure we went to Sunday school and summer camp, and when it came time to graduate, he paid my way through four years at Cal Poly."

"You adore them."

"Oh yeah. I'd do anything for those two. But..." She laid a hand on her heart. "Inside here I have this need to find out what happened to Micah. A hole in my heart that can't be filled by anything or anyone. Thankfully they understand this obsession I have to get at the truth. I'm not sure why it's taken such a hold on me, but I can't let Micah go without at least trying to make him part of my family again. I'd feel just awful if I didn't give it my best shot."

"Sounds perfectly reasonable to me. You've lived with this hanging over your head for most of your life. It won't let go because Micah is still a huge part of who you are."

She smiled at his understanding. "Not many people get it. I've had relationships that didn't work out because my amateur detective work got old real fast. When I get in that mode, when I'm sitting at the computer for hours at a time, looking for something, and won't let up, it's hard to pull me back."

"You ever hire a detective?"

She shook her head. "I've done most of the research myself. I've dug into the pasts of my birth parents, Robert and Laura Lambert, until I feel like I know every detail about them."

She leaned across the space to get closer. "I don't expect you to understand this, but I even drive that Suburban because it used to belong to my father. The SUV was sitting in the driveway the day it all happened. It's the last image I have of that house. Outside everything seemed so...normal. But inside...I don't even want to picture what kind of carnage a six-year-old could have walked in on, if not for everyone else already on the scene."

Caleb took her hand. "How on earth did you ever find the Suburban though? It must've been like looking for a needle in a haystack."

"I'm resourceful. One of my classmates had a father who worked at the DMV. After explaining my situation to him in detail, he tracked it down, got an address, and the next day I set out to find it."

"Just like that?"

"Hey, once I turned eighteen I needed my own wheels." She lifted a shoulder. "Denton had promised me if I could find one, he'd foot the bill. He had no idea I'd already located what I wanted. And it wasn't even for sale. Before he could stop me, I'd wrangled a friend into driving me and we traipsed off to Big Sur to track down the Suburban. I spent my entire savings on it because first I had to sweet-talk the owner, a park ranger, into selling it to me. Imagine my horror when I discovered it had the original three-speed manual transmission."

Caleb laughed. "And you were too stubborn to give up on the idea by then."

"Oh yeah. I had to learn to drive that thing or eat crow. Turns out, it wasn't that difficult once I got the hang of it and stopped stalling out."

"So, all this time, you've played Nancy Drew hoping to find out something that leads you to what happened to Micah?"

"It's been an obsession—there's no other word for it—that I can't shake. I've spent years learning everything about my parents, where they both went to elementary school, where they went to high school, where they worked. I know where they went to church, even where they exchanged their vows. They weren't bad people, Caleb. They'd never been arrested for so much as a parking ticket before that day. They'd never been in trouble with the law. They paid their taxes on time, worked hard, and mowed their grass every weekend like clockwork. Sure, my dad could yell and scream at times. But even then, if the cops came, they never once dragged my father off to jail. I checked. There was no drug use that I could turn up. And not much drinking involved. We didn't have the money back then for a lot of extras like booze. As far as I've been able to tell, they were just two ordinary, hardworking people who woke up one morning and the world as they knew it exploded with rage and violence. After all these years, I still don't understand it."

"How can we ever really understand the mind of a sociopath or a psychopath?"

"Doesn't mean I haven't tried."

Caleb thought it was time to change the subject. "So, you have a degree from Cal Poly? Impressive. Majoring in what?"

"Don't laugh. Enology."

He chuckled. "The study of wine."

"Yep. Learning to grow grapes."

"Why would I laugh at that?"

"Because most people do. After Christine died, Denton decided to chuck his nine to five job. He took Christine's life insurance money and bought a winery, a small one outside San Mateo. We moved to the country permanently when I was twelve so Denton, Dad, could grow grapes."

She narrowed her gaze on him. "Okay, Mr. Landscaper, it's your turn. I've spilled my mysterious past that you so wanted to know. You've learned all my so-called secrets. My mysterious side is no longer so mysterious."

"What else could you possibly want to know about me? You already know my predetermined genetics. The stuff running through my veins is inherited directly from a narcissistic psychopath. It's not exactly something I usually tell my dates, let alone coming clean like this on the first."

Under the table, she bumped his knee with hers. "Technically it's our second date. Let's hope neither one of us inherited any predisposition for that kind of violence. Tell me something simple, something benign, like where you went to school."

"That one's easy. UC Davis. Got a degree in horticulture like Landon, like Shelby." He leaned back in his chair. He thought he'd be able to let her story go, but it, so much like his own, fascinated him. "I think I'm beginning to get the picture. You came here to find Micah, didn't you? Something or someone led you to believe that your brother's living here?"

She winced at the question and it changed her demeanor. But she put her wine glass down and cleared her throat. "I'm here because about four months back one of those ghosts you mentioned earlier started bugging me and wouldn't let me rest until I packed my bags and headed south."

"Whoa. That's a story in itself."

"It's nuts. Dad and Cassie thought I might be losing it."

"I bet. Are you planning to tell me the rest?"

"Hey, since graduating college—and for the past three years—I've had a pretty normal life working at Denton's winery. It's doing okay, not great, but he and Cassie and I get by. Everything was fine until one day I was out in the field with one of the growers and I looked up and there was this man I recognized from a couple of dreams I'd had. Only this time it wasn't the middle of the night. There I was in broad daylight and this guy is just standing there watching me. With the sun at his back, he had sort of a halo-looking circle over his head. At least that's what I thought at the time. That guy turned out to be Scott Phillips. Your Scott Phillips from Pelican Pointe. After that day, he started showing up regularly. Each time, he'd spout the same message. 'Micah is still waiting for you to find him.' Which got my attention. And then he'd disappear until the same thing happened the next day and the next. This went on for about a month. For a while there, I thought I might be losing my mind. For real. I even checked to see if my birth parents, if Robert or Laura, had any type of insanity in their family tree."

"But they didn't?"

"None that I could find."

"Wow. So, based on a message from a ghost, you packed up your Suburban and came down here, just like that, because of what Scott said to you?"

"Sounds crazy, doesn't it?"

"No, not crazy. Like I said before, eerie."

"Oh, well, you want to hear something *really* eerie, there's more."

He sat up straighter in his chair. "Sure."

"I don't think my father was the one who did the killing that day. I remember he could be a little nutty at times, a little volatile, a little loud, but at the end of the day, he loved my mother. I don't think he would've ever killed her. And I don't think he would've ever taken his own life."

"Then who? Ah. The woman who took Micah. She shot them both to get to Micah. Murdered two people. Kidnapped the baby. And she conveniently makes the scene look like a murder/suicide."

"You got it. But why? And how do I prove it? Because right now I have nothing. After all these years of looking, I have absolutely zip, zero, not a thing concrete to prove my dad didn't kill anyone. And how would I ever find out the identity of who *that woman* really is. Some days I feel it may go unsolved forever and I'll never find Micah."

"You know what they say about a hunch, right? Follow it until it no longer exists as a hunch, put it to rest. That way you've proved the hunch wrong. What you have, Hannah, is great intuition. We just sat here over dinner tonight and proved that."

"Uh huh. And maybe we both have it. What do you have to say about that?"

"That we had lousy traumatic events occur before we were adopted."

"You can do better than that."

"I believe I can, but not with you sitting way over there."

"This is where you put me. You did the seating arrangement."

Without warning, he blurted out. "I talk to Scott, too. About six months ago he approached me in my study. He usually shows up there about the same time of night. The first time it occurred it was after I'd broken up with a woman. I thought he was trying to console me in some way. Now, I'm not so sure. Maybe it was all about you coming here."

"I knew it! I knew you were hiding something! What was his message to you?"

"Simple at first but vague. He told me I needed to focus on my work and put aside the social aspects for a while."

"Social aspects? You mean, like dating? How strange."

"Yeah. He talked about me waiting for the right woman to come along some day. I think he was talking about you."

"Whoa. Wait a minute. I'm just here to find the connection to Micah."

"Let me guess, Scott treats this like a scavenger hunt where he drops little nuggets of information in hopes of stringing you along with just enough to keep you on the hook."

"That's why you need to keep in mind that when I'm done I'll be heading back to the winery to work for Denton."

"Sure, I understand." But he shook his head and smiled. "Frankly, I'm glad I got that admission off my chest. It's embarrassing to confess that I talk to a man who's been dead for several years."

Hannah let out a low sigh. "I know. But I can't focus on the dead part. I have to focus on Scott leading me to what I want to know." She stood up to start clearing the table.

Caleb joined her at the sink. "I say we start a fire and listen to some music, see where the mood takes us."

She poked a finger in his chest. "I'm not sleeping with you on our first date, Caleb. But I am interested in something you've got."

He yanked her against him. She smelled like a walk through a thousand orange blossoms. "It would surprise me if you weren't. Many women can't resist my…charm and good looks."

She stifled a chuckle. "As drawn as I am to your charm, I was referring to your video game collection. If I'm not mistaken, I spotted a vintage version of Pac-Man in there, just waiting for someone like me to play it."

"Hmm, sounds reasonable enough. What if I told you I also have Goldeneye 007?"

"Get out! With multi-player death match mode?"

"That's the original version, baby. No true gamer would be caught without death match mode."

"Then what are we waiting for? Shooter to shooter, the challenge is on."

The rest of the evening they spent playing an assortment of videos. He reigned supreme at Star Wars while she kicked his ass at Goldeneye. They bonded over Jedi lore and dragons, before moving on to prehistoric dinosaurs. They talked about Nintendo versus Atari and the dawn of Xbox.

By the time, Caleb drove her back to her house, the rain had stopped. The clouds had moved further east, leaving the sky crystal clear. The stars had popped out like a string of giant diamond bracelets, layered and glittering bright, twinkling down from the heavens above them.

From where they stood on the driveway, they could almost hear the waves lapping against the pier straight down Crescent Street.

Hannah angled her head skyward. "I had fun tonight. Thanks. It wasn't as bad as I thought it would be talking about all that stuff with you."

"Same here." He drew her closer, tilted her chin up. "I've decided to wait for the traditional, but lame, third date to sleep with you."

She snorted with laughter. "Oh really. That's big of you, almost saintly even."

"Saintly I'm not," Caleb admitted. To prove it, he crushed his mouth to hers. A burst, brighter than any star, surged high and hot. The moment he let go, he rested his head on her brow. "Are you sure you want to wait?"

"You're the one who mentioned the third date. Besides, there are reasons we should."

"Yeah. But right now, I'm having a hard time coming up with one."

"Small town, people talk. I've already risen to number one by knocking off Nellie. I don't want to stay at the top because I'm boinking the hunky landscaper."

"Talking dirty is no way to get me to leave."

She cupped the back of his neck and brought his lips down to meet hers again. The heat spiked. The air heated. "Okay, so we have chemistry. One excellent reason to slow things down before jumping in the sack."

"I was afraid you'd see it that way." He held on to her hand, brought it to his lips. "One thing you need to know. You're worth the wait."

Six

Caleb started his day early at Bradford House with his mind on Hannah. He'd discovered her quirky personality also came with an off-the-wall sense of humor and an outlook on life that many would call fearless.

As he worked the Bobcat into position, he started the process of digging out the first plot of earth that would become the flower garden.

In his estimate, the little Bobcat worked faster and better than any backhoe ever could. Landon preferred using the backhoe. But over the years Caleb had found that digging with the smaller machinery proved more versatile on a job site. With the digger attachment, he could dig trenches, loosen hard-packed soil, remove stubborn rocks and stumps, all without ever stopping to remove and replace the attachment.

That's why he was surprised when the thicket of trees proved to be a bit of a problem maneuvering around each large cypress to scoop out the soil.

As he performed the mindless work, his mind drifted again to Hannah. What other woman would spend an entire evening in front of an almost twenty-year-old video game and enjoy herself? He didn't know many females who would even have suggested passing the time like that, let alone been happy about it.

Sometimes during the work, he'd glance up from the chore to enjoy the sunlight dancing off the water, reminding him that January in Pelican Pointe didn't come close to the freezing cold back east. From his vantage point next to the cliffs, the view gave him a beautiful perspective of the ocean.

There wasn't a cloud in the sky as he sat back and directed the equipment to scoop up sections of dirt around the old trellis.

It took about an hour to carve out the right length and width before he moved on to another section. The area near the boulders proved difficult. Mainly because someone at some point had taken the trouble to pile them up near the corner of the house. It took another hour to take each large rock and move it to another part of the yard where the stone could easily be loaded and carted off. Once he finally got down to the dirt left underneath, he started to scoop out what was left of the ground. He was working on a nice size hole, lifting out chunks of the earth, when something small and white appeared in his line of vision.

He cut the engine and hopped down to take a closer look. Caleb stood frozen for several seconds, staring into the carved out mass of dirt, unable to move. When he did come out of his daze, he reached in his pocket for his cell phone. Still staring at what he'd uncovered, he waited for Brent Cody to pick up on the other end.

"Hey, Brent, this is Caleb Jennings. I'm over at Bradford House, clearing some land. I think you need to drop what you're doing and get over here, quick. I think I've discovered what looks like bones, remains."

"Are you sure?"

"I'm fairly certain."

"I'm on my way."

While Caleb waited at the curb, the scene became chaotic almost before his eyes. First Brent got there. The police chief, who wore his hair longer than he had when he'd been sheriff of Santa Cruz County, spent a long time staring into the hole in the ground, studying the unmistakable small skull.

"Those are human, right?" Caleb wondered from some twenty yards away. "It looks like it belongs to a small child, maybe even a baby."

"Yep. I'd say no more than a year old," Brent agreed. "We'd better get in touch with Quentin and let him know what's about to happen here."

"I already called him after I called you. He said he'd be here as soon as he could finish up with Prissy Gates. It seems Prissy took a tumble this morning and hit her head on the coffee table. The wound needed ten stitches to close."

"Okay then, I'll call the county and make arrangements for a forensic team to bring their proper gear for a dig."

"How long do you think this will take? I'm guessing a week. They'll have to dig up the rest of the yard, won't they?"

"I'm afraid so."

About that time, Eastlyn pulled up. She got out, walked to the hole and pulled her sunglasses down her nose to get a better look. "That's disturbing. Forensics will have this place looking like giant gophers burrowed their way across the lawn, probably before sundown."

"They'll dig that far down?" Caleb asked.

"On something like this? You bet they will," Eastlyn stated. "They'll probably dig up the entire front yard before they release the property back to Quentin."

Brent slapped Caleb on the back. "Look at it this way, they'll likely do some of your work for you."

Caleb took off his ball cap, a black and silver Raider hat, and mopped his brow. At the sound of a car engine, he turned and spotted Quentin's vintage Woodie rolling into the lane.

Quentin and Sydney made a mad dash over to the hole to look at what was there for themselves.

"What do you make of it?" Brent asked Quentin. "Take a long look now before the medical examiner gets here, maybe tell me what we're dealing with ahead of the curve."

Quentin squatted down to get a closer look. "It's definitely the remains of a child, a small one, maybe even a newborn. The body's been in the ground for a very long time." A sick thought ran through his head about his uncle. Maybe there was a dark side to the old man that he hadn't known about. "How long did Douglas live here exactly?"

Brent scratched his chin. "Thirty years. Maybe more. He built the place after the lot sat vacant for a long while. That was during a time when Pelican Pointe was becoming a ghost town. Everyone was moving out, headed someplace else. I remember my grandmother saying how strange it was to see someone as prosperous as Douglas deciding to settle here. And building a house as grand as this one was almost unheard of."

Quentin squinted toward the cliffs. "Makes you wonder why a professor would pick here to retire, to build his house, no academic world around, closest university is fifty miles into Santa Cruz. I'd have to agree with your grandmother."

"Yeah, that's all I recall from her days living here, at least, off the top of my head. Murphy would probably be able to remember more, like who Doug purchased the land from, maybe even why he ended up here. If not, it's all speculation. As it is, I'll have to go through public tax records to learn who owned it originally."

Quentin stood up and stared at Brent, then over to Eastlyn. "You know what this means, right? My uncle could've been involved in this. Although I have no idea what 'this' is at the moment. The dead body of a child wouldn't exactly be a boon to the former mayor's reputation."

"It's way too early to go jumping to conclusions like that," Eastlyn cautioned. "Let's at least pinpoint a timeframe before we start accusing anyone of something this despicable."

"She's right," Sydney said, slipping her hand into Quentin's. "Let's try to keep an open mind at least until we find out the history. After all, the land's accessible to just about anyone. The bones being here doesn't preclude someone coming here to bury a body, even that of a child."

"I don't buy that," Caleb tossed out. "Look how close it is to the house. You'd make noise digging that far down."

"I agree," Quentin added.

Sydney stubbornly held out for false hope. "Maybe it happened while Douglas was out of town or something."

"Like I said," Brent began. "A simple check with the county tax assessor's office and we should have our answers pretty quick as to who owned the property before Douglas built the house. It's possible Douglas wasn't involved."

Quentin rubbed the back of his neck. "I'm not sure how you figure that. And I just thought of another problem. We'll have to keep Beckham away from here until the remains have been dealt with and removed. With his grandmother dying last month, he's already had enough of death to last a lifetime. The kid doesn't need to come home from school and see this."

"Agreed. I'll go pick him up, make sure I'm there after his last class," Sydney offered. "That way I can prepare him a little on the ride home."

"Good idea," Brent said. "But you should know the crime scene techs could take a week or more before they clear this area. They'll want to dig for more bodies. You'll have to make arrangements to stay away that long."

"We'll be okay," Sydney stressed. "We'll stay at my house until the forensic team has done their thing and gone."

"Do you still want to live here?" Quentin asked. "Maybe it's not such a great idea to come back at all."

Sydney's head was beginning to throb. Because she'd rushed out of the clinic in a hurry, she'd left her sweater behind. She shivered in the January breeze. "Do I have to give you an answer right this minute? We've put so much time and effort into our ideas for redoing this place, now the yard. I hate to back off all those plans. But…"

Quentin put his arm around her waist. "I know. Plus, it hasn't even been a week since we signed the papers to make it ours. What's the likelihood we could unload it on anyone else, especially after this?"

Sydney rested her head on his shoulder. "I say we stick it out until we find out more. There has to be a reasonable explanation why an infant is buried in this location. Maybe it's very old. You know, Chumash old, or belonged to settlers who lived in the area."

Quentin exchanged looks with Brent. "Don't bet on that outcome. For one, those bones haven't been in the ground long enough to be from a Chumash settlement, or Spanish missionaries. If I had to ballpark a guess, I'd say less than a quarter of a century."

"That covers quite a span of time right there," Brent reiterated. He pivoted to where Caleb stood. "Maybe you could move your machinery around to the side of the house for now. The county will probably want to use it to dig up the rest of the yard and not bother with bringing in their own equipment. Would you be okay with that?"

Caleb was still having trouble getting the image of that skull out of his head. "I don't mind. The job's on hold anyway. Not much anyone can do about it."

Quentin ran his hands through his hair. "I'm so glad Beckham is at school right now. After what he's gone through with his grandmother, I'm glad he wasn't here to see this. What if he'd come upon that skull—"

"It's unnerving even for the rest of us," Brent added. When his cell phone buzzed, the chief of police went into an all-business mode. "Yeah, I'm standing right here staring at what amounts to a baby's grave. I've got the local physician here with me onsite, and he's also the homeowner. The doc confirms it's the bones of a small child. So yeah, I'd appreciate it if you'd assemble your team together and get over here as soon as possible. Thanks."

Brent ended the call and stood back near Eastlyn. "Coroner is on his way. Dumbass actually wanted to know if I was sure it was human remains before he made the trip from Santa Cruz."

Eastlyn shook her head. "Same old county response. That's the very reason we have our own chopper. But this...there's no getting around the medical examiner. It has to be done by the book."

"It is a rather unbelievable find," Caleb pointed out. "I had to get rid of all those boulders stacked up there just to get down to the dirt enough to dig. What are the odds that the first day I start ripping up the yard I stumble upon buried remains?"

Sydney latched onto Caleb's arm. "Oh, my God. Maybe that's the reason I got the willies every time I got close to that rocky flower bed. It didn't look right to me. Now I guess I know why."

Caleb nodded. "It looked like it didn't belong here. For an out-of-place tower of rocks so neatly stacked, someone put a lot of effort into piling them up like that on purpose. They didn't end up shaped in the form of a cairn by themselves. Bradford must've had them put there as a memorial."

Sydney could only agree. "With no name? What a jerk. First time I saw it, I thought maybe Quentin's uncle must've had a gardener at one time who tried his hand at an artistic flair to give the yard some...pizzazz. I feel silly now."

"No need for that," Eastlyn said. "Think of it this way. If not for you two moving into this place, then buying it, who knows how long that body could've remained here under the ground without anyone knowing about it."

"Good point," Brent added. "At least this way there's hope that we'll be able to get the child a proper burial, maybe back where he needs to be, not dumped in a flower bed."

Caleb stuck around until the coroner got there, mulling over a lead no one else knew about. This skull, these remains, had to belong to Hannah's little brother. But when the media from Santa Cruz showed up to video the forensic team setting up and picking away the dirt, Caleb got out of there. He went to hunt Hannah and tell her the news before she heard it from anyone else.

He found her Suburban parked on Landings Bay in front of the Donnelly house. She was loading up her cleaning supplies into the back.

"Hey, fancy meeting you here," she called out as soon as she spotted Caleb getting out of his pickup.

"Are you done here?"

"Yep, just finishing up."

"How about some lunch?"

She looked at her watch. "At two-thirty? Sure. Why not? All I've had is the apple I grabbed around noon. I could eat." She noticed he seemed bothered by something. "What's wrong? Didn't you start the Bradford House job this morning?"

"I'll tell you over a burger and fries. Why don't you follow me to the diner?"

But by the time they reached the eatery, word had spread about what Caleb had unearthed. As soon as the two walked inside, all heads turned to stare at Caleb as if he'd dug up the devil himself.

Hannah took notice. "Did you just rob the bank or something? What's going on?"

Caleb took hold of her elbow and scooted her along to a booth near the window. Margie Rosterman, the owner, followed them to the table, throwing down a couple of menus for them to peruse. Margie stared Caleb down. "Worked up an appetite, did ya? I wonder why. Who do you think might be in that grave up there on the hill?"

A shiver ran up Hannah's arms. "Grave? Okay, what are you guys talking about?"

"You don't know?" Margie bobbed her head toward Caleb. "Since he's the guy who dug it up, I'll let him tell you what he found."

"How about bringing us a couple of coffees?" Caleb suggested, trying to get rid of Margie long enough for him to let Hannah in on the news.

"Humph," was Margie's response as she turned on her heel and went to fetch the drinks.

With Margie out of earshot, Caleb squirmed in his seat as he relayed the morning's events. "The thing is, as I stood there watching the scene unfold to what it is now, I thought of you. You don't think those remains could belong to your baby brother who got kidnapped, do you?"

Hannah's appetite had suddenly vanished. "I don't know what to think. The guy who brought me here, who's supposed to have all the answers, has gone MIA these past few days. Getting any clear-cut answers out of him is darn near impossible."

"I hate it when that happens," Caleb said, trying to lighten the mood.

She got the humor, took it in stride, but was clearly upset by the day's events. "Yeah. Well, when I see Scott again I plan to give him a piece of my mind about that. I can't believe this is his idea of finding my little brother. Who does that sort of thing? Bring me here so I'll settle for finding bones? That's…not fair."

"But at least by unearthing the remains, you'd know what happened to him. It would give you some closure."

"How? How does closure work when I have no idea who could have stolen him in the first place and brought him here? Now I have more questions than I ever did."

"Hold up. We're both getting way ahead of ourselves. Sydney told Quentin to wait before jumping to conclusions and I think that's sound advice. We should take a step back before heading down the definitive path that those remains belong to Micah."

"Oh really?" She chewed her lip. Her voice took on a more serious tone. "Call it a gut instinct, but they have to belong to him. Why else would I be sitting here? What other baby in the area is missing? I'm prepared to yell at Scott for bringing me all this way, but—"

She stopped talking long enough for Margie to bring over two steaming cups of coffee.

"What do you guys want for chow?" the owner asked. "The special is meatloaf."

Caleb had only glanced at the menu, but he wanted Margie to leave them alone for longer than a few minutes. "I'll take a cheeseburger with the works and a side of fries."

Hannah wasn't so eager. "I'll…uh…I guess I'll have the tuna melt on wheat." She dug in her purse for the small bottle of aspirin she kept there. "And could you bring me a glass of water?"

"Will do. I'll get your food started."

After Margie had gone, Caleb picked up where he'd left off. "You think Scott's work might be done. He got you here and I found the remains. That's why he's MIA now. There's nothing left of the mystery anymore."

"Exactly. Now it's a wait and see kind of thing and I'm not very good at waiting. How long do you think it'll be before Brent gets the results back as to the child's age and how long he's been in the ground?"

"Could be months. That's why I think you should pay a visit to Brent after we eat and tell him the entire story just so he has a better grasp of the situation. You have to let him know that the baby might be Micah, Hannah. There's no other way."

She let out a sigh and turned slightly sick at her stomach again at the prospect of talking to Brent. "I know you're right, but the idea of this getting out and everyone knowing about it is…I don't know how I feel about that."

"You want answers though, right?"

"Of course I do."

"Brent is your only hope of that happening. You have an obligation now for full disclosure."

"I know. But I'm not happy about it."

Seven

While the forensic team shoveled out more dirt, that afternoon Brent called a meeting in his office. He asked anyone who had anything to do with Bradford House to be there. That included Quentin and a slew of friends Douglas had before his death. It included people the former professor had known before and after he became a politician. Which left Brent's office full of former supporters who were there to staunchly defend their friend.

Jack Prescott, the retired town doctor, emphasized his belief in Douglas by tapping the desk with his index finger...repeatedly. "I want to go on record right now stating that Belle and I never knew Doug to have a mean bone in his body. And I knew the man before he became a teacher at UC Davis. Doug and I go way back. So don't even try to suggest those bones happened on his watch. Those remains had to have already been buried there when he built the house."

Quentin took exception to that. "No way, Jack. Those bones were buried in that specific spot after the house had been built. That does make it happen on Doug's watch."

Jack wheeled in his chair. "You don't know that for certain. You're a physician, not a builder."

"That's true, but digging a foundation requires digging down several feet into the ground. The grave was too close to the house, which says you're wrong."

But the current mayor was also on Doug's side. Murphy couldn't recall the people who'd sold Doug the land, at least not off the top of his head. "That's been thirty years or more and these days I have a tough time remembering what I ate for breakfast. But I'm with Jack on this. Doug had a good heart. Whatever happened, he wasn't a part of it."

"I'm working on finding out more about the property owners," Brent admitted. "So far I've turned up records at the county that show a couple by the name of Pryce and Adelia Townsend owned the land. I ran a background check on both. They're both still alive, living in a retirement community near Sausalito. I called and talked to Adelia. Her husband Pryce suffers from dementia. According to the wife, they bought the land with every intention of settling here. But once they realized it wasn't the thriving little town they'd hoped for, they scrubbed the idea of building their own house and put the property on the market. It sat for almost three years before Douglas snatched it up for a song. To eliminate them, I asked Adelia if she'd ever had kids. She claims she didn't, which I intend to verify."

"I doubt this couple had a kid who died back in the San Francisco area and they decided to drive down here to bury it in a vacant lot," Eastlyn said, shaking her head. "Long drive just to dispose of a body. But I suppose there's no logic when it comes to something as sinister as this."

"Ah, yes. Now I remember those two, Pryce and Adelia," Murphy admitted. "Pryce made his money in San Francisco real estate. He was looking to buy land with an ocean view. That's how they ended up here. Land was less expensive here than in the Bay Area. But the wife didn't like the idea that, economically, things here looked bleak.

She didn't want to shell out a bundle on building a house that wouldn't hold its value."

Hannah and Caleb could hear the discussion as soon as they stepped inside the police station. Brent's office was full of so many people, they could see the overflow had spilled out into the hallway.

At the sound of the door opening, Eastlyn backed out of the room, greeting them in the reception area. "Hey, what are you guys doing here?"

"I need to see Brent," Hannah said, her face showing distress.

"He's a little busy right now trying to work out a few of the background details on the Bradford property."

Caleb cleared his throat. "I think he'll want to hear what Hannah has to say."

Eastlyn eyebrows rose in curiosity. "Okay. Take a seat and I'll see if I can pull him away from the group."

They watched as Eastlyn burrowed her way through the throng until she reached Brent's desk, where she leaned over and whispered something in the chief's ear.

A few seconds later, Brent emerged from the room. "What's this about? I'm kind of in the middle of something. If it can wait—"

"It can't. I need to talk to you," Hannah began. "It's about those remains. I might know who they belong to."

Creases formed on Brent's forehead as he eyed Hannah's agitated state. "Oh, really? Then let's head down the hallway where we can talk."

He led them to what looked like a small interrogation room. It was barely big enough for three people. "Have a seat."

Nervous, Hannah shook her head. "No thanks. I do my best talking on my feet." She went into the backstory about Micah and what had happened so long ago in Turlock to her entire family.

The information took Brent so much by surprise that he wasn't sure what to ask first. He scrubbed his hands over his face and quickly regained his composure. His years of police training kicked in. "Ah. That's what brought you here. You came to town to locate your brother?"

"Yes."

"I wish you'd come to me for help when you first arrived."

"I'm sorry. It never even crossed my mind to ask for help."

Brent leaned back in his chair. "Tell me something. Did you ever add your DNA to a national registry for missing people, a database specifically used by law enforcement that looks to match relatives with bones, in hopes of getting a match to your brother?"

She met the chief's eyes. "Yes. I did. As soon as I learned about its existence, I added my DNA hoping it would never apply to Micah."

"Well, before you leave I'll need another sample to check for a familial match."

"Anything you need. I want answers too."

"Eastlyn!" Brent called out. "I need a DNA test kit back here." He turned back to Hannah and motioned for her to sit down. "You like needles?"

"Not particularly."

Hannah looked so tense he tried for a bit of humor. "Then get off your feet. You don't want Eastlyn drawing blood while you're standing up." He held up his hands. "I'm trying to lighten the mood here. Taking DNA these days means a swab to the mouth, nothing more."

Hannah gave him a half smile. "I knew that."

"What do you want to bet Eastlyn has trouble finding the kits? That woman's always organizing and rearranging a cabinet or a storage closet. She's a real go-getter, but there are days she drives me nuts."

After a few minutes ticked by, Eastlyn appeared in the doorway holding the plastic baggie with everything needed for collection. She looked from Caleb to Hannah. "Which one of you gets swabbed?"

Hannah sent the cop a wave. "That would be me."

"Want me to do it?" Eastlyn asked Brent, even though she'd already started snapping on latex gloves.

"Be my guest," Brent said, shifting in his chair toward Hannah. "You understand the medical examiner may have a long list of questions for you. At the top of that, will be whatever you can tell him about your brother, what hospital he was born in, date of birth, things of that nature. IDing the remains is priority one. The results of your swab should come back within the week. If it's a match, we have a definite kidnapping in play that resulted in death. That falls within an FBI investigation, which means you'll likely have to start from square one, repeating your story for their benefit. Prepare for a media blitz. They love spewing this kind of story out for breakfast."

Hannah had been holding her breath while Eastlyn swabbed the insides of her mouth. She waited until the cop had stepped back before adding, "Sounds like a long, nasty ordeal ahead. Will the FBI really need to get involved?"

"It depends on whether the remains belong to Micah Lambert. If it's a match to you, the feds will likely drive over here from the Santa Cruz office, more for show than to actually work a case."

"It doesn't sound like you care too much for the feds," Caleb surmised.

"I've dealt with them before. I'd rather not have them on my turf. It's my case," Brent pressed. "I don't need the FBI poking their noses into a local homicide. But I will cooperate with them if they come knocking."

Eastlyn finished capping the tube and placed the swab inside an evidence bag. She looked at her boss. "Want me to drive this to the lab now, put a rush on it, and let the coroner know it could assist him in the identification process? I'm happy to do it."

"See what I mean? A real go-getter. Sure. It'd save me a lot of leg work. I'll call and tell him you're on the way." Brent swiveled in his chair to face Hannah. "Something else you need to know. When it's a child's death like this, the medical examiner will step up his game to find out how this baby died. And that could be tricky with such old bones. As of this moment, I'll shift my focus to doing research and learning the details of your case. It'll likely mean contacting the sheriff in Stanislaus County to see what he can share with me. All this will no doubt dredge up old memories for you. And like I said before, when the press gets wind of it…"

Patient up to this point, Caleb stood up. "When it comes to finding Micah, Hannah's already done quite a bit of research on her own. She's been searching years for answers."

Brent eyed Caleb and then Hannah. "I'm curious as to what brought you here specifically. What did you think you'd find in Pelican Pointe? Why here of all places?" When Hannah just sat there without saying anything, Brent went on, "How did you come by the information that was good enough of a lead to think you'd find Micah here?"

Hannah cut Brent a look before glancing up at Caleb and then back across the desk at Brent. "If I tell you, it's likely I'll be admitting to an embarrassing situation. If you insist though, I suppose I'd describe how I got the information…as…something…not quite in the realm of your usual leads, not entirely within normal investigative methods."

Fascinated, Brent sat up straighter in his chair. "You're telling me you broke the law?"

"Um, no."

"Okay." Then it hit him. "How out of the realm are we talking about? Like paranormal out of the realm stuff?"

"I got a tip from someone," Hannah finally blurted out. "Someone that seemed determined to get me here. I took it as a sign that karma or whatever it was had finally cooperated and pointed me in the right direction. I had hope."

"Ah." Brent bobbed his head. "By any chance would that have come from Scott Phillips?"

"Cut the BS, Brent?" Caleb snapped. "You know damn well how Scott likes to dabble in other people's lives. He did it with Hannah back in San Mateo. One day she's there living her life and then Scott enters the picture and dangles the possibility that she'd find Micah here. She packed up and here we are. Of course, Scott left out a crucial detail. He failed to mention that Micah would already be dead and buried at Bradford House."

Brent pointed a finger at Caleb. "But we don't know that for certain, do we? It is interesting though because Scott rarely interferes by dropping all those hints only to end up wrong. I have to consider Micah's abduction a viable change of direction."

"But you're missing the mystery here," Hannah stressed. "How did baby Micah get from Turlock to here?"

"Oh, I'm not missing a thing about the mystery. I get it," Brent insisted. "I'm aware there's still a lot of legwork yet to be done to find out how that baby came to be buried at Bradford House. You're staying put here in town, right?"

"I'm not going anywhere until I find out what happened to my brother," Hannah snapped.

"Good. Because I'm sure I'll have more questions. In fact, I want you to go home and write this all out. I want you to share what you've discovered in your research over the years. Whatever it might be, no matter how trivial or unimportant you think it is. Was your investigation done through a private investigator or on your own?"

"I did it all myself, using a few leads from what I remembered at six, and going back to the day it happened. Since I didn't have the money to hire a proper investigator, everything I know came from a lot of hard work and Internet searches." Hannah got to her feet on shaky legs. "Before I go, I want you to promise me that you'll keep me in the loop, no matter what."

Brent bobbed his head in agreement. "I don't have a problem with that. If it were me, I'd feel the same way."

Hannah blew out a breath. "Could it be this simple? Micah's been in that hole for decades? Could that poor little baby have been snatched out of his crib that day by a psychopath only to wind up buried in the ground? It doesn't make a whole lot of sense to me."

"Psychopaths don't have to make sense," Brent concluded.

"That's the scariest thing. But he was just a little baby, unable to fight back, unable to hurt anyone. There was no need to kill him."

Brent got to his feet as well. "I agree with that. Look, I don't want you leaving here rushing headlong into a preconceived notion. I admit it sounds very much like we've already solved this thing. But years as a police officer have taught me one thing. Jumping to conclusions will get you off track, get you wearing blinders. No good cop should ever put on those blinders. I caution you not to make that leap until we get the DNA back. Once that happens and it's a match, then we'll start working backward twenty years."

Hannah nodded. "Okay. I'm a little numb. I still need to process all this anyway. And you gave me homework. If not for Caleb I wouldn't have come in here today."

"But I'm glad you did. It was the right thing to do. It gives me another angle to look it and saves weeks of guesswork."

"If it is Micah I want him buried next to my parents back in Turlock."

Caleb stretched his arm around her waist. "Let's take one step at a time for now. We have to get through this next week first."

"There is one more thing you should know," Hannah added. "I'm not convinced that my father is the one who shot my mother. I don't think he took his own life that day. Which means it wasn't a murder/suicide at all. I don't think my father shot anyone."

"Yeah," Brent said with a nod. "I'd already thought of that possibility. How else was this woman planning to get her hands on the baby?"

"There's just one problem with that theory," Hannah said. "I've never been able to figure out the one missing ingredient about that day. If she was already in the house, if this woman had just murdered my mom and dad, then why did she pretend to be a social worker? Wouldn't she have fled the scene *with* the baby and driven off? She didn't need to pretend anything if she already had the baby."

Brent sat back down. "Not necessarily."

Hannah sat back down as well. "You want to explain that?"

"It's a possibility the cops showed up before she could get out of the house with your brother. You see where I'm going with this?"

"Not really."

"Off the top of my head, let's take it from the little you've told me so far. Let's say, this woman is brazen enough to commit a double homicide to get a baby. After all, we think that's the sole reason she's picked your family. She's determined, maybe a little off her rocker and she knows what she wants, even if it means eliminating your parents to get it done. Somehow, she gains access into the house. Maybe she pretends to be a door to door salesperson or a survey taker. Whatever it is, it gets her inside the living room and your mother asks her if she'd like something to drink. She waits until your mom turns her back to head into the kitchen, and then takes out the weapon. She pulls the trigger."

Getting caught up in setting the stage, Hannah licked her lips and provided the tidbits she'd learned over the years. "They were shot with a 9-millimeter. The gun was left at the scene right next to my father, hence the murder/suicide angle."

"You've seen the police report?"

"I have copies of it. I believe my dad had been asleep in the bedroom but came out to the living room for some reason. That's where the police found both bodies. Because the gun was there I guess they assumed they'd gotten into a fierce argument and my dad shot my mom.

He saw what he'd done and then turned the gun on himself."

"Okay, let's go with where the bodies and gun were found minus the suicide. For this scenario, your dad is sound asleep in the bedroom. He hears what he thinks is a gunshot. He responds by getting out of bed and hurrying into the living room. Our perp fires again. She drops the gun near your dad. The neighbors, who heard the first shot minutes earlier, have already dialed 911. It's the middle of the day, a slack time for the police. Maybe there's already a uniform cruising the neighborhood, maybe he's sitting around the corner for whatever reason and responds immediately to the call over his radio. The perp's just murdered two people in cold blood. She looks out the window and sees the cop car pulling up to the curb before she even has time to jerk the baby out of his crib. She panics. She runs out the back. At some point, she realizes she didn't get what she came for. She's stewing about it, thinking long and hard about how to remedy that. She wanted that baby more than anything else in the world, enough to commit double murder, so she comes up with what she believes is a bold, daring move. She circles the block, maybe a couple of times, then she turns down your street to assess the situation. She pulls up behind a cruiser, puts the car in park and sits there to take in the scene. She realizes the police presence is growing with every tick of the clock. But it's a chaotic mess. First responders are inside walking the crime scene already. Baby Micah is wailing in the background, screaming his lungs out. The perp can hear him from her spot at the curb. You can bet there's a police officer on scene charged to care for the infant, but he can't calm the baby down. No matter what he does the kid keeps wailing. Our perpetrator simply walks in the door, claims to be the social worker who's gonna take baby Micah off the guy's hands. Believe me, in that situation any uniform will tell you they're relieved when Child Services show up. The uniform gladly relinquishes the baby to the first person who offers. That's our perp. He hands the baby over without a squabble. She walks out of the house, gets back to her car, and takes off. By the time anyone figures out that she isn't who she claims to be, it's too late."

Hannah exchanged looks with Caleb before staring into Brent's face. "Wow. You've figured out what I was never able to in less than five minutes. Why aren't you kicking ass in some huge police department somewhere else?"

He gave her a smile. "I don't want to live somewhere else. Did I get close?"

"Incredibly close. Your version of events solves the gaping hole in my theory. By any chance did you ever work homicide?"

Brent's lips curved wider. "A time or two. So that fits more in line with what you already know?"

"Yes. There's another issue that's bothered me for years. If you get in touch with the sheriff up in Stanislaus County, ask him why no one ever bothered to check to see if the murder weapon actually belonged to my dad. I don't think it did. I might be wrong about this since I was just a little kid, but the type of gun I remember my dad owning was more like a .22 rifle, a long gun. It wasn't a short weapon. The first time I read the report it mentioned a 9-millimeter. I started looking through scads of pictures on the Internet. At the time, I didn't know anything about guns, but I do know one thing. The weapon my dad owned didn't look anything like an automatic handgun, not even close. Try comparing a rifle to a handgun. A child knows there's a difference."

"Okay, that's good information. It'll make me sound like I know something about the case that maybe he doesn't. Have you ever spoken to a member of law enforcement face to face about the murders other than obtaining a copy of the police report?"

"A couple of times when I was in college I contacted the sheriff's department, but they never called me back. So, one day I drove there, had to sit in the lobby for the better part of an afternoon before a detective came out to talk to me. His name was Morrissey, Jeb Morrissey. I'm pretty sure he retired last summer. He's the one who felt sorry for me and got me a copy of the autopsies and the police report. But that was the only time I sat down with anyone…official."

Brent stood up, offering his hand. "Hannah, you've done an amazing job to get this far. It's okay to let me handle the rest."

"I don't know if I can let go. Cops usually have so much on their plates. They don't have time to go back and revisit a case like mine, a case where I'm trying to find my only brother but also trying to prove my father wasn't a murderer. This case is my life, finding the truth is all I've ever truly wanted."

"This is Pelican Pointe. We rarely have a crime wave here that fills up my plate. I'll do everything I can to help you find the truth. I promise."

It was almost five o'clock when veterinarians Keegan and Cord Bennett opened the door to the police station and looked around.

"Is Brent here?" Keegan asked Eastlyn.

"Sure. Go on in. After a super busy day, things have finally slacked off. I guess you heard."

"That's why we're here."

"Is it the noise? Because there's not much we can do about the digging. And even if Caleb hadn't found the remains, he'd be the one making just as much of a racket."

"It isn't the noise," Keegan said. "I think I might have some information about the remains."

"Really? Wow. You and half the town."

Brent overheard part of the conversation and walked out into the small lobby. "Cord, Keegan, how's it going?" He noted Keegan looked worried, similar to how Hannah had looked earlier.

Keegan stood wringing her hands. "It was fine until I came back to shore—someone reported an injured seal south of here near Wilder State Park. I went out to see if I could locate it. But when I got back I saw the commotion next door and heard about what Caleb found."

Cord eyed Brent as if trying to convey something with his facial expression. "Keegan has something to tell you about something she witnessed a long time ago."

"No problem. Come on in to the office. You look like you could use something to drink."

"I don't suppose you have a margarita back here with a double shot of tequila," Keegan quipped.

"Best I can offer you is a cupful of water from our dispenser. Have a seat."

"I'll take it."

Brent went out to the water cooler in the lobby and filled a paper cup, brought it back to Keegan. "What's up? You're upset about something."

Keegan guzzled down the contents and set the cup down on Brent's desk. "I know who buried those remains at Bradford House. It was the owner. But he wasn't alone."

Eight

The air had left the room by the time Brent recovered enough to speak. "You saw him do that?"

Keegan nodded and leaned closer to the desk. "I remembered an incident from when I was a kid. But before I explain that, you know I grew up right next door to Bradford House."

"Sure. The Fanning Rescue Center is right next door."

"My grandparents, Porter and Mary, raised me in that house where Cord and I live now. But that huge estate next door wasn't always there. At first it was a vacant lot. My grandparents wanted to buy that acreage from the couple who owned it. Townsend was their name I found it this afternoon in a bunch of old papers belonging to my grandparents. According to those papers, the plan was to extend the rescue center beyond its borders and make it larger. My grandfather had been eyeing that property for years and couldn't get the owners to budge off the price. There are notations in the papers I found that say Douglas knew my grandparents wanted the land and went behind their back to get it. My grandfather makes it clear that Douglas drove up to San Francisco for the sole purpose of wining and dining the Townsends to get them to sell him the property. It worked. And, you see the results. Douglas got the land, built the big mansion, and proceeded to act like a frat boy by throwing a string of loud, obnoxious, lavish parties, for the next several decades. The man eventually became the mayor and the talk of the town. It seems fitting now that he still is."

"You mentioned an incident. What did you see?"

"I was about thirteen. It was winter. I was in the process of doing my chores before school, which included feeding our resident patients. At the time, we had a very large elephant seal who barked a lot. That morning, he was causing his usual ruckus and I was trying to calm him down. From next door came this booming voice. It was Douglas yelling at me to keep the animal quiet. I won't repeat the string of obscenities that sailed out of his mouth. If not for his making a scene at the time, I probably wouldn't even have looked over the fence. But I did. I saw Douglas and a woman digging a hole, right about where the forensic team is focusing now. I watched them toss a bundle, something wrapped in a blanket, striped, in that damn pit they'd dug. That's what I remember. They dropped the striped blanket in the hole and started shoveling dirt back in almost immediately."

Brent sat back in his chair. "Did you ever tell anyone about this?"

"I didn't know it was a baby!" Keegan shouted. "How could I have known that? I went on to school and didn't think twice about the incident."

"I'm sorry. Could you recognize the woman again if I showed you a picture?"

Keegan let out a shaky sigh and looked over at Cord. "Didn't I tell you he would ask me that?"

"You did."

Keegan swiped a hand through her hair. "The one thing you need to know about Douglas is he had a parade of women that came and went. It was hard to keep up and difficult to differentiate one from another. Men, too, stopped in at all hours of the day and night. But if I had to give you a description from that day, I'd say…I remember red hair like mine, only more…stylish, not as wild, but more tamed. She was tall, like a model. Whenever she'd come for the weekend I remembered her car, she drove a fancy red BMW, sporty thing."

Eastlyn stood listening from the doorway and traded knowing looks with Brent. "She's a good witness, Brent."

"Yep. Very. Good account of what went down, Keegan. You may have just saved me a lot of investigative time."

"So, it helps? What I saw that day so long ago helps? Because try to imagine what I felt like today when I learned what was in that hole. I was sick, Brent. Ask Cord. I've been mortified ever since I learned they threw a baby away. I have to live with that."

"It's not your fault. You were just a young kid. No one could've predicted they were burying a child. No one could have imagined that kind of evil living right next door. What you've just unloaded is a huge break in the case for us. We're grateful you came in and didn't keep this to yourself."

"How could I keep that kind of thing to myself? Not after what I remembered seeing, the callous, nonchalant way Bradford yelled at me that morning, as if that was the most important thing, getting the seal to stop barking instead of the fact he was burying an infant."

Brent stood up. "You go on home now. I'll write up an official report based on everything you told me for the file. You can bet I'll be in touch. I'll ask you to sign your account of what you saw. Cord, you see to it Keegan stops worrying about this, at least for tonight. There's nothing she could've done at thirteen to prevent this from coming back to haunt us all."

Cord took his wife's hand and started for the door. "She knows that, but she also knows that even an animal deserves a better burial than what this baby got. In fact, in our business when an animal dies we give it a little ceremony. What bothers Keegan is that this child was tossed away like garbage. That's something the rest of us with a working heart have a tough time understanding."

Caleb had driven Hannah back home and stayed to fix her something to eat. It was the first time he'd been inside the same little bungalow that his sister-in-law had once occupied.

"I'm perfectly capable of making my own dinner," Hannah grumbled, even though she was secretly glad he'd trailed her home.

"I know you are, but you've had a rough afternoon."

"And you haven't? It isn't every day a person finds a skull belonging to a baby."

"Still trying to get that out of my head, thank you. Here's hoping that keeping busy will do the trick. What do you have on hand to eat?"

Caleb paced the kitchen throwing open cabinet doors and peering in like he was taking inventory, and then concluded the result on his own. "You don't have much in the way of food here."

"The space doesn't hold a lot. I told you it was tiny," Hannah explained as she watched Caleb move around the mini kitchen, looking in every nook and cranny.

"Yeah, but I had no idea you have zero cabinet space to speak of and barely enough room to turn around. Where do you put your canned goods or cereal or snack foods?"

"What is it with you and this thing you have about a huge pantry?"

"I like having a place to unload the groceries. Every kitchen needs one. I don't think I could live here in something this small."

"I make do." She walked over to a little door near the back and opened it up. "Eastlyn added some shelves to the broom closet and started using it to hold groceries. This is a simple guest house and not much more. I was lucky to find it. I couldn't believe how little Keegan and Cord were asking for rent on this place."

Caleb inspected the tiny cupboard and shook his head. "We need to buy groceries. You go take a hot shower and relax. I'll run to Murphy's Market and pick up two ribeyes, some potatoes for baking, and the makings for a salad. How's that sound?"

"Sounds wonderful. But you don't have to do all that."

He met her halfway in the middle of the kitchen and took her chin, tipped it up. "After what happened today, I don't want to spend tonight alone."

"That makes two of us."

"Then it's settled." He gave her a friendly swat on her backside and started out the door. "I'll be back in half an hour."

Left alone, Hannah knew what she had to do. She had to call Denton and Cassie to let them know what was going on. She didn't want either one hearing about the remains on the six o'clock newscast.

She took out her cell phone, found Denton's name in her contacts, and hit the number to dial.

The voice on the other end was a warm reminder she had family. "What's up, baby girl?"

"Hi, Dad. I've had kind of a rough day." She started to cry and through a blubbering explanation, she was finally able to tell Denton what she suspected.

While Hannah explained things to her family, Caleb pushed a cart up and down the aisles at the market, chunking in what he needed to make dinner. He didn't expect to run into Beckham. The teenager was with his girlfriend Faye, a little brunette with big chocolate eyes who had a guarded demeanor around other people.

Since Beckham had found a home with Quentin and Sydney, Caleb decided the teenager had put on some much-needed weight.

Beckham eyed the stuff Caleb had in his cart. "You actually eat arugula? You know that's dandelion weeds, right?"

Caleb slapped Beckham on the back. "Wrong. They're two different plants altogether. Arugula is an annual with a peppery taste while dandelion is a perennial with a much more bitter flavor. You'd know that if you studied that plant chart I gave you."

Beckham made a face. "It sounded too much like homework."

From the side, Faye inched closer to Caleb. In a low voice, she murmured, "You're the one who found that poor little baby."

"Unfortunately I am. Are the news vans still parked on Ocean Street?"

"They're crawling around like ants," Beckham replied and clutched the basket he carried in his hand a little tighter. "Such a terrible thing to do to a tiny kid like that. Who do you think put it there?"

"No idea. That's what Brent's working on." Caleb was convinced he needed to change the subject. "What are you guys up to?"

"Sydney sent me out of the house to shop for supper. It's an excuse to get rid of me, us, so she and Dad can talk about what to do once the cops get done with the yard. I think for us Bradford House might be history."

"Are they thinking of moving out of there permanently?" Caleb asked.

"Maybe. They might keep the house. But they don't know what to do about, you know, marking the spot or whatever for…later. They think something should be done, something put there, like a marker. They're still batting the subject around. I'm just not sure, they'll want to move back in, even though some of our stuff is still there."

Faye shifted her feet. "It was my idea to put up the marker once they find out the baby's identity, of course."

"That's not a bad plan," Caleb said.

"Who do you think she is?" Faye wondered.

Caleb turned to look at Faye. "She? What makes you think it was a girl?"

It was Beckham who went into detail. "Those guys doing the digging found a multi-colored blanket with pink stripes on it. Faye and I were looking through a pair of binoculars when we saw them drag it out of the dirt."

"You guys were spying?"

Beckham grinned. "We used the trail that leads around to the cliffs. Not even the reporters have found it yet."

"Pink points to one specific gender," Faye reminded them. "At least that's what Sydney says. She thinks most baby boys wouldn't have pink stripes on a blanket. What do you think?"

"I think she's right. I wouldn't want a pink blanket," Beckham added.

"You would if you were cold," Faye pointed out. "A baby would be way too young to know the difference anyway."

Caleb stared at the wise Faye. "You're pretty smart. Women would know more about stuff like that than I would." But an interesting turn of events, he thought. And he couldn't wait to pass that information along to Hannah.

"We gotta go," Beckham announced. "Sydney's waiting on us to get back with the fixings for spaghetti."

"See you guys later. Take care."

Caleb wheeled his cart into the frozen food aisle intending to pick up ice cream. He was bent at the waist over the freezer section when a heavy object banged him across the back. He straightened up in time to see Phyllis Caldwell drawing back to whack him again with her purse.

"What the hell are you doing?" Caleb cried out. "Quit that!"

Phyllis had to be near seventy. But for an older woman, she packed a punch. "It's what you deserve, disturbing that little baby the way you did. How dare you dig him up like that!"

He caught the woman's arm in mid-swing. "I was hired to do a landscaping job. I had no idea I'd stumble on a body buried there. It's not like I dug it up on purpose."

Phyllis didn't shirk from her mission and landed another blow, this time to Caleb's shoulder, knocking him back a step.

"What's wrong with you? Cut it out! Now! Why are you doing this?" He narrowed his eyes. "Unless...do you know who that baby belongs to?"

"No! And I don't care who it belongs to. It doesn't matter. I heard the bones came up in pieces. Shame on you, Caleb Jennings. It isn't enough you belong to that murderer, that mentally disturbed Eleanor Richmond, the one who's responsible for killing my niece. Brooke was a sweetheart and your mother took her away from us. And now, today, I hear you have to go and dig up a baby's body right out of the ground."

Murphy walked up about that time and grabbed Phyllis's arm. "What the hell is going on here?"

"Ask Mrs. Caldwell," Caleb grumbled as he pushed his cart out of Phyllis's reach. "She's talking crazy. That body has nothing to do with her niece."

"Yeah, well, if Brooke hadn't fallen for your spineless father she wouldn't be dead now. She'd probably have a couple of kids of her own." Phyllis dabbed at her eyes. "I didn't even get to plan her wedding. Her brother Ryan, and I miss her every single day."

"I thought you guys lived over in Scotts Valley," Murphy noted.

Phyllis opened her purse and brought out a tissue. "We used to. But an opening came up at the elementary school and Julianne, the principal, offered Ryan a position there to teach fourth grade. This is his second semester there."

"You can't come in here, Phyllis, and start attacking people with your purse," Murphy explained while directing Caleb to move down the aisle.

Caleb took the hint and headed for checkout.

By the time he got back to Hannah's place, he'd calmed down enough to start dinner. But Hannah met him at the door with a frown.

"Durke called me in to work tonight. It seems it's Darla's night on, but she caught her baby's cold and Geniece isn't picking up her cell. On weeknights, there's usually just the one waitress on duty. Looks like tonight it's me."

"Why am I not surprised? I guess spending time alone tonight just wasn't in the cards. Did you talk to your family?"

"I did. Dad was ready to jump in the car with Cassie and head here tonight. But I persuaded him to hold off and wait for confirmation." She noticed the strained look on Caleb's face and took his chin in her hand. "What happened while you were gone?"

He set the bags on the counter and started unloading the steaks and perishable items into the fridge. "It's amazing what you can learn at the grocery store. According to Beckham and Faye, the forensic team found a pink-striped blanket in the hole with the bones."

"Already? Uh, that would indicate the baby was a girl."

"That seems to be the general consensus, and if true, changes things quite a bit for you."

"That means the baby might not be Micah." Relief moved through her like a bolt of lightning. But that still didn't explain Caleb's demeanor. "You aren't this upset learning about a blanket. What else happened?"

He told her about the run-in with Phyllis Caldwell. "She's Brooke Caldwell's aunt. Like everyone else in town somehow Phyllis got wind of the news at Bradford House. I guess it brought back bad memories. Once she spotted me at Murphy's, she lit into me and decided to remind me that my so-called mother is the reason Brooke's dead."

"That's ridiculous."

"Not really. There's probably some truth in that statement. But even though I had nothing to do with it, for a few minutes there this afternoon, I was the closest thing Phyllis could bop on the head out of frustration."

"I'm so sorry. That isn't fair to you."

"Nothing about my parents has ever landed in the fair column."

Hannah pressed her lips to his. "Look, why don't you come to the bar tonight and I'll buy you dinner. I know chicken wings is a poor substitute for steak but it's the best I can do."

"Maybe I will…later. I think for now I'll head home and get cleaned up."

"Okay, but text me if you change your mind."

Nine

The Shipwreck on a weeknight was far less crowded than on the weekends. But stalwart regulars still showed up for happy hour. In addition to the permanent cast of characters that walked in the door, Hannah waited on a group of grad students—three guys and two girls—who were in town from UC Santa Cruz. They'd spent all day touring the Chumash Museum for their evolutionary biology class and were ready to party.

"I'm gonna need to see IDs all around," Hannah stated after they ordered beers and wings.

"Hey, gorgeous," one of the fresh-faced young men began. "How about you and me going out to my car for a quickie? Did I mention it's an Audi?"

Hannah rolled her eyes. "As silver-tongued as you think you are, I'm still gonna need to see your ID."

"Problem?" Durke called out from behind the bar.

Hannah stared the young man down. "Is there a problem here or should I just bring sodas all around for everybody with the wings?"

"I'm twenty-three," one of the man proclaimed, proving it by lifting his butt off his chair and taking out his wallet. He held up his driver's license. The other three members of the party followed suit, producing photo IDs proving they were over twenty-one.

"Four beers and a soda then," Hannah concluded, still glaring at the asshole with the attitude.

"Wait. Okay. Fine," the stubborn man said, finally slipping the ID out of his wallet. Instead of handing it to her though, he tossed it on the table.

After confirming it was a genuine California license that showed a birth date making him twenty-six, only then did Hannah take her time and head over to the bar to get the draft beers.

She gave Kirby the wings order and greeted members of the Santa Cruz County forensic team who had decided to spend their first evening in Pelican Pointe checking out the drink specials. Hannah supplied them with gin and tonics, a couple of mojitos, and whiskey sours until they finally ordered what had become the bar's specialty...the wings.

She tried to linger around the crime scene techs hoping to pick up on what they'd found so far, maybe learn something scientific. But all she heard was a string of excuses that explained the reason for happy hour. She got the impression that the scene at Bradford House had prompted tonight's alcohol consumption. It seemed most were looking to drown out what they'd seen with a steady dose of hard liquor.

Hannah couldn't blame them. She wasn't certain a bottle of rum was the answer, but it couldn't hurt sipping an Irish coffee in front of a roaring fire. She wished she was home now—eating steaks, sitting with Caleb and commiserating about their lousy day.

A bit disappointed that he hadn't sent her a text and it was almost ten-thirty, she considered sending him one.

But when the pigheaded twenty-four-year grad student signaled he needed a refill, Hannah lost her train of thought. The man had been flirting with her all evening. Each time she got near his table, his hands tried to grab and feel her ass. She took most of the behavior in stride as part waitressing in a bar. It wasn't the first time a man had gotten fresh with her while trying to do her job. But when this guy started getting seriously drunk and surly, she turned to Durke for help.

"See that asshole over there. Do you think it might be time to cut him off? For several hours he's been getting more and more rude with each draft."

"I'll talk to him."

"And say what?" Hannah wanted to know. "Keep your hands to yourself. I tried that about an hour ago. I've been avoiding him. If Darla or Geniece were here I would've simply switched tables. Me solo. Won't happen."

"Hey, gorgeous redhead," the grad student yelled, waving his empty mug in the air. "Over here. 'Nother beer. Move it now, bitch!"

"See what I mean."

Before Durke could round the bar and boot the man out the door, Caleb walked in and caught the derogatory comment. Even now, he headed toward the drunk.

Sensing an ugly scene, Hannah dashed that way but Caleb beat her to the man's table.

He stood behind the sloshed guy, gripping the drunk's shoulders hard, his fingers digging in for emphasis. Those fingers that did routine manual labor held the man in place and got his attention.

"I don't recognize you, so I'll cut you some slack because you're a stranger in town. But in these parts, we don't talk to women like that. Understand?"

Because the guy nodded and seemed agreeable to changing his attitude, Caleb let go. But the drunk wasn't going to stop without a fight. He came up out of the chair, swinging at Caleb.

Caleb ducked and clocked the guy with one punch, right in the nose. The inebriated man swayed and fell back where he stood.

The drunk's friends gathered over him and tried to help him to his feet.

Caleb looked up to see Eastlyn swagger over to where he stood. She patted her brother-in-law's shoulder. "Hey there, slugger, how's it going?"

"No fair," the drunk grunted, holding his nose. "You guys know each other."

"True," Eastlyn stated. "But the owner isn't my brother-in-law and he says you've been harassing the wait staff all night. That would be the redhead you've been hitting on for most of the evening."

Hannah appeared at Eastlyn's elbow. "He's been a pest every time I get near the table, trying to put his hands on me, using inappropriate language, and won't take 'no' for an answer."

Eastlyn let one hand rest on her weapon just to make sure the drunk understood he shouldn't take this lightly. "Ah. Now see, you're not allowed to do that, not here, not in Santa Cruz, not anywhere, bub."

"But the local tough guy is allowed to break my fucking nose? Is that it?"

"I'll call the doc and let him take a look at that bloody mess you call a nose. It's obviously broken. But before you go making a fuss, think twice. I could arrest you for drunk and disorderly and you'd spend the night in jail. But because you're bleeding like a stuck pig, I'm letting you off the hook for the public drunkenness. That is, as long as your friends get you of here now, and drive you back to wherever you came from…tonight. Got that?"

The man finally nodded.

"Great. I'll call the doctor and your friends can see to it that you get over to the clinic without a problem. But if I ever see you in town again, I'll lock you up on sight. Take my advice. Learn some manners before you get your nose smashed again, otherwise you won't have such a pretty face for long."

Hannah took Caleb's hand. "Thanks for showing up when you did."

He slid his arm around her waist. "No problem. That guy was ramping up, ready to get nasty in a heartbeat."

"I sensed that. It made me uneasy. I'd been the brunt of his raunchy attitude for most of the night."

"You don't have to take this crap, Hannah. There are other jobs in town."

She slid her hand across his chest. "It's one incident, Caleb. Besides, I'm already talking to Isabella about running the co-op in town on a permanent basis. Maybe even growing a few grapes one day."

"Now you're talking. Since Eastlyn's here, why don't we see if she can confirm the rumor about the blanket."

"Great idea. But see those guys sitting at that table in the corner? That group is part of the forensic team. I don't think Eastlyn will answer any questions as long as we ask her here."

"Good point. Then let's question her outside."

"I could take my break now. Hold on. Let me tell Durke." Hannah scooted around the end of the bar and whispered something to her boss. A few minutes later she came running back, following Eastlyn out into the parking lot.

When she'd caught up with the cop, Hannah blurted out, "Mind if we ask you something?"

"Go ahead. Doesn't mean I'll answer it though."

"The thing is…we heard, Caleb heard this afternoon, the forensic people found a pink blanket with the rest of the bones."

Eastlyn lifted her head skyward. "Don't believe everything you hear. That's just plain wrong information."

"I see. Someone told Caleb there was a pink blanket found at the site. So, it isn't true?"

Eastlyn huffed out a breath. "They found tattered pieces of a blanket. The only pink I know about was the faded blood spots on the shredded pieces."

Hannah was a little unsteady on her feet. "Oh. So, I guess that means Micah is still very much a possibility for a match."

"'Fraid so."

Empathy for the woman had Eastlyn leaning against her car. "I shouldn't be discussing this with you two at all. But this afternoon, I sensed that Brent cut you some slack so I will, as well. I can confirm there was fabric discovered at the scene believed to be what was left of a blanket. It wasn't intact. The faded blood made it look pinkish in color. Keep in mind, that thing's been in the ground for almost two decades. But those forensic guys tested it and confirmed it was human blood on the material."

The news caused Hannah to wince. "Blood is a serious indication that baby suffered a catastrophic event. Caleb and I thought that if the blanket was pink it might rule out Micah."

Eastlyn shook her head. "No such luck I'm afraid. Your little brother is still the best lead we have in IDing those remains."

"I was hoping for a different answer."

"Sorry. I wish I could've provided one. Look, I gotta go and follow up with that jerk at the clinic, make sure he hightails it out of town with his friends." Eastlyn opened the door to her squad car. "For what it's worth, my advice is to get your mind off the results. I'm serious. You have a week to wait. Don't spend the next seven days stressing out about it. Stressing out won't change a thing."

With that, Hannah and Caleb watched her zoom out of the parking lot.

Hannah crossed her arms over her chest. "How exactly do I not stress out about it?"

"Eastlyn has a typical cop mentality about most everything, all business. And she's probably right. Worrying yourself silly won't help the outcome."

Hannah blew out a breath that lingered in the chilly air like fog. "This is turning out to be a really crappy January. I lost one of my major clients today. I certainly won't be cleaning the Bradford House any time soon. When they say a week, you watch, count on it taking two."

"Yeah, I had a hunch that might be the case. Quentin's yard makeover is on hold, which leaves me with a huge gap in revenue."

"Great way to start out the new year, huh? I could drop by the nursery tomorrow, throw a little business your way, and pick up a lemon tree. I've been wanting to try my hand at growing one."

He put his arm around her shoulder. "Thanks. I can rest easy now, stop worrying about January sales, and send in that pesky mortgage payment."

The simple sarcasm had her leaning into his body. "Thank goodness I still have the job at the B&B. How about some of those wings I promised you?"

"I guess I could choke down a couple with a beer."

She stuck her arm through his. "Good. I like being able to glance across the bar and see you sitting there."

"Why didn't you say that earlier?"

"Because you already have the advantage."

"I do? Mind pointing it out to me?"

"You already know I plan to sleep with you."

After her shift ended, he followed her home in his truck.

"You can't come in."

"But you said…"

"I know what I said…earlier. It's just that I have a long day tomorrow at the B&B and if you come in we'll stay up all night making love. I need to be sharp because after I finish at Promise Cove I plan to do some…research."

"What kind of research? Ah. You plan to go behind Brent's back and still hunt down information? Great. I want in on that."

"Be sure because I'll likely piss off the police chief. I'm not from here, but you are."

"It's a light day at the nursery tomorrow. I'll take the afternoon off and come with you. Besides, I want to make sure I reserve that making-love-all-night thing. I'm not letting you off the hook."

"I don't want off the hook. But I think I know what will happen once we get together. I feel there's something building between us. Seriously building. Don't you feel it, too?"

For an answer, he yanked her against him and covered her mouth. The air sizzled between them.

"Is that what you had in mind?"

"Yeah. Do me a favor. Promise you'll dedicate an entire night to that right there."

Ten

As in most small towns when something out of the ordinary happens it didn't take long for the news to make the rounds.

There'd been a flurry of buzzing rumors since the discovery, and it seemed Hannah was the target. She'd heard whispers behind her back from her first stop at the diner to get coffee that morning to her next stop at the bank. The long stare from the teller had surprised her. She'd dropped in to deposit the check Kinsey Donnelly had given her yesterday for the weekly cleaning job and was amazed that so many customers there had become gawkers. Rubbernecking at an accident was one thing, but downright staring reminded her too much of the day she'd lost her parents.

Maybe the frosty treatment at the bank should've prepared her for the reception at Promise Cove. But it still surprised her. As soon as she opened the front door, Jordan greeted her with kid-glove treatment. The innkeeper shoved a cup of coffee in her hand and ushered her past the living room, down the hallway, and into the kitchen.

"The chores can wait for a bit. Come in here and sit down. Tell me everything. Don't leave anything out. I had no idea your reason for being here was to find your baby brother. How heartbreaking that your long search might end at Bradford House."

A little self-conscious, Hannah sat down at the farmhouse-style table in the familiar cozy kitchen and watched Jordan fuss over a pan of gooey cinnamon rolls. The warmth in the room reminded her what it might've been like if she'd had an older sister, someone to talk to and share her fears and feelings.

Hannah realized then she'd have to go over the turn of events again for Jordan's benefit. "Everyone keeps telling me that I shouldn't jump to that one basic conclusion. But it's hard not to believe it's Micah in that hole."

Jordan brought over a serving tray filled with chocolate croissants and sat down across from Hannah. The innkeeper dished out one of the tasty treats and slid it onto a plate. When she caught Hannah staring, she added, "Would you prefer a cinnamon roll? I didn't even think to ask."

Hannah grinned. "Not at all. It's as if you knew the chocolate croissant fit my mood better than the other. It's just that you're such a remarkable woman, so talented in the kitchen. It's a wonder your guests don't leave here twenty pounds heavier."

"So what if they do? Life should be enjoyed. That includes indulgences now and then. Guests come here to be pampered. It's one reason I'm good at this job. I believe we ought to treat ourselves at times when life's just too hard to handle."

Hannah took her first bite of the croissant. "This is delicious."

"It's my mother's recipe. I've been making them for almost twenty years. I never get tired of watching someone take that first sample and seeing their reaction. It's heavenly, isn't it?"

"Downright decadent."

Jordan picked up her coffee cup and went on with the purpose of the chat. "If it isn't Micah buried there, who else could it be? What other baby could possibly be left that way in such a prominent location? You might not be able to tell it from the road but anyone who's lived here for very long knows that house at one time was *the* showplace in town. It was where all the Christmas parties were held, elegant costume balls, Fourth of July barbecues, and New Year's Eve bashes. Douglas had a flair for entertaining. That all slowed down when he retired as mayor. And then he got sick and it all but ended his party days. But you need to understand that for a body to be discovered there, especially that of a child, it's the biggest news since Carl Knudsen was arrested for serial murder. This story is more than a little mystifying to all the locals."

Hannah added cream to her mug and a little sugar. "Ah. I guess that's why everyone stared at me at the bank as if I intended to make off with the cash."

"Oh, no. Did they?"

"Yeah. Big time. Isn't the first time people have whispered behind my back. Foster care in a new school was much the same way when I was a kid. My point is, I think I should be cautious about making this a foregone conclusion. Micah might be alive. I feel hope is the only thing I have now. Over the years, there have been other times that I thought I was close to answers, only to get let down and discover I had the wrong person in my sights. Wrong birth date. Wrong description. It stands to reason it might not be Micah at all. I can't help wondering how could it be this easy? After my long pursuit of the truth, how could Caleb just stumble on the remains like he did? You see why I'm skeptical."

"What does Scott say?"

Hannah almost choked on her coffee. "I can't exactly conjure him up, Jordan. Maybe you can, but I haven't seen him since New Year's Eve or rather New Year's morning. He must be staying away for a reason."

"What do you suppose that means?"

"It might mean that I've found Micah and his work is done. There. He got me here and…" Hannah's voice trailed off. She dropped her head into her hands. "I don't know. I'm so confused about it all. One minute I'm sure it's Micah and the next I've changed my mind and it's not."

"But that doesn't sound much like the way Scott works. He usually finishes what he starts. At least that's my perspective." But instead of delving into that arena, Jordan waved off the thought and peppered Hannah with a long list of troubling questions. "Maybe I just need more details."

Hannah caught her up with the remainder of the backstory just as she'd told Brent the day before.

Jordan leaned back in her chair. "Something doesn't add up. How is it the police blamed your father for the shooting when clearly this woman who took the baby is the one responsible and made it look like a murder/suicide."

Hannah threw up her hands. "Thank you. I've been thinking that same thing for…forever…or at least since I was old enough to grasp the circumstances of how Micah disappeared."

Jordan patted her hand. "Girl, you have a huge mystery on your hands. You need to get Brent thinking that same way, make sure you're both on the same page with this."

"Brent surprised me. I got the impression he's leaning that way. Although he found it interesting enough, that's one way to go."

Jordan's eyes settled on Hannah in stern fashion. "Oh, honey, please tell me you aren't thinking of trying to run down leads on your own? That won't go over well at all with Brent."

"But technically, this isn't his case."

"Did he say that? If that's Micah, it's his murder investigation."

"And if it isn't…the original kidnapping happened in Stanislaus County, the double murders were there."

Jordan shifted in her seat. "All I know is that Brent is like most members of law enforcement. He's very territorial when it comes to protecting this town. He used to be the county sheriff. No more. Since leaving that job it's like he has something to prove to everyone. That's why you better believe he'll do his best to solve this thing. Trust me on that."

Jordan chewed her lip. "You know, when we first heard the news yesterday, Nick and I thought of something that might be relevant. It just so happens I have a ton of photos Scott took of Bradford House. Scott started taking pictures back in high school. He fancied himself a photographer and worked on the yearbook and the high school newspaper. Add to that, in his spare time, he was quite good at capturing things around town in pictures, black and white mostly. You may have noticed upstairs, I had some of his treasured photographs framed and used them as artwork to display around the house. Through the years, he must have taken at least a hundred photos of Bradford House. Nick and I discovered them a couple months back when we went to the attic to get out the Christmas decorations. There was a box of photos sitting out, big as life in the middle of the room as if Scott wanted us to find them. Once we got the tree up, we began sorting through the box and found some stunning photos taken on Bradford grounds and the surrounding cliffs. I'd planned to give them to Quentin at some point as a housewarming gift. But with the busy holidays I haven't had the chance."

"I'd love to see them."

Jordan got up from the table and retrieved a large manila envelope stuffed with pictures, some taken in vivid color, others snapped in black and white. She spread them out so Hannah could peruse through the stacks.

Hannah went through at least three dozen images and began to pick up on a pattern. "Some of these were obviously taken before the yard was fully landscaped as it appears today. See? There's a smooth patch of grass where eventually that rock wall will be located. Right here is where they found the skull." She pointed to the western part of the lawn. "But in these photos there are no rocks visible. None stacked the way Caleb found them yesterday." She flipped over the back of the picture, hoping for a date, but the reverse side was blank. "When do you suppose these were taken?"

"No idea. I'm sorry. Scott would know for certain."

That wouldn't help her much unless Scott decided to make an appearance. And soon. "Look, do you mind if I take a few of these with me? Not all, just the ones that show the specific area of the lawn where the forensic team is digging. There's a difference in how the same plot looked through the years."

"No, of course not. I have a feeling Scott wanted us to find them for a reason. Maybe this was it."

Later that afternoon after Hannah finished up her work, she went by the nursery. Inside Caleb's office, she laid out the pictures for him to see.

"Wow, this is like looking back in time when the old house was in its best shape ever. New. Same can be said of the yard. We have to find out who built that rock wall and when."

"I was hoping you'd say that. Are you certain The Plant Habitat wasn't involved with the yard makeover back then? I mean, you might not know the answer to that since you couldn't have been more than six or seven at the time. But think about it, if it wasn't your family's company, then who was doing that kind of work?"

Caleb's face looked stunned. "That's a great question. And one I should ask Landon. I'll be right back."

"Uh-uh, not without me."

They found Landon in the greenhouse, bent over a worktable, clipping the stems on a hybrid orchid that would one day be as easy to grow as a daisy.

Hannah fanned her face. "It's so much warmer in here than out there."

"We keep it a toasty eighty degrees," Caleb told her.

"Look at this," Landon stated with pride. "I think I'm getting close to coming up with one hardy orchidaceae, resistant to disease, over-watering, and root rot. One that offers a new color, a blend between lavender and purple."

Hannah moved closer to get a better look. "That's the most gorgeous orchid I've ever seen."

"This is the man in his element," Caleb said to Hannah. "Landon is the quintessential plant architect. You want to know how to grow grapes, this is the guy to ask."

"So you're much more than 'the flower guy,'" Hannah teased. "Not sure you know it, but that's the term Drea lovingly uses to refer to your expertise in all matters of the growing cycle."

"'Flower guy' suits me just fine," Landon said with a grin. "But I spend equal amounts of time with fruits, vegetables, and herbs as I do with the geraniums and the daffodils she sells. Although I do favor coming up with better-tasting apples and easier-to-grow asparagus."

"I'm not a big fan of asparagus," Hannah admitted.

"Hannah wants to grow grapes," Caleb announced. "Her father owns a vineyard."

"A small one on the outskirts of San Mateo, out in the rolling countryside."

"Beautiful place to grow grapes," Landon replied, wiping the dirt off his hands with a towel. He tossed the rag on the counter and leaned back against the workbench prepared to talk a while. "You guys look like you have something on your mind other than my approach to gardening."

"Were you the original landscaper at Bradford House?" Caleb asked. "I mean, did you put in the yard and flower beds for Douglas once he got the house built?"

Landon rubbed his jaw. "Funny thing about that job. Douglas Bradford pissed me off when he went over to San Sebastian and hired a contractor to do the work instead of keeping things local. Didn't even bother knocking on my door to see if I could do it."

"Why? Did you guys have some kind of falling out?" Hannah piped up.

"Nope. Not that I knew of anyway. Back then, Doug hadn't been here long enough for me to squabble with him about much of anything. I'd say he'd been in town less than a year when he started digging up his yard himself, trying to put in a sprinkler system for the St. Augustine grass he planted. Didn't buy that from me either. So, when it started to die off, I thought he'd come to me for help. But that didn't happen. Imagine, not even bothering to get an estimate on how I could remedy it for him. Because it wasn't my problem I didn't offer to do squat to fix the situation. Within three months, every square foot of that sod had turned brown and died, every inch of yard had to be replaced. This was before he threw his hat in the ring to run for mayor. Needless to say, his attitude ticked me off enough that when he did run, Mr. Bradford did not get my vote."

"Show him the pictures, Caleb," Hannah urged. "Most of them were taken using black and white film but a few are in color and give you a better comparison of the difference as the years went by."

Caleb spread the photos on the workbench, dividing them into two categories. "These were taken at Bradford House before the rock wall was completed. And these show the place after it was built."

Landon shook his head. "That rock wall wasn't put up until at least ten years after Doug moved there. See the difference in the house itself. This color photo shows the paint fading just a tad. Rumor was, that the wall was supposedly built to fix a drainage problem. Doug didn't want a repeat of his grass getting overwatered and dying out. What little bit of the rock you saw there and carted away yesterday was what was left of a piss-poor attempt at construction. The concrete wasn't done right to begin with. It didn't take long for it to crumble away after a few years. What with the salt air around here, it didn't last more than five, not in totality anyway. You saw what was left of it, nothing more than seven feet in length, if that."

"Wait a minute. It just hit me what you're saying. That wall went up around twenty years or so ago." Hannah turned to Caleb. "That's about the right timeframe. That's how long the initial estimate is that the bones were in the ground. That can't be a coincidence. It means Douglas is on the hook for that wall going up. You don't allow such a thing on your property unless it's your own idea."

"And if he had firsthand knowledge constructing the wall, then he had to know what was underneath it."

"Good Lord," Landon said with a frown. "You actually believe Douglas had a hand in killing that baby?"

"I don't know," Hannah admitted. "Who knows if it was Douglas or not? But if the wall went up fast, in a sloppy, hurried fashion, it sounds like whoever dug the line and hauled in all those rocks must have taken advantage of the event. They dug a long trench that wouldn't give off an air of suspicion, made up a reasonable explanation like repairing a plumbing problem and..."

"And then plopped a baby's body down underneath the boulders," Caleb finished. "A perfect way to hide a sinister act and do it quickly without drawing attention to the burial itself."

"But I doubt Douglas dug the ditch himself," Hannah said as she chewed her lip.

Landon agreed. "Douglas wasn't the kind to get his hands dirty. He hired a contractor, a man by the name of Ridge Faulkner, who built that house from the ground up."

Caleb started to pace back and forth in front of the windows to think. "But you said Doug started putting in his own sprinkler system. A man who doesn't like to get his hands dirty doesn't do that."

"I just assumed that's the moment Douglas found out he was way out of his element. That's when he hired Joe Wheeler, the landscaper out of San Sebastian. Joe showed up to finish installing the sprinkler system and stayed to build that pergola in the back."

"Interesting. Maybe this Faulkner and Wheeler could shed light on what they know about Bradford," Caleb suggested. "You don't hang around on a big job for months at a time without learning something about the client."

Landon crossed his arms over his chest. "Ridge could probably add something to the story, but won't. Faulkner died about five years ago from a spill he took in his kitchen."

Hannah's shoulders slumped. "And it's for that reason we may never learn how that baby came to be buried there. Everyone's either dead or disappeared."

"Are you sure that's all you can remember about Bradford putting in the wall?" Caleb wanted to know.

"If I think of anything else, I'll write it down. How's that?"

"It'll have to do. What now?" Caleb asked Hannah.

"I'd like to drive over to Turlock. If you're planning to help me with this, you need to see where it all began."

"Won't that be too painful for you?"

She laid her hand on his cheek. "That's sweet of you to think of my feelings. But it won't be the first time I've gone back there, more like a dozen times at least. For a long time now I've been determined to get at the truth and I've never been shy about visiting as many times as it took for me to do that."

Hannah did the driving as they set out on the two-and-a-half-hour drive to Turlock.

Overhead, the sky brewed with furious gray clouds that formed to the west. The billowing mass kept building up, looking like it was about to slam into them with heavy rain. A clap of thunder announced the cloudburst right before the downpour began in earnest.

"I hope Wally checked my windshield wipers," Hannah declared, flipping on the switch. "I forgot to ask him to do that."

"Wally is a thorough mechanic. When he works on a car he gives it his complete attention." But Caleb's mind kept drifting from the bad weather to something else. His curiosity stoked, he began to ply her with questions. "Why have you gone back to Turlock so many times? It has to be a gut-wrenching experience for you. Why put yourself through that?"

She blew out a breath. "You're right about that. I guess I'm hoping to see the house differently each time and hope it sparks something inside me, a memory that might lead to a miracle. I don't know exactly. What can I say? The house keeps pulling me back."

"And has it ever had that effect? Have you ever felt that miracle memory pop up?"

"Since I'm still trying to find Micah that would be a big, fat no."

"You were only six. What kind of a memory could it ignite, except for the one where you walk up and see dozens of police cars out front?"

Fat drops of rain splattered the windshield in a deluge. It seemed like more black clouds opened up and sent a pounding barrage, battering the SUV. The wind whipped the vehicle onto the shoulder as if it weighed nothing. Hannah held the wheel steady while she slid the defroster to high, and turned up the heat. She took her foot off the gas and reduced her speed down to fifty.

"At this rate it'll take us twice as long to make the trip."

"That's okay," Caleb said. "I'd like to make a suggestion. Why don't we go to the house and then check into one of the hotels in the area, spend the night? With the weather this stormy, it wouldn't hurt to get off the road."

Without taking her eyes off the traffic, Hannah smiled. "I didn't bring my toothbrush. Or a bag. Or a change of clothes."

He ran a finger down the side of her jaw and along her throat. "A toothbrush is easy enough to pick up. We don't need a change of clothes since we likely won't be wearing anything for very long anyway. What do you say?"

"I say if you can find a hotel room, sure. It's a go."

It took them three hours to make their way to the Turlock city limits sign. Hannah cruised past a string of churches; it seemed like there was a different one on every corner, representing a wide variety of religions—Mormon,

Roman Catholic, Methodist, Church of Christ, and mosques.

"After coming here for so many years, I've gone through the town's history. Twice. It was named after Turlough, a village in County Mayo, Ireland. And it's more culturally diverse than you might think. It started out with immigrants from Sweden. But with the Central Pacific Railroad expansion, people started pouring in from all over to work the acres and acres of crops in the area. Land was reasonably priced back then. It boomed with all kinds of people, a melting pot, a mixed bag of ethnicity. The town is literally made up of people from all over the world—the Middle East, Syria, Iran, Iraq, Europe. You name a cultural part of the globe and they probably are represented here."

She made a right into the older section of town and meandered through tree-lined streets until she got to El Capitan Drive. A left took her past a familiar little house she used to call home.

When Hannah pulled to a stop she noted the change in appearance since the last time she'd been here. "The house must have another new owner. The outside is blue again. Last time it was an off-white with brown shutters."

She took out her phone to snap photos she'd print out later and stick in the file she kept, making sure to keep track of the color changes.

Caleb tried to picture the scene, tried to wrap his mind around how an innocent first-grader would react to happening upon the chaotic scene of a murder/suicide. "You must've been so overwhelmed that day."

"And scared. Total strangers I'd never met before were about to cart me off to live somewhere else for the rest of my life. I didn't understand what was happening until late that night. I knew something was very wrong but I didn't know what. I didn't know I'd never see Mom or Dad ever again. Six-year-olds don't process that kind of thing. Even though that's the line everyone kept repeating, I couldn't comprehend any of it. For the next six years or so, the nightmares plagued me and wouldn't let up."

"Why did they eventually stop?"

"Because I willed them to. I made up my mind I was tired of going back to that day. It didn't do any good so I decided to change my way of thinking. I made my mind up that the only way to get peace of mind was to find Micah."

"Did you ever wonder how that woman knew to find a baby here, at this particular address, in this house, in this neighborhood, in this town, of all the places she could've picked, why here?"

"Are you kidding? A thousand times I've wondered that. Look around. What do you see? A simple, ordinary, working-class neighborhood. What made the Lambert household so special? Why did we stand out? Was it six-month-old Micah? Did the woman want a baby so badly that she followed my mother home from the grocery store one day to grab him? Why did she have to shoot them? Why didn't she snatch Micah out of his stroller or something? She could've distracted my mother and grabbed him when Mom wasn't looking. But that's not what happened. I've gone over it in my mind a thousand times. It doesn't make sense."

"Because your parents could identify her," Caleb stated flatly.

Hannah pushed her hair off her face and pivoted in her seat. "That's a terrific theory with one problem. My freshman year of college, I made up a list of women that my parents knew. Any female who'd ever come in contact with them over the years—neighbors, casual acquaintances from work, you name it—they ended up on the list. I even hunted up my old babysitter who sat with us a couple of times before the kidnapping. Cheryl Baines was her name. She's still in town by the way, lives over on Baker Street, two blocks west of here, married to the supermarket manager. It wasn't Cheryl that day or any one of the twenty-five women I checked out."

"But there has to be something you overlooked. Someone that didn't make it onto that list."

"Maybe, or maybe my family crossed paths with a psychopath who steals babies and kills people for the thrill of it."

"You have my word that I'll do everything in my power to help you solve this. You deserve that much. Whether it's Micah in that grave or not, I won't stop until we're satisfied with the outcome."

"Jordan says we may have a problem with Brent. That the police chief won't condone our interfering with his investigation."

"Then we won't let him find out." He wanted to wipe that look of despair off her face so he took out his cell phone, started the search for the nearest hotel.

"Any luck?"

"Looks like lodging choices come down to the typical roadside motels. Unless…are you up for a crazy detour?"

"Depends. How crazy?"

"Two hours due west of here is the family cabin, a cool-looking abode that sits high on Cutter Mountain. If we hustle we could be there in time for a relaxing meal in front of the fireplace. We might have to settle for what's on hand, like canned goods, but the place is well-stocked. What do you say? We'd be that much closer to home."

"What about work tomorrow?"

"I can take a day off. How about you?"

"I was supposed to clean Bradford House. That means my schedule is wide open. Sounds like a no-brainer. After all, I brought you all the way out here, practically on my wild goose chase for nothing. So why not? I could use an adventure."

"Then if we're done here, how about we hit the road? Why don't I drive? You look wiped."

"Be my guest," she said, opening the driver's side door. "I'll let you tackle the bad weather and slick roads."

Eleven

On the drive to Cutter Mountain, slick roads were the least of their problems. Manipulating the twisting, mountainous two-lane blacktop in the dark, climbing uphill, was stressful and tedious. As the elevation increased, so did the scenery.

Through the windshield, Hannah noted towering pine, cedar, and redwood appear off and on in the headlights. She rolled down the passenger window, inhaling the fragrant air filled with cedar and pine. "It's a shame we're missing out on seeing such beautiful landscape in the dark."

"You'll see it tomorrow. We'll go on a hike before heading back to town. You'll get the full impact of the rolling foothills."

"Promise? Because I could really use a big dose of Mother Nature."

"There's a waterfall about four miles from the cabin. Cooper and I used to hike up there to swim. And it's a great place for a picnic."

"Please don't mention food because right now I could clean out the buffet at Pizza Palace."

"There's a diner about ten miles up the road. I say we make a pit stop for burgers and a bathroom break."

"Maybe by the time we finish eating, the rain will have stopped."

The diner turned out to be a rundown dive, a former gas station left over from the 1950s that claimed to serve the best cheeseburgers and beer-battered fries within a hundred-mile radius.

"Who knew their advertising would turn out to be the real thing and not a marketing ploy? You've eaten here before?"

Caleb slurped the chocolate shake they were sharing. "About a dozen times. Dad used to bring us up here for that special one on one time. He'd reminisce about my grandfather. Apparently there was a tight bond there before my grandfather died. For all I know it could've been nothing more than in Dad's head."

"Why do you say that?"

"Well, because to hear Eleanor tell it, she had Euell, that was my grandfather, wrapped around her little finger. So I guess to Dad, this cabin represents those memorable occasions when Euell took the time to spend with just him."

"I take it your dad brought you up here a lot."

"He and Mom had a routine. They always made sure they took each kid somewhere special. Cooper's was museums, the planetarium, concert venues, or galleries. Drea liked going to the zoo, or taking a shopping trip up to San Francisco. Me? I liked getting away to the mountains. While Dad and I were spending quality time here with each other, there were lots of things to do, hiking, fishing, or just talking. The cabin is where Dad gave me the 'sex talk' for the first time. Now that I think about it, he really did go out of his way to make sure I knew how much he loved me. He coached Little League, helped me with my algebra problems, and made me feel like a normal kid."

"It meant a great deal to you to feel normal because it helped you forget about the abnormal beginning," Hannah concluded. "I completely get it."

He took her hand. "I realize now why I felt that connection to you the first time I saw you. Scott saw it too."

"A ghost gets us together. Now there's a story for later. How much farther do we have to go to get to the cabin?"

"About twenty miles." He glanced out the window. "And look, the rain's stopped."

"Then let's pay the bill and get out of here. I'm exhausted."

Half an hour later Caleb turned the Suburban onto a long, curvy lane. By this time, the clouds had drifted further east, allowing the moon to come out and the brilliant umbrella of stars to glisten overhead.

Once he pulled to a stop, Hannah got her first look at the rustic retreat, sitting in the middle of a forest of sequoias. Even in the pitch black of darkness, the gables and wraparound porch surprised her. This was no drafty shack, but a good-sized hideaway that long ago had embraced its lodge-like architectural design.

She hopped out and breathed in the crisp mountain cedar mingled with the recent rain.

She took one step toward the porch and stopped. There was something off about the way the shadows danced on the front door that didn't look right.

"Caleb, was there a fire here recently?"

"Not that I know of. Why?"

She lowered her voice to a whisper. "Look at the front door. What is that? Soot?"

Caleb darted up the steps to run his hand along the wood and realized the door was partially opened. "Damn. I think someone's broken in. Go back and get in the car."

"Not a chance. I'm not letting you go in there alone."

He let out a sigh. "Fine. But we'll need a flashlight."

"Better still, a tire iron." They retraced their steps back to the truck where Hannah found the flashlight and Caleb grabbed the hunk of steel metal out of the back.

"Stay behind me."

"Since all we have for protection is a hunk of metal and my Swiss Army knife, I intend to."

Caleb stepped inside, reaching first to flip on the light. He threw the switch back and forth several times without success. "That's what I thought, no electricity."

After shining the beam around the room, his heart broke. The place had been tossed, furniture turned over, the place ransacked, leaving behind a mess to clean up.

"It looks like they stayed here for a few weeks and then trashed the place before they took off."

"Call me paranoid, but why do I get the feeling this has Eleanor's stamp all over it. Who else would know the location of this place?"

"Why would you say that? Isn't she locked up?"

"She is, yeah."

"Then how would she pull something like this off?"

"I've been told the friends she makes on the inside have lately been deemed parole-worthy. She could've easily pointed them in the right direction. Think about it. Great place to stay off the radar."

Caleb went room to room, taking inventory of the mess. "We can't stay here tonight, Hannah. Whoever did this has eaten everything that was stored away in the pantry. And if they didn't consume it, they wasted everything else. The only thing left is a jar of olives and a bottle of V8 juice. Looks like the fridge isn't working. They probably cut the power lines. I'll have to check before we leave."

Hannah stood in the bedroom doorway. "Yeah, well, they also poured gasoline on the mattress in here."

"Check the other bedrooms, will you?"

She walked down to the next doorway. "Same thing in here." She stuck her head into the bathroom and came back waving her hand in front of her face. "The toilet's backed up. The smell in there is just awful."

"I wouldn't feel safe falling asleep here. They might decide to come back at any moment."

"Come back? To what? There's nothing left to trash."

"Yes, but it's still shelter, four walls, a place to hide out, away from prying eyes."

"Okay. You've convinced me. Let's get back on the road."

Caleb spent twenty minutes taking pictures of the damage with his camera phone. "Let's get out of here. I'll come back this weekend and clean it all up. I'm sorry about this, Hannah."

"Don't be. It isn't your fault. I'm sorry someone did such an awful thing to a beautiful, serene spot like this. People suck."

"I was thinking the same thing. You'll stay with me tonight?"

"Absolutely. I wasn't planning on going home alone."

Once they got back on the road, the trip seemed to take longer than two hours. Hannah had fallen asleep, slumped against the passenger door. To keep himself awake, Caleb changed CDs several times, going back and forth from the light rock sound he used when he made his deliveries to heavy metal.

But his mind wasn't on the music. He kept trying to work out what he'd seen at the cabin. He had a hard time coming to grips with why Eleanor's asshole friends would've sought out refuge there, only to vandalize the place.

Whoever had been in the cabin had stayed for much longer than a week, probably two. He was sure of that. But nothing about it made any sense. If it wasn't Eleanor's buddies, then how had they known about the cabin? The property was too far off the main road for a vagrant to simply discover on his own. A person had to know where to turn, not once but twice, just to make it to the cutoff. From there the road was so narrow in places it would be difficult for a stranger to simply "happen upon" the cabin unless they were specifically looking for it.

Add to that, for a hiker to be out exploring the trails nearby one would have to risk getting lost in dangerous mountainous terrain. The paths were more like overgrown patches of thick forest than a jaunt through a greenbelt. There were treacherous ridges and cliffs, jagged landscape, not easy to cross on foot, let alone in a vehicle. The land just wasn't a place where someone could get lost without a great deal of effort.

No, the only reasonable explanation for him was that Eleanor had shared the details about the cabin with one or more of her prison cellmates.

It deeply disturbed and angered him. Escaping Eleanor's clutches was proving to be more difficult than he'd assumed. He should've listened to Cooper. His brother had claimed all along that getting off the woman's radar would be damn near impossible. Now he understood the full impact of that.

He took the exit off the highway and wound his way around to the 101. He could tell he was nearing the coast when the road conditions changed to fog. When his headlights finally illuminated the city limits sign of home, he breathed a sigh of relief. The clock on the dash read half past midnight.

He took his eyes off the road long enough to glance over at Hannah. He didn't want to wake her, so he decided to forego stopping to pick up the remote control for the gate. It was still in his truck parked at the nursery. There was no need to make an extra stop just to retrieve it when he could access the gate with the code.

He turned down Cape May and drove until the streetlights disappeared. For the first time in a while, the remote location gave him cause for alarm. He pulled up to his house in the dark with only the headlights of the car for light. He had to jump out and manually key in the numbers on the keypad to open the gate.

Inside the Suburban, the movement caused Hannah to jerk awake. She bolted upright, bleary-eyed, and looked around, breathing a quick sigh of relief when she spotted Caleb standing off to the side punching in the code.

But something caused her to turn her head to the right. Farther down the lane, toward the vacant area where beach grass grew tall and thick, stood a figure of what she assumed was a man wearing a hooded jacket and jeans.

Hannah frantically rolled down the window enough that she could be heard. At the top of her voice, she yelled and pointed in the direction of the man. "Caleb, we aren't alone. Get back in the truck. Now!"

In the time it took Caleb to respond to the warning, the man disappeared into the tall grass.

Skirting the front of the truck, Caleb climbed back inside, immediately jerking the gear into drive and popping the clutch. He stepped on the gas and took off toward the garage at the side of the house.

"Damn, the garage door opener is in my truck." He shifted into reverse, backing all the way up to where he could park right in front of the door. "Are you sure it wasn't Scott you saw?"

Hannah shook her head. "I know what Scott looks like. It wasn't him. I think the guy might have taken off toward the rolling hills behind your house. The other day you pointed out that drainage ditch back there. That would make a perfect place to hide."

"The canal? Why do you say that? How can you be so sure?"

"Because I think that's where he came from. That concrete canal is so deep it could hide a man. It was my first thought the first time you took me on a tour back there."

"Okay. Let's get you settled inside and I'll go take a look around."

She grabbed his arm. "No, you won't. Not alone. You're calling Brent or Eastlyn. Do it, Caleb."

"Do we really need to get them involved? It's so late. Besides, what do we tell them exactly?"

"Are you kidding? We tell them we saw a man lurking around your house in the middle of the night, a prowler."

"Maybe you were still half asleep."

"You think I was dreaming?" She acted insulted but had to concede she might've been seeing things that weren't there. "You're saying you didn't see the guy at all?"

"I didn't see anyone. You yelled, I turned to look at you and saw nothing but the headlights glaring in my eyes."

"Fine. We won't call Brent then. But I know what I saw. Let's just get out of the car. I'm sick of sitting here."

Caleb unlocked the front door and quickly flipped on the lights. Inside the entryway, they stood there shedding their jackets until they plopped down on the bench to take off their shoes.

Caleb finally blew out an exhausted sigh. "Look, I know you're tired. It's okay by me if our first night together is spent doing nothing more than curling up together to sleep."

Hannah tilted her head to stare at him. "That's…very noble of you. But I'm tired, not dead."

He flashed her a grin. "I was hoping you'd feel that way."

"I won't lie. That whole episode back at the cabin rattled me more than I let on. And just now, I guess I wasn't awake yet. I guess I was still spooked and thought I saw someone standing in the dark spying on us."

He stood up, snatched her hand. "Come on. Let's go to bed. I promise I won't let anything happen to you."

"You know, I truly believe that." She got to her feet but began to bounce on her toes. "Right this minute, I need to pee. The long drive and all that soda are catching up with me."

He led her to the master bedroom and pointed her in the direction of the adjoining bathroom. As she dashed off to take care of business, he swatted her fanny. "Don't fall in."

A few minutes later she came back out and couldn't believe what he'd accomplished in a short span of time. The bedroom was aglow in flickering shadows. He'd lit scented candles and set them on the dresser, the chest, the nightstand. The smell of vanilla and perhaps a hint of spice floated in the air.

He'd turned down the bed sheets in silky invitation.

"You really know how to set the scene. You don't have to seduce me."

"Every woman should know the pleasure of being seduced into bed."

His hands went around her waist before roaming lean fingers down to her hips. Caressing the muscles in her rump, he whispered in her ear, "You've been sitting too long. Let me loosen you up with a massage. You have the sexiest neck." He proved it by nibbling at a sensitive spot before slowly using his tongue to trail a path to her chin. He saved her lips for last. "Your mouth makes me want to dive right in."

The moment he deepened the kiss, she was mesmerized, hit by sensations that felt like a blast of potent moonlight. That power built along her spine, tingling right to her toes. He began to unbutton her blouse. After baring a shoulder, he grazed along her flesh, setting her skin ablaze with fiery heat.

Her hands got busy helping him out of his jeans.

Urgency had him reaching around to get rid of her bra. He held up the lace. "Nice. But these are even nicer bare." He lovingly touched the curve of a breast, flicking his tongue around a nipple. The slightest brush backward and they both tumbled down to the mattress.

But his weight felt light as air. His fingers fumbled with her jeans. She helped him by lifting her hips so he could jerk them down and off.

He took her under by focusing on her breasts, one nipple at a time. With each pull from his mouth it took away another layer of inhibition. He moved down her body leaving wet kisses on each precious spot.

His hand slid down between her legs, curved over the sweet core. Her head lolled back. She raised her hips again. With each stroke of a finger, the crescendo built. That little slice of heaven soon built to a groundswell. She slid toward a shattering quake. Like a raging fire, she erupted.

She came as sparks splintered into a thousand white-hot embers. It was like a wild inferno that left her struggling for her next breath of air.

With her heart thudding to a fast beat, she arched her back. Her arms went around him as he slipped into the wet heat.

He clasped his fingers in hers, then stretched their joined arms above her head. He felt her body hum, vibrate beneath him. He captured her breathy sighs. Each left him with that heady feeling of strength and power. It gave him purpose.

"Come for me again, Hannah." His body urged hers to sync in rhythm. The woman beneath him moaned. His mouth roamed down her jaw to her neck. His pace quickened.

She felt his muscles bunch. That back and forth dance kept her wrapped in a blurry haze of need. Her senses battered, she rode out the sensations, layer by silky layer.

He made her feel like smooth satin, like she was lying on a bed of velvet grass, racing toward that hot pool of release. That bolt of pleasure yanked her over the edge, dragging him up and over right along with her. They soared high, plunging off the cliff together.

Limp from the tidal wave that had swept them up, they washed up on a soft sandy beach, sated but exhausted.

"I don't think I can move," she whispered, breathless.

"Then don't. I will." He rolled off her with all the energy of a snail.

"That was…intense."

"Amazing. But I'm fading fast. Long drive. Hot sex. Sleepy." With one yank, he nestled her into his side, placed a light kiss on that messy mane of red, and promptly closed his eyes.

Hannah watched him fall asleep as fatigue set in, and soon, she too drifted off.

Twelve

The sex had been phenomenal, but when he woke at six-fifteen, he decided he had too much on his mind to go back to sleep. He crawled out of bed because there was something he had to take care of before he did anything else. Reluctantly, he left Hannah sacked out under the warm covers.

He didn't even bother with a shower. Instead, he grabbed the clothes off the floor from last night and hurriedly got dressed, scribbled a note to Hannah in case she woke up before he got back, and left it on the dresser.

He headed out the front door, bypassing the kitchen and the coffee pot.

Hannah's Suburban was his only means of transportation, so he climbed into the vehicle and set out for his dad's house. Explaining to his parents about the condition of the cabin wouldn't be easy. But it had to be done.

Landon and Shelby lived practically next door to The Plant Habitat. It was early when he circled around to the back door and came in through the kitchen. His parents were sitting at the table eating breakfast.

"To what do we owe this early morning visit?" Shelby asked. "Not that we aren't glad to see you but I thought you and Hannah were headed out of town."

"Turlock," Caleb grunted. "Been there and back already. Long night."

"I see that," Shelby said. "Want me to scramble you some eggs?"

He kissed his mother's forehead. "Finish yours first. I can wait. I'll take coffee though and hope it's strong enough to wake me up. I left Hannah sleeping." He went to the cabinet for a cup, and then stood in front of the Mr. Coffee Shelby had purchased fifteen years ago. "I can't believe this old thing still works. What happened to that one I gave you for Christmas several years back?"

Shelby looked amused. "We're waiting for 'that old thing' to take its last dying breath. So far it hasn't. It just keeps brewing coffee the way we like it. Why change it out until we have to?"

"Some changes can't be helped," Caleb muttered.

Landon and Shelby traded looks. "Is there something on your mind other than Bradford House?" Landon asked.

Caleb turned around to face the people who'd raised him, and shifted his feet. "I might as well rip off the Band-Aid and be done with it. After leaving Hannah's old homestead in Turlock, I got this brilliant idea to take her to the cabin."

"Nothing wrong with that," Shelby said.

"Exactly. Great getaway to the mountains, take her mind off the childhood drama she went through as a kid, not to mention distancing herself from the remains I unearthed at Bradford House. For me, seeing that skull was a little too much to handle. I could only imagine what it was like for her. Anyway, I had this great plan. I'll take her mind off all the bad stuff, give her beautiful scenery to look at, and see if I can talk her into spending the night with me. Things are going pretty well until we get to the cabin, and we discover the place totally trashed. I mean, the food in the pantry has either been eaten or flat-out wasted, cans opened and left to rot, flour and other stuff tossed all over the floor, garbage piled up, ants crawling around in the sugar, gasoline poured on the beds. You name it, they did it. Every vile thing they could think of doing went into tearing the place up. A place I've enjoyed my entire life now looks like someone piled garbage in a heap and walked away."

Because his anger was ramping up all over again, he had to wait a beat before going on. "I've been seeing red ever since. And this is the most hurtful part of it all. I think it was Eleanor's pals who did it, parolees from her cell block who went there to do Eleanor's bidding. And before you say anything about how crazy that sounds…"

"We don't think you're nuts," Landon muttered before taking a swig of his coffee. "It sounds just like something she would do to get back at all of us for some slight she's feeling at being locked up. Grab your coffee and take a seat. Did you report the vandalism?"

"Not yet."

"That's fine. Let me do it. I'll put a call in to the sheriff up there. Next, I'll call the park ranger and let him know to be on the lookout for trespassers. Then I'll call our closest neighbor. Remember Tahoe Jones?"

"The Choctaw Indian? Sure. Best fisherman I ever saw, could catch a fish with his bare hands if he had to."

"That's right. Tahoe will gladly keep an eye on the place with that double-gauge shotgun he carries."

Caleb leaned back in his chair. For the first time thinking about the mess at the cabin, he could relax. "I remember Tahoe taking me fishing out on the lake in his canoe. He's a great resource if you want to know anything about the fish in the area or the wildlife. That is, if you can get him to talk. As a rule, the man doesn't say two words unless prompted. Grunts a lot. But I'll check in with him once I get there."

Shelby shook her head. "You can't go back up there alone. Landon and I could close the nursery for a few days. Landon won't be much good to you since he hurt his back but—"

Caleb held up a hand. "I have to go back because someone has to clean up the mess. We can't let it sit there another week like it is. Both toilets are clogged and the place is beginning to stink. And just because we have eyes on the cabin in the future, doesn't mean a whole lot if we don't take the necessary steps to prevent it from happening again."

Landon rubbed the side of his unshaven jaw. "What did you have in mind?"

"I don't know yet. I plan to run a few things by Cooper. When's the last time you guys were up there?"

"The weekend right after Halloween," Shelby answered without hesitation. "We spent Saturday and Sunday taking in the autumn air and generally kicking back from the hectic rush of summer. We took the time off, like we always do, to get ready to deal with what would come with Thanksgiving and Christmas."

"I forgot about that. You guys always fit in a trip up there sandwiched between Halloween and Thanksgiving. It's like someone knew the routine. They waited until after you guys were there. The thing is, with it sitting vacant most of the time, what happens when the asshole comes back? Cleaning the place up will all be for nothing. They'll just repeat their performance."

"You think they'll return?" Landon asked.

"Yeah, I do. For spite. I think Eleanor purposely sent them with instructions to do as much damage as they could."

"But why? What makes her do things like that?" Shelby said.

"The same reason she's a murdering narcissist. To show us how much contempt she has for all of us and the life we live."

"I'll say it again and again. That sounds like Eleanor. Most selfish female I've ever known," Landon uttered in agreement. "But if you believe this guy's coming back, should you really go back alone? I may not be in great physical shape to lift anything, but I can damn well bring my rifle with me."

"It's okay. If I feel like I need help, I'll corner Cooper into making the trip. That place holds special memories for me. That's why I don't intend to let Eleanor ruin what I have there, especially after she's poisoned so much of my life already."

Shelby started to clear away the breakfast dishes and take them to the sink. "Did you experience anything else suspicious while you were there?"

"Other than the heartbreak of seeing the walls and floors ruined? No. But when we got back last night Hannah did think she saw a strange man taking a walk near the front gate of my house."

Shelby didn't like the sound of that. "Taking a walk in your neck of the woods? That sounds out of place. There's nothing much out where you live that would cause anyone to just get the urge to go for a walk. Even the people who live on Cape May generally don't head east to stroll past your front gate."

"Yeah, that occurred to me around five a.m. Anyone who wants to take a walk usually heads west toward the pier and the beach. I feel bad now because when it happened, I did my best to shoot down Hannah's anxiety about it. But I think she was on to something. She wanted to call Brent then and there, but I thought she was seeing things."

"That girl seems to have good instincts," Landon stated. "Maybe you should have listened."

"Next time." Caleb stood up, drained the contents of his mug. "I can remedy my mistake now though. I'll go talk to Brent and make it official. Then I need to get back home. Hannah's probably hungry and I want to be there to fix her my special eggs."

Shelby turned from the sink to pat his cheek. "That's a detour from the old Caleb. You only fix those eggs for family. How serious are you about her?"

Caleb smiled. "I'll have to let you know on that score, mostly cause I'm just getting started."

Landon shifted in his chair. "Don't worry about the time off. Take whatever days you need to work on the cabin."

"For starters, give me two days off, add Saturday and Sunday to that, and it'll probably take those four days to shovel out the trash and make it look like new again."

Landon chuckled. "Good luck with that. Because it'll take a helluva lot more than four days to get those old walls looking like new, especially since it's been standing on that same spot since 1952."

"Then you won't be disappointed with the results," Caleb shot back with a grin.

Landon chewed the inside of his jaw. "You know what might work? Installing a camera. Let the surveillance speak for itself. That way we'd know who this bastard is and be able to take the video to the law."

"Great minds think alike. That's one of my ideas. I'll check into it before I leave. Cooper is the tech guy in this family. I'll see if he thinks technology will work that far out in the boonies."

"Are you taking Hannah with you?"

"If I can sweet talk her into spending the next four days scrubbing out an old cabin in the middle of nowhere, you bet."

Caleb found Brent and Eastlyn writing out parking tickets along Ocean Street to all the tourists who'd illegally parked there overnight.

"Doesn't anyone read a sign anymore," Brent grumbled as he ripped off another piece of paper from his pad.

"You can't blame all the visitors to town who want to park here and gander out over the water," Caleb noted.

"I suppose that's true. Especially when they spend their hard-earned cash here eating and buying souvenirs."

"It seems a shame they'll leave with a ticket in hand."

"Don't try to soften me up," Brent said.

Eastlyn strolled up to join them, one hand resting on her weapon. "Besides, I've given most of these same cars warnings for the past two days. Now, it's time they take our ordinances seriously."

Brent sized up Caleb's mood. "What's on your mind? If you're about to ask me how the case is going on the Bradford House deal, don't bother. There's no news and no new updates. I haven't heard a cause of death from the medical examiner yet. The forensic team is still digging the same ground as they were before. And the lab hasn't finished processing the DNA yet. So, there's absolutely nothing to pass along."

Caleb held up his hands. "I'm just here to report a prowler last night near my property and to bring you up to speed on a few more details about what happened to our family cabin up in Stanislaus County." He went into the short version and finally went for the bonus round. "My opinion is that it was one of Eleanor's associates from jail who recently made parole. It's the only thing that makes sense. The cabin is hard to find without a map and then it's still difficult to get to without having some readily available knowledge of the area."

Eastlyn's face flushed with alarm. "Does Cooper know yet?"

"Nope. But I'm headed to the train store next to make sure he gets a heads up."

Eastlyn made a face and rocked back on her heels. "I already printed out a list of potential parolees from Eleanor's cell block. Just because she's incarcerated with a bunch of women, doesn't mean they're any less dangerous felons."

"You got that right," Caleb muttered.

"Cooper and I routinely keep track of her visitors, which are mostly male. We also monitor her known associates in jail just for this very reason. Some of the women locked up with Eleanor have committed violent assaults, not all homicides mind you, but serious offenses.

We didn't even consider she might send her pals to wreck the cabin."

Caleb stuck his hands in his pockets. "I don't know who's responsible yet, but I intend to find out."

Eastlyn tried to soothe his temper. "If it's any consolation, we've focused our attention mostly on strangers hanging out around town. You know, people showing up at Drea's shop or the nursery or the train store, maybe even lurking around any of our homes. Coop's always been convinced she'd lash out in some way by using people on the outside to get to one of you."

"Yeah, well, he would know. Eleanor's good at using just about anyone she comes into contact with. Whether that includes writing fanciful letters, or going through the meet and greet on visitors' day, she's gone through all the family she has. She's down to relying on brainwashing strangers to do her bidding. God knows she's good at convincing people she's gotten a raw deal in life. Her pitch isn't that hard to spot if you know what to look for. Unfortunately, some people are so gullible they're taken with her appearance. She doesn't look like a monster. They get caught up in her words. They don't know how evil she truly is until it's too late."

"She has a few devoted followers that visit every other week or so," Eastlyn announced. "Mostly men, a few women, but mostly males."

"Makes me sick at my stomach. It's a good thing I haven't eaten breakfast yet, otherwise I'd upchuck right here and now. What is it about murderers who are locked up that fascinates these idiots on the outside to become a fan?"

Brent leaned back against the red Corvette with Arizona plates where he'd just tucked a ticket under the windshield wiper blade. "It's a phenomenon no one can really explain. Women sending pictures of themselves to killers who've targeted little girls is beyond comprehension. But it happens."

"That's disgusting. These guys don't have a clue what kind of woman Eleanor is."

"I don't think they care. It's an excitement to them, a macabre addition to their otherwise dull lives," Brent explained. "Look, is there anything you want us to do officially about the prowler? Eastlyn and I are fine with taking turns doing drive bys at your place."

"That's a good idea, especially over the next four or five days when I'll be out of town getting the cabin cleaned up."

"Cooper and I could go with you," Eastlyn offered. She looked at Brent. "Surely I'm due a vacation day or two."

Caleb grinned at his sister-in-law. "Thanks for the offer. But it's not necessary. Hang on to your vacation days and use them to get away from the grind. I'll take care of it. I do need Cooper's input on a few things, though. Is he at work now?"

"Probably not. The store doesn't open until nine-thirty."

"Then I'll head to the house. See you guys later."

Caleb made the block and pulled up to a hacienda, a totally California look that had Spanish Mission style written on all over it. The house looked like it could've easily stood during the old West when the Spaniards colonized the area.

He opened the gate and walked past the courtyard. Standing under an ornate archway, he rang the bell.

Cooper opened the door still wearing his robe, gripping a cup of coffee in one hand and a book in the other.

"Look at that. Did I wake you, princess?" Caleb jabbed. "You're still lounging in your PJs at this hour while your wife is hard at work handing out parking tickets along the pier. Shame on you."

Cooper's mouth curved up. "Oh, she loves that sort of thing. Gets all jazzed and righteous about the tourists who can't read a damned street sign located in plain sight. She'll go on for hours about how they have no respect for posted city ordinances. She's in her element when she's up there writing out tickets. Come on in. Want coffee?"

"I would, but I need to get back home." Instead of making small talk, Caleb got right to the point, going over the story for a third time that morning. He watched as Cooper digested the seriousness of the news and wasn't surprised to see his brother slump into one of the benches in the entryway.

"I told Eastlyn she was planning something. I didn't know what exactly. But trashing the cabin is a new low even for Eleanor."

"And petty," Caleb tossed back. He took out his cell phone and brought up the pictures he'd taken of the damage. "This is what Eleanor's pal left us to deal with."

Perusing the photos sucked the joy out of Cooper's morning. He knew how much the cabin meant to Caleb and empathized with the hurt. "I'm sorry, Caleb. She's evil."

"And then some. Eastlyn volunteered to continue going over the list of parolees who reside or have resided on Eleanor's cellblock. She promised to focus on the last few weeks. In the meantime, I'm going back up to Cutter Mountain to set things right. I thought I'd install a camera while I'm at it. We might get lucky and catch the bastard in the act."

Cooper scratched his chin. "So you're going to clean the place up and hope the asshole returns to do the same thing again? Caleb, that's nuts."

"If you have any better suggestions, I'm all ears. Landon is in the process of calling the sheriff, the park ranger, and old Tahoe. Remember him? He taught us how to hunt and fish. Anyway, maybe between the three of them they'll be able to catch this asshole and keep him from doing it again, especially if I install an alarm system along with the camera."

"It's worth a shot. I'd be glad to go up there with you, close the store, and spend the weekend helping out."

"I'd planned to take Hannah with me. She doesn't even know about it yet. I needed to run the camera thing by you first. I'm hoping you'll tell me that installing it so far up the mountaintop won't prevent the camera from working."

"Nope. Not at all. If you aren't installing anything that needs Internet connection and Wi-Fi, you'll be fine."

"I thought I'd buy one of those cameras triggered by a motion detector."

"Those are pricey, but they'll definitely get the job done. Are you sure you don't want me to close the store and put in the grunt work with you?"

Caleb's resolve seemed to waver. He paced a few steps away and then back again. "Tell you what. Let me see if I can persuade Hannah to leave behind all this Bradford House business and come with me. Give us two days of solitude together and then plan on joining us. Otherwise, I'll just be calling you and nagging you for help with the installation. Alarm systems aren't my thing."

"I can do that. In fact, maybe Eastlyn can use the chopper to fly me up there and avoid all the weekend traffic on I-5."

"Lucky you. It still amazes me how she flies that thing with a prosthetic foot."

"I know. She's an amazing woman. She does physical things all the time that I won't even try."

"Then we'll plan on doing that. I gotta get back now. I've been gone way too long as it is." He turned toward the front door and stopped. "And Cooper, watch your back, watch out for anyone hanging around your house who looks like they don't belong for one reason or another. Eastlyn will tell you all about one of those types when she gets the chance. But for now, don't take any unnecessary chances with strangers."

"I won't. I know the drill." Cooper ran his hands through his hair. "Caleb, do you think this harassment from her will ever stop?"

A sad look crossed Caleb's face. "I wish I could be optimistic, but the truth is, as long as Eleanor's alive to wreak havoc, she'll forever be a thorn in our side."

Thirteen

Caleb considered how grim those words were as he made the trip home. When he reached the gate, he was surprised when it opened on its own. Either Hannah was operating the console from inside the house or something was wrong. Maybe the guy from last night had broken in. Maybe he was holding her hostage.

Edgy and nervous, Caleb went on alert and picked up his phone to send her a text.

Are you okay?

Yes. Where've you been? I called you but your phone went to voicemail.

Caleb checked his calls and sure enough he'd missed several from Hannah. *Sorry. Was running errands. Thanks for opening the gate.*

No problem. You took my car. I had no way to get home unless I walked.

Sorry.

He was still formulating that last part of the text when she opened the front door.

He hopped out of her Suburban and darted up the front steps. "I had to take your car because mine's still at work. I hope you haven't eaten breakfast. I wanted to fix you my scrambled egg special."

She let out a sigh. "I woke up and you were gone. I took a shower, put the same clothes on as last night, and you still weren't back yet. I thought you'd probably gone to the diner to get a to-go order or something and would be back in ten minutes. And when you didn't call me back, I began to get worried. Before I knew it, that worry began to morph into a feeling that I was being watched. It creeped me out."

He saw unshed tears shimmer in her eyes. His arms went around her. "I'm sorry I left. I didn't mean to scare you."

"You didn't, but he did. Just now when I went into the kitchen to put on coffee, I saw that guy again from last night. He was poking his head up out of the drainage ditch and staring toward the house right into the kitchen."

"I'll call Brent right now."

"I already did. I took the initiative myself this time." She pointed to the police cruiser pulling up to the gate and hit the button again to let the vehicle enter. "Looks like Brent brought Eastlyn."

"Where'd you last see this guy?" Eastlyn called out as she brought out her nightstick.

"In the back," Hannah answered, wrapping the sweater she wore tighter around her body.

In response, Brent signaled for Eastlyn to head to the right corner of the house while he took the left side.

Caleb went into his study and opened the desk drawer. He reached in, gripped the Beretta in his fist, and headed toward the kitchen.

"What are you planning to do with that?" Hannah asked. "You should let Brent and Eastlyn handle this."

Caleb stood in front of the slider that went out to the deck, his eyes searching the landscape between the house and the drainage ditch. "I intend to, but I want to be ready if things go south and that guy hightails it up the hill. What did this guy look like?"

"Tall, reddish-brown hair, cropped in a military-style cut, wearing camouflage pants and jacket. He looked to be in his late thirties."

"Good description."

"I'm detail-oriented."

"So I've noticed." He spotted Eastlyn and Brent meeting up from two different directions near the easement as they approached the canal. He watched as the cops took a long time studying something in the beach grass. "Looks like he took off already."

Hannah moved to stand beside Caleb and watched as Eastlyn and Brent took their time perusing the area back toward the house.

"Someone's definitely been camping out down there," Brent noted. "Guy left in a hurry but not before leaving behind his bedroll and a canteen. We'll confiscate it all for evidence if it should come to that."

The police chief spotted the Beretta in Caleb's hand. "Put that thing back where you got it or holster it. I don't want you firing at what might be nothing more than a trespassing vagrant. I understand you think it's related to Eleanor. But if it isn't, there could be a simple explanation, some drifter who thought he'd found the perfect spot to set up camp for a few days and go unnoticed. After all, you just spotted him last night, correct?"

"That's true," Caleb admitted.

"Then let me collect DNA off what he left behind and check the system for matches, see if he was ever in lockup or has a violent history. Just promise me until I know for certain this is related to Eleanor, leave the intimidation to me. Scaring him off with that gun might be a good idea to you, but this is what I do. Are we clear on that?"

"Understood," Caleb said, reluctant to put the weapon back in its drawer.

Eastlyn tried to smooth over the directive. "Look, we understand you're concerned about strangers lurking around here, especially if they're here to spy on you for Eleanor's sake. No one wants you to take unnecessary chances. But—and this is the part that Brent's trying to convey—what if this guy is simply a homeless person without an agenda? Many of these transients are mentally ill, some schizophrenic with violent tendencies. Without daily medication to keep them calm they get rattled and lash out."

Brent took in the panic on Hannah's face and cut his eyes toward his partner. "Eastlyn, you might be making it a tad worse with that explanation."

"Oh. Sorry. What we're trying to say is let us do our job. As for me, I'm happy to drive by, even come back here after dark to see if he's returned. That's what I get paid to do, Caleb."

"Okay. Okay. I get the picture. Fine. A bigger presence out here from you guys will hopefully deter him from sticking around. That's fine by me. I just want him to move on and stop scaring Hannah."

"We'll take care of it," Brent assured him. "You guys get some breakfast and enjoy your morning while we get back to work."

After Brent and Eastlyn disappeared back down the hill to the culvert to bag the so-called evidence, Hannah huffed out a breath. "Nothing like a lecture from law enforcement before having your first bowl of cereal."

"No cereal. I'd planned to make you my special eggs."

"So you keep promising."

He handed her the Beretta. "Could you put this back in the desk drawer for me while I whip us up some breakfast." To his surprise, she handled the weapon like a pro. "By any chance do you know how to shoot that thing?"

She gave him a disgusted look. "You don't grow up trying to find out who murdered your parents and why it happened without taking a course or two in self-defense. That includes several classes in gun safety and how to hit a target. I know martial arts, own a first-rate Taser, and have a licensed Glock 17, just in case."

He got out a carton of eggs and began to crack them into a bowl. "If the camouflaged guy had managed to break in here, you could've handled yourself, right?"

"I like to think so. But I was a little uneasy about being here all by myself. This isn't my house. I wasn't exactly sure how nosy I could get in order to find things like a weapon. Should I go through your closet to borrow this sweater I'm wearing, or not? In the end, I decided you wouldn't mind."

He leaned in to give her a kiss. "You look better in it than I do."

After beating the eggs, he added milk and cheese to the concoction. "I'm really sorry you were that uneasy alone. It never even dawned on me that you'd wake up before I got back. I left you a note on the dresser."

"You did?" She lifted a shoulder. "Oops. I guess I must've missed it. What did it say?"

"That I had to tell Mom and Dad about the cabin. Then stop by the police station to talk to Brent and report to him what you saw last night."

"What caused the change of heart?"

"I couldn't get past the fact that it's fairly remote out here. I like it that way. But as distance goes, I know full well it's probably a mile from the nearest house on this end of Cape May. I've clocked it a time or two. Plus, it's rare for anyone to amble out this way just for a walk. I can't remember it happening in the last year, that's how rare it is. And when people want some fresh air, they usually head in the opposite direction to the beach. After I did some thinking on it, I realized what you saw had to be real."

"Want a hand with those eggs?"

"Could you get out the mushrooms and the spinach, maybe chop them up for me?"

"Sure. Where's your cutting board?"

She got busy slicing and dicing and then dumped the veggies into Caleb's egg mixture.

He plated the omelets while she got out the orange juice. All the while he stalled, wondering how he could ask her to go back to the cabin. In the back of his mind he had the perfect argument. After sitting down to enjoy the meal, he worked through his pitch before actually beginning the conversation.

"Someone has to go back up to Cutter Mountain and haul out the garbage at the cabin."

She angled her head to catch the look in his eyes. "Let me guess. That someone is you?"

"I volunteered. I want you to go with me."

"You know I can't. Jordan needs me on Fridays at Promise Cove. And today, at eleven o'clock, I have a standing job to clean the mayor's house. Then there's the bar on the weekends. And I should really hang around here and poke into the Bradford House angle, do a lot more research."

"I hate to remind you but you're forbidden to go anywhere near Bradford House. Brent was very specific about that. Not to mention when he finds out you're poking into his case, he'll be furious. We can postpone that if you're out of town. Besides, when you think about it, what has all this boatload of research done for you so far?"

Hannah's face fell, truly offended. "How can you say that? I'm here, aren't I?"

"Because you listened to Scott, not because you stumbled on a clue from your own investigation."

She made a guttural sound in her throat. "Okay, point for you. But work is different—"

"I happen to know Jordan isn't full up. She has two guests staying at the B&B. Two. It's January here, Hannah. Winter is slow along the coast for everyone."

"I know what month it is," she snapped. "So I'll change the sheets in two rooms instead of six."

He picked up her hand. "It's just that winter along the coast isn't exactly anyone's busy season. Business slacks off."

"That isn't entirely true. Durke does pretty well on the weekend. And I could use the money. Which is the main reason I can't go. It's unfair to leave Durke short-handed."

"Hear me out. You still have five days or so before the DNA comes back, right? That's a lifetime hanging around town waiting. Even if you do manage to keep your mind off those remains for one day, will you be able to do it for four or five?"

"I have to. And another reason why I should keep busy with work and research."

"And I say during the time you're waiting, grab yourself a little R&R. Four days to clear your head. I'm offering four days, Hannah. Then we come back on Sunday night, Monday morning at the latest. After which, we start peeling off the layers of this thing like an onion. For starters, we locate Wheeler and anyone else who worked on Bradford House during the twenty-year time span in question. In the event the remains don't belong to Micah, I say we go through public records to show all the baby boys in Micah's age group who registered for school from here."

She pushed her hair back behind her ear and chewed her lip. "That's not a bad plan. I'm impressed. I admit it's quite possible I could go nuts waiting for the lab to call Brent and for him to call me. The idea of waiting so long is maddening. That's why I jumped in the car yesterday and went back to Turlock. You've obviously put some thought into your pitch. Let's say I agree to ask Jordan and Durke for the time off. Haven't you forgotten one little detail? What happened to the place being uninhabitable? Have you forgotten the toilets won't even flush?"

"I have a solution to that. There's a four-star lodge within twenty miles of the cabin. We sleep there in the evenings and then during the day I work on everything else, plumbing included. I'm not expecting you to do hard labor, Hannah. But I do expect you to relax and enjoy getting away in the mountains. Cooper promised that he and Eastlyn would come up on Saturday to help me with the work."

"Four-star hotel, huh? If I give up my weekend shift, the place better be nice with room service."

He saw the first crack in her resolve and added more fuel. "It's more like a resort."

"With a spa? Hmm. Honestly this is sounding better and better. Okay, all things considered, how can I turn down another adventure with the guy who was so romantic last night?"

"Then we're good to go?"

"I guess." She looked around for her handbag and spotted it on the counter. She dug out her Day-Timer and phone. "I'll have to cancel on the mayor and reschedule. I'll put him in the slot that belonged to Bradford House. Jordan deserves to know the reason I'm leaving her in the lurch, as well as Durke. Then I need to go home and pack. I'm sick of wearing these same clothes."

Caleb got up to clear the plates and put them in the dishwasher. "You pack while I make the reservations at the lodge."

"You haven't made the reservations yet? What if they're full up? I've cancelled my jobs for nothing."

"They won't be full up. It's January."

"People do travel in January, Caleb. Especially to the mountains."

"I know that. But it isn't like it's summer and warm weather. And the area doesn't get a lot of skiers up that way. We'll be okay. I'll need you to drop me back at my truck. I also need to find a place to buy an alarm system and a surveillance camera, then pack up my toolbox and anything else I'll need for the job."

"Sounds like we're throwing this trip together on the fly. I don't think half an hour is enough time for you to get everything you need. Who sells surveillance equipment in town?"

"Yeah, that's a problem. I hadn't thought of making a trip to San Sebastian to buy that stuff. You'd better give me more like an hour."

"Here's a thought. Why not have Cooper pick up the alarm system and camera and bring all of it up with him when he comes? You need his help to install it anyway."

"That would work. Good thinking. I'll do that." He turned from the sink and picked her up in a hug. He kissed her hair, nibbled on her ear, and finally got to her mouth. "Thanks for coming with me."

"Thanks for asking. I think I should get away from Pelican Pointe, even if it's just for a few days. I've been thinking about this. I should drop off those pictures Scott took before we leave, and let Brent judge the differences in the images for himself. They're almost like a time capsule."

"Probably a good idea. And gives merit to Bradford's involvement."

"I'm beginning to get excited about the trip."

"Good. It'll give you a chance to bring your Glock."

Her eyes bugged out at the implication. "I hope you're alluding to target practice. Or am I there as more like your backup?"

"Let's hope a bunch of tin cans is all we have to worry about."

Fourteen

Caleb loaded up his pickup, locked up his house and set the alarm. He checked in with Eastlyn on his way to pick up Hannah.

"Make sure you swing by the house at least once in the morning and again at night."

"Stop worrying. Brent and I have this covered. We're making sweeps by the flower shop, the nursery, our place, your place, and everything in between. If the guy comes back, chances are we'll spot him before he has a chance to hurt anyone."

"How do you intend to be everywhere when you're flying Cooper up to the cabin Saturday morning?"

"I'm just dropping him off."

"You aren't staying?"

"Nope. We're bringing the equipment up and then I'm taking off. He's coming back with you guys Sunday or Monday. It's okay to take the extra day. It'll give you both more time to install the security measures we talked about. Without those, you're setting yourself up for another disappointing round."

"I know this guy will come back if we don't catch him."

"One thing we know for sure. He can't be in two places at once. He's either running around the woods near the cabin or he's left there for good and decided to hang around town in the peeping Tom role. You and Hannah be careful, stay alert."

"Will do. Same goes for you."

By noon, Caleb and Hannah were heading north, past thick forest land on winding roads that went through scenic foothills.

Behind the wheel, Caleb pointed to the landscape. "I'm always amazed by the beauty along the coast."

Hannah rolled her window down and breathed in the fresh air. "What is it about the ocean and a beach that makes people dream?"

"Romantic setting maybe? What did Brent say when you dropped off the photos?"

"Mostly he was surprised that I shared them with him. I also gave him a great deal of my research. Not all, but enough. I got the sense that he knows a lot more than he's telling us."

"Sounds like a typical cop."

"It does, doesn't it?"

"What did Durke and Jordan say about you taking the time off? Were they upset?"

"Jordan was clearly disappointed that I won't be there tomorrow, but she wasn't upset. I think she misses our conversations more than my work. Sometimes I think she gets lonely out there during the day when Nick is at the bank. At least that's my impression."

"Why do you say that?"

"Because I don't really do all that much. I mean, don't get me wrong, I did at first. I dusted everything in sight, including the light fixtures. I cleaned toilets and showers and bathtubs. I polished the silver, the furniture, the banister, even the doors. I even picked up trash around the property. But lately, it's been different. Jordan steers me into the kitchen, where we usually sit down and have a cup of coffee, maybe a cinnamon roll, and just have a gabfest. The girl talk goes on for a good hour before she decides, only then, I should go upstairs and get to work. If I didn't know better, I'd say she's paying me to come out there so she'll have someone to talk to."

"You think she's that lonely?"

"I do. The thing is she lives a good distance from town. Sometimes I wonder if people forget she's out there. Think about it. The only time she gets to talk to others is when she drops Hutton off at school, takes little Scottie to preschool, or runs errands around town. Otherwise, she's stuck out there with no one to talk to."

"Very perceptive on your part. Drea mentioned the same thing to me last summer when she delivered flowers out there and Jordan talked her ear off."

"I wonder if her husband is aware of it."

"Nick stays busy at the bank. I go in there once or twice a week and he's invariably got three people waiting to talk to him."

"The price of success, I suppose."

"It shouldn't be that way. How about Durke? Was he mad at you?"

"Not really. Durke's a laidback kind of guy. He said he could cover both Saturday and Sunday shifts if Darla and Geniece show up as scheduled, which isn't as definitive as it sounds. I think those two definitely take advantage of Durke's good-natured approach to management."

"Believe it or not, I got that impression, too."

"Durke's a nice guy to work for, really understanding and patient. He even told me to make sure I enjoyed my days off. How sweet is that?"

"I know you. You'll likely spend the next four days worried about letting Jordan and Durke down. I hope you don't do that because you absolutely need to take this time to come to grips with the idea that Micah was left in that hole, which is horrible in its own right."

"In other words, prepare for the worst."

"Unfortunately, yes. While on the other hand, the second scenario is that it isn't Micah, which means you should take this time to prepare a whole new game plan knowing your kid brother is out there somewhere. Alive. Making his way in the world the best he can until—"

"Until I find him," she stressed.

"Until you find him," Caleb repeated.

"I'm looking forward to this, even helping you out with the work at the cabin. I just need to get my head on straight before I take on Isabella's co-op."

He raised a brow, took his eyes off the road long enough to glance at her. "Is that a done deal?"

"Yeah. She made me an offer with benefits and vacation days, the whole bit. I couldn't believe it. I haven't had time to talk it over with my dad but it's a good job, one where I can eventually grow grapes on part of the land."

"Which part?"

"The spread that backs up to the woods."

"So, you're staying in town no matter what happens with the DNA?"

"Surprised me, too. We have a busy weekend ahead, don't we?"

He picked up her hand and placed a kiss on the palm. "It won't be so bad. We'll spend our nights sleeping on Egyptian cotton sheets and calling room service. But it will get busy over the next four days. I called an electrician to come out tomorrow to replace the cabin's outside wiring, update it to twenty-first century standards."

"And the plumber?"

"Can't forget the plumber. I also had to order three new mattresses, one for each bedroom, scheduled delivery for Friday afternoon."

"This little stunt your mother pulled must be costing you a fortune."

"We all pooled our money, the family did. That's the usual way we handle things. And please, in the future, never refer to Eleanor as my mother. That woman has the maternal instincts of a tiger shark."

"You think we'll run into this guy up here?"

"I hope not."

"That makes two of us."

The Cutter Legacy Resort was fancier than Hannah expected. It looked like a chalet that belonged in Aspen where celebrities came to ski. It wasn't all that large, but it sat at the foothills nestled against the mountainside. It had three-hundred-and-sixty-degree panoramic views of the little valley where tall junipers and sequoias battled for space. A copse of hemlock and pine guarded the circled driveway entrance.

The posh lobby had a massive floor to ceiling stone fireplace on one end and at the other, a wall of windows overlooking the valley.

"You were picturing something more rustic maybe with a bearskin rug on the floor?" Caleb whispered.

She elbowed him lightly in the ribs. "You know exactly what I was thinking and it wasn't this."

"Never in a million years would I presume to know what's in your head. But some developer built this thing about five years ago to pick off some of the tech crowd coming down from San Jose for the weekend. I guess it worked."

After check-in, a bellboy delivered their luggage to their room, a luxurious suite with a king-sized bed. She fell back on the mattress testing the bounce. "I feel like I just won a three-night stay at the Waldorf. It's freezing in here. Could you turn up the heat?"

He leaned over, letting his body fall on top of hers. "Let's see if I can warm you up instead."

She ran a slim finger down his throat. "I think you know the answer to that already."

They undressed each other in the soft afternoon glow of waning winter light. They dived under the covers with momentum carrying them down. Her hair spread out on the pillow as he nipped her bottom lip. He slid one hand down her body, stroking each silky curve, focusing on each bend and arch. He worked his way lower, his tongue trailing over her. Like a laser, he locked in on that special point. His teeth nipping until she exploded like a beam wrapped in glorious sensations.

When she could catch her breath, her hand swept along his muscled chest down to his lean waist. She arched her body and used it as leverage to flip their positions until she was on top. She straddled him, wrapping her thighs around his. Their eyes locked as he moved inside her. Wet and slick, they drove. Her body on fire, loose and rushing to that point of surrender. Up, up, and higher still. Beyond the deepening blue to the next wild layer of indigo, their world slid into a kaleidoscope that exploded in a rush of need and swirling heat.

She collapsed on his chest in a limp heap, listening to his heartbeat as she tried to recover enough to move.

He stroked her hair.

"Caleb?"

"What?"

"I didn't think you could top last night." She finally found the energy to slide off to the side. "Please tell me we don't have to move from this spot."

"I wish. Why don't you unpack, get settled, and I'll go start work on the cabin."

"I'm not letting you go out there alone."

"Let's not start the weekend off with this argument again. I'll be fine. I should be back around five-thirty or so."

She sat up on one elbow and enjoyed the sight of watching his naked body crawl out of bed. He unzipped his bag and started throwing his things into one of the dresser drawers. "Since it took you all of ten seconds to unpack, I'll do the same. Because I'm going with you. There's no point in having a fight about it, either. That's one of the reasons I made the trip so we would be together. Splitting up isn't part of the deal."

"Any other female would likely stay put and enjoy the room, maybe binge watch some TV, take a long soak in that Jacuzzi tub."

"I should probably do all that since I already know what's out there waiting for both of us—backed up toilets, smelly garbage steaming with flies and ants."

"Yuck, even I think that sounds repulsive. That's why you should stay put."

"You forget that I'm used to getting my hands dirty. I run my own cleaning service *and* I don't mind digging in the dirt. The clogged toilets, however, are all yours. I know nothing about plumbing anyway."

"That's why I called a plumber. He's scheduled for tomorrow along with the electrician."

"I'm a fan of both. They take care of the big stuff while we go out there and haul off trash. It leaves us more time to make use of this divine room."

A spurt of protectiveness about the cabin he loved so much reared its head. "It isn't a bad place. Spruced up, it's always been nice and homey."

"Aww, I didn't mean anything by suggesting we stay here. It was your idea. I'm sure I'll be able to see the cabin's potential once we get past the filth."

"Come on, we'll spend an hour there doing just that before dark, two tops."

Once they got dressed and left the hotel, they stopped at a grocery store to pick up supplies—garbage bags, six kinds of spray cleaners, paper towels, bleach, and an extra mop and broom. They needed paint to cover the stains on the walls and found it at a big box store out on the highway.

Perusing the paint aisle, Hannah watched him pick up a gallon of bland interior white. "So, you're going with the same boring color you had on the walls before this incident forced you to repaint?"

"You have other ideas?"

She spread out the color wheel and began to flip through the choices. "A ton. But due to our time constraints we keep it simple. Since there's no paneling to deal with, how about a nice French Oak for the living room, Summer Sage for the kitchen, and Glass Slipper or River Blue for the bedrooms?"

"It's better than white, huh?"

"Infinitely. Plus, if you're going to take the time to slap on paint, why not liven up the place with a fresh look? Get rid of that dingy, outdated feel. When's the last time it was redecorated?"

"The main room did have paneling until 2000. That summer Shelby had us rip it out and put in new sheetrock, which we painted white to lighten up the room."

"Ah. Do you think she'd mind if you swapped out for color?"

"Nah. She's been complaining about the walls for years, too ascetic." He decided right there to take her advice and opt for color.

After hailing the salesperson, they continued to shop while they waited for the clerk to mix the paint. They picked up new rollers and brushes and several tarps to protect the hardwood floors from drips and spills.

Armed with determination, provisions, and a decorating plan, Caleb pulled out of the store parking lot as fat snowflakes began to fall. At the higher elevation, the wind had a bite to it.

"This is amazing. I don't see snow that often. It's so exciting."

"When you're freezing that pretty little ass of yours off, I'll remind you how much you like the cold."

"If it's simply cold, that's different. Snow is much more appealing somehow."

"You must think there's logic in that statement…somewhere. Have you forgotten, in order to get snow, it's gotta be around freezing? And I don't like being cold. That's why I live where I live."

"And you're making fun of my logic? It gets cold near the coast. Try San Francisco."

"Much further north than Pelican Pointe. The weather back home is downright balmy in the summertime. Stick around and you'll see I'm right. It makes for a terrific growing season."

The snow picked up as he made the turn into the lane. They'd reached the cabin with daylight to spare. But the truck fishtailed on the slick pavement, skidding onto the shoulder.

"Whoa, please tell me we won't get stranded here tonight without power."

"Don't worry. I can get us out of here and back to the hotel. We'll drop off our supplies and make a list of everything that needs doing. We're here an hour tops."

Once they were inside, she stuck close to the front door and the living area because the smell didn't seem as bad there as in the rest of the house.

"It's freezing in here. It must be fifty degrees."

"I'll make a fire. There's plenty of wood left in the crate. Funny, that's the only useful thing the guy seemed to have left untouched."

"That's probably because he had a working furnace," she said with her teeth clattering in the frigid room. After that, she stayed glued to the fireplace while he went through the house, making detailed notes in the spiral notebook he'd brought.

When he came back his face said it all.

"You're really pissed off."

"Yeah. But I'll have to get past it. There's too much to do." He sat down at the massive wooden desk in the corner while she curled up in one of the leather chairs nearby.

She liked watching him mull over an idea. The way his mouth quirked up at the corners whenever he found the solution to a problem.

"What are you staring at?" he asked, glancing up from his notebook.

"You," she answered, getting to her feet to run her fingers through his hair. "I just realized how cute you are sitting there all serious and thoughtful. What is all this in your binder?"

"I've been keeping a journal of sorts filled with a bunch of facts and figures about the cabin. Ever since I've been coming here going back twenty years. That's how I know when Shelby changed out the original décor and when we last had someone up here to look at the furnace."

Peering over his shoulder, her eyes bugged out at the length of the list. "Caleb, there's no way we can get all this done in the three days we have left."

"I know. But I'll focus on the big stuff and maybe come back this spring, when the weather's warmer. I think the roof's giving out. It might be coming to the end of its lifespan, which has nothing to do with our vandal."

"You know what occurs to me. Why didn't this guy just set the place on fire? If Eleanor wanted to make a big statement, burning it to the ground would've been a doozy."

"What are you getting at?"

"Maybe the guy was here to retrieve something and he didn't find it."

"Wow, you may have a point. I never considered that."

They stayed for another hour, well past dark, but only because they did another room to room search jotting down as many hiding places as they could think to look. By the time they left, she'd convinced Caleb there was something in the cabin worth turning it upside down.

Which meant the guy would eventually come back for a second look.

Fifteen

The next morning it was after seven when room service knocked on the door to deliver their breakfast order—a stack of pancakes and Eggs Palermo—two poached eggs nestled atop a grilled Portobello mushroom, prosciutto, and fresh spinach.

Hannah opened the door to a man dressed in a red jacket and black pants, who wheeled a cart laden with food into the room. She signed the receipt, added a tip, and called out to Caleb. "Food's here. I'm starving."

Without waiting, Hannah dug in with gusto.

Caleb was a little slower to get out of bed. "How'd you sleep?"

Hannah poured herself a cup of coffee from a silver pot. "Like a rock. How about you?"

"I kept trying to come up with what's inside the cabin that Eleanor would want. She never showed the slightest bit of interest in anything there before."

Hannah waved her fork at him in between bites. "I don't want to split hairs here, but technically we don't know for sure that she has anything to do with the vandalism at all. At this point, you're just guessing."

"Because I know the devious side to Eleanor."

"Okay, you have knowledge that I don't, your own history makes her immediately a suspect. But think about it. If Eleanor hid something in the cabin that she needed to retrieve years later, she'd be able to tell whoever was there exactly where to find it. Am I right? Why didn't she do that? He obviously tore the place up looking."

Caleb scratched his head. Try as he might to dispute that logic, he couldn't. But he wasn't about to give up the notion that Eleanor had been involved somehow. "Maybe he found what he was looking for and tore the place up because he's a first-rate asshole."

"No argument there. These eggs are delicious. Try a bite before they get stone cold."

Caleb pulled on his jeans and plopped down at the end of the bed so he could reach the cart. He finally picked up a fork and cut into his eggs. "Not bad. Tasty. How did you know to order this?"

"Eggs Palermo was listed on the menu left on the door last night as one of the choices. I'd never had it before but it sounded interesting."

Caleb scarfed down the remaining pancakes and let out a sigh. "We need to get going. I need to call Tahoe Jones to have him meet us at the cabin. Are you ready to be there when the plumber and electrician arrive?"

"I'm ready for a working toilet and a furnace that blasts out heat."

"Then let's get on the road."

"We'll need to stop for sandwiches."

He grinned. "You're thinking ahead about lunch? You're my kind of woman."

The snow had long ended by the time they reached the cabin where Tahoe Jones was waiting.

Hannah discovered the elderly man was short—no taller than five foot five. Maybe that's why he had the habit of carrying a shotgun with him wherever he went. The weapon was almost as tall as he was and weighed about as much. On the skinny side, Tahoe's wrinkled face had warm brown eyes that twinkled with a sense of humor. Leaning up against his beat-up, older model Ford pickup truck, he gave Caleb a toothy grin.

Tahoe held out a hand in greeting. "Been a long time. Do you still take off running whenever you see a raccoon?"

Caleb pumped the man's hand and laughed. "Not since I was five." He angled his head toward Hannah. "Long story, short version. I came up here once and made the mistake of finding a baby raccoon hiding under the porch. I thought it was a kitten so I tried to pull it out of its little cubbyhole so I could hold it and pet it. Big mistake. The thing chomped down on my thumb and wouldn't let go. They carted me off to the ER where I got three stitches and a series of shots that hurt like hell."

"Ouch. I see why you ran."

"A little too late," Tahoe said with a chuckle. "Your dad let me know you've had a break-in. Too bad I didn't catch the bastard in the act." He held up his gun. "If I had, me and The Boss here would've handled it already. Good news is I haven't seen hide nor hair of anyone hanging around since Landon's phone call. And I've been on guard. If it could happen here it could happen at my place when I leave to go to town."

"Thanks for that. Have you seen Sheriff Hines or the park ranger?"

"Not Hines himself, but several sweeps in the area from his deputies, as has Mick Daily, the park ranger."

At the sound of a truck engine, they all turned to watch a white van turn into the lane.

"Let's hope that's the plumber," Hannah sang out with hope.

Sure enough the van had a plumbing logo on the side. When a bearded man crawled out of the driver's side, Hannah pumped a fist in the air and did a little jig. "I hope you don't mind big, dirty jobs."

"Nothing to 'em," the plumber boasted. "They're right up my alley."

"I'm glad you feel that way," Caleb began. "Let me show you the worst of the bathrooms."

While the plumber did his thing, Hannah and Caleb hauled out the gasoline soaked bedding to the front of the house so the delivery drivers could remove the old mattresses and box springs.

It was cold outside but within ten minutes neither one of them felt the chill. In fact, Caleb was sweating so much he took off his jacket.

From there, they took each room one by one, beginning with the kitchen. They began by scooping up flour, sugar, and cereal from the floor and shoveling crap off the counters. It all ended up in a large, aluminum bucket, before getting dumped into garbage bags and then hauled out to huge trash cans pulled down to the road. They bagged up sacks of nasty, rotting food from the refrigerator, bundling the sacks together in the one remaining metal garbage can on hand, and locking it down near the road so the county refuse truck could cart it off to the landfill as soon as possible.

The electrician showed up thirty minutes later with a flair for playing detective. "How on earth did every wire running to the electric box get severed?"

"Ever heard of a narcissistic sociopath with a very sharp box cutter and a distorted view of the world?" Caleb fired back.

The man's jaw dropped. "I hope no one got hurt."

"Not yet. That's why I need the entire electrical box moved inside."

Once the cabin had working toilets and a clean interior, the atmosphere inside changed, especially when the furnace kicked in and the heat came on, warming up all parties involved.

Hannah and Caleb put the kitchen back together, starting with the refrigerator. They swabbed the tile floor to a shine. They washed what dishes, glasses, and cups hadn't been broken and tossed the pile of shards into the trash heap. They restacked the plates in the cabinet, put away pots and pans.

They got out the brushes and rollers and celebrated when the first coat of sage green went on the walls before noon.

From there, they moved into the living room, shoveling out the trash in there. They mopped the hardwood floor twice, working comfortably side by side until they broke for lunch. They spread out one of the tarps in front of the fireplace and devoured roast beef sandwiches along with a bag of Fritos they'd picked up at a grocery store.

"Not the freshest rye bread I've ever had but it fills the belly," Hannah said as she munched on her chips.

Sitting on the floor, Caleb relaxed and stretched out his long legs. He polished off his bottle of cream soda and stared at Hannah. "What is it you like most about working in a vineyard?"

She leaned back against the leather chair, gazing out the window as if putting thought into her answer. "I'd have to say I love walking between the rows of vines just as they start to bud out, just as the sprout appears on the vine. But it's a tough call because I love every part of the vine cycle, from nurturing the baby plant along to blooming, to smelling the dirt, to reaching out and feeling the shape of the bud with my fingertips, and knowing that first little shoot will develop into a sweet-tasting grape one day."

It warmed Caleb's heart to realize they had so much in common. "I love working around plants. Growing things is the most contentment I could ever have and get paid for it. Gardening's in my blood."

"When did you know that's what you wanted to do?"

"Six maybe, following along behind my dad, emulating what he did in the greenhouse. And then later, I loved watching that hybrid become a different kind of plant no one had ever heard of before. There's something calming about it."

"I'm planning to ask my father to help me get started at the co-op, helping me pick out the grapes best suited for the soil near the lighthouse." She tilted her head and looked at Caleb. "But it occurs to me you could probably contribute to that subject. The plan is to bring in the best grapes, not just for wine, but jam and jelly as well. I have this idea to turn the keeper's cottage into a store, where we sell a portion of what we grow and make to the tourists. The co-op could use the jam and jelly items as a fundraiser, a moneymaker, and then put the cash back into the crop. I like the way Isabella structured what she grows to benefit the people in the town. She told me about all the times they stop in, those who need the harvest to make ends meet. I can't wait to be a part of something like that."

The waning light had her gathering up her trash. "Shouldn't we get going on the living room paint if we want to get out of here soon?"

"Yeah, but it's peaceful sitting in this spot watching the trees sway in the wind."

"You were right about this place. Spruced up, new paint, heat, a john that flushes, I can see what you love about it. If you want to, we can check out of the hotel tomorrow morning and stay here Saturday and Sunday night."

"You wouldn't mind?"

"I won't lie, I'll miss the room service. But I'll survive. I see that look in your eyes as the cabin slowly comes back to life again. That look is priceless. It's obviously important to you, which tells me about who you are as a person. You'd do anything for your family and I really like that about you."

He ran a finger down her cheek. "At the risk of having it go to your head, I love just about everything about you. Your determination to find Micah is one of the all-time examples of not giving up. I adore that about you."

"If we don't get up from here and finish the painting, I get the sense we'll end up in bed soon."

"Not unless the mattresses get here."

She gave him a wry smile. "If you're the conventional sort, sure."

He cocked a brow. "The floor? I'm up for that."

She let out a laugh. "No. Raincheck. Hotel room. Three hours from now. Whaddya say to that?"

"You're on."

With sex on their minds, they picked up their paint rollers and reluctantly went back to work.

They were spreading French Oak, a soft creamy brown color, on the living room walls when they heard a delivery truck pull up just before five. Two men unloaded three sets of queen mattresses and box springs and carted them into the much cleaner-smelling bedrooms.

That night before they left, they stood back admiring the work they'd put in.

"It'll break my heart if this asshole repeats his performance," Hannah admitted. "What if he comes back tonight before you and Cooper install the alarm system and ruins everything we've done here?"

"Good call. I'll contact the sheriff's department and make sure someone can keep an eye on the place tonight."

"But what happens in between their drive bys? It won't be enough."

"I know, but it's the best we can do without sleeping here."

"I honestly hate to leave and risk it."

"Me too."

They did eventually lock up and take off. But they were still worried about the cabin on the drive to the lodge.

Once they got back, they went up to their room to shower off the dirt and sweat.

As Hannah got out of her filthy jeans and top, she noticed Caleb watching her. "What?"

"You look beautiful. So much you blow me away."

"Okay, now I know you're lying. My hair's greasy and smells like gasoline. I have paint on my chin and a scratch on my nose where a box fell on it."

"Poor baby." He kicked off his work boots, yanked his shirt over his head, and unbuttoned his jeans. He held out a hand in invitation. "You look beautiful. And I'll say it as many times as you want me to because it's true. Take a shower with me, Hannah."

She stepped into his arms, took his face between her hands. "You're a charmer, Mr. Jennings."

He shed his jeans and backed her into the bathroom. "So formal and proper. Let's see how long that lasts." He turned on the water. As he maneuvered her under the spray and into the steam, he lowered his mouth to hers.

Their hands spread soapy foam over curves and angles, hips and breasts. Slick, wet, they went after each other.

Caught up in her, he slipped his hands under her butt and lifted her off the tile floor. She straddled his legs, lowered herself onto him. Joined, she held on as satiny smooth met up against hard. They rocked and raced with only one goal in mind. Fire and heat surged. They shuddered, exploding in frenzy, surrendering to each other.

He rested his head on hers, out of breath. "That's one way to cap off a hardworking day."

"I could get used to this."

He ran his hands up her back. "God, so could I. Are you hungry?"

"Starving."

Later, they opted for room service again and ate Pacific salmon, cozied up in bed.

Before going to sleep, Hannah got out her laptop to catch up on her emails. To Brent, she asked for an update on the case. To Isabella, she sent a list of ideas for the co-op, repeating how excited she was about her new job. To Durke, she made sure Geniece and Darla had showed up without incident to cover her shift. To Jordan, she wanted to know just how booked up the B&B was for the upcoming week. She made certain Jordan knew she'd be there, on time and without fail. It seemed polite to keep a dialogue going until she could update Jordan about the co-op job.

"What are you doing?" Caleb asked.

"Keeping the lines of communication open while I'm gone."

"You've sent emails to practically everyone you know. You'll be back before noon on Monday."

"Sue me if I'm thorough."

He went over to where she sat at the desk, head bent at the keyboard. He began to nip his way along her neck. "Our last night in this luxurious room. We're supposed to make the most of it, but with you way over here...that's hard to do."

She shut the lid on her laptop. "That's okay. I can remedy that."

Sixteen

Saturday morning, they checked out of the hotel and returned to the cabin, arriving around eight o'clock. As the sun tipped over the mountaintop, they stopped to enjoy the sight.

"I didn't see anyone hanging around getting here. Looks like the cabin made it through the night without another fire," Hannah said as she grabbed the coffee and croissants they'd brought for breakfast.

Caleb unlocked the front door and breathed in the still lingering smell of freshly painted walls. He looked around, cautious and afraid of what he might find. But the cabin was empty and looked the same as they'd left it the night before.

They ate breakfast in the spotless kitchen, the fresh paint smell in the air around them.

"You made the right call with the sage green color," Caleb noted.

"Thanks. I hope Shelby shares that opinion. What's the plan today?"

"We've shoveled out most of the trash, made the kitchen look like a new room, cleaned out the living room, now we tackle the bedrooms."

She raised her cardboard mug of coffee. "Here's to that. If we plan to sleep here tonight, I want the sleeping quarters comfy and clean. That means loads of laundry to get the bedding sanitized. I looked in the linen closet and there are plenty of towels, lots of sheets and comforters. I'm washing all of it just in case that…pervert…touched any of them. The amazing thing is the utility room is the one place he left untouched."

"The washing machine works. I tested it out yesterday," Caleb said in assurance. "Didn't try the dryer."

"That's okay. I'll turn it on before I load up a lot of clothes. The last thing I want is to have to cart baskets of wet towels to a laundromat on the other side of the mountain. I'm anxious to have fresh towels and a clean place to sleep tonight. When's Cooper due?"

"While we were loading up the truck I got a text from him early this morning saying his ETA is ten o'clock. Since we don't have cell service here, that's the last update."

He stuffed the last of the croissant in his mouth. "I'll start carrying out whatever needs to go from the bedrooms."

Hannah emptied the linen closet, making several trips to the laundry room. She tested the dryer. After finding it in working order, she put on the first load of towels. While that washed, she took another spray bottle of cleaner and got to work on the sink and tub in the master bathroom. She mopped the floors again before throwing the towels in to dry. She loaded up the washer with sheets and went back to finish the hall bathroom.

She heard the wop wop wop of chopper blades circling the house and met Caleb at the front door in time to see Eastlyn and Cooper touching down on the one open area that was big enough for the helicopter to land.

Cooper began unloading boxes of equipment and setting them on the ground. He tossed out a duffel bag and stepped back away from the blades. As soon as he got far enough away from the rotors, Eastlyn waved and lifted off.

Caleb ran up to help him lug the gear up to the house. Both men acted as pack mules to get all the stuff he'd brought to the front doorstep.

Cooper set down one of the boxes on the porch. "Hey, Hannah. How's it going?"

"We've made great progress on getting the cabin clean. But we're anxious to get the alarm system working."

Cooper dug out a piece of paper from his pocket, shoved it toward Caleb. "I found this before I left this morning, taped to my front door. You were right from the start, thinking this was Eleanor's doing."

Caleb read the note and gave it to Hannah to read.

"It says your mother sends her love," Hannah uttered aloud. "Oh, my God, that creepy feeling is inching up my spine again just reading those words."

Caleb rubbed his forehead. "So, her friend is basically taunting us? But why? Hannah thinks there's something in this cabin she wants."

A brow arched up over Cooper's right eye. "An interesting theory. I take it you haven't come across anything that would be of value to her?"

Caleb shook his head. "Not yet. It isn't like we haven't tried. We've been through every room, cleaned out cabinets, linen closets, dresser drawers, you name it. So far…nada."

Hannah opened the door wide and led the way inside. Standing in the middle of the living room, she held out her arms. "What do you think?"

Cooper's jaw dropped. "Wow! There's new paint on the walls. This looks fantastic."

"French Oak," Hannah noted, beaming. "There's new paint in every room except the utility room and bathrooms."

Cooper turned in a circle. "You guys got this much done in two days? According to the photos Caleb showed me this place was in sad shape. I'm impressed. It looks amazing. This old place hasn't looked this good since it was new. I'm taking pictures of the improvements and sending them to Mom and Dad. It'll blow them away."

"You can't. No Internet," Caleb reminded him. "You forget how remote this place really is. You come up here used to Wi-Fi and modern conveniences and have to rough it. It takes some getting used to. That's why I asked whether the alarm system would work."

"Right. Well, no problem. I'll adjust. I've been to my share of remote locales. The surrounding beauty makes up for lack of cell phone service. Where do you want the cameras?"

"Mounted in the most obvious of places, the front porch, the back deck, as conspicuous as possible. That way anyone who gets close to the perimeter will know without a doubt they're being videoed. And I found the perfect spot for the alarm system, a place where they'll have to breach all the new locks to get inside. And if they want to shut it off, they'll have to go down to the basement to do it. I had the electrician put in a brand-new box down there specifically for that purpose."

Cooper slapped his baby brother on the back. "That's smart thinking. I say we get started."

While the guys worked on the security system, Hannah continued to deal with the mountain of laundry, stuffing each comforter into its own load. She folded stacks of towels, repeated the process with another load and gathered up the massive quantity of sheets she used to make up the beds.

She was in the third bedroom, struggling with the stubborn corner of a fitted sheet, grumbling that she didn't have enough room to work, when she tripped over a gap in the floorboard. She looked down to see a plank that seemed out of place, and stomped on the raised hazard.

"Well that's gonna cause somebody to break a toe," Hannah muttered under her breath. "As it is there's not enough room to maneuver around in here since the bed is pushed up against the wall."

She gave the bed a good shove out of frustration, and noticed the ill-fitting board wobble against the rest.

"Bad repair job," she decided as she tried to poke the offending board with the toe of her shoe. She watched the wide plank give way more than it should have.

She got down on all fours and tried to get the plank to come up, using her fingers. That's when she realized just how much higher it was from the rest of the flooring.

Not in the mood to give up, she ran to the utility room and opened Caleb's tool chest. She found a small metal crowbar and grabbed the flashlight.

Back in the bedroom she wedged the crowbar in between the gap and put enough leverage on the other end to get the wooden plank to pop up. Hannah stared at an empty vent space, perhaps twelve inches deep. She picked up the flashlight and aimed the beam into the small cavern.

"Ick, cobwebs," she uttered as she stuck the light farther into the hole, past the spider webs. When the beam fell on what looked like a bulge of something lodged in the corner, she gingerly used the flashlight to poke at the lump. When it didn't move, she used the crowbar to work it in position where she could see what it was.

The lump turned out to be an old bank bag made from canvas. It had dark green lettering stenciled on the front that read, "The First Bank of Pelican Pointe."

She recognized the logo—a likeness of the bank building in town, silk-screened onto the fabric at one time, but it had faded badly, almost peeling off completely, leaving behind bits of green ink attached to the material.

Hannah worked her fingers between the drawstring and tugged it open. She sat back on her heels before plopping her butt down on the floor, realizing she'd literally stumbled on the very thing Eleanor had sought to find.

Seventeen

Caleb and Cooper stared at the kitchen table where Hannah had dumped out the contents of the canvas bag.

"An old bank bag filled with enough Krugerrands to buy a tropical island," Caleb noted with disgust. He used his fingers to comb through his hair. "How could our intruder have missed this?"

"It wasn't that easy to find. I wouldn't have gotten lucky either if I hadn't been stooping over struggling with the fitted sheet. That side of the bed couldn't be more than six inches from the baseboard. Unless he was tidying up changing the sheets there's no way he would've even seen the loose board."

"But we were in there yesterday with the delivery guys. And then we swiped paint on the walls. Neither one of us saw anything wrong with the floor."

"We weren't really looking down at the floor or under the bed," Hannah insisted. "We were focused on moving what little furniture is in there enough to paint."

"Hey, I'm just glad you found it," Cooper said as he examined one of the gold coins. "Most of these were minted in 1970, only three years after their initial debut in South Africa. This explains why Eleanor sent an emissary to tear this place apart since she couldn't exactly conduct the search herself."

"But why come after the bag now?" Hannah wondered.

"Maybe she forgot where she hid them until recently," Caleb proffered. "Mental lapse. She is getting up there in years."

Cooper sent his brother a look of disbelief. "Yeah. Right. Not likely. Eleanor forget about gold coins? Nope. Not buying that."

"You're both missing the larger picture here," Hannah began. "This asshole obviously thinks you guys already found the bag. That's why he's hanging around town and creeping around your houses. He thinks you have the gold."

When Cooper started to reply to that, she held up her hand. "Not done yet. Hear me out. How did your...er...Eleanor...come by this many South African Krugerrands, in of all places, Pelican Pointe? Did she ever travel extensively abroad?"

"Not until she went on the run after murdering two people," Caleb grumbled. "I'm sure she saw plenty of scenery between here and Georgia. But I doubt that little journey explains thousands of dollars in South African gold."

Caleb stopped talking and exchanged a long look with Cooper. "You know who might be the best source for that, someone who'd know how she came by these? Dad. He knows Eleanor infinitely better than anyone else."

"Yeah. But in the meantime, we're sitting on a fortune out in the middle of nowhere. We're sitting ducks. You know damn well this guy's coming after this...eventually. If Hannah's right, Eastlyn could be danger right now."

"And Shelby and Landon and Drea," Hannah pointed out.

"Exactly." Sweat popped out on Cooper's brow. "It's just a matter of time before Eleanor pressures her cohort to ramp up the effort."

"Then we better finish running the coaxial cable and get the whole system wired. It's a good thing you bought a DVR with a five-hundred gigabyte hard drive, enough for several weeks of recording. Who knows how long this guy will wait before he takes another run at us?"

Cooper stood back, crossed his arms over his chest. "Yeah. Well. Maybe we should think about getting this kind of security for our own homes."

"One problem at a time," Caleb muttered. "Besides, I already have an alarm system."

"Not like this one. At least if he pays us a return visit here, we'll be better prepared than letting him stick a note to the door or lurk around where we live without fear of getting caught."

That one idea had Cooper grabbing his jacket.

"Where are you going?" Hannah asked.

"I need to borrow the truck and drive somewhere until I get cell phone service. Eastlyn needs to know what's going on so she isn't taken by surprise in the event he breaks in there looking for this bag."

Hannah swept a hand through her hair. "I've no doubt Eastlyn can take care of herself."

"Of course she can, but I need her to get in touch with Mom, Dad, and Drea, and make sure they're all aware of the situation."

Caleb paced the length of the kitchen. "Good idea. I just hope while you're gone I'll be able to finish the wiring."

"Do the best you can. I'll be back soon."

Without Cooper, Caleb had trouble getting the alarm system where it worked with the cameras, but after fiddling with the DVR, he finally managed to get everything in sync.

With Hannah's help, he tested the motion detectors and performed several dry runs before he was completely satisfied with the solidness of the security.

When Cooper got back, he found out firsthand what Caleb's state of the art system could do. The minute he got within thirty yards of the front door, lights popped on, the camera kicked in, and the alarm went off, loud enough that

Cooper had to cover his ears. "I take it you were successful in getting it up and running?"

"It has very sensitive triggers."

Cooper held up a bag from one of the local restaurant chains. "I brought food. Burgers and fries so nobody has to cook."

"What did Eastlyn say?"

"That Drea saw a man this afternoon hanging around the flower shop. He fit the description of our lurker. Tucker's spending the night at her place for a few days until we find this guy."

"I wonder if our bold vandal will stay in town or make the trip out here?" Hannah wondered aloud. "It's only a two-hour drive."

They ate supper with that thought hanging over their heads.

After dinner, they went back into the third bedroom, deciding to make sure they'd uncovered all of Eleanor's hidden loot.

"I'm pretty sure this was the room Drea used whenever we came up here as kids," Caleb noted. "Cooper and I shared the middle bedroom."

Cooper nodded. "That sounds about right. I don't ever remember crawling underneath the bed though, which is pretty much how the loose board must've gone unnoticed."

Hannah opened the closet, rifled through its contents. But all she found were a string of outdated shirts hanging on wire hangers and several old board games stacked on the top shelf. She ran her hands around the walls of the closet, knocking on the drywall. "Sorry to say, no hidden panels in here."

Caleb plopped down on the bed. "Once we get back to town what do we do with that bag of gold?"

"I guess we take it to Nick and it goes in the bank vault. I don't want it hanging around my house, tempting some loser to break in."

"Same here. Now that I think about it, we have nothing to do for the rest of the evening. We could jack up the stereo."

Hannah's eyes landed on the tower of board games. "That's not entirely true." She picked up Scrabble off the top. "Are you guys any good?"

For the next several hours they listened to old vinyl albums and passed the time playing Scrabble, then a few hands of gin rummy, before settling on a wicked game of cutthroat Monopoly.

Hannah handily beat them both. "Sorry, guys. But I spent three years in foster care where all we did was pass the time playing one kind of game or another. Monopoly was popular until video games had us arguing over the controls. The adults sent us packing back to the kitchen table, preferring Monopoly to the fighting."

"No wonder you played like a pro," Cooper grunted. "I'm going to bed. You guys can sleep in the master. I'll be fine in the middle bedroom."

"Are you sure?" Hannah asked, as she packed away the game pieces and stuffed the fake money back into the box.

"Positive. Just try to keep the noise down. I don't want to hear Caleb screaming in the heat of passion."

Caleb responded by taking off his shoe and tossing it in the direction of his brother, barely missing Cooper's head.

Cooper hooted with laughter and disappeared down the hallway.

"I feel a lot better knowing that security system is up and running," Hannah noted while she cleaned up their paper plates from supper.

"If the bastard makes it past either door, it'll be up to the Beretta and the Glock to stop him."

She threw a clean dish towel at his head. "Oh great. That'll help me sleep like a baby tonight. Not."

"Nope. That's what I'm for." His arms circled her waist while his mouth moved to her neck.

"You heard Cooper. We have to keep it down."

"Where's the fun in that? Come on, we'll give him nightmares."

Eighteen

Two hours later, an ear-piercing, high-pitched siren shattered their slumber. The incessant woo woo woo sound—a sound that only an alarm system from hell could produce—kept screeching, splitting every nerve in the eardrum.

Caleb grabbed his gun and stumbled out of bed. Throwing back the bedroom door, he stepped out into the hallway and ran smack into Cooper.

"Where are you going?" whispered Cooper.

"To check the monitor in the living room."

"Maybe the monitor and kill switch should be in the bedroom."

Caleb sent him a deadly look. "Where was that suggestion when I hooked up the damn thing six hours ago…by myself."

Hannah snatched up her robe and didn't even think to grab the Glock. She shadowed the men down the hall until they reached the living room.

One look at the video screen had Caleb lowering the pistol. Out of the darkness, a lone raccoon came into view. The animal, guilty of setting off the alarm, sauntered across the back deck before scurrying off into the night.

"The sensors definitely need recalibrating," Cooper lamented. "Otherwise that thing will pick up every squirrel from here to Tahoe's property line."

"Yeah, yeah, yeah," Caleb groused. "I'll go tweak the damn thing." He disappeared down the basement steps to get it done.

But ninety minutes later, the alarm went off again. This time when Caleb checked the monitor he saw a trio of possums roaming carefree in the backyard, thirty or so feet from the back door.

"This time I'll do it," Cooper offered. "I'll bring the sensor field in, shrink the area, so it won't pick up movement from that far away."

Forty-five minutes later, the woo woo woo sound from hell erupted again.

Caleb threw back the covers, picked up his gun, marched out into the hallway, heading toward the living room.

Cooper staggered to the doorway and followed his brother. "What the hell is wrong with that thing?"

"I don't know, but I'm about ready to shoot the monitor on sight." For the third time that night, Caleb stood there watching the same raccoon as before, only this time he'd brought a well-fed friend. The two looked as if they were casing the joint and were trying to figure out the best way to gain entry.

Caleb let out a deep sigh. "I'll go calibrate the sensors so it'll detect an even greater amount of movement before the alarm goes off." Pissed off, down he went into the basement again to fiddle with the motion detector.

After that, the trio slept soundly until six-forty-five when Hannah woke up and couldn't get back to sleep. She got dressed and tiptoed out of the room, leaving Caleb snoring softly.

She headed to the kitchen to put on coffee, selected the strong, Italian roast from the cupboard and loaded up the water. While the machine rattled to life, she decided instead of waiting around she'd check to see what was happening with the monitor in the living room.

For five minutes her eyes stayed glued to the screen, but she saw nothing out of the ordinary and went to pour herself a shot of much-needed caffeine.

She grabbed her jacket and a blanket from the utility room and took her coffee outside to the back deck. It was chilly, but she sat down in one of the Adirondack chairs and spread the blanket across her legs. Her first sip was accompanied by a feel-good contentment that only caffeine produces. But it was more than that. She hadn't felt this happy in…maybe she'd never felt this happy.

She watched the sun peek out through a smattering of clouds and turn the sky a brilliant pinkish orange and wondered what had happened to that hike Caleb had promised, the one where she'd planned on communing with nature. She had a feeling this was as close as she was going to get.

A noise to her left had her eyes darting to check out the family of possums pawing beneath the winter sand. She sucked in a breath waiting for the alarm to go off and let out a sigh of relief when nothing happened. The silence indicated Caleb had finally tweaked the sensors to get the proper setting. Or maybe it had been Cooper.

A cone dropped down from a large sequoia and landed softly in a mass of crumpled wet fronds. In the still of the morning dawn, a rustling noise drew her attention back to where the determined possums seemed eager to paw at the ground. They were certainly sniffing along the dirt on the scent of something.

Curious, she got up from the warmth of the blanket, set her cup down on the railing. But as soon as she started walking toward the pile of leaves, the possums scattered.

As she got closer, she spotted it then, the clump of fur left behind. Her first instinct was to back away because she thought the animal was dead, it was that still.

But then she heard a pitiful whine, saw the thing open one eye and move one of its legs. There among the melted snow, lying in the sand, was the ugliest dog she'd ever seen. The mutt had tried to burrow under the leaves to die but probably ran out of energy.

The poor thing had the wiry coat of an Airedale but the body of a Jack Russell, complete with a dirty cream-colored coat mixed with patches of brown. But where the terrier was less defined, the mutt influence took over, mostly around the snout. There was no denying the filthy, matted fur, or the saddest, biggest pair of chocolate brown eyes she'd ever seen.

Hannah kneeled to the ground next to it. "You poor little half-starved thing. Are you hurt? Of course, you're hurt. I see blood on your hip. Let's get a better look at you. Ah, a female. Well, girl, you barely have the strength to hold your head up, don't you? What you need is food, water. Don't go anywhere, I'll be right back."

She got to her feet and dashed back to the house where she grabbed a bottle of water and a bag of crackers, stuffed both into her jacket pockets. She reached in the cabinet, took down one of the bowls.

She raced back outside and brought out the water, poured it into the bowl and held it out so the dog could lap it up. Next, she opened the sleeve of crackers, mashing several up in the palm of her hand. She held out the crumbs and watched the mutt lick her hand clean.

"What are you doing?" Caleb asked from behind her.

Hannah jumped at the question and the dog yelped.

"Don't scare me like that," Hannah cautioned. "Say something before you sneak up on a person."

Caleb took in the animal's poor condition and looked back at Hannah. "I'll ask again. What are you doing? And what is that?"

"What does it look like? It's a puppy, a poor little starved-to-death thing left out here to die. See how skinny she is. She's so thin you can see her ribs. Poor baby. Her coat's filled with burrs and tangles, and she's barely got enough strength left to roll over."

But just as Hannah got that last part out, the dog defied her and rolled to a belly position before crawling to get closer to Hannah.

As a reward, Hannah ran her fingers through the dog's mane. "You're such a frail thing. I bet you're still hungry. Huh, girl? We should take it slow with the food though. How long's it been since you've had anything decent to eat anyway?"

"Hannah, that dog needs a vet."

"I know that. That's why we can't leave her out here to fend for herself. She's miles from anyone, Tahoe included."

"You want to take that flea-ridden thing back with us?"

Insulted, Hannah's back went up. "I'm not leaving her in the middle of nowhere to starve, Caleb Jennings. I bet Cord will be able to patch her up like new. I'm keeping her. I'm calling her Molly. You're a good girl, aren't you, Molly? Just unlucky enough in life to get dumped out here in the boonies with no one around to take care of you."

It was that last statement that smacked Caleb between the eyes. Hard. He bent down in the dirt to examine the dog more closely. "She's crawling because she can't stand up. There's something wrong with all four of her paws. And see the blood on her hind leg. That wound's from a BB gun. It's probably still lodged in there."

Hannah's mouth dropped open. "Someone shot her? What kind of asshole does that? We need to get her up to the house, pour some antiseptic on that leg and see what other injuries she has. Peroxide will have to do until we can get her back home and let Cord treat it properly. She needs a bath, too."

"We'll use the shed out back to scrub the dirt off. It has an old metal tub that'll work just fine. Plus, it has hot and cold running water."

But Hannah was thinking beyond that. "We'll need dog food and a brush, maybe a pair of clippers to get the tangles out of her coat."

Caleb lugged Molly into the shed. The pup didn't weigh more than twenty pounds. He set her down on top of a table and got the tub down from where it hung on the wall.

Molly didn't seem to mind the water. It soothed her paws and the wound left by the BB gun. They also discovered Molly suffered from a cut on her shoulder near the back of her neck.

"That looks like it came from a knife," Hannah noted with disdain. "What's wrong with people that they would do something like that to a defenseless animal."

"That's definitely a knife wound. See? It's too perfect a line to have come from anything else, which means she had contact with an ugly human."

"Maybe our vandal?"

"I'd say that's a distinct possibility. Which might mean he doesn't carry an honest to goodness weapon on him."

Hannah bored a hole in him with a beady-eyed stare. "If he did, Molly here would likely be dead by now."

"A sobering thought. Although, think about it. Molly wasn't out there when we arrived on Thursday. We would've seen her when we hauled out that mountain of trash. I walked past that very spot at least half a dozen times on Thursday alone just to get tools out of the shed."

"Then where's she been hiding all this time?"

"Not here."

After they scrubbed off the filth, they poured peroxide into Molly's wound.

"The BB's still in there. You can feel it," Caleb declared.

By the time they carried Molly into the house, they found Cooper cracking eggs into a bowl.

He turned from the stove. "Well now, who do we have here?"

"Cooper, meet Molly," Hannah said. "I found her this morning under the giant sequoia. The possums were pawing at her because she was half dead. She's my first dog."

Caleb pivoted toward Hannah. "You've never had a dog before? You didn't mention that earlier."

"No. Things in life didn't exactly work out in that department, I guess."

Cooper eyed the tail-wagging mutt. "She looks perky enough now. I'll make more eggs. Molly looks like she could use a meal."

Molly devoured an entire plateful of scrambled eggs all the while staying wrapped around Hannah's feet.

"It's a nice day for a walk," Cooper announced after breakfast. "Why don't you guys head outside for a while?"

Hannah chewed her lip. "I'd love to go on a hike but it hurts for Molly to walk. I don't want to leave her alone."

"How about we take turns? I'll stay here and look after Molly while you guys go. When you guys come back, I'll take my turn. I brought my camera with me and I'm itching to take some photographs of the area that I can display in the store and add to my website."

Hannah laid a hand on Cooper's arm. "I sometimes forget you make a living other than selling trains."

"I'd pretty much starve to death if all I had going for me were locomotives and box cars. Not that I don't love trains and memories of Dad, but the storefront also acts as a gallery of sorts."

"I know. I have one of the pictures you took of the crops growing near the lighthouse. The way the sun filters through the trees takes my breath away. You captured that one special moment at the right time of day perfectly. I haven't even had a chance to hang it yet."

"I don't remember you coming in and buying that," Cooper said before turning his head to stare at his brother. "Ah. That was for Hannah."

Caleb smiled and took Hannah's hand in his. "I'm convinced it was how I got her to go out with me the second time. We'd had coffee together but I had to leave before we were done talking. I wanted to make it up to her. I needed something—not flowers because I thought she'd think I was showing off—but rather something that made an impact. Anyway, I looked for a gift that would reflect the town, but in an out of the ordinary sort of way. I walked in your shop after work one day and saw that hanging on the wall. It was beautiful and breathtaking and exactly what I was looking for. You have an amazing talent, my brother."

"I don't think you've ever told me that before. Thanks. It means a lot. What about the fact that you're an amazing gardener? You grow these beautiful plants and wait for them to…blossom, sometimes for years, something that would drive me nuts. Me. Zero patience on that score."

Cooper cut his eyes over to Hannah. "So, did the photo intrigue you enough that it won you over for that second date?"

Hannah felt her cheeks flush. "I'm here, aren't I? The truth is he sent Beckham to my house to deliver the package."

"I paid him five bucks to make sure he handed it to you personally."

"And he did. I unwrapped the thing immediately, and it blew me away. I sent Beckham back with a 'thank you' note."

"I got it. And pretty much knew from that moment I wanted the chance to ask you out because I knew you'd say yes."

"You guys get out of here," Cooper reiterated. "I'll do the breakfast dishes and keep an eye on Molly."

To make Molly more comfortable while she was gone, Hannah decided the dog needed a bed. Before she left she decided to find something she could use for one. Surely the shed, with all its junk, could provide a box or a basket.

She started for the back door and before she could step outside, she heard Molly whine and belly crawl an inch or two toward her. "I'll be right back. You stay put. There's no need to miss me."

But as she made her way to that ramshackle outbuilding, Hannah realized she felt warm inside. The dog liked her enough to miss her. She'd never had that before.

Digging through the jumble of stuff, she found an old wicker laundry basket that would work perfectly. She went back inside to the laundry room and retrieved one of the clean blankets she still had piled on top of the dryer. She folded it over several times until it fit in the bottom and would make a nice thick, soft spot to sleep.

Hannah picked Molly up and set her down on the bed. "There. How's that feel?"

"Not bad," Caleb said from the doorway. "You have your own little crib, Molly."

The dog promptly tried to get out.

"Maybe she has to go potty. I'll take her out before we go."

Caleb followed them outside. "You're reluctant to go on the hike without Molly, right? I have an idea." He headed off in the direction of the shed. A few minutes later he came back pulling a rusted-out wagon with faded red wooden rails around the bed. He'd thrown in a strip of old carpeting to make it snug and cozy.

"Oh, my God, this'll work. What a great idea." Hannah plucked Molly off the ground and into the wagon to get the dog's reaction. "Let's tell Cooper we're taking her with us and hit the trail."

It didn't take long pulling the wagon behind her to realize the ground was way too bumpy for a sick dog.

"We should keep to the pavement, stick to the blacktop," Caleb suggested. "Once we get out to the road, we can hug the shoulder. It'll still be a pretty walk among the pine trees."

"I'm just happy to be outside."

They walked for almost a mile without saying anything to each other until Caleb got curious.

"Is everything okay? I've never seen you this quiet for this long." Thinking she was worried about the dog, he added, "I'm sure Molly will be fine."

"It isn't that. I've every reason to think Cord or Keegan will be able to fix her up."

"Then what is it?"

"I don't think Micah ended up at Bradford House, Caleb. I don't think that's him in the ground."

"When did you come to that conclusion?"

"Don't laugh. But I've always had this 'connection' to him, even though the only image I have is that of a little baby. At least I think that's what it is, some kind of link because we're siblings. Don't you have that with yours?"

"I guess. To some extent."

"I think I'd know if Micah was dead. He's alive, Caleb. I'm sure of it. I feel it in my heart. He's somewhere living his life like most twenty-year-olds do, doing normal things. I just hope that his life is in Pelican Pointe and this whole thing hasn't been for nothing."

"It hasn't been for nothing. We found each other, didn't we?"

She ran a hand along his cheek. "I didn't mean it like that. You've been the one bright spot for me in all this."

"Same here. I can't think of another woman who would put up with coming here in the sticks to put herself at risk. Not to mention leaving her jobs to make the trip."

"I needed this. To get away for a few days. And look, I found Molly."

"Not to mention a fortune in Krugerrands."

Hannah laughed. "There is that. It still mystifies me how that amount of gold got here at the cabin. I thought you said she bitched about your father not making enough money. If she had access to that kind of wealth, why did she bicker about the money factor?"

"Eleanor had to make a fuss about something. Her unhappiness with my Dad wasn't due to anything he did. She just didn't like her life. If there was no immediate chaos, she'd make sure to create it. Don't you understand that? Why else would she disappear that night not knowing whether Cooper could get us back to shore safely? Turns out, he couldn't. If it hadn't been for a fisherman coming along when he did we'd likely have drifted farther out to sea. And I wouldn't be standing here now."

"That's a scary thought."

"For sane people, it is. Not so much for Eleanor."

"But if she wanted a new life why didn't she just take off with the gold when she left?"

"Yeah, I can't figure that one out either. That must be what makes it a mystery."

"We're a pair, aren't we?"

He draped an arm over her shoulder. "But you aren't part of a dangerous psycho."

"Who says? If I can't prove my father is innocent, it'll always be out there for people to speculate that he's a monster. It'll be hanging over my head for the rest of my life."

She stopped walking. "Where is this waterfall you mentioned?"

He pointed ahead of them. "Due north. We've probably walked less than a mile."

Hannah made a face. "Really? So, another three and a half miles that way? Ugh."

"Why?"

"I guess maybe Cooper could take a picture of it for me. Let's head back."

When it was Cooper's turn for a hike, he took his time touring the landscape he'd known as a child. On his way to the waterfall he took pictures of the rolling countryside, the sun as it filtered through towering sequoias, and plenty of colorful birds nesting in the pine trees.

Never one to take the most direct route, he detoured off the road and took the scenic path he'd been taking since he was a boy.

After Landon and Shelby had taken in three damaged kids, they'd seen to it that the siblings had plenty of distractions. The cabin became one of those places, a destination that soon offered Cooper a reason to grab the Nikon he'd gotten for his birthday.

It didn't take him long coming back here every summer to realize it was nature's paradise. The mountainous terrain became a favorite subject that brought him full circle to his love of landscape. Here, he could lose himself in the picturesque trails for hours and forget about what he'd helped Eleanor do the night his father had been murdered. The beauty of the area had helped him heal back then just as it often had on his other travels throughout the world.

Today, the thick forest of mountain pine and cedar sprinkled with sequoia still staggered him each time he experienced their magnificent reaches. He'd made this same hike to the waterfall dozens of times before. But it still took him half an hour in, before he realized someone was dogging him. He could sense he wasn't alone. A couple of times, he'd picked up the footsteps, the rustling, the sound of someone unfamiliar with the dense underbrush following him from off the trail.

He wasn't exactly sure what to do. Should he continue to the waterfall to get the guy out in the open or backtrack on a parallel course and head back to the cabin?

He decided to circle back using a trail that was off the beaten path. It was higher in elevation and not as well-traveled, but it would likely be the best way to lose whoever had trailed him this far.

Cooper picked up his pace and made it to where the terrain became more rugged. He took out a bottle of water from his backpack and drank generously trying to hydrate himself in anticipation for the higher altitude. With any luck, the guy behind him might not be as well-prepared. If his tracker hadn't brought the right provisions for the tougher trail and higher elevation, the man wouldn't be able to keep up.

Once he reached the first rocky slope, he began the ascent toward the peak. He clambered to top of a boulder and realized he was high enough that he could see the footpath behind him. He stood there trying to pick up any movements of other hikers using the same trail. But he saw nothing. He was about to scramble up through the narrow gap when he caught sight of a man doggedly trying to scale the same side of the mountain he'd just climbed.

He wished he'd brought the binoculars, without them he couldn't make out anything more than a tall man with a paunch trying to keep up.

"Struggling mightily, aren't you?" he murmured to himself with some satisfaction. "Let's see if you can stay with me through the pass."

It took Cooper ninety minutes to get back to the cabin from his jagged route around the mountain.

When he did, he found Caleb and Hannah sitting on the front porch with Molly.

"Did you get the picture of the waterfall?" Hannah questioned.

"Nope. But I did manage to dodge the son of a bitch that likely tore up the cabin."

Nineteen

"Let's face it, I'm hoping that having the dog will take Hannah's mind off waiting for the DNA to come back," Caleb confessed to Cooper after he'd dropped her off at the little bungalow on Monday morning.

He'd helped her with her luggage and Molly's basket knowing full well she intended to hurry over to the veterinarian clinic before going anywhere else.

"I don't have a stool sample," Hannah muttered. "When I made the appointment online once we got cell phone service, Cord's website said I should bring one with me."

"Don't worry about it. Just be glad they could work you in today," Caleb assured her. "Text me as soon as you get done here."

"Good thing we share a driveway. What are you and Cooper planning to do?"

"Family meeting first, and then I'll keep you posted what else after that." He placed a kiss on her forehead. "Don't be nervous. Cord and Keegan are good at what they do. They'll fix up Molly."

She hoped that was true as she waved goodbye to Caleb and Cooper. Toting Molly in her arms, she made a beeline for the veterinarian clinic where she was greeted by the receptionist, Irene Odana.

Irene had given up her dead-end job telemarketing just three months earlier for a full-time position working for Cord and Keegan. At barely five-two, the woman had a mop of silvery streaks running through her black hair even though she hadn't yet celebrated her thirty-eighth birthday. She wore a pair of big-framed eyeglasses that she seemed to forever be pushing up on her nose.

"I have a new patient for Cord. Or Keegan," Hannah announced, keeping a tight hold on Molly. "The online appointment form didn't specify which vet we'd be seeing."

"Mondays belong to Cord, although depending on what emergencies come up, Keegan can run over from the rescue center if she's needed." Irene shoved a clipboard across the counter toward Hannah. "Fill this out and Jessica will be with you directly."

Hannah already knew Jessica St. John was Cord's technical assistant. Jessica had recently completed two years at Santa Rosa Junior College. She'd finished all her certifications to become Cord's nurse, radiologist, and his all-around medical tech. She could take blood, start IVs, give injections, and was the go-to person on patient education, a program Keegan and Cord started and believed benefited the animals as much as it did their owners.

Hannah had barely finished the paperwork when Jessica showed her to an exam room. On the walk down the hall, the young tech went over what she'd do.

"My job is to go over Molly's medical history, get her vitals, and assess her overall health before Cord gets in the room."

Instead of putting Molly down on the exam table, Hannah let the dog sit in her lap. "That might be a problem. I'm afraid there isn't much information I can offer other than what I filled out on the form. I have no idea how old Molly is or how she came to be in this condition."

Jessica perused the form. "Ah, so she's a stray, and you found her with these injuries, one cut across the shoulder and the BB shot still lodged under her skin?"

"*Was* a stray. She's not anymore. She's mine now," Hannah maintained.

Jessica smiled and ran a hand across the BB pellet on Molly's hip. "Such a shame that there are people out there who'd shoot a defenseless dog. She's lucky you found her. I have all I need for now. Give Cord a few minutes and he'll be in here shortly. He's almost done stitching up a cat he just neutered."

Hannah and Molly waited for about ten minutes before Cord came in wearing a white lab coat and carrying a file folder in his hands. Hannah looked up at her landlord and smiled. "Surprise. I suppose you'll be needing a pet deposit from me now?"

Cord grinned. "From one animal lover to another, I think we can waive that. Since when did you get a dog, though?"

Hannah told him the story. "Then on top of the gash near her neck, some asshole shot her with a BB gun in the hip. See? It's still in there. Feel."

Cord ran his hand along the dog's hip. When he reached the sensitive spot, Molly reacted with a yelp. "I'll get that out of there to prevent infection. Let's look at this gash."

Hannah held the dog still while Cord examined the knife wound.

Cord shook his head. "It always surprises me at the inhumanity of man. It shouldn't, but it does. Looks like it's been at least a week since it happened, older wound. It's healed about as well as it can on its own. I'll give you some antibiotics to help it along even more."

"She has fleas but with the wounds we didn't think we should give her a flea bath."

"A wise decision." He noted Hannah looked adoringly at the pup and the gesture told him everything he needed to know about their bonding. "You know, Keegan and I pegged you for an animal lover the first time we met you. Good to know you saved this little girl. Let's start out by seeing how much she weighs."

Cord's big hands plucked Molly out of Hannah's arms and plopped her down on the scale. The dog trembled like she expected an executioner to pop out of the cabinet any minute.

"Twenty-one pounds. Definitely underweight. But we can take care of that with a consistently better diet."

He picked the pup back up and put her down on the exam table. "I'd say she's maybe five months old, a mutt of mixed breeding for sure. Since she's so young and a stray to boot, she probably needs all her shots. I'll run what's known as a titer test to determine if she's built up any antibodies in her system."

Cord picked up an otoscope to look in Molly's ears. "Plenty of dirt in there. I'd say this girl has been roaming around probably since shortly after her birth. I'll have Jessica clean them out and give you some drops to keep away infection."

Cord jotted down a few notes in Molly's chart. "We'll also get a stool sample and test for intestinal worms and the dreaded heartworm. Right now, I'll treat her injuries with betadine and see if the knife cut would benefit from stitching, which I doubt at this late date. It's obvious you cleaned the wound and gave her a bath already."

"She seemed to like the water. It gave her some relief from the flea bites."

"Probably felt good on these aching paws, too. Huh, girl?" Molly thumped her tail and Cord got to work, getting out a syringe and a vial from the cabinet. "The BB wound is fresh, probably less than three days old. So, I'm giving her a local anesthetic that'll let me take it out without putting her to sleep. The knife wound likely occurred more than a week earlier."

"So two separate incidents? That seems odd."

"Yeah. Weird. Molly was probably hanging around where she wasn't wanted and whoever she let close enough tried to cut her. She likely dodged the knife but not before it left a shallow gash. The good thing is it isn't that deep. That's probably why it healed fairly quickly."

Cord's surgical skills had the BB out of Molly within minutes. The dog immediately turned her head and licked his gloved hand.

"That a girl," Cord said in a soothing voice, snapping off the latex. He slid his fingers through the dog's fur. Again, Molly wagged her tail. "You're gonna be fine in a couple of weeks. I'll send Jessica back in to collect the samples and draw some blood. I'll be back in a few to go over the test results."

Jessica came in with a tray. "This'll be quick and mostly painless, just a quick couple of pricks and a little discomfort from the fecal swab and then it's over. Cleaning out the ears won't hurt at all. In fact, it might even help her hear better. Be sure to get her a flea collar after that gash on the neck heals. If you have any problems with anything else, be sure to let us know."

Half an hour ticked by before Cord came back in with the test results.

When he did open the door, he brought a bag of doggie treats with him. He gave one to Molly. "Negative on the heartworm, so she's good to go for the monthly treatment to prevent it. Don't miss a dose. But she does have roundworms. I'll deworm her before she leaves today and plan on another in two weeks. The good news is roundworms don't do as much damage as other types of parasites. But with continued treatment, Molly should be worm-free before you know it. I strongly suggest feeding her a dog food that's high in protein and a source that comes from chicken and egg. Dry to me is best. But that's because I've seen better results using dry in strays that haven't had a particularly good start in life. Getting rid of the worms and getting the right dog food in her should turn things around for Molly in a big way. Once the worms are gone and her wounds heal, you should notice a huge difference in her energy level. She'll feel more like running around and playing."

"I look forward to that. Is she okay to be around other dogs?"

"I wouldn't. Not until the second deworming, at least. But the heartworm meds will also treat the other parasite. Do you have any other questions for me?"

"I'm feeling a little overwhelmed. If I can't take her with me to work, then do you know any good dog sitters?"

"Feeling overwhelmed, that's normal. And yes, I have two great people I recommend for dog sitting jobs or dog walkers in general. Francie Odana is Irene's younger sister. She's available for dog sitting during the week." He rattled off her number. "You need someone after school or on the weekend, it's Faye DeMarco. She's only thirteen, but very reliable." He recited her number from memory. "Any other questions?"

"I guess not."

"Then relax and enjoy the new addition to Team Hannah."

Hannah tried to do just that. Since she couldn't very well take Molly to work with her, she contacted Francie Odana to watch the dog for a few hours while she picked up her routine from the week before.

Her first stop was Promise Cove. She had to make sure Jordan was okay with the time off she'd taken. But she needn't have worried.

"I'm glad you were able to relax for a few days," Jordan assured her. "Waiting for Brent to get back to you has to be stressful. You needed the break."

"You're taking this awfully well. Am I fired? Because I had a long talk with Isabella before I left and I agreed to take the job at the co-op. Full-time."

"That's wonderful. No, you aren't fired. I suppose this is your two-week notice then?"

"Sadly, yes. Can I ask you something? It might border on odd."

"If it's about Scott…?"

"I need to know where he's buried. It came to me last night at the cabin what's missing. If he won't come to me, maybe I should go to him."

Jordan put her arm around Hannah. "Honey, you're welcome to go to the cemetery, but Scott has his reasons for not coming around now. Didn't he mention to you that you had to find out things on your own, in due time. You're impatient for answers. Sometimes it just takes time to get where you want to go."

"Who needs Scott when I have you for a friend?"

"I'm glad you feel that way. You're easy to talk to. I'll miss your visits."

"Are you lonely out here, Jordan?" The words had barely landed when Hannah's hand flew to her mouth as if embarrassed at the acknowledgment. "I don't know why I blurted that out. I'm sorry."

Jordan took a seat at the kitchen table. "A little, especially since Hutton started school and Scott goes to preschool three times a week."

"Mondays, Wednesdays, and Fridays," Hannah supplied.

Jordan's cheeks flushed red with humiliation. "Am I that obvious? It's true, I don't like the fact that Nick took the job at the bank. I never did. Although it's been years, I still miss him here, putzing around, keeping me company, doing little chores here and there, like touch-up painting, mending a broken rail, or having a second cup of coffee with a muffin in the kitchen when the house is quiet. I know how silly that sounds. I know he needs to work, to feel that same sense of accomplishment he had back in L.A. when he worked for a huge corporate bank."

"Does Nick know how you feel?"

"No, not even a little bit. I've hidden my feelings well. I miss him being here, doing the things we'd planned here together. I thought that's what he wanted, too."

"I'm no expert on relationships, but I'd say the first step in maintaining happiness in one is honesty. I think you should tell him how you feel."

"But I don't want to disrupt the work he does at the bank. He does good work, Hannah. He approves loans that let residents purchase their first houses, car loans that allow people to drive a decent vehicle. He's brought the bank back from a cold, heartless entity to its original purpose—a partnership with the community."

"Maybe he could do that from here? Bank managers have home offices all the time."

"Initially that's what he talked about doing. But little by little the bank business picked up. There are days he seems overwhelmed. Sometimes he doesn't get home until after seven in the evening."

"Then maybe he should hire an assistant loan officer. Maybe the two of you should sit down and revisit your original plans and dreams for this place. What if he isn't happy either?"

Jordan's eyes grew wide at the notion. "He has complained about the workload."

"There. See. You should talk to him about it. Pick a time when the kids are tucked in for the night and the guests are asleep. Take a walk around the grounds so there are no distractions. In fact, maybe the two of you should have your own quiet weekend in the mountains."

"I'm not even sure that's possible."

"If I can leave all my part-time jobs behind for four days, surely you can break away for a couple of nights."

"I could ask my sister and her husband to watch the kids for us this weekend."

"Go for it. Don't spend another day miserable. It's not worth it. Life's too short for that."

After their talk, Hannah went upstairs to get to work. There were bathrooms to clean, beds to strip, laundry to get done, and beds to remake with fresh sheets.

The guests in one of the larger rooms had checked out earlier that morning—a couple visiting from Seattle—so she started in there. She opened the French doors to let in ocean air and began the chore of pulling bedding off into a pile to wash.

She sprayed foaming bubbles on the sink, tub and shower, and let it set before scrubbing them to a shine. Bundling the sheets on the floor into her arms, she headed downstairs to the laundry room.

While stuffing the clothes into the washer, her thoughts ran to Molly. She hoped the dog could shake her health problems and be good as new without more worry and meds. She wondered what Caleb was up to and fought the urge to text him.

But there was too much to get done. She took the stairs at the back of the kitchen and looped around to the linen closet to get clean sheets. Arms full, she backed up and looked squarely into Scott's eyes.

"What the—? Ghostly, my ass. When did you become corporeal?"

"I'm not. It's an illusion. You wanted to talk to me? Here I am."

"I…where've you been? What have you been doing with yourself? Don't tell me you've been too busy to know about what's happened at Bradford House. Did that grave belong to Micah? Where've you been all this time?"

"Do I bombard you with personal questions?"

"No, you just show up in a field of grapes and scare the crap out of me."

"Point for you."

"If we're keeping score, you're way ahead. Is that Micah at Bradford House or not? Tell me the truth."

Hannah heard Jordan walk to the bottom of the stairs. "Hannah, are you okay up there? Are you talking to me? If so, how about coming back down here for a conversation."

Hannah gave Scott a flustered look before finally answering Jordan, yelling down the staircase to her. "Uh…talking on my cell phone. Sorry to be so loud."

She whirled on Scott and lowered her voice. "See what you've done. Now I'm lying to Jordan."

"Who asked you to lie? Why not just tell her you were talking to me?"

"You disappear for days without a word, no direction as to what I'm supposed to do, and then you show up here of all places."

"I live here. This was my home a long time before it was Jordan's. Although I do appreciate you giving her advice that makes her happier, Nick, too. They could both use a new outlook on life."

"Oh, stuff it. Getting a straight answer out of you is damn near impossible." By the time she'd finished getting the words out, Scott had taken off...again.

She made a growling sound in her throat. "Get back here and finish this, you ghostly galoot!"

Hannah heard a noise behind her and whirled to prepare for another face off. But it was Jordan, bringing up fresh water for the upstairs plants.

"Problem?" Jordan asked with a little smile forming at the corners of her mouth. "Frustrating, isn't he? Even on the best days when we were married, he could be the most exasperating man I'd ever known. Always was like that, too. Used to drive me up the wall."

"You must've had the patience of a saint," Hannah said, raising her voice so Scott would hear the declaration. "The man could no doubt make a priest spit fire."

Getting back to work, she stayed busy for the next several hours. When she did head for home, for some reason, she felt better about things. Even the scene with Scott couldn't dampen her good mood.

Maybe it was because she wanted to check on Molly. Whatever the reason, she had shopping to do. Doggies needed supplies.

Twenty

While Hannah picked up where she'd left off, Caleb wasn't as lucky.

He and Cooper got the family together in the office at The Plant Habitat to discuss what to do with the Krugerrands. They didn't have a choice in the matter. Someone was out there who wanted the gold. They had to come up with a viable plan.

"Where do we put the gold while we work out a solution?" Shelby asked. "It makes me nervous just looking at it."

"You have to secure it. Best way to do that is take it to the bank as soon as possible," Eastlyn suggested. "Toss it into an existing safety deposit box."

"What other option do we have?" Drea pointed out, glancing from one to the other. "I don't want all that money in my loft."

"That was my first thought," Cooper muttered in agreement. "I don't want it anywhere near the house. Something else to consider is that once it gets out that we have a bag full of gold coins—we stopped counting at five hundred—things are bound to change."

"Which on today's market equates to over six hundred thousand dollars," Caleb informed them.

Landon let out a low whistle. "That's a lot of dough."

"Exactly," Cooper stated. "My point is, I'm not sure what the repercussions are for letting that info get past these four walls. All I know is there will be a major downside to it. Thoughts?"

"I agree," Drea said quickly. "That amount of money will change us. And if not us, the people around us. They'll likely view us differently."

Eastlyn wasn't thinking about appearances. What bothered her were the inconsistences. There was a mystery here that didn't make sense, beginning with the bag itself. "Can we spend a few minutes figuring out how that bag came to be at the cabin in the first place?"

Landon cleared his throat. "I have some idea about that, only I'm not sure you'll believe me."

"Why wouldn't we?" Caleb wanted to know. "Does it have anything to do with Eleanor ripping off our grandfather?"

Landon's eyes bugged out. "It seems you've already gotten from point A to point B without me."

Caleb stuck his hands in his pockets. "Only because we hashed it out on the trip back to town. We all know the story about how Euell Jennings lost everything. That's why he supposedly shot himself in the barn that day. His investments had tanked. He was out of money." He spun around to Landon. "You said yourself you thought Eleanor made it look like suicide."

Landon looked like he might throw up. To relate what he knew, he had to swallow down the bile. "Dad had a bag of coins just like that one. He got this wild idea that Krugerrands were the future. So he tracked down a coin dealer out of San Francisco with an inroad to bringing them into the country. Dad paid cash, kept the transaction low-key, and hid the gold away in the safe in his study. By the time he died, he'd had them for years. Hours after he died, it was Eleanor who started the rumor Dad was broke. Then after the funeral we were coming up on probating the will. I knew about the bag, same as Eleanor did, knew it would probably be revealed during probate. I thought if the cash in the bank is gone we still have a backup plan, a plan B. I wasn't worried because I was sure we still had the gold. Those Krugerrands were Dad's ace in the hole. So after we buried him, that afternoon I opened the safe. Imagine my surprise to find it empty, cleaned out. The gold was gone and so was the bag. I never laid eyes on it again until today."

"So basically, it's your inheritance, yours and Eleanor's," Caleb stated.

"I suppose. But Eleanor never liked to share. Now, I don't want any part of it," Landon declared, looking over at Shelby. "Do you?"

"Well, I won't lie, it would go a long way to fattening up our nest egg, building it up wouldn't hurt. But no, you guys should probably split it between the three of you. That seems fair after everything she's put you through."

Caleb exchanged glances with Cooper and Drea. "Is that what you guys want?"

Cooper tightened his jaw. "You're forgetting Eleanor in that equation. She believes she's still entitled to it. She tried to cut us out once. Literally. If the guy she sent had found it before we did, we wouldn't even be huddled in the office like this discussing the topic. So the question remains what do we do about Eleanor and this guy who keeps hanging around spooking everyone?"

"Catch this dude," Eastlyn stated in a no-nonsense voice. "Get the town involved in the hunt. If we can find him, maybe we can get him to turn on Eleanor and end this for good."

Drea nodded. "I like that idea. I don't much care what happens to Eleanor after they find him."

"I could get on board with ratting out Eleanor," Caleb said. He angled his head to look at Eastlyn. "Please tell me you have a brilliant, sure-fire, military strategy guaranteed to work."

"Nothing's guaranteed. But I need more information before coming up with a strategy."

"Like what?" Cooper asked.

"There are a few things nagging me about the gold that just won't let go."

"Okay. Maybe you should just spit 'em out," Cooper stated.

She stared at her husband, let her hands rest on her hips. "From what you told me of the story that night, Eleanor lit out of here after jumping in the water, leaving you guys stranded. She disappeared, left you guys in Smuggler's Bay without a backward glance. Why didn't she immediately head to the cabin and retrieve her stash? That gold would've kept her off the radar and made life on the run infinitely easier. Why didn't she take it with her that night?"

Cooper scrubbed his hands down his face. Would all this speculation ever end? He stood up, angry. "Maybe because that night she was bat-shit crazy. She'd just killed two people. She had to enlist her own nine-year-old son to help get rid of the bodies. Her mindset was... How can I put this? Run away...get away, far, far away. Get the hell out of Dodge before the kid decides to blab and turn her in to the cops. I honestly think she thought the three of us wouldn't make it back to shore that night, that we would die right out there on the water. I'm absolutely convinced that's what she was hoping for. But she didn't hang around long enough for me to ask about her plans or to ask whether she gave a shit about any of us. I'm fucking tired of trying to explain the reason Eleanor does anything. The truth is we may never know. And I'm so tired of this...her...this part of my life. I just don't want to deal with it anymore."

Eastlyn knew her doubts would strike a nerve. She also knew Cooper's fury wasn't directed at her but at himself and at Eleanor. She wanted to soothe his rage. But first, she needed to offer a solution, something that might end this once and for all.

She put her arms around his back. "You're right. I'm not able to argue with a single point you made. You deserve to end it here...now. That's why I'm willing to go see Eleanor behind bars and interview her…officially…get her on the record."

"Been there, done that," Cooper fired back. "Didn't do one bit of good."

"I'll think of another angle for the interview. When I went with you before, I wasn't a cop. I'd like to see her squirm, see if I can get her to admit what went wrong with her plan that night. Did you ever wonder who helped her escape? Someone did, someone here in town. She doesn't do anything on her own, including cleaning up after herself. She couldn't have set the plan in motion without major help."

Cooper dropped into a chair. "Fine. Go talk to her. Go ask all the questions you want. But you won't get the truth. You'll get everything but that."

"Maybe. But then I've got all the gold in Pelican Pointe to use as incentive, don't I? I've got what she wants more than anything else."

"You plan to reward her?" Cooper ground out, indignant at the prospect.

"Dangle. I plan to dangle it just within her reach. But first I have to catch this guy who's after the loot. To do that, I propose holding a town hall meeting and get the community involved. Julianne's already offered to let us use the auditorium tonight. I want the whole town on the lookout for this guy."

After depositing the bag of gold in the bank, Caleb and Cooper needed a drink. They ended up walking in the door at The Shipwreck in the middle of the afternoon, something Caleb couldn't ever remember doing before.

"Do people drink shots before three o'clock?" he asked Cooper.

"Alcoholics do it all the time."

"Thanks, that makes it so much more special for me."

With a keen eye of observation, Durke took one look at his early bar patrons and knew something was wrong. "Rough day?" he asked Caleb.

Caleb slid onto one the bar stools and Cooper did the same. "You have no idea. Ever wish you could pick and choose your family?"

"Uh oh. Trouble between siblings? That's probably why I relish the fact I'm an only child. No disputes to deal with over toys or territory. What can I get you guys?"

"Two draft beers will get us started. No problem between siblings," Cooper explained. "But other aspects of genealogy come into play when you're dealing with a cold-stone narcissist who, by some unfortunate turn of events, happens to have been the one who gave birth to us."

Caleb punched his brother in the ribs and nodded toward the guy sitting alone at a table. The man was mid-thirties, heavily tattooed, and had prison inmate written all over his demeanor.

"Who's that?" Caleb whispered to Durke. "I don't recognize him."

Durke set down two pint glasses and glanced over at the man in question. "Some guy who's been coming in here off and on for the past two weeks. He's a loner, sits by himself, and usually nurses the whiskey he orders for hours."

Caleb exchanged a look with his brother. "Am I getting paranoid or could that be another Eleanor devotee waiting to come after us?"

"Paranoia is contagious. Let it go. It's not worth trying to keep up with Eleanor's fans. I'm so tired of talking about her, thinking about her, even remembering how her damn voice sounds turns my stomach."

"We should drink our beers and go home then, stop all this running around in a frenzy reacting to something Eleanor's either threatened to do or already done." In truth, he couldn't wait to get home to Hannah and have a relaxing evening. She'd be worried about the dog and they could deal with the pup together. They could fix dinner in a calm and completely ordinary way, like most other people probably took for granted, maybe tell each other about the kind of day they'd had, go over problems in a reasonable fashion. Then they'd head off to bed and make love before falling asleep.

Normal. When had the idea of normal ever been so appealing or so sexy?

Cooper interrupted those thoughts with a grunt toward the stranger. "He's on the move. Should we follow him?"

"You just told me to drop it."

"I know. But someone followed me yesterday on the hike. It sort of looks like him. We should find out who this guy is."

Caleb drained his glass. "Sure. Why not? Let's see if Eleanor sent this bastard to spy on us?"

It was a crazy thing to do—following a tough guy with an obvious prison persona about him and not knowing what he would do.

Cooper sat shotgun while Caleb crawled behind the wheel of his truck. But they didn't have to go far.

The man had a Harley parked curbside down at the pier and took off just as Caleb got within forty yards.

"Go after him," Cooper urged.

Caleb responded by gunning the engine. They trailed the guy as the bike looped around to Main Street and headed back through town to the north.

He managed to stay behind at a safe distance from the stranger until the Harley pulled to the shoulder of the road just before Taggert Farms and came to a stop.

"What do we do now?" Caleb asked.

"There's two of us and only one of him. I say we confront him."

Before they could finalize their decision, Caleb saw the guy get off his bike and head toward them. Standing well over six feet, their stranger stood in the middle of the road and shouted toward the truck, "What is it with you guys? Why are you following me?"

Caleb watched as Cooper stuck his head out the window. "Who sent you to spy on us? We know it was Eleanor."

"What? What are you talking about? I don't even know who you guys are. I saw you at the bar, though. My name's Bremmer, Simon Bremmer. I'm a friend of Cord's and Nick's. Ask them, they'll vouch for me."

"What are you doing here?" Cooper asked his voice getting louder. "Did Eleanor send you?"

Simon thumbed a hand toward Taggert Farms. "I'm working here, helping Silas and Sammy with the planting season. I just got back from three tours overseas."

"Are those military tattoos?" Caleb asked, beginning to believe they were way off the mark.

"Yeah. Army ranger. Why?"

Caleb punched his brother's arm, pulling him back in from the window. He began to try to apologize. "Sorry. Sorry. Major mistaken identity. Our fault. I'm Caleb Jennings. This, raving, paranoid delusional just happens to be my brother Cooper Richmond. So…uh…sorry for yelling at you. Sorry for following you. Sorry in general. If you'll stop by The Plant Habitat I'll make sure you get a free lemon tree as a housewarming gift. No harm done. Well, it's been nice meeting you, but we have get back to town now. See you around. Welcome. Have a great life."

After rambling, Caleb pulled the truck into a U-turn, leaving Bremmer standing in the middle of the road looking confused and more than a little perturbed.

"Way to go, genius," Caleb muttered to Cooper.

Cooper shook his head. "I really do hate my life. Did I mention that?"

"You did what?" Hannah shouted, standing in her little kitchen dicing veggies for a stew. "Do you have any idea how dangerous that was, confronting a total stranger like that? What if he'd been armed? What if he'd taken out a gun and shot you both right there on the road?"

"Bremmer seemed like a nice enough guy," Caleb declared as he finished browning the beef and added his made-from-scratch sauce into the pot to let it simmer. "It was Cooper's idea."

"But you didn't have to go along with it, now did you?"

His hands, free now, roamed down to her rear end where he ran his fingers along her firm ass. "I love watching your outrage. I'm more embarrassed than anything else. I haven't made such a fool out of myself like that since high school when I tried playing tough guy defending Olivia Watson's honor."

"What happened?"

"Joey Hendricks cold-cocked me and broke my nose. Blood went everywhere."

"Poor baby." Hannah slithered her way up his body until he picked her up. Her legs went around his waist. "Want to fool around while the stew simmers?"

Reaching behind her with one free hand, he fumbled with the burner on her tiny stove, finally turning it down to low. "That's the best idea I've heard all day."

Across the room, Molly let out a couple of approving yips and danced in place at the end of the bed.

Caleb's head snapped around at the sound. "Is she okay?"

"Oh yeah. I think she's letting us know she's happy and safe and fitting right in here with us."

Twenty-One

The turnout was better than Eastlyn expected. Everyone in the auditorium talked at once.

The town hall meeting, it seemed, was seriously in jeopardy of sliding into chaos before it ever got started.

Eastlyn tried to gain control, but to be heard over the crowd she had to use the microphone and had to wait for Brent to hook it up backstage.

Once he gave her the go ahead, she looked out over the multitude, and began her pitch, only to have a screechy feedback kick in.

Brent adjusted the volume control on the speakers and Eastlyn took a deep breath and got her lines out in one long spiel. "Okay, people. Sit down and listen up! I'm bringing this meeting to order. I need your attention. Now! We have a situation…"

Most everyone settled down except for the front row where Myrtle Pettibone, Ruthie Porter, and Marabelle Crawford were arguing over who'd seen the man in question last week. All three claimed to have already shooed him off their property a time or two.

Prissie Gates and Emma Colter, who occupied seats in the second row, kept trying to shush the old ladies so they could hear Eastlyn.

For the most part, Eastlyn ignored the ruckus and held up a sketch she'd asked Lilly Pierce to draw and had the school kids hand out at the door.

"This is our peeping Tom. This is the man who's been seen around town lurking near several houses and businesses. Note the description. He's about six feet tall, dark brown hair, and has a somewhat raggedy appearance. If you spot him, don't approach him, don't try to detain him yourself. Call Brent or me."

Cora Bigelow, the postmistress, held up her hand. "Why don't I put one of these posters up in the post office right next to the new stamp machine? Everybody in town stops there and stares up at the wanted posters."

"There you go," Eastlyn said. "Community involvement is how we'll catch this guy. That's a fine idea, Cora. And to everyone else, feel free to put up one in every window along Main Street until we nab this guy."

Barton Pearson, the new funeral director, cleared his throat. "I saw this guy on Saturday. I'm sure of it. He was hanging out between Drea's Flowers and the Snip N Curl."

Barton turned to Drea, who was sitting at the end of the row, for confirmation. "It was when I stopped in around noon to place the order for Margaret Henderson's memorial service. We decided on a cascade of lovely purple orchids, purple being Margaret's favorite color. Remember?"

"I do. But that isn't the only time he was there. He kept staring at the store for several hours," Drea added. "He was there most of the day on Saturday. Ask Fern Schiebel. She came in to order roses for her daughter's birthday and even commented about how the guy wouldn't stop glowering at her."

Tucker let out a sigh. "I wish you'd called me. I'm right down the street. I would've confronted him —"

Eastlyn pointed a finger at Tucker. "Now see, right there, that's what we don't want anyone to do. It isn't against the law to lean up against a lamp post and stare at a business or glower at people. But we have had reports that he's been peering into windows at night and during the early morning hours."

Sitting in the back row, Hannah bumped Caleb's shoulder. "Is this really a good idea? What if there's an innocent explanation for this guy hanging around? I thought we agreed that maybe he's a transient."

"It sounds like Eastlyn might be making this stuff up as she goes along. Maybe we are pushing the panic button a little too early. We're all just a little on edge. Maybe he's just a homeless person with no place to go. I mean, Cooper swears he was being following on Sunday. This mystery man can't be in two places at once."

"And where's his car? No one's seen him driving around town. Walking yes, driving no."

"Good point. Let's see where Eastlyn goes with this before we start panning the idea."

Hannah felt someone tap her on the shoulder. She turned to see Sydney standing off to the side.

"Hey. I've been meaning to tell you how very sorry I am   about…about…those   remains…that could…maybe…turn out be…your…brother."

Hannah got to her feet so she could hear Sydney better. "Thanks. Maybe we should go out in the lobby so we can talk."

"Good idea. My voice tends to carry. It's the ER nurse in me. I don't know how to whisper."

The two women moved into the foyer near the trophy case.

"Do you miss being at Bradford House?" Hannah asked. "I sorta miss cleaning all those rooms. I didn't think that was possible."

"Yeah, me too. It's a great old house, or it was before this. It's sad really. Quentin, Beckham and I were enjoying living there. We're still debating the issue, back and forth, mainly because Quentin just spent a bundle on buying the place. I tend to think that'll play a huge role in our decision."

"No matter what the DNA results are, I think you guys should move back in there. The house has so much character that you don't see in houses these days. And that view is…spectacular."

"I don't know. It's a lot to process having that kind of thing found in your yard. Do you think you could ever get past having a dead body discovered where you live? A baby no less? And what if we find out it's your brother? How would you feel then?"

"I see your point."

"See. I'm not sure what to do. It's weighing on me…a lot. Brent says they'll be done digging by the end of the week and we can pick up with the yard renovation. But I'm just not sure it's the right thing to do. It's so strange. You think the remains belong to your brother while Quentin is convinced that baby has something to do with his uncle."

"Just goes to show no one seems to have any answers. Yet. Are the three of you comfortable where you are now? At your house?"

"My house isn't as large, that's a fact. But Beckham seems happy there, which means we don't have to have the big house. It's just that…if we put it back on the market…who else will want to buy it after…this?"

"Don't forget the real estate market is bouncing back. There's always someone out there looking for the biggest house on the block with an ocean view."

"But here, in Pelican Pointe? It might be tough to unload," Sydney pointed out. Lowering her voice, she leaned in closer. "So…you and Caleb, huh?"

"Looks like."

"You guys should come to my house for dinner Friday night. It'll give Quentin a chance to cook out. Don't expect anything fancier than burgers and hot dogs, not at our house anyway."

"Burgers are fine with us. What time?"

"Sevenish? I'll see if I can round up a few others to make it a blowout end of the week party. I have to run now and round up Beckham and Faye. They're here…somewhere."

"Faye? Is that Faye DeMarco? I just recently found a stray, a puppy, and Cord mentioned that Faye dog sits on weekends."

"That's one and the same. You can ask her yourself about dog sitting Friday night. She'll be at the get-together. She's Beckham's little girlfriend. Those two are practically inseparable. I'm not sure it's completely healthy at this point, but then, if it's a solid friendship what can it hurt, right? They like the same books, like watching the same movies, and keep up their grades by helping each other with their homework. They rarely argue about anything."

"Sounds better than a few of my past relationships," Hannah added.

"Isn't that the truth?" Sydney said in agreement, glancing at her watch. "Oh, look at the time. I gotta find those kids and get out of here. See you Friday night."

After the meeting broke up, Caleb grabbed Hannah and went in search of Eastlyn and Brent. Surrounded by a slew of people, he nudged them off to the side so he could gauge how it went. "Do you think this did any good at all?"

Like any cop who'd just held court, Brent had a certain confidence about him. "Are you kidding? When this town comes together for one main cause, I've seen it have a domino effect. Look at the size of the crowd tonight. That tells me the residents are into catching this guy. He'll be lucky if someone doesn't shoot his ass trying to peek in the window before the end of the week."

"People love a common goal, nothing like trying to find a peeping Tom to jumpstart a community effort," Eastlyn added.

Brent nodded. "I predict within forty-eight hours we'll have our man. Someone here will cross paths with him. He can't keep eluding us in such a small area for long."

Drea walked up with Tucker in tow. She angled toward Eastlyn with something on her mind. "I've given this some thought. I'd like to volunteer to go with you when you make the trip to see Eleanor."

"As much as I'd like the company," Eastlyn began. "I need to do this without a member of the family there."

"I'm not family," Hannah stated. "I'll go with you. Pass me off as your assistant or whatever, maybe another cop. I'll do it."

Eastlyn's lips curved up. "Now we're talking. Okay, here's the deal. Brent and I have gone over a strategy that he thinks—based on other conversations he's had with law enforcement about Eleanor's personality type—should be most effective at getting her to talk. Without family members around, there's a good chance she'll drop that 'poor me' attitude, maybe drop her guard, and we can get past two decades of lies."

"Or bring popcorn for the show," Cooper finished, still cynical. "Eleanor loves performing for people and not in a good way. She excels at showing off. Since her time spent in Georgia she's even perfected a southern accent."

Caleb rolled his eyes. "Yeah, California girl goes Scarlett O'Hara. Drama queen with a little southern belle thrown in."

Drea slapped Caleb on the arm. "I wish you guys would stop being so negative. It makes sense not to have family confront her since that seems to be what triggers Eleanor's buttons." She looked over at Eastlyn. "I should give you some of the letters she's written me. That insight might be just the thing that gives you the edge, get a peek into her psychobabble and maybe you'll be able to get her to leave us alone."

Eastlyn rocked back on her heels. "Good idea. Caleb? What about the letters she's sent you? Cooper's let me read most of her correspondence to him. But before I make the trip, I'll round up yours and bone up on where Eleanor's head is. Every little bit helps to know the personality we'll be dealing with." She turned to Hannah.

"You should probably do the same and then we'll compare notes on the drive up."

"But not before we catch this guy, right?" Hannah confirmed. "I'd really like to feel safe again in my own home. The dog helps but I'm not sure she's strong enough yet to attack a predator just yet."

Eastlyn patted her on the arm. "Don't worry. We won't go anywhere until we can catch this bastard."

After everyone went their separate ways Caleb walked Hannah out to the parking lot. "What did Sydney want earlier?"

"She invited us over Friday night for a barbecue. I accepted. I hope that's all right. I did it without even talking to you first."

"It's fine with me. It'll give me a chance to bug Beckham. I like that kid. He's a go-getter, smart, too."

"I got the feeling Sydney wants to discuss the…situation with the…remains."

"But we don't even know who it is yet."

"Whatever the reason, Sydney mentioned they might not go back to the house, which affects your project there."

"I've been expecting that. I won't hold them to the contract they signed. Doesn't matter. My heart's no longer in it anyway. Redoing the yard seems…way down on the list of priorities."

Once they reached the Suburban, Hannah peered inside at Molly. She'd left the dog wrapped in a layer of blankets so she wouldn't catch a chill.

While staring at the dog, an idea hit that she thought might cheer Caleb up. "Let's take Molly for a short walk around the park. Cord took a quick look at her hip this afternoon on his way home and pronounced her officially on the mend. He thinks her leg is ready for some light exercise."

"Without the wagon?"

"Yup. Whaddya say? I want to be the first to show her the town." She nestled into his chest and threw out a tempting offer. "Afterward, I'll buy you ice cream at the diner."

"Make it a triple chocolate cone and you have a deal."

"Done."

The walk proved cathartic and gave them a chance to see how Molly took to her new collar and the leash. The pup didn't like either one at first, chewing and nipping at the constraint around her neck. But that only lasted until Hannah distracted the dog with a couple of treats she'd brought with her. "I want Molly to get well so I'm able to take her with me to work."

"You aren't talking about cleaning houses, are you?"

"Nope. I'm already looking ahead to beginning my job at the co-op. I have another meeting set up with Isabella for next Monday. And after that, she'll be turning the entire operation over to me. With two kids, one a newborn, she swears she won't have time for anything but to pop in from time to time. That means she's committed to not meddling in my decisions. It also means the success of the place rests on my shoulders. I'm a little nervous about it, wondering if I've bitten off too much."

"Stop it. You'll be fine, more than. You already have an idea of what grows well in the soil. Learn to rotate whatever crop you deem the most successful and that's half the battle."

"What if I kill every living thing growing there now? What if all the tomatoes die? What if the lettuce turns brown and tastes yucky? What if the blueberries rot on the vine?"

"In that case, I'd have to test your nitrogen and phosphorus levels."

She bumped his shoulder. "I'm pretty sure you've already done that, more than a couple of times."

He nibbled her jaw. "Yeah, but not nearly enough."

Twenty-Two

Brent's prediction turned out to be accurate. A mere six hours after the town hall meeting ended, at two-thirty in the morning, the phone next to his bed rang.

Sound asleep, he struggled to recognize Tucker Ferguson's voice on the line. From what Brent could make out from the man's whispering, the silent alarm had been triggered inside Drea's Flowers. "We can hear someone moving around down there. Want me to see if I can corner him until you get here?"

"No!" Brent snapped out into the phone. "Weren't you listening earlier tonight? I'm on my way. Stay put upstairs until I get there. Do not go downstairs."

Brent crawled out of bed to get dressed. While pulling on his jeans, he put in a call to Eastlyn. "We have a confirmed sighting. Drea's Flowers. I'm en route now."

"Will meet you there," said the sleepy voice on the other end of the line.

Brent arrived first but waited for his backup to get there. A few minutes later, Eastlyn pulled up at the curb.

Gun drawn, Eastlyn calmly wanted to know, "How do you want to handle this?"

"You. Front. I'll take the back."

From the alleyway, Brent noticed the back door had been left ajar. He didn't know who this guy was, but he did know the man was sloppy—a deaf man could've heard the noise coming from the storage area.

Brent pushed open the door and spotted a figure rifling through the boxes Drea had stowed on the shelves. Midway from the end, the guy still had an entire side yet to go.

"Police. Hands up. Now."

From the other side of the room, Eastlyn darted forward to frisk their intruder. "Weapon," she shouted, and pulled a .38 from the band of the guy's waist. She lifted his wallet from his back pocket, and slung open the billfold. "Name on his driver's license is Delbert Delashaw, address out of Columbus, Georgia."

Delashaw threw an elbow toward Eastlyn and used his body to shove her backward. She landed against the other side of the shelving, making it wobble. Despite falling backward, she lost her balance briefly, but caught herself before taking a full tumble.

In Delashaw's effort to bolt toward the door, the guy met resistance from Brent. The chief of police met him head-on with a fist smack in the face, cold-cocking Delbert with one punch to the nose.

From behind, Eastlyn kicked his legs out from under him, causing the suspect to fall to his knees. With her boot pressed to his back, she pushed Delashaw face down on the floor. She managed to jerk his hands behind his back to slap a pair of handcuffs around his wrists.

Brent yanked him to his feet.

"You broke my nose!" Delashaw protested.

"Probably. We'll get the doctor to look at that. But right now, you're under arrest for breaking and entering, trespassing, resisting arrest, and attempted assault on a police officer. You have the right to remain…" He read Delashaw his rights and drove him to the station.

After taking his fingerprints, snapping a mugshot, and formally booking their guest for the night, Eastlyn brought him, still handcuffed, into the interrogation room, plopped him down in a chair. "He doesn't say much."

"What would be the point?" the man asked in a nasally southern accent. "What about my nose?"

Brent, who had brewed a pot of coffee, leaned back in his chair, sipping the caffeine, calm as a priest. "Does that still hurt? Eastlyn, what's the status on the Doc?"

"Last I talked to him Quentin was getting dressed. He'll be here directly, I'm sure." She turned to stare at Delashaw's face. "Don't worry. We'll get you patched up real soon."

Brent studied the paperwork on the man before glancing up at their prisoner. "Now see, the doctor's probably on his way right now. How about answering our questions while we're waiting? That sounds reasonable, doesn't it? For starters, what's a man from Georgia doing in our little neck of the woods?"

"Just taking in the sights along the coast."

Having been woken up out of a deep sleep, Brent was in no mood for games. "Really? Inside a flower shop at three in the morning? Are you sure that's the story you want to stick with?"

Eastlyn stood to the side with her arms crossed over her chest. "Mr. Delashaw's driver's license says he's forty-two. But he looks thirty-five to me. DL might be phony though. I ran him through the system anyway. Turns out, the Georgia boys want him for murder one. Looks like we have us a celebrity here in our little jail."

Brent noticed that statement had Delashaw looking panic-stricken. "Nose hurts like hell, doesn't it? Any reason why the Georgia authorities would think you might've murdered somebody, Delashaw? Aren't you mildly curious what Eleanor's gotten you into? Oh. Wait. Maybe you knew her as Loretta Eikenberry."

Stony silence from Delashaw had Eastlyn picking up the casual-like tone. "Where've you been staying while in our fair city?"

"You know where. I made camp in that drainage ditch until it rained me out and you guys confiscated most of my stuff."

"Near Caleb's place? Yeah. We saw that. Mind telling us why you've been hanging around a member of the Jennings family for the better part of a week?"

"Look, you already know Eleanor sent me. Okay? I've been trying to deliver a message to her family, somebody ought to care what happens to her. Eleanor and I are getting married. She wants y'all to know she didn't do what they said she did."

That brought a genuine chuckle out of Brent. "You mean murder two people? Possibly three?"

"She didn't murder nobody."

"That's interesting. Her own brother believes she murdered their father when she was a teenager. If she didn't kill anyone then why do you suppose she pled guilty? She stood in a courtroom and told everyone she murdered her husband and another woman in cold blood, signed the paperwork saying she did it. Before she shot them with a .38 she'd been trying to poison her hubby with arsenic for months."

Eastlyn leaned in toward Delbert. "Good thing for you she's locked up. Otherwise, you might be next, Delbert."

Brent waited a beat to let that soak in, and went on, "Traditionally speaking, that puts your wife-to-be in the classification of a serial killer. Like serial killers, do you, Delbert?" He watched as the man became visibly more nervous. "When did you first meet Eleanor or Loretta or whatever she was calling herself at the time?"

"When she moved in to her house in Georgia, I lived down the street. I was twenty-two when we met. That was long before the U.S. Marshalls dragged her back here."

"Go for older women, do you?" Eastlyn asked. "She must be a good fifteen years older than you are."

"She said she was forty-five."

Eastlyn guffawed with laughter. "Maybe a dozen years ago. What's your angle in all this? What's in it for you? Besides half the gold, that is."

A sheepish look crossed Delbert's face. "Damn it, I told her you guys beat me to it."

"So you're the guy who did all that damage to the cabin?" Brent asked. "Why?"

"She said she didn't like that place and for me to tear it up after I found the gold. I tried to set it on fire but even that didn't work."

"Where did she tell you the gold was supposed to be?"

"A panel in the back of a lower kitchen cabinet. I kicked that thing in and found it empty. I tore that place apart and it wasn't in no cabinet anywhere. It was gone. That got her plenty pissed off when she found that out."

"You communicated that to her? How?"

"One of the guards likes her. He lets her use the phone in the office. I call her on that line all the time."

"Lucky Eleanor."

"I kept trying to tell her it was hard to break into all the houses she wanted me to search. But she insisted. Not even when that dude went out of town could I get past his fancy alarm system. Ellie got mad at me, threw a downright hissy fit."

"Ellie? How sweet," Eastlyn said in a demure voice. "You do realize that you aren't the first person Eleanor has used to do her bidding, right? She has a son, Jonathan Matthews, almost as old as you are. Poor Jonathan's doing a stretch in Corcoran because she talked him into attempted kidnapping some months back. From what I hear, Jonathan makes sure he writes to 'mommy' every single day without fail, though."

"Ellie has another kid?" Delbert asked in disgust. "What else hasn't she told me?"

"I imagine the list is as long as your arm." Eastlyn exchanged looks with Brent. "Are you thinking what I'm thinking?"

A sleepy-eyed Quentin appeared in the doorway, holding his black bag. "Is this the guy who needs a doctor?"

Brent stood up. "Sorry to say, his nose got in the way of a fist. Shame he tried to take off running when he saw us. See what you can do to make him more comfortable because our guest isn't getting out of here anytime soon."

Quentin set his bag down, studied the prisoner. "Broken nose. I'll reset it and tape him up. Any other problems I should know about?"

Brent rubbed the back of his neck and stood up. "Unfortunately, I don't think you can fix stupid or make this Georgia boy less gullible."

Eastlyn bobbed her head in the direction of the hallway toward Brent so he'd follow her out of the room but still allow them to keep an eye on their prisoner. "If Eleanor's using a guard on the inside, she could be tapping into all kinds of other illegal activities using those special privileges. She's obviously using every dumbass she encounters for her own purposes."

"I'll contact the warden and put a stop to it. She'll end up in solitary, which means she'll be desperate to talk when the right time comes. It's the .38 I'm wondering about. Did you see how old that gun is?"

"I thought Cooper was sure he buried it in the backyard that night with the bodies."

"Memories from a little boy so long ago are hardly concrete. And she might have gone back to dig it up after she swam out of the Bay."

"Delashaw did have access to Eleanor's possessions back in Georgia. That might explain how the murder weapon ended up circling back here after all these years."

"That's why I'll have to send it to ballistics."

"We're a hotbed of police activity," Eastlyn noted with a little too much joy in her voice.

"And I'm sensing you're loving every minute of it."

"Well, a girl's gotta do what a girl's gotta do to stay on her toes—especially when half of those toes are gone."

Twenty-Three

Once word made the rounds through the Jennings family that Delbert Delashaw was behind bars, they decided to get together for brunch at Caleb's house.

Caleb and Hannah prepared omelets while Molly looked on from a corner of the kitchen. The dog could get around now without a limp and with several days of antibiotics, the pup acted friskier than ever before.

Hannah plated a cheesy concoction of peppers and ham for Landon and served it to him with diced potatoes and fruit on the side.

Landon rubbed his hands together. "This looks delicious. This girl can cook, a plus in my book. It was nice putting that closed sign on the door in the middle of the week, letting people know we'd be back at two o'clock. Taking a breather for lunch like this, we should do it more often."

"It's a special occasion," Cooper cited. "I like how Eastlyn's plan came together."

"We all do," Caleb began. "But there's something I still don't understand. Eleanor told this Delbert guy the gold was in the kitchen. If it's true, then how did it end up in a bedroom under the floorboard?"

"Bothers me, too," Eastlyn threw in. "I'm convinced Delbert was telling the truth. According to the pictures Caleb took, Delashaw concentrated most of his efforts in the kitchen, upset that he couldn't find the loot in there.

I'm also convinced that, at some point, someone moved it from a seventeen-year-old girl's original hiding place to the bedroom. It would also explain why she didn't take the gold with her when she left that night after dumping her kids and disappearing into the night."

"She didn't know where it was," Hannah concluded.

"You got it," Eastlyn stated. She watched as every member of the Jennings family glanced around the table, accusing eyes on each other.

"You think one of us moved the bag?" Drea determined.

Eastlyn looked around the room. Her eyes stopped at Landon and stayed there. She waited for him to come clean by boring a hole in him with the cop's glare she'd perfected over several months.

Beads of sweat popped out on Landon's brow. "I lied. The other day I told you guys I hadn't laid eyes on that bag until then."

"But that wasn't the truth," Cooper stated. It wasn't a question.

"No, it wasn't. After the bag disappeared from the safe, it wasn't difficult to figure out who'd taken it. But I had no idea where she'd hidden it. One day I figured out that every time Eleanor left town she came back with a new outfit. About a week later, I followed her out of town and discovered she was making trips to the cabin. She'd grab a coin or two, and then head to San Francisco for a shopping spree. You guys were just babies the first time I caught on to what she was doing. But it didn't take long for me to get tired of watching her flaunt the money in my face when my business struggled every month. At one point, Shelby and I were down to our last thousand dollars. So, one day I followed her ass up there, parked my truck out of sight, and hiked back on foot. I saw her through the kitchen window running her fingers through the coins like a genuine Ebenezer Scrooge, only female, acting slightly more irrational. The bag was sitting out on the table. I waited until she put it back behind the panel and stayed hidden until she left. Once I discovered her hiding place, I went in and took several hundred coins out of the bag."

"Oh, Landon," Shelby groaned. "You didn't?"

"To save our business, you bet I did. I took the bag and hid it in the bedroom that was mine as a kid. I knew about the hole in the floorboard. I didn't want her squandering any more of the money. I knew she'd never find it there, and I was right. I took those coins to a dealer, got close to twenty-five thousand dollars for them, which I put right back into the business. Every time I needed an influx of cash, I went back to that bag. But there was a huge price for my deception that I didn't count on happening."

Landon took a deep breath before going on. "After that, when Eleanor would make trips to the cabin and couldn't locate the gold, she started acting crazier than ever. She'd go, and I'm paraphrasing Cooper here, 'she'd go bat-shit crazy' a little more off the deep end each time she couldn't find the gold. It became evident in the way she started panicking over every little thing. From something Layne did to something you kids would do. She'd go nuts, screaming fits, and threatening to do dire things. She'd always treated Layne and you kids like shit, but she got much worse after not having access to the money."

Landon put his head in his hands. "It's my fault. All of it. What happened to Layne and Brooke was all my fault. I knew she wanted out of her life and I sabotaged her effort by taking that gold away from her, withholding her access to what she considered her fortune. I honestly think it drove her insane. I'm sorry. I shouldn't have lied to everyone about it, but I was ashamed of what I'd done."

"It was as much yours as it was Eleanor's," Caleb voiced aloud. "Eleanor's the one who stole it, killed to get it, and then refused to share it with anyone else. I don't see how that's your fault."

Landon looked up at Shelby. "I'm sorry, honey. To think I'm the one who pushed Eleanor to kill Layne and Brooke. She came damn close to killing the kids. I've had to live with that for…way too long."

"Nonsense," Shelby said, running her fingers through his hair. "You did no such thing. The Eleanor I know has never cared a whit about anyone but herself. The narcissist is responsible for deciding to commit murder, not you."

"On that I'm sure we all agree," Eastlyn declared. "Okay, that's one part of the mystery solved. We can accept the fact that Eleanor went to the cabin that night to make one last desperate effort to locate the bag. She must've gone totally off the rails without finding the gold."

"Wonder who she turned to for help without having access to the gold?" Hannah speculated. "It had to be someone in town she could trust."

"We've always believed she had help. That's the second part of the mystery," Caleb stated. "But we may never know the truth."

Landon glanced up at Eastlyn. "How'd you know it was me who moved the bag?"

"I wish everything was that easy to figure out. You're the only one who had access and a reason. I knew you'd eventually crack from what you saw as guilt. I just had to keep badgering you with a look every now and again until you came clean."

Cooper noticed his wife's demeanor. She chewed on her thumbnail until he finally said, "There's something else?"

"Maybe I shouldn't even be discussing the case like this, but I think you need to know the rest. GBI, that's the Georgia Bureau of Investigations, got back to us about an hour ago. Delashaw isn't just wanted for murder, but he also has a string of felony convictions for credit card fraud, theft, and burglary. There's been a warrant out for his arrest since he skipped town about the same time Eleanor was extradited back to California. In other words, Delashaw followed Eleanor here and he's been on the run ever since. Georgia expects California to return the favor and extradite Delashaw back to their stomping ground. But that isn't the biggie. When we arrested him, he had a .38 in his possession. Brent reminded me that a .38 was used to kill Layne and Brooke."

"Surely you aren't suggesting that it's the same weapon?" Cooper asked. "I buried it in the backyard."

Eastlyn rested her hand on Cooper's shoulder. "All I can tell you is what I know. It's an older model gun manufactured five months before the murders. That fits the timeframe. Eleanor likely went back that night and retrieved it. Brent's already sent the gun off to the firearm's specialist in Santa Cruz. We'll know soon enough if it's the murder weapon. But get this, we discovered it was originally registered to Douglas Bradford."

"Wow, that's a telling piece of evidence," Hannah declared. "If only Bradford were still alive, he'd have some explaining to do."

For Caleb, the stench of the past hung over the rest of the day and put him in a foul mood. He snapped at Cora Bigelow for asking a simple question about potting soil. He did the same with Marabelle Crawford who wanted to know how to grow a jade plant. And then to top it all off, he forgot to deliver a pallet of rosemary seedlings earmarked for Promise Cove.

By the time he got off work, he was in such a state that he decided he wasn't fit to be around anyone else. For the past several hours he hadn't even answered Hannah's texts. And then around seven-thirty they stopped coming in altogether.

He sat in the dark in his study listening to Samuel Barber's *Adagio for Strings*. For someone who claimed the past didn't bother him much, Eleanor had fully gotten under his skin. The way she reached out from inside a cell to play puppeteer showed a power that made his stomach churn. After all these years, she still held them all in the palm of her hand. Going over Delbert Delashaw's pattern of devotion, it made him wonder if there were others out there, and if so, how many. She had the ability to talk people, especially males, into doing whatever chore she wanted them to do for her.

It creeped him out. But mostly, it pissed him off.

A day ago, he was wishing for a life without a past, one closer to what everybody else had. But now, he had to admit, those ordinary and normal things would never be there for him. Sometimes normal just wasn't meant to be. He had to face facts. Fate had dealt him a mother with a heartless outlook on life and a mental problem. He couldn't deny he'd come from a monster, a woman with no soul, no heart, no empathy for anyone but herself.

What the hell was he doing wishing for things he couldn't have? What the hell did he know about anything other than the psychopath that made him?

Hannah's joy at having a dog circled around to one indisputable truth. She no longer walked in the door to an empty house. In just a few days her little cottage had seemed to take on a different personality.

Because Molly still needed looking after during the day, Hannah had brought in Francie Odana to take up the slack.

Thirty-four-year old Francie had suffered a brain injury during her teen years. She'd been the only survivor of a car accident that had taken three other lives. After spending almost two years in a coma, she woke up one day only to realize she'd have to learn how to walk and talk all over again.

Accomplishing that feat had taken her another two years in an assisted living facility. Even though her speech was slow and she would always walk with a limp, Francie decided she wanted to leave the group home and move in with her sister. Irene owned a one-story house on Sandpiper Lane where Francie didn't have to climb stairs.

The two sisters had found contentment living together for the past ten years.

While Irene spent her days on the phone selling cable TV packages, Francie picked up odd jobs doing whatever she could to make money around town. She raked leaves, washed dishes, and sometimes swept up after church services on Sunday afternoons. She was also a part-time custodian at Murphy's Market, sweeping up, mopping the floors, and taking out trash. But what Francie loved most of all was taking care of her own Welsh Corgi, a service dog she'd had for almost eight years.

When Cord and Keegan took over the animal clinic, Francie begged them for a job feeding and caring for the animals, some of which had to stay overnight to recover from surgery. Once Cord and Keegan discovered Francie's knack with the patients and the loving way she treated each cat, dog, or injured ferret, they snapped the woman up. She was so good, she sometimes took on the difficult task of subbing at the rescue center, working around the seals and sea otters.

It hadn't taken long for Hannah to realize Francie was a gentle soul who cared for Molly like the dog was her own pet.

When Hannah walked in the door that afternoon after work, the house buzzed with energy. Francie sat on the floor, which Hannah had come to realize was her favorite spot, playing tug-of-war with Molly. The dog held onto a rawhide chew toy for dear life.

"How was she today, Francie?"

In her slow drawl, Francie went into detail. "It's a joy watching Moll-y get strong-er each time I'm with her. She was down-right frisk-y to-day."

"Did she finally eat her dry food?"

"Better. She likes it better than before."

"Want to stay for dinner? I thought I'd fix stir-fry."

"Thanks but I-rene ordered us piz-za."

"Lucky you. Then you better get on home before it gets cold." Hannah reached in her pocket and pulled out the cash to pay her tab. "Thanks. I don't know what Molly would do during the day without you."

"S'okay. I like Molly."

"She likes you, too. Next week, I should be able to bring Molly to work with me. She'll be able to be around other dogs by then. But I might need you to sit with her when I work my last shift at the bar this weekend."

"No prob-lem. Let me know."

After Francie left, Hannah plopped down on the couch with the dog in her lap. Molly stretched out to enjoy the rubs. When Hannah moved to scratch the dog's belly, she couldn't help but glance at her cell phone. She picked it up, only to see there were no texts from Caleb. Disappointment roiled in her stomach like bad fish. He hadn't bothered answering her texts, which told her he didn't want company.

That was fine by Hannah.

"Stupid man," she muttered. "So what if he refuses to text me back. Who cares? Let him act like an idiot." She let out a sigh. "Why do men have to be so dumb, Molly? Tell me that."

Molly yipped and got to her feet. Her short tail wagged with excitement.

"Maybe you're right. Maybe we should go check on him."

Hannah bagged up the fixings for her stir-fry recipe to take to Caleb's for supper. "I doubt the man's eaten. What would he do without us, huh Molly? What?"

She clipped the leash onto Molly's collar and led her out to the SUV.

Five minutes later, she reached the dead-end circle on Cape May. The house was dark, not a light on anywhere inside. And of course since he'd probably parked his truck in the garage, she couldn't even tell if he was home.

"Would you look at that? The man's taken to his bed like a spoiled teenager." She reached for the phone and tried one more time to text Caleb.

I'm sitting out by the gate. Open up. I brought dinner.

A few seconds ticked by before the gate swung open.

He met her at the front door with a sheepish, hangdog look. "What are you doing here?"

"I thought my text pretty much summed it up." She set Molly down on the pavement and held up her bag. "I figured you probably hadn't eaten yet."

"Hannah, I had a lousy day and I'm afraid I'd just take out my bad mood on you tonight. That's why I really need to be alone."

"Are you telling me I should leave?"

His shoulders drooped. "No, of course not. Come in." He bent down to scrub the dog's ears. "How are you doing, girl?"

Molly tried to give him a head butt and settled for licking his hands.

"What did you bring to eat?"

"Oh, so now you're interested in what's in the bag. Why didn't you text me back? There are people who might possibly worry about you."

"Because I'm not fit to be around anyone just now, especially you."

"Hear that, Molly? For your information, we don't have to talk…about anything. But we all do need to eat. Step aside while I make supper. You may not be hungry, but I'm starving."

Stepping inside his house, she flipped on lights all the way to the kitchen. Molly trotted in behind her. It was Caleb who brought up the rear.

Hannah dumped rice into a steamer, poured olive oil into a skillet for grilling the chicken, and then chopped up enough garlic to hold off several vampires. She threw in fresh ginger and nodded toward Caleb, who stood on the other side of the kitchen, watching it all play out. "If you intend to just stand there gawking, make yourself useful. Chop up the red and yellow peppers. See if you have any broccoli. It's the one thing I didn't bring."

Dutifully, Caleb dug in the fridge for anything green. In the crisper, he found a bag of snap peas and celery. "Will these do?"

She snatched them out of his hand. "Perfect. Thank you."

"No. I should be thanking you."

"Yes, you should. But that's okay. I don't hold grudges. Much." She turned back to the stove to mind the chicken. Deftly she seared the veggies to a tender, golden edge before scooping out rice, and plating the food.

"Do I at least get a glass of wine for my effort?"

"Sure. Sorry." His wine cooler held a variety of merlot and white. He selected a chardonnay with a fruity hint of peach and spice. As he peeled off the foil, he watched her flitting from counter to counter and realized he was feeling much better about…his life. Hannah had managed to bring him out of the doldrums with one well-timed meal.

"This looks delicious." With the first bite, her culinary skills were evident. "How'd you get the chicken to turn out like this?"

"It's called marinade," she said with a grin.

"Do you like the taste of the grape?"

She picked up her glass, took a generous taste. "It's delightful."

"I'm sorry I pissed you off. But as I look at my plate, maybe I should do it more often if it gets me a meal like this."

"You're just lucky I didn't leave you here to sulk."

"I know that now."

"What is it that put you in this kind of mood? Are you upset with Landon because he took some of the gold?"

"He was entitled to his share. No, that wasn't what set it off."

"Then what?"

"Something inside me clicked this afternoon. I realized that, to some extent, Cooper's been right all along. Eleanor will always be this monster that won't let go. She'll never accept defeat. How will I ever have kids and be able to explain to them what I come from?"

"Do you want children, Caleb?"

"I don't know. Don't you?"

She tried for levity. "I have a few goals before I reach that point to find out."

She took his hand when she realized how deep his hurt went. "I get your concern. I felt much the same way after reading the police report and what they said my father did. When I was old enough to understand it, I was devastated. How could I pass that kind of madness on to my children? Surely I would have to remain childless for the rest of my life."

"It's not the same, Hannah. Your father most likely didn't kill anyone. There's hope for you. Not for me, I'm afraid. There's no mistaking the destructive path my mother created. To some degree, she's still making sure there are plenty of victims—her kids, her brother—you get the point. Simply put, she's most likely a serial murderer."

"But she's locked up. She isn't getting out. It's entirely up to you whether you continue to remain under her thumb like this. You can't let her get to you every time she gets the urge. You can't allow her to mess with your head. This isn't you, locking yourself in the dark like this. Look at what you've done, Caleb, what you've accomplished. You have a beautiful home, a wonderful job, a family who loves you. What more do you need?"

He stood up and went to her. "Right now, I'm pretty sure all I need is you."

Twenty-Four

Hannah was doing a load of laundry at Murphy's house when the call came in from Brent.

"I don't want to tell you over the phone so could you come into the station so we can sit down and talk."

"Sure. It's bad news, isn't it?"

"Hannah, let me do this my way, okay?" Brent said. "I prefer to see your face when we go over the DNA. I'm not trying to sound mysterious, but I really need you down at the station. Now."

"Is it okay if I bring Caleb?"

"Absolutely. Bring anyone you want."

After she hung up, she sent Caleb a text message to meet her there.

They pulled up at almost the same time in front of the station. She watched as Caleb got out of his truck and skirted the hood to put his arms around her.

"No matter what I said Sunday, I'm nervous," Hannah admitted.

"It'll be all right."

"I feel like this is the first drop of rain, Caleb, like we're prepping for a storm before the flood waters rise and this is the first round of the devastation."

"You're strong. Remember that. But it wouldn't hurt to remember that we're stronger together. We'll get through this. Whatever Brent tells us in there, we'll deal with it together. That's a promise."

"Thanks for being here with me."

Once inside, Brent escorted them into his office and motioned for Hannah to sit down. "I'm sorry it took so long even after I put a rush on things, but...the lab had some trouble getting...sufficient...DNA...out of the...bone marrow. The little bones were so brittle and dried up that the poor little thing—" His voice trailed off and he stopped in mid-sentence. "Sorry. I'm sure you get the picture."

He studied the paper on his desk and looked across the room at Hannah. "Anyway, the DNA from that baby—it was a girl by the way—did not come back as a match to you."

Hannah wasn't sure she'd heard correctly. "I thought..." Her shoulders dropped. She let out a loud sigh. "I thought you were going to tell me..."

"I know what you thought."

"Then it's good news for me, for Micah. Although I still have to figure out what happened to him, and who took him. Nothing's solved. I don't understand. I'm not sure why I'm here, why Scott pointed me in this direction."

"You said it yourself," Caleb reminded her. "Micah's alive. We just have to find him."

"Exactly," Brent said. "And I have to find out who killed our mystery baby. I have some ideas on that. Several witnesses have come forward. Now that I have a DNA profile I plan to start with Douglas Bradford. Since the remains were found on his property, he's under the most scrutiny. Quentin has agreed to provide a swab to send to the lab."

"What good does that do?" Hannah wanted to know.

"I'm hoping to get a familial result," Brent concluded. "Truth is, if that baby belonged to Douglas, then Quentin's DNA will come back having at least a few markers that match up to the baby's. I'm still amazed that science is able to narrow it down like that."

"And if those few markers are present…?"

"Then I get a court order and head to Eternal Gardens, exhume Douglas. Until then, I try to narrow down the list of all those who had relationships with…our former mayor…of the intimate variety."

Hannah chewed the inside of her jaw. "So, before I go, a little help in the right direction would be nice. Last week you said you wished I had stopped in here first to let you know about Micah. Now I'm sitting here asking for your help. Where exactly would I go to find a list of twenty-year-old men living in Pelican Pointe?"

"Have you thought about starting with one of the online sites about adoptions and genealogy? Maybe he's figured out he's adopted and is trying to find you."

"You aren't serious, are you? I registered with those sites as soon as I turned eighteen. I had hope back then, until someone pointed out to me that Micah was stolen. His adoption is probably nonexistent, as in, illegal."

Brent looked chastised. "Right. Sorry. I wasn't thinking."

"This is the reason I have a tough time letting go, putting my faith in anyone but myself to do the job."

Caleb straightened in his chair and raised his eyes to meet Brent's. "Why couldn't you just run DMV records for her, records that list all the guys who turned twenty in the area? Micah has to have a driver's license."

"I suppose I could do that. Give me twenty-four hours and I'll get Eastlyn to run it over to you."

"And just like that I'm still left to wonder."

"Sorry," Brent added. "But think of it this way. There's still hope."

After Hannah and Caleb left his office, though, Brent went over to see Quentin at the clinic. He had to wait thirty minutes for the Doc to finish seeing all his patients for the day.

Once the last patient, Oliver Danson, paid his bill, Sydney led Brent into Quentin's office. "It won't be long. He's on the phone with a patient trying to help them with a problem. I'm heading home to start dinner. Remind Quentin that he has to help Beckham with his science project later tonight."

"Will do. What's the project?"

"Something about growing bacteria, which is why Quentin is trying to prove a point to Beckham about washing his hands more often."

"Ah, teenage boys."

"Exactly. They aren't what you'd call clean freaks."

A couple of minutes later, Quentin came into the room and plopped down at his desk. "I bet you're here for the swab."

Brent handed him the test kit he'd brought with him. "That, and to pick your brain about what the coroner told me."

"Let's hear it."

"Female, probably less than three months old, approximate age, because anything definitive is just not possible after such a long time in the ground. He speculates that she most likely died shortly after birth."

"Newborn? That's…heartbreaking."

"Do you think the mother could've suffered from that thing River had? What was it you called it?"

"Postpartum hysteria, not to be confused with postpartum psychosis. No."

"Why not?"

"It's true postpartum hysteria most often deals with depression, but sometimes it surfaces when the mother starts having weird thoughts. Now those weird thoughts can and do morph into having scary thoughts directed toward the baby. The baby doesn't look right, he's not acting right, in other words, something's off or just plain wrong. As I recall in River's case, Eli wasn't crying enough. Mommy's thoughts might seem harmless enough but can turn into bigger problems over time. Especially when the new mom stops sleeping, has crying jags, starts coming up with even weirder ideas in her head. Postpartum hysteria is a fairly common problem, occurring in one in seven women after giving birth. There's a fine line between it and the more serious illness known as postpartum psychosis. That's the one that can end up with deadly consequences if left untreated. But make no mistake, new mothers can experience symptoms from both categories, inconsequential and serious. If you're about to ask me if this baby, this newborn at Bradford House, could've been the victim of such an occurrence, the answer is simple. I would have no way of knowing that with absolute certainty without a lot more information. You said it yourself. After such a long time, you may not even be able to find this woman."

"I think I can. What about the other category, the more serious one?"

"Postpartum psychosis is rare. It occurs in one or maybe two out of one thousand births. It's treatable. Doctors have been making great strides in researching the subject. I find it highly unlikely that what you're dealing with at Bradford House would ever link back to postpartum psychosis."

"You're saying it's more than likely, outright deliberate murder?"

Quentin gave him a cold stare. "Not without an autopsy report stating that fact. Did the medical examiner speculate about stillbirth, an accident at birth, sudden infant death syndrome, anything along those lines that would indicate the baby stopped breathing because of a medical reason?"

"I see your point. That must be why he listed the cause of death as unexplained. I shouldn't jump to a conclusion then?"

"I don't see how you can unless there were broken bones, arms, legs, skull. Was the hyoid bone intact? That's the horseshoe-shaped bone at the neck that breaks easily when pressed, as in strangulation. The baby could've even been smothered, which wouldn't leave a mark on her."

"Maybe you should talk to the coroner."

"Sure. If you think it'll help, I'd be happy to."

"Tomorrow?"

"Set it up. I'll make myself available."

"Thanks. Is there anything you remember about your uncle that might help me understand this guy any better? From what I've found out he's either a rock-solid saint—that came from Jack Prescott, by the way. Or, he's a cad, a playboy, a real ladies' man—that came from Murphy and one of my eyewitnesses."

Quentin unpacked the contents of the test kit. "It's easier to give you DNA than to tell you anything worthwhile about Douglas. He was a mystery. He didn't go out of his way to keep in touch with his only link to family, his sister, my mother. I grew up seeing him maybe twice before my father was killed. I think Douglas came for a visit to Tahoma about that many times. I remember him acting strange, as though our little town was beneath him. I don't think he cared much for my mother's choice of husbands. A Native American wasn't high on his list of suitors."

Quentin swabbed his own mouth in front of Brent, slipped the Q-tip into a vial, and capped the sample closed before continuing. "Certainly, after my mother took her own life, Douglas was even less involved. He seemed even more distant and determined not to have anything to do with me or Nonnie. When I got older, Nonnie let me read my mother's journal. In it, I learned she missed having contact with her brother. It became obvious she thought the reason he kept his distance was because he had a secret life he didn't want anyone to know about. That secret, according to my mother, was that Douglas was gay. She believed it and I took that for the truth, and didn't think any more about it."

After scrawling his name on the sample, Quentin handed it off to Brent. "Imagine my surprise coming here and discovering no one thought that at all. In fact, it was just the opposite. I learned from Charlotte, Beckham's grandmother, that the former mayor gave so many lavish parties that he often had a string of female companions who routinely stayed overnight. Douglas took them on trips with him to conventions, on cruises and to resorts, fancy dinners at nice restaurants. He even bought them cars. That little tidbit came from Kinsey, who as his lawyer might know a helluva lot more about the guy than I do. The point to all this is I didn't really know Douglas Bradford at all. The last time I saw him he came to college graduation, strutting around because his little Native American nephew had set his sights on the medical profession. I'm downright sorry I can't be more help to you, especially now."

"You think that baby belonged to Douglas?"

"Yeah. I do. But what I think isn't as important as what you think."

"Right. It's just that I have a witness who saw Douglas burying something right near that spot. That event took place during the right timeframe. And he wasn't alone."

"From what I've heard Douglas rarely was…alone, that is. Now all you have to do is ID the woman your witness saw. My guess is that would be the baby's mother."

"Do you think I'm dealing with a murder?"

"I'll be better able to answer that after I talk to the coroner."

Twenty-Five

That evening a cold winter rain battered the coast with a line of storms packing forty mile per hour wind gusts.

While the weather outside worsened, Caleb and Hannah settled down in front of a toasty, crackling fire with Molly snuggled in her bed. The laundry basket had been replaced by a cozy insert made from foam and covered in soft denim that hadn't been cheap.

Caleb knew full well Hannah felt down. She'd had the blues ever since leaving the meeting with Brent. But like she'd done with him and pulled him out of the doldrums, he intended to do the same with her. "I won't let you spend another minute wallowing in self-pity."

"Am I that obvious?"

"You know what's great on a rainy, winter evening like this?"

"Reading a good book in front of a cozy fire?" she quipped.

"There is that, but that's not where my mind went first. Keeping one eye on your mood, I'd say having a bout of hot, sweaty sex tops just about anything else. It'll make you feel better." He crooked a finger. "Come closer so I can see your eyes. Let's make it interesting. You're a lover of games. Let's play chess. *Strip* chess."

"Talk about incentive. That isn't bad. Okay, you have my attention. So how would it work? Every time I capture one of your game pieces, you lose a piece of clothing? Is that it?"

He cocked a brow. "You think you can beat me at chess?"

"Scared?"

"Not a bit. But let's go over the rules. Let's say I take *your* bishop, rook, knight, or king."

"As if."

"Oh, it's gonna happen."

"Really? That's a shame since I'm already picturing you without that shirt you're wearing and minus the pants."

"Hmm. Maybe I'll lose on purpose."

"That would be the smart way to go. Let's throw in one caveat for good measure, though."

"What's that?"

"You have to dance. Can you dance an Irish jig, Caleb? Move your feet to an Irish beat?"

"You mean like a Riverdance sort of thing? If it gets you naked, absolutely."

Hannah went over to his wall of shelves, where the stereo had a prominent place in the middle. But there were no CDs with an Irish theme. "Do you have something against the Irish? There's not a hornpipe or a reel or a fiddle here."

Caleb came up behind her, picked one, and slid it into the player. He held out his hand. "Will you settle for a round of Scottish bagpipes and the drums instead?"

Her arms went around him. "I don't think I've ever seen a man striptease to bagpipes before."

"There's a first time for everything."

Twenty-Six

Sydney's end-of-the-week party turned out to be a large backyard event that overflowed with such a crowd she had to scramble to defrost more hamburger meat.

"Thank goodness everyone brought a side dish," she exclaimed, flitting from kitchen stove to the outdoor grill where Quentin kept searing more hot dogs.

"It'll be fine," he assured her. "Brent and River brought a casserole, Nick and Jordan brought a rib roast, Thane and Isabella brought pizzas, and Kinsey and Logan stopped and picked up cake and ice cream. I don't think anyone will go home hungry."

Ethan slapped him on the back. "And Hayden just had to make up a batch of her chocolate chip cookies. I'll no doubt leave here five pounds heavier."

"It seems like you invited the entire town," Hannah remarked, looking out over the backyard.

Sydney lifted a shoulder. "Word of mouth has a way of spreading. Now that we don't have to worry about a peeping Tom, everyone just wants to relax and enjoy themselves. They all hired sitters to watch their broods while they live it up on a rare night out."

But Caleb noticed it didn't take long for the guests to slant their conversations to the situation at Bradford House. Especially the group of men who stood around

Quentin at the grill. They were full of questions aimed directly at Brent.

"Any word yet on who that baby was?" Logan said to Brent.

"The lab assures me they'll have Quentin's DNA back by next week."

Nick was just as curious as every other guy. "Lots of ideas floating around. The probability is high that the baby belongs to Douglas. His property. His playboy lifestyle."

"No one's substantiated anything to me yet. You know something I don't?"

Nick shrugged. "I wasn't living here back then. But people talk when they come into the bank. Everyone seems to agree the former mayor had quite the social life."

"I'm aware Douglas entertained on a rotation basis. I'm trying to hunt down the list of people he entertained. Any names pop up during these conversations?"

"More than a couple. But the women's names don't mean much to me since they've long since moved out of town. Some say Flynn McCready is the guy you should talk to."

Brent stared at Nick. "Really? That's a new direction. How so?"

"Prissie Gates told me that Flynn and Douglas were thick as thieves back then," Nick provided.

"I thought Jack Prescott was Bradford's best friend."

Nick shook his head. "Jack was supposedly happily married. Think about it. Unless Jack fooled around on Belle, the horndog mayor would likely be drawn to a best friend with no attachments, someone just like him, someone he could party with. In my book, that description fits what I know about Flynn perfectly."

Brent took out his cell phone to make notations of everything Nick had given him.

Quentin brought over a cooler containing beer and began handing them out to the men.

"Just the guy I want to see," Brent said. "Did you get a chance to talk to the coroner?"

"Late last night. After he sent me copies of the slides from the autopsy, we agreed the images show a hairline fracture across the baby's skull. That makes it another type of evil. He's convinced now it was homicide. I suspect that's probably what he'll ultimately list on the autopsy. Is that what you wanted to know? Does it help?"

"It does, gives me a leg up on the investigation. Thanks."

"Is it true you've decided to ditch the house because of all this?" Logan asked Quentin.

"Still kicking it around. Shame too. Beckham seemed to be settling in there. He likes that spot on the beach where he was inducted into the Miwok tribe. He doesn't complain about it, but we know he's missing his room there."

"Then why don't you hold a cleansing ceremony that covers the entire grounds?" Kinsey suggested. "Call out Marcus Cody or one of your own, like Nonnie and Stone. Get them back in town to perform the ceremony. Cleanse the place of the evil. Make a big deal out of it."

Quentin cocked his head to stare at the lawyer. "That's not a bad idea. Natives do that all the time." He met Logan's eyes. "How is it you so keenly married someone who's so obviously ten times smarter than you are?"

Logan's face broke into a wide grin. "Let me tell you it took some adjustment. What makes it especially hard is that she never rubs it in my face."

"Much," Kinsey tossed back, a sparkle in her eye. "The ceremony could act as a rebirth, not only for you guys but for Bradford House as a whole. Invite the entire town to participate. You might even consider renaming it Blackwood Manor."

"I don't know about that," Quentin returned. "It sounds about as pretentious as Bradford House. I'll kick it around with Sydney and Beckham. Those two always come up with a list of great ideas that would never occur to me."

Jordan sought out Hannah and pulled her aside. "I wanted to thank you. Nick and I had this long talk last night until the wee hours. Turns out, he's as unhappy as I am about the long hours he's spending away from Promise Cove. He wants to make changes to his schedule, take more time off to spend at home. I…we owe it all to you."

"Don't be silly. I'm just happy that it's something Nick wanted as much as you did. This way, I won't worry about you out there by yourself after I start my new job."

"Does Durke know yet?"

"Not yet. That's on my to-do list. I have a question for you, though. Have you had the opportunity to use Faye DeMarco to dog sit Quake?"

"No, unfortunately we're too far out of town for her. But if you're interested in getting to know her, she's right over there sitting next to Beckham under that giant oak tree."

Hannah tugged Caleb away from the buffet table to go with her to meet Faye. It became apparent to Hannah the closer they got that the two teens were holding some type of ceremony using Buckley, a lab and golden retriever mix, as some sort of stand-in for the ritual.

Brown-haired Faye was no bigger than a sprite. The girl had huge brown eyes that looked too big for her face. Faye held a turtle, the size of a small dog, on her lap that seemed at home around humans, or maybe just used to the girl's feeding and handling of him.

Caleb broke the ice. "Hey, Beckham, how the heck are you? Haven't seen you since Christmas. What are you guys up to?"

"We're getting ready for a Miwok celebration. It's a tradition practiced during the winter to mark the seven constellations that make up the Big Dipper. The time is right when the stars are at their brightest."

"It's the start of the tribe's spiritual year," Faye supplied. "A very important, somber occasion that requires the right music and traditionally prepared food. We're putting it all together."

"Ah. You're certainly getting into learning about your new Native customs," Caleb remarked.

Beckham nodded with pride. "Now that I'm a true Blackwood—and the court says I am because we filled out a bunch of paperwork—Faye and I research all the customs at the school library. We've already scheduled them on the calendar for the entire upcoming year."

"Every month our goal is to celebrate a new one," Faye added. "It's fun mapping out all the different traditions and assigning them a month."

"Not to mention we get extra credit for it in social studies," Beckham owned up.

Hannah chuckled at their enthusiasm. "It's still amazing that you'd go to the trouble of doing that, shows initiative."

She sat down next to Faye on the grass. "I spoke to Cord, the veterinarian. It seems you come highly recommended as a first-rate dog sitter and dog walker. Since I have a new puppy, I'm in the market. I'll probably be needing your services soon."

That perked Faye up. Her face turned from concentrating on the task at hand to Hannah's compliment. "Sure. What kind of dog do you have?"

Hannah went into a description that showed her pleasure at having a dog in her life. "Her name's Molly and she's about five months old, still growing, a cross between an Airedale and a Jack Russell, which I suppose makes her some kind of small terrier."

"Molly sounds sweet. If I'm not available on Saturdays and Sundays—I'm limited to taking paying jobs on the weekends because of school—my brother Andy can dog sit." Faye pointed to a man standing next to the grill helping Quentin with the burgers and hot dogs.

Hannah followed the track of Faye's eyes to a tall man with a mahogany mop of brown hair. Her jaw dropped. For several long seconds, she couldn't take her eyes off Faye's brother. "I'm sorry, what did you say his name was?"

"Andy."

"Andy DeMarco," Hannah said aloud. "That sounds Italian."

"Pretty much. Andy and I don't look a lot alike though. My hair's much darker than his. He has more reddish brown for some reason. It's odd because neither one of our parents ever had red hair. They're originally from someplace in Italy, Palermo, I think."

Hannah swallowed hard enough to get the words past her lips. "And where are your parents? Are they here tonight?"

"They died in a car accident two years ago."

"Oh, honey, that's terrible. I'm so sorry."

"Hannah already knows my grandmother died before Christmas," Beckham explained to Faye. "I told her the first time she came to Bradford House. That's where I met her, but Hannah had already heard about it. I guess the whole town had."

Caleb noticed Hannah still staring at Andy and leaned over to whisper, "What's wrong with you?"

But Hannah couldn't stop staring at Andy. "I'm…nothing. You know, the first time I showed up to clean Bradford House and Beckham was there, I shared my story with him. I lost my parents when I was six. I know how rough it can be. How old is your brother, Faye?"

"Andy? He's twenty. Did you get dumped into the system when your parents died? Because Andy didn't want that to happen to me. He's a lot older than me. That's why Social Services wasn't much interested in shipping him off to live with strangers. They didn't much care what Andy did. All I know is that Andy could stay put in Pelican Pointe no matter what. But me, if I couldn't stay with Andy, I'd have to go live with a foster family. Good thing he wanted to keep me around."

"That's really nice of Andy."

"Oh yeah. Andy's super smart and takes care of everything at home. He does everything a parent does, even checks my homework before I go to bed. He makes me follow the rules, though. So, did you? Did you get dumped in the system?"

"I did, for a little more than three years or so. Then I got adopted. I thought it was a miracle at the time. You sound very worldly for a girl your age, talking about Social Services like that."

"At my age—I'm almost fourteen—I'm way too old to get adopted by anyone now. And I wouldn't want to leave my brother alone anyway. That's why I'm lucky to be here, living with him. This way, I get to stay in my own room and see Beckham and go to the same school and nothing much changed for me. But it could've been…horrible."

"It sounds like you're very lucky to have Andy. But you know, Social Services isn't as terrible as you make it out to be. Those social workers have been known to do good work for kids by finding them decent homes, sometimes more stable than the ones they had to leave. Were your parents good to you and Andy when they were…alive?"

"Sure. I guess. But they always worked too hard. They never had any time to come see me at school or go to parent-teacher conferences. The day it happened, they were racing back to their jobs in Vegas when they were killed, probably going too fast and driving carelessly." Faye put the turtle down on the grass and the animal began to nibble the ripe blades of St. Augustine. "My birthday's in two weeks. Andy says I get to have a party like this one. Would you and Caleb like to come?"

"We'd love to. Where do you live?"

Faye rattled off an address on Cape May. Suddenly chatty, Faye went on, "We're planning to plant a garden out here. We had plotted out a place at Bradford House, but…that might not happen now. And if it gets closer to spring we'll need to have a backup plan."

"I find a garden is one of the most soothing places to spend time. You can read a book. Or sit out in the sun. What do you plan to grow?"

"Flowers mostly. Maybe a few things Oogway Putney—that's my turtle over there—likes to eat. Nonnie, that's Quentin's grandmother, called it a memory garden. Nonnie came up with the idea."

Beckham finally managed to get a word in. "Nonnie and Sydney suggested we plant it in memory of my grandmother, Charlotte Dowling, and Faye's parents. That way, we can remember them by picking flowers out of the garden, and taking them out to Eternal Gardens and putting them on their graves at the cemetery." He turned to Caleb. "Faye and I planned to ask you for advice when we get the seedlings in the ground."

"That's a super idea and touching. I'm happy to help. Or Hannah. Pretty soon she'll be managing the co-op next month, growing vegetables for the town. So if I'm ever not available, you can always ask her for advice."

That caused the teenagers to go into a litany of questions that lasted almost until the party began to wind down.

Later, when Caleb finally got Hannah alone in the kitchen, he nudged her into the laundry room for privacy. "What was that all about with Andy?"

"What do you think is wrong? Faye said Andy was twenty. And look at him."

"Oh, come on. You practically stopped breathing just looking at him. To me, he looks like Andy. What do you see?"

Hannah put her hands over her face. "He's the spitting image of my father. I swear I'm not making this up, but Andy looks exactly my dad. And he's the right age, Caleb. I think Andy could be Micah, Micah *Andrew* Lambert."

Caleb blinked in surprise. "What? You never said anything about Micah's middle name being Andrew."

"Why would I? Who would've ever thought that he'd be using his middle name? Not me. But that can't be a coincidence. Now, all I have to do is find out whether his birthday is in August. If it is, I've just found my little brother."

"With Brent dragging his heels on that list, maybe I know a way we can bypass the DMV info. I'll be right back." Caleb left her in the kitchen to hunt down Julianne McLachlan.

Julianne sat in a circle with a group of other women talking about making another trip out to Cleef's farmhouse to pick up an old fireplace screen she'd found there.

"I hate to interrupt but I was wondering if I could have a word with Julianne," Caleb interjected. "It'll only take a minute."

Hannah was waiting for Caleb at the side of the house in the little courtyard. It was the one spot that wasn't teeming with people and would afford them a level of privacy. Hannah explained her predicament to the school principal.

"You want me to what? No. I will not snoop into a student's records from another school in the district. San Sebastian High is off limits to me," Julianne declared. She shook her head for emphasis. "I'd have no reason accessing their computer records. Nope, no way."

"Former student," Hannah corrected.

"Doesn't matter. I can't go searching through anyone's school records for no good reason. That's a violation of so many privacy laws I won't even bother to list them. Look, I sympathize with your predicament but surely you understand why I can't do it."

"Absolutely. But do you have any other advice as to where to look for a person's records, someone who might've graduated say, two years ago?"

Julianne narrowed her gaze at Hannah. "You have someone already in mind, don't you?"

"Of course I do."

Julianne let out a sigh. "You tell me specifically what you're looking for and I'll see if I can come up with a...reasonable explanation as to why I need that person's info. Who is it and what do you want to know?"

"I need to know if Andy DeMarco was born in August."

Julianne scanned the backyard until she spotted Andy having a conversation with Thane. "But Andy's standing right over there. Why don't you just walk twenty yards or so and ask him yourself when he was born?" Like a brick falling off the roof, it hit Julianne then. "Oh, my God. You think Andy might be your brother?"

"Shh. Don't say it so loud," Hannah cautioned. "It wouldn't be fair to him finding out that way. I need to work up to it. Make sure of my facts before I approach him."

"Okay, look. I can take care of this here and now without breaking any laws or rules. It's simple. I'll go ask Faye. How's that?"

"Sure. August 9th, that's Micah's birthday," Hannah blurted out quickly when Julianne turned to fulfill the mission.

But then the principal stopped, turned back around, looking somewhat confused. "Micah?"

"That's his birth name," Hannah added. "Micah Andrew Lambert, my brother."

"Ah. Fine. Wait here. I'll be right back."

It took Julianne less than five minutes to run back with the news. "Faye confirms Andy's birth date is the same. I think you have either a major coincidence here, or you just won the brother lottery. Congratulations."

Hannah grabbed Julianne's arm just as she was about to whoop louder. "No. You can't say anything to anyone. Not even to Ryder. I need more proof before I go turning this kid's life upside down."

"But…"

"No buts. A minute ago you were lecturing me about rules and regulations…and laws. I can't just go over there and say, 'Hey, Andy, guess what? I'm your sister.' I need to know a lot more facts before I do anything like that."

"Like what?"

"Like anything concrete about his parents. Who were they? Has he ever suspected that he was adopted? Does he look like his parents? Faye says no, but what does he think? There are steps, Julianne, to confirming it."

Julianne held up her hands. "Sorry. You're right. I got carried away. You know who would know more about Andy than just about anyone else, besides Quentin, of course?"

"Why Quentin?"

"He befriended Andy, reached out to him long before anyone else did. Quentin is the one who sent Andy to Ryder for a job working on the new hospital. Andy owes his steady income to Quentin."

"And Ryder who hired him," Caleb tossed in.

"Exactly. So, whether you like it or not, Ryder spends a lot of time with Andy every day, five days a week. He could ask Andy all kinds of things while they're at work, casually, without raising red flags. Believe me, these construction guys have eight hours, sometimes more, to talk about all kinds of personal stuff while they're on the clock. So, do I get to tell Ryder now about what's going on or not?"

Hannah's shoulders relaxed. "Sure. If he has any questions, tell him to call me. I'll even make up a list of things to ask Andy if he needs it."

Hannah started to walk away and then stopped. "And it wouldn't hurt if Ryder wanted to go that extra mile and swipe some DNA off one of Andy's soda cans or his thermos."

Julianne couldn't believe what she was hearing. "Jeez, I think you've been watching too many crime shows. This is getting more covert by the minute."

"So, do you think Ryder will do it?"

"I don't know. We'll see. Ryder does like those crime shows. He never misses an episode of *Forensic Files*."

"Great. Then he should feel on top of the world knowing he helped solve a twenty-year-old mystery."

Twenty-Seven

Hannah waited an excruciating twelve hours before hearing back from Julianne that Ryder had agreed to casually ask Andy a series of questions. That morning, she also learned that Ryder had called Andy in to work on the hospital project under the guise they could finish framing out what would be the operating room.

"It's on," she told Caleb before heading out the door to her shift at The Shipwreck. "I don't suppose you could offer to lend your muscle by helping them out? It is Saturday."

"You want me to help build a hospital all the while eavesdropping on Ryder's conversation and Andy's answers?"

"When you put it like that? Yes."

He snatched her around the waist, rested his brow on hers. "I never knew you were such a sneaky little minx. I like it. But I can't just pop in and offer to help out of the blue without raising some major red flags. It's better if Andy feels completely at ease with Ryder. And if I understand the plan, the two guys will be alone in the building."

"You're right. Bad plan. Bad Hannah. I'm anxious, is all. Good thing I have my shift at the bar to keep my mind off Andy."

"Yeah. Right. Like that'll make a difference. Look, I hate to bring it up, but are you still planning to go with Eastlyn when she talks to Eleanor?"

"I was. Do you not want me to go?"

"I don't. Not really. You'll probably have to take a long, hot shower afterward. Because getting that close to Eleanor will leave you feeling...tainted."

"As I understand the process, there'll be a glass wall between us. It's like a separate room."

"Won't matter. Getting within ten feet of Eleanor presents a certain risk factor...to you. You need to understand that you'll be on her radar after the visit."

"You're afraid she'll somehow convert me into one of her followers? I'm not that easily influenced, Caleb. I'm hardly naïve or gullible."

"Were you able to bone up on her past?"

"Caleb, I know practically everything Eastlyn does. She's caught me up in a quick course she calls Eleanor-ology."

"That's cute, but this is no joking matter."

"Stop worrying. I'll be fine. I gotta run. But if you hear anything from Ryder, text me."

While Hannah dealt with a Saturday afternoon crowd at The Shipwreck, Caleb loaded Molly up in his truck and headed to Promise Cove to deliver that pallet of herbs, overdue by several days.

Not long after leaving the city limits, he and the dog drove past a coastline packed with lush scenery. The view became a forest of cypress, alongside woodsy redwood that bumped up against the staggering coastal cliffs. The landscape whizzed past Molly as the dog rested her chin on the pickup's window frame.

It took less than twelve minutes for Caleb to reach the turnoff that led to the Bed & Breakfast. He bumped along over a new bridge Nick had built because of heavy rains in the area.

Caleb pulled into the driveway and parked behind an older model Volkswagen Golf with out-of-state plates. It looked as though a tourist from Nevada had found lodging at Promise Cove for the weekend, a typical occurrence since this was the only place to stay within a fifty-mile radius off the interstate.

Caleb set Molly down outside his pickup in case she needed a potty break. "You stay put right there, and don't go running off, or Hannah will have my head if you get lost."

As he strolled past the little station wagon, curiosity had him peeking inside. One look told him something seemed amiss. The interior was littered with food wrappers, aluminum cans, and other trash, as if the driver had been living out of the car.

Not such a typical occurrence, considering the pricey rates at Promise Cove, he thought now.

Caleb headed up the steps to the wide wraparound porch, and rapped on the door. No one answered. He waited and then knocked again. When there was still no answer, he started back down the steps only to hear what sounded like a muffled scream coming from inside the house.

In an instant, he made the decision without thinking. He flung open the front door. To his left, he spotted a man standing in the living room holding a gun, the barrel pointed at Nick's head while Jordan and two frightened little kids looked on.

"Come any closer and I'll shoot the boy. All I want is the gold," the man said to Caleb.

"Excuse me," Caleb said, playing dumb. "What gold?"

"You know damn well what gold. That bag you stuffed into a safe deposit box on Monday," the man snarled through clenched teeth. For emphasis, the gun-wielding guy used the weapon to bump against the back of Nick's head. "It's tucked away in his bank. And I want it."

Caleb held up his hands in mock surrender. Out of the corner of his eye, he caught movement from the doorway. In a stealth effort, Molly inched her way up to the door on her belly. The dog positioned herself right behind Caleb.

Stalling for time, Caleb shifted his feet and went into an insulting rant in hopes of rattling the gun-wielding guy.

"What kind of an idiot are you, man? I mean, you look like the dumbest SOB on the planet. Don't you realize the bank's closed now, locked up tight until Monday with an alarm system that doesn't operate until nine a.m.? Didn't you explain that to him, Nick? Or is this guy too stupid to grasp something that simple?"

"Already tried that," Nick stated, blood trickling out of the corner of his mouth. "I tried telling him I can't very well retrieve the bag if I'm sitting here."

The stranger turned the gun toward Caleb. "You're here now, you're gonna get it for me or I'll kill this entire family. I'm not waiting till Monday."

Until that point, Molly had been hidden out of sight. But the dog shot out from behind the door, leaping at the guy's legs, which is the only thing little Molly could reach.

The distraction gave Caleb an opportunity to bull rush the man's midsection. He hit him so hard that he drove the man halfway across the room and into the wall. Pictures fell to the floor and shattered.

Once the man's back hit the wall, Caleb could feel the air rush out of the man's lungs. He heard the gun clatter on the hardwood floor and skid somewhere under the window.

Caleb pounced. His fists began to fly. He pounded the guy's face, pummeling him with wild fury. He sent all his pent-up rage into every punch. Blow after blow obliterated the man's jaw and nose. While he gave the guy a beating, Molly chewed on the man's leg, taking hunks out of his ankle.

Nick picked up the weapon as he shuttled Jordan, Hutton, and Scott into the entryway. "I want you guys to run as fast as you can out of the house."

"What about you, Daddy?" Scott shouted.

"I have to help Caleb. You go with Mommy. No argument. Go! Now!"

The kids went scurrying down the hallway with their mother. Once Nick knew they were on their way to safety and away from the asshole, he turned back to help Caleb.

He took one look at Caleb's relentless onslaught and realized it was over. Latching onto Caleb's arm in motion, Nick put an end to the fight. "You've got him now. It's okay. You can quit now. He's unconscious. He's not going anywhere."

Out of breath, Caleb sat back on his heels, wiped the sweat out of his eyes. "Who is this bastard?"

"No idea. He showed up about twenty minutes before you got here pretending to be lost and needing a room. We let him in," Nick said with a shrug. "I guess it's one of the pitfalls of owning a B&B."

Nick bent down to pick up Molly, stroking the pup's head and held her to his chest. "And who is this little angel?"

"That's Molly. Hannah found her a week ago in the mountains, half-starved, and brought her back to town with us. I've always heard mutts make the best guard dogs. Now I know it's true."

"This asshole locked our Quake up in the laundry room off the kitchen. Otherwise, I think Quake could've done what Molly did. I'm grateful you two came along when you did."

Caleb looked down at the man on the floor. "What do we do with him?"

"I want him out of my house. Let's drag him outside and tie him to the nearest tree until Brent shows up."

"Sounds like a plan. You have blood on your mouth."

"Yeah. The bastard pulled the gun on Jordan first and when I reacted, he hit me across the mouth with the pistol."

Caleb took in the stranger's nose, bloody and crooked. "I think I got him back for you."

Nick slapped him on the back. "Any time you and Hannah want a weekend out here, just say the word. Accommodations are on the house. Bring Molly with you. There's always room for the dog."

While Nick and Caleb secured the man so he couldn't go anywhere, Jordan had called Brent. As they took the time to loop a rope around the stranger's feet and body, they heard sirens approaching in the distance.

Two patrol cars pulled into the lane. Brent got out of one, Eastlyn, the other.

"What the hell happened?" Brent wanted to know.

Nick replayed the scene again.

"I'll go see if he has ID," Eastlyn volunteered. A few minutes later she came back. "Nevada driver's license identifies him as Craig Mooney, age 46. I also found this letter in his jeans pocket, return address says Eleanor Jennings, Chowchilla Correctional."

Caleb's jaw tightened with rage. "I figured as much since he was after the gold. So we're dealing with another asshole fan of Eleanor's?"

Eastlyn shook her head. "I'm fascinated by how she gets these guys to do whatever she wants—from behind bars no less. I checked, she doesn't even qualify for conjugal visits."

"Yeah, well, it seems her power of persuasion is off the charts. But you be sure to ask her about it when you sit down with her. It seems all she has to do is demand, and these poor schmucks are willing to commit kidnapping and murder to get it done for her."

"You'll charge him with kidnapping, won't you?" Nick asked. "I want him charged with assault. I'm pressing charges to the max."

Brent rocked back on his heels. "He threatened to kill a child, so yeah. I'll throw every charge I can at this guy just to make sure he doesn't bond out."

"That's some comfort anyway," Nick groused. "Now it's time to explain to my kids what the hell just happened. They're scared to death."

"Don't worry. That'll be in the report we send to the DA's office."

Hannah heard the news from Caleb via text. But a more lengthy, colorful version circulated around town from Tandy Gilliam when he came in to play pool with Archer Gates.

"Got yourself a real warrior there, Hannah," Tandy said. "Not every dog would've pounced like that, 'specially a little bitty thing like Molly. Maybe you shoulda called her Xena, warrior princess."

Hannah smiled and traded Tandy's empty glass for a full one. "Maybe. First time I saw her though I knew she had a strong spirit and a true heart. I knew she'd be fierce and loyal."

"You can just tell like that?" Caleb asked from the doorway, holding Molly.

Hannah went over to inspect his face. She took his chin in her hand. "You look fine, don't even look like you've been in a fight, not a scratch on either one of you."

"That's because the guy never landed a punch. Did he, Molly?"

"Lucky me. I have my very own hero *and* a warrior dog." She fluffed Molly's wiry coat. "And you? Such a tough little girl disguised as a guard dog. You get extra Kibble tonight."

"Don't I get anything special?" Caleb wanted to know.

Hannah fluffed the hair on his head, and whispered, "You get the same thing you got last night."

"I can live with that," he said, placing a kiss on her cheek.

From behind the long mahogany bar, Durke cleared his throat. "Technically no dogs are allowed in here."

Caleb held up Molly. "Haven't you heard? She's my service dog. She eases my stress."

Durke grinned and swatted his rag on the counter. "I'm feeling the love here already. Never let it be said I'm so rigid that I can't make an exception for a therapy dog."

"There you go," Hannah said, and promptly reached over and gave Durke a hug. "I'm going to miss working for you."

Durke's brow creased. "Are you leaving town and never coming back? I thought you were just going up to the hilltop to grow stuff and do good for all vegetables everywhere? Grow me some wine, girl. Grow me a nice Chianti and then we'll talk."

She patted the side of his face. "I'll no doubt be back in to eat, drink, and make merry like a regular customer. I look forward to not being on my feet for eight hours, carting beer back and forth."

"You'll miss the tips," Durke quipped.

"And you'll miss your stalwart employee."

"No argument from me."

Caleb and Molly were still hanging around when Ryder showed up.

Hannah had to suppress the urge to rush him with a bunch of questions. Caleb picked up on that and did it for her.

"So...any progress with Andy? Did he suspect you were grilling him?"

"Yes. No. At least I don't think so. One thing I do know for sure is the kid definitely doesn't have a clue he's adopted. Although he did hint at one particular weird incident."

"Which was?"

"When he started kindergarten, he remembered there was a big deal about his birth certificate. He recalled how the situation got worse because his parents panicked. It was so apparent that his mom homeschooled him for the first two years despite having a full-time job."

"How did that work exactly?"

"Babysitter, I suppose. Anyway, it went on like that until one day the school district knocked on their door.

From what Andy said there was an embarrassing scene. By this time, he was about eight and his mother had given up her regular job to stay home with Faye, who was only two at the time. He said he recalled conversations that centered around trying to figure out a way to do something about his birth records."

"Hmm," Hannah said. "He remembers all that? How do you suppose his parents finally worked it out?"

Ryder had done some thinking on that. "Applied for a social security number and from there dummied one up. It's not unheard of." He pulled an empty soda can resting inside a zip lock baggie out of his pocket and put it on the counter. "I felt a little silly collecting this. But this is the can that Andy drank from with his sandwich today. I'm one-hundred-percent certain."

Caleb grinned. "I didn't think you could pull it off. Thanks."

"Neither did I. But he turned his back at just the right moment and I snapped it up, Andy none the wiser."

"I hate doing this behind his back," Hannah admitted, chewing her lip. But she was thinking about the next step. "Based on what you learned so far, what do you think my next move should be?"

Ryder bobbed his head toward the dog. "Ask him to puppy sit and see where it goes. Andy's a sucker for animals. And he's always looking ahead, looking to make some extra cash. My advice would be to get to know him a little better before you yell, 'Surprise! I'm your sister.' It wouldn't hurt to let him see that you don't have an ulterior motive in what you're about to do."

Hannah took the advice to heart. That's why she suggested to Caleb that a circle of friends might be the answer. "They could help me coordinate a campaign, one that would show Andy I could be the perfect big sister if given the opportunity."

The plan meant enlisting the help of several people, mostly those Andy had encountered for one reason or another, and trusted. Neighbors like Kinsey, who'd helped

Andy battle Social Services. His employer Ryder, and others like Quentin and Sydney he knew he could depend on, if necessary.

But before the first phase could become operational, Hannah needed a favor from Eastlyn.

"You have to take this soda can to the lab and have it tested for Andy's DNA."

"Hannah, I'm a sworn officer of the court. I'm not allowed to just send in DNA samples at will from every Tom, Dick, and Harry who comes along. It's...unethical."

"Ah, come on, I'd do it for you. This is my family we're talking about, my only living relative. I have to know for certain before I make an ass out of myself. So what if he just happens to have the same birthday as Micah. So what if Micah's middle name is Andrew. What if it's all just a crazy coincidence? Then what?"

Eastlyn looked at the woman who'd become her friend. "You know it's not a coincidence."

Hannah grinned. "That's the point. I know Andy's my brother. I believe it with every fiber in my body."

"Fine. Okay. Give me the damn soda can."

Hannah threw her arms around Eastlyn's neck. "How long do you think it'll take?"

"I'll drive it to the lab myself and put a rush on it. Another rush, you know, like the one before, the one that took a week for the baby's DNA to get back. Does that tell you anything?"

"Yes, it tells me you're turning into my very best friend."

Twenty-Eight

While Hannah waited for the DNA, Caleb went on another kind of mission. He needed to know more about Delbert Delashaw and Craig Mooney. He started with a visit to the police station where he hoped to learn how Eleanor kept coming up with her own personal minions.

"Is there any way to put a stop to this? We've tried following all the regular protocol—from contacting the warden to taking out protection orders—nothing's worked."

Since arresting Mooney on Saturday, Brent had been expecting this conversation. "I don't know what to tell you. Prison officials won't keep Eleanor locked up in solitary for longer than a few weeks at a time. Then she's right back to actively seeking people who'll act as her warriors in the field."

"That's just it. After a few weeks of solitary confinement, she gets back to her cell and goes right back to making friends with anyone she can talk into committing these horrible acts. Nick and his family could've been killed. How does she meet these lowlife followers?"

"Through other prison inmates," Brent supplied. "This Mooney fellow has a sister, Tara Diablo, who's serving time on the same cell block for assaulting a neighbor. It's as simple as Tara giving Eleanor her brother's contact info and him striking up a friendship with her via letters. From that point, Mooney is just a drive away from his home in Nevada. Delbert Delashaw is another matter entirely because Eleanor met him back in Georgia. Those two go way back together. And I suspect she somehow gains access to the Internet to expand her social network, even though it's off limits."

"With all these followers, she probably has someone on the outside recruiting these people."

"Could be. Let's face it, there's no telling how many more Mooneys or Delashaws are out there waiting to strike. In case you were wondering, Mooney admitted that Eleanor sent him to the cabin to keep an eye on you guys."

"So while Delashaw was locked up, she had someone else out there to spy on us."

"Had it not been for the security system you guys installed, Mooney would've tried to get in the cabin."

"See, this is what I'm talking about. I bet this Mooney is the one who followed Cooper. It wasn't like Coop carried the gold inside his backpack."

"Yeah, but Mooney thought Cooper might lead him to a secret hiding place and leave the stash."

Caleb ran his hands through his hair. "Isn't there any way to cut off her communication with the outside world and stop her from using these people to stalk us? At this point, I'm ready to try anything."

"Brent personally got the guard fired that had taken a shine to her," Eastlyn let it be known. "Not sure how long it will take her to find a replacement stooge. If only we could find some way to put the fear of God into her so she'd stop this harassment. But whatever it is we come up with, we should do it before Hannah and I make the trip to Chowchilla. Make it the icing on the cake."

"We could just give her the damn gold with the caveat that she leaves us alone," Caleb suggested.

Eastlyn let out a whistle. "Cooper will *never* agree to that, not ever. And besides, Caleb, you can't give in to a blackmailer. Once you do, the demands never end. She'll just keep hounding you guys, upping the ante, again and again."

Brent sat back in his chair. "I agree with Eastlyn. Her type will always think of another way to scam."

Caleb let out a sigh. "Then it's hopeless."

"Did he actually say that?" Hannah asked Eastlyn on their way to Chowchilla, referring to Caleb's dire assessment.

"I'm afraid he and Cooper have given up trying to stop Eleanor. They know she's capable of sending in her mercenaries whenever she gets the urge. I must admit Caleb might be right when he says it's hopeless."

"Not necessarily," Hannah uttered as she looked over at Eastlyn sitting behind the wheel of her tan and red Bronco.

"If you have an idea, now's the time to give it a platform."

"Well, we both desperately want to ease Cooper and Caleb's stress level, right? They're so anxious about her that it's becoming a daily battle to keep their cool. So why not scare Eleanor into complying. Let's say we run a bluff on her, maybe make her believe we have the evidence we need against her to file charges in the death of her father. We use the threat to make her stop this campaign against her kids."

"That's not a bad idea, except for one small detail. I'm a sworn officer—"

"Officer of the court," Hannah finished. "Yeah, yeah, I get it. So you keep saying. Your ethics won't allow you to sit down in front of her and pretend you have evidence when you don't. Okay, well, it was just an idea."

"Damn good one, too," Eastlyn muttered as she made the turn to get on to the freeway. After merging into traffic, she lowered the volume on the radio so the two could talk. "I can't believe you're giving up that easily."

"What?"

"Don't you want to work on me during the trip, get me to see your side of that argument in a more positive light?"

"But you just said…" Hannah's shoulders dropped. "Let me get this straight, you want me to keep pitching the idea even though you're clearly against doing anything that would compromise your job as a police officer?"

"For the next three hours I'm a captive audience, aren't I? I'm not going anywhere. I've suddenly decided to listen with an open mind. How's that for considering our options?"

"Why?"

"Because I don't like seeing Cooper upset every time the phone rings. He looks at it like it's the device from hell. I don't like seeing him agonize over whether the next customer who comes into the train store is there because they were sent by Eleanor. It's a sad situation. So, if I have to bend the rules to ease his mind, then…so be it."

"Fine. I just thought that cops dupe a suspect every day somewhere in America to get them to confess. They make the suspect believe something that isn't real, right? Why not work the con on Eleanor? Who better to fake out than Eleanor? Especially after the hell she's put Cooper through."

"Now see, that's a superb argument and one I could clearly support."

"How did you get her to agree to talk to us in the first place?"

"I told her you were thinking about writing a book about her."

"You did what? You lied?" Hannah started laughing and couldn't stop. It went on for almost a full minute until her sides hurt. "Like that's any different than what I'm proposing? Jeez. What happened to ethics? Well, I did write a grant proposal once back in college."

Eastlyn snickered. "That's okay. I laid it on pretty thick. I asked her if she'd ever heard of the writer, Ethan Cody, from Pelican Pointe. I dangled the fact that Ethan's writing that book about the serial killer, Carl Knudsen, the one that's finally coming out this summer. Anyway, I made you sound like the next Ethan Cody, only *your* subject is the cunning femme fatale, Eleanor Jennings Richmond."

"Hmm. That's…sneaky….and quietly brilliant." Hannah lifted a shoulder. "I suppose whatever works, I'll play along. But I'm letting you do most of the talking. Between you and me, I'm nervous about this whole thing."

"So am I."

"You're kidding?"

"Nope."

"But at least you've met her once before."

"I wouldn't call it a meeting. I've seen her through a glass partition while Cooper—bless his heart—went toe to toe with her. Big difference."

"Is she…does she look…sinister?"

"She looks like she could be anyone's grandmother. Just keep in mind that by most accounts this woman has murdered three people without showing a smidgen of remorse. Cooper's right to think she's heartless."

"Caleb once said she had the maternal instincts of a tiger shark. At the time I thought he was exaggerating. Now I know better."

"Then why not stick it to her with a good dose of acting? Okay, I'll do it. I'll tell her we've uncovered new evidence that she killed her father."

Hannah went quiet, considering that approach. "No. No. That won't work. It won't be enough of a threat."

"Why the hell not?"

"Because she won't care about anyone knowing she murdered her father, not at this late date. She's already suspected of doing that anyway. It won't be enough to get her to leave Cooper and Caleb alone. We need something outlandish, something completely out of left field that we can really hold over her head. Maybe it should be a murder case that's totally off the wall."

Eastlyn snapped her fingers. "Like the baby's death at Bradford House."

"Maybe. But tricky. What happens when Brent finds the real killer? Might work until that happens but then we're right back to the harassment."

"Then I don't know what you're angling for," Eastlyn concluded.

"You said Delashaw was wanted for murder back in Georgia, right? That he killed some poor woman for her insurance money. What if we led Eleanor to believe that her would-be husband planned to testify against her and blame her for that murder?"

"I'm not following. What's the difference if we use her own father's murder and some stranger down in Georgia?"

Hannah held up her hand and ticked off the merits. "Georgia, not California. Active death penalty there, not here. Lethal injection. Eyewitness testimony in the form of Delashaw that claims she did the killing." Hannah took out her cell phone. "Delashaw hasn't been moved to the county jail yet, has he?"

"Nope. Still sitting there right next to Mooney."

"Okay then. We get Brent to grill Delashaw. We need more details out of the guy, more firepower to put the fear of God into Eleanor and sound believable. Getting extradited back to Georgia where she could sit on death row makes Chowchilla look like a three-star hotel."

"Nice. I like the way your mind works. I'll throw it out there and gauge her reaction. It'll be fun watching a psychopath squirm at the prospect of lethal injection."

When Eastlyn pulled up to the parking lot for the California Correctional Facility it was almost eleven o'clock.

"We have to catch the shuttle that takes us to another building. Let's practice our spiel."

After clearing security, a pat down for Hannah, and for Eastlyn a guard with a handheld wand, surveillance cameras followed them down a hallway to the visiting room. Here, they waited for the inmate to make her grand appearance.

Eleanor walked through a door at the rear of the room in handcuffs and leg chains. She wore a light blue two-piece outfit that consisted of a top with a white T-shirt underneath and matching pants with elastic at the waist. The guard removed the cuffs but left the restraints around her ankles.

When she picked up the phone on the wall, Eastlyn noted the difference in Eleanor's appearance from the last time. For one, the mass of long hair had been reduced to a short, almost manly cut. Her face looked older, leaner, and tougher.

Without introduction, Eleanor went on the offensive. She took one look at Hannah sitting next to Eastlyn and stared a hole through the glass. "Who's the redhead?"

"She's the writer I told you about. Hannah Summers."

"Uh-huh. So my daughter-in-law's brought another whore to the party? Great."

"Always a pleasure talking to you, Eleanor," Eastlyn said, her voice dripping with sarcasm. "I can see why your kids are so very fond of you. What happened to the debutante who once thought herself too classy for Pelican Pointe?"

Eleanor didn't bother to answer the question. Instead, like any predator, she seemed to size up the weaker of the two women. "Shouldn't *Hannah Summers* be the one asking me the questions instead of my son's cop wife?"

"No problem. I'll have to take a shower when I leave here anyway," Eastlyn said as she handed the phone off to Hannah.

Hannah sucked in a deep breath, determined to play her part like a pro.

"Are you really writing a book about me?"

"Oh, yes ma'am," Hannah replied in a polite drawl. "You fascinate me. Women serial killers are rare. Finding one like you is even rarer still."

Eleanor let out a smoker's raspy cough that hung like a laugh on the air. "You got the wrong idea about me, honey. I didn't kill anybody."

"Really? Then I guess there won't be a book. If there's nothing to write about I made the trip for nothing. Come on, Eastlyn, we're wasting our time here." Hannah completed the bluff by getting to her feet.

Eleanor sat there so long glaring back without saying anything, that Hannah thought for sure she'd blown the first phase.

While the women sized each other up, Hannah could tell there was a war going on inside Eleanor. The killer seemed conflicted. On one hand, the demure grandmother-type wanted to proclaim her innocence. That side was at odds with the serial killer who wanted full-blown coverage of her deeds. Attention from a book would more than let the world know what a clever woman could do with a little creativity and a devious mindset.

"Oh, sit down," Eleanor finally huffed out. "What is it you want to know for this book you intend to write?"

"We're all curious why you left your kids and disappeared that night without taking the gold with you. Delbert Delashaw was quite adamant that you wanted him to find it. After so many years, you figured he had to eliminate the cabin as a potential hiding place. There was only one reason he was there, and that was to retrieve the gold. What baffles everyone is why you didn't take the gold with you that night? I guess you didn't have time to go to the cabin before you took off."

Hannah watched as the narcissist finally sprang to life. "If you're going to tell a story, dear, you should get it right. Of course I went to the cabin that night to retrieve *my* gold. My gold," she emphasized. "I wasn't about to leave it inside that horrid, filthy hut."

"How'd you get there? Who in town helped you?"

"Ah. That's new. No one's wanted to know that from me before. Maybe you're not so dumb, after all. I had friends back then, good ones, people who liked me. It always pays to keep friends in high places. Remember that. Douglas Bradford, you know Douglas, the mayor. Dougie boy and I were quite close back then. He's the one who drove me up to the cabin. I was so tired I wanted to fall into bed, but Dougie said no, that I should get the gold and keep moving. So, I went into the kitchen, where I'd kept it since I was seventeen and I slid back the panel underneath the bottom cabinet, just where I'd left it, like I'd done so many times before, and found the cubby empty. The bag was gone. I went into a rage until Doug got me to calm down. I wanted to go back to town right then, and confront Landon. Of course it was my idiot brother who discovered my stash and stole it out from under me. I was rattled that night and wasn't thinking straight so I had to rely on Douglas to tell me what I should do."

Eleanor sniffed and ran her fingers through her short mane. "Never trust a man, honey. Not ever."

Hannah knew the story didn't quite jive with what Landon had already told them. But she needed to know how far Eleanor would go with the lie. "What did Douglas tell you to do?"

"'Forget about the gold for now,' he said. Focus on getting out of town. He'd keep looking for it and take care of sending it to me whenever he found where Landon had hidden it. What a fool I was back then."

"I take it Douglas didn't keep his word?"

"A politician who keeps his word? Doesn't exist. But that was my stupid and naïve stage. Never again."

"But if you believed Landon took the money then why send Delashaw to the cabin to retrieve it?"

Caught in a lie, for a second time, Hannah watched Eleanor's face transform into someone else. And then it hit her. "Ah. You didn't really believe the gold was in the cabin after so long a time and that many years had gone by, did you? You just wanted to shake up the family, send Delashaw to do a little recon and stir things up with everyone—Landon, Cooper, Caleb, and Drea. If Delashaw burned down the cabin, so what? You didn't care. You hated the mountains anyway. And it was a subtle reminder, something that would surely be construed as payback and a way to mess with everyone."

"Aren't you the clever girl?" Eleanor said, gripping the phone tighter until her knuckles turned white. "As you might've guessed by now I turned that cabin upside down looking for the gold back when it disappeared. I truly believe that rat bastard Douglas was in cahoots with Landon. After all, Dougie stopped answering my phone calls and my letters shortly after I left town. He wanted no part of me and apparently didn't have a problem moving on to the next little whore that came along."

"My guess is you divided the gold at some point. Long before you ever decided to murder Layne and leave town. There were two bags back then. The night you murdered Layne and Brooke, Douglas drove you to the location where you'd stashed the portion you'd kept for yourself. It had to be somewhere close by, somewhere that only you knew of its whereabouts."

Eleanor batted her eyes. "I do have my wits about me in a crisis."

"If you swooped in and took one bag with you to Georgia, what happened to the other?" Hannah asked, innocently.

Eleanor's smile was like a Cheshire cat's. "Oh now, let's not be condescending. Craig told me it's safely tucked into The First Bank of Pelican Pointe right where Caleb and Cooper left it. I know Craig failed to get the gold out of there. I'm not without my sources. I do get my updates on a regular basis."

"Don't you think your kids should have the remaining gold after everything you've put them through?"

"That would work out perfectly for a little gold digger like you, wouldn't it? Like I don't know that if my kids get their hands on it, they'll be spending money that rightly belongs to me."

"How do you figure it belongs to you?" Hannah fired back.

"I'm the one who worked for it. I'm the one who figured out a way to keep it before my father spent every dime of it on that stupid ranch. Giving it to my so-called offspring is not an option. Not happening, my dear." Her hands flitted in the air. "As you can plainly see, I'm paying my debt to the state of California. But that money's mine. I could use it for things I need in the commissary. No one in my family sends money to take care of *me*. I rely on the kindness of strangers. So, make no mistake, one way or the other, I'll get my hands on it…eventually. Be sure to pass *that* message along to my little darlings back in Pelican Pointe."

Eastlyn had heard enough. She snatched the phone out of Hannah's hands. "I don't think so, Eleanor. You're gonna stop all the threats. Here. Now. Today. You're gonna stop coming after the money and leave your kids alone."

"Like hell I will," Eleanor declared.

"Fine. We figured you'd say that. Then here's the way this is gonna go down. We have Delbert Delashaw, your longtime boyfriend from Columbus, Georgia, in custody. Delbert is wanted for murdering an elderly woman, Orinda Salazar, for her insurance. Does the name do anything for you, Eleanor? It should. You collected half a million dollars in an insurance scam. We happen to know that's part of what you used to live on during your life in Columbus. There are records back in Georgia showing as much."

Eastlyn put her face closer to the glass. "But here's the thing, Eleanor. Delbert's ratted you out. He's turned on his wife-to-be and decided to cop a plea in exchange for giving them you. For the past several hours he's been calmly explaining how you're the one who executed the old lady and controlled all the money. You're facing the death penalty in Georgia, Eleanor. Delbert's already talking to the state investigators. And they like what they're hearing."

"Damn you to hell! Damn all of you to hell!" Eleanor pounded the counter with her rolled up fists. "What the hell do you want from me? I've given you people everything there is to give!"

The guard came over to take Eleanor's arm and cut the interview short. "If you can't control yourself, then I'll take you back to your cell."

Hannah sent a pleading look toward the guard and took the phone back from Eastlyn. "It's very simple. We want you to stop contacting your children. Forget about the gold. Let your kids have the money. You go to Georgia where death row is a lot more active than it is in California and you're looking at vastly different accommodations there versus here. You'll be facing lethal injection, Eleanor. They'll put your mug and profile on their website for the world to see. No more getting outside for an hour. No more opportunities to get cozy with the guards. No more warm and fuzzy phone calls to your adoring men friends. Death row is different from the regular prison population."

Eleanor's eyes became dead pools of gray. "You wouldn't dare. No one crosses me."

"It's already in the works, Eleanor. Unless you stop harassing your kids. That's the only way you stay in California. Orinda Salazar is coming back to haunt you, every single time you send another asshole to Pelican Pointe. If I see one stranger trying to get in Caleb's face, or Cooper's, or Drea's, I'm personally seeing to it that your ass is carted off to Georgia right alongside Delbert's. Are we clear?"

"No one tells me what to do."

"Okay then," Hannah said calmly. "Interview over. But if I were you I'd start learning the lyrics to *Georgia On My Mind* real fast, because the clock's ticking and they're coming for you very soon."

"You were great back there," Eastlyn said once they reached the shuttle bus.

"Let's just hope Caleb thinks so." Hannah held up her phone. "He sent me fifteen messages in the last hour. He's anxious to hear what happened. Aw, he wants to know if I'm all right."

"What'd you tell him?"

"Nothing yet. But I'm going to suggest we enjoy our evening to the max." Hannah keyed in her thoughts to Caleb.

Let's grab something to eat and sit on your back deck. We'll watch the sun go down from there.

Sounds good to me. So, you're okay?

Never better. What'd you do while I was gone?

Worried. Mostly. But I started a new project.

Really? I can top that. I spent the afternoon ending one.

Three and a half hours later Eastlyn dropped Hannah off at Caleb's house. When she stepped inside the front door Molly greeted her while Caleb simply slipped his arms around her waist and gave her a kiss on the ear. "I made tacos, hope that's okay."

"Anything. I'm starving. How was Molly?"

"I took her for a walk through the meadow behind the house. Come on, let's eat before the food gets cold. What did you think of Eleanor?"

Hannah smiled. "You're nothing like her. Don't ever think you are. There's something missing inside her, some part of her heart that doesn't work like the rest of us."

"The sociopath who has no empathy," Caleb concluded.

They watched the sun go down over the rolling field of clover behind the house, nibbling on the tacos he'd made and drinking bottled beer.

"You want to talk about what happened?"

She shook her head. "Maybe later. Eleanor will either leave you alone or she won't. But I can go to sleep tonight knowing I did my best. Talking about it more than that might ruin this moment. And I don't want to do that."

Caleb didn't either. It was at that point he realized he had everything he needed—a loving woman who possessed an abundance of empathy, a clever and brave dog, and a place like this to eat tacos and watch the sunset from his back deck.

He didn't need anything else.

Twenty-Nine

While Eastlyn and Hannah finished squaring off with Eleanor in one prison, Brent started his day signing in at another. At the Correctional Facility known as Soledad, Brent was there to see Flynn McCready. He'd run out of leads to pursue in the Bradford House murder and not much to lose by sitting down listening to a story or two out of the former bar owner.

Flynn had been a longtime resident in Pelican Pointe and knew a lot of its history and its secrets. If not for his participation in the distribution of meth, Flynn would still be an institution there.

Now, he was inmate number 704597621 and still so new to the system that he wore an ugly, garish orange two-piece uniform, baggy in size, and ugly in everything else.

When Brent plopped down on the other side of a glass partition, Flynn looked much older than his years. Brent still had trouble believing the business owner he'd known for such a long time could've been stupid enough to get involved with something as serious as meth. What Flynn's involvement taught him was a valuable lesson. Everyone could have a darker side. Flynn's seemed to have originated with greed.

"How're they treating you?" Brent began.

"If you're here to talk to me about that bullshit Eleanor keeps shoveling about how I killed Layne and Brooke, you can just kiss my ass."

"Still denying that, are you?"

"Damn straight because it never happened. Eleanor Jennings is a lying piece of shit trying to get out of jail on a lie. She's guilty as hell. She's right where she needs to be."

"Then I guess you'll be glad to hear that's not why I made the trip."

"Then why?"

"I've got a dead baby, buried on Bradford House grounds. It's beginning to look like Douglas Bradford's past reappeared in a big way."

"Why ask me?"

"Because there are a lot of people in town that still remember you and Douglas used to be drinking buddies. You were his wingman or so the stories go. Plus, if I find out that you had anything to do with that baby's death, you're looking at a whole new ballgame. You'll be in here until they carry you out in a box."

"Now, you just wait a minute. Don't come in here accusing me of every fucking thing that ever went wrong in Pelican Pointe. That's not fair. I'm no killer, for God's sake. You know that. You know me, Brent."

"I thought I did...once. What do you know about the baby, Flynn?"

"I know if I tell you it ought to be enough to get me out of here and into a better place."

"Okay. You start talking, tell me a story, and I'll listen."

Flynn eyed the guard and then leaned closer to the partition. "It was a long time ago back when Doug still lived that swinging lifestyle he loved so much. But it came with a hefty price. He got mixed up with this crazy chick named Felicia Atherton, tall, model-thin, gorgeous redheaded goddess she was. They dated for about six months. All that time Felicia was all about becoming first lady of Pelican Pointe, if you know what I mean. She was after marriage, pestering Doug every other day to head to Vegas for one of those funky, quirky weddings. That's all she ever talked about. Felicia threw out a lot of bait, but Doug just wouldn't bite. Somewhere in all this, she got pregnant. At first, Doug didn't believe her, didn't even think it was his. Dumb bastard. But when she started showing fairly quick that proved him wrong. A few months went by and she goes into labor. Doug runs her over to Santa Cruz to the hospital there where she delivers the baby, a little girl. They come back to Bradford House and I think all is well with the two of them. I figure any day now Doug's gonna take that leap into marriage. Never happened. Before two months go by, the baby's gone. No more baby. Doug claims he thinks Felicia did something to it while he was out of town on one of his trips to San Francisco."

"That's convenient."

"Yeah. That crossed my mind. But since Doug was always the luckiest son of a bitch I ever knew, I thought…well maybe. Whatever happened, it happened quick, because the baby was gone. One night, Doug comes into the bar and gets drunker than I've ever seen him. Finishes off a bottle of vodka and starts on another. He tells me this story about how he helped bury the baby in the yard because he didn't want anyone to know Felicia had killed it, didn't want his constituents to know he'd been a part of it."

"You should probably know at this point, I have a reliable witness to that event. So be sure your facts line up with what I already know."

Flynn's eyes got big. "I'm telling you everything Doug told me. But there's more. Felicia isn't done with Doug quite yet. One day out of the blue, she shows up with another kid, this one a little older and a baby boy. I guess she figured with another baby in the picture, Doug would give in and marry her. But by this time, Doug realized Felicia was off her rocker. I mean, bat-shit, crack-whore crazy. He decides to end this thing once and for all. He takes the baby to a couple he knows in town who's been trying to adopt. It's Carla and James DeMarco's lucky day. You remember the DeMarcos, right? That Italian couple over on Cape May. Anyway, there's no doubt Carla and James are overjoyed, just ecstatic, at the idea they're finally about to become parents. After that, they think Doug hung the moon because he says a few words over the baby and pronounces it adopted, done deal. Since Felicia kept calling the baby Andy, and had already made up a birth date, Doug stuck with that on the phony paperwork. Because after all, Doug didn't have a clue where the kid came from or a single piece of paper to show that it was even adoptable. To this day, I have no idea where Felicia got a baby that fast and neither did Doug. But it didn't matter much to him where the baby came from as long as he could get the little guy out the door. He'd made the DeMarcos happy. The kid was no longer his responsibility. All ends well, right?"

"What happened to Felicia?"

"Doug sent her off to a mental hospital outside Visalia. Woman stayed there for damn near three years before she finally got out. Last I checked, she lived in a trailer park back in Turlock."

"Turlock? Why Turlock?"

"I guess that's where her people were from. I don't know. Now is that enough to get me out of here and transferred to the Men's Colony down in San Luis Obispo?"

"Depends."

"On what?"

"If what you told me just now checks out. If it does, I'll be in touch. Thanks, Flynn. I'll be talking to you soon."

After Brent's visit with Flynn, a lot happened quickly over the next few days with the case. He spent a several days in Turlock, cooperating with the sheriff's department there, helping them track down Felicia Atherton. They let him stay to watch the Atherton woman's interview that ended up lasting more than five hours.

After the third day, Brent checked out of the motel, glad to be heading back home. He drove back with the knowledge that when he arrived in Pelican Pointe, he'd have an update that would satisfy everyone.

Brent decided to get all the parties involved in one place. He picked Bradford House because it served several purposes. One, he wouldn't have to repeat the story more than once if everyone heard it at the same time. And two, he could provide a visual because it was important to show how the story had developed over time.

He was certain he'd covered all his bases by the time a steady stream of people gathered in the main living room. He stood near the huge picture window, looking out over the piles of dirt dug up across the front yard.

He looked out at Hannah and Eastlyn. "The guards tell me that since your visit Eleanor has gone nuts. She's gotten in several fights and lost all her privileges. She's back in solitary confinement."

Hannah let out a sigh. "You know what they say happens when a psychopath loses control. They say the results are never pretty."

Caleb squeezed her hand. "Brilliantly played, because, above all else, narcissists love themselves. They fear death. Look at what Bundy did in Florida once he was convicted. He fought against getting the chair. He'd killed at least thirty-five women, and yet, didn't want to die himself. Add to that, Eleanor, like Bundy, doesn't want to lose the attention, attention is what she thrives on, making people's lives messy and full of chaos."

Cooper shifted in his chair and looked at Eastlyn. "Brent says all that stuff you guys said to Eleanor might actually come true. Delbert really has decided to testify against her to save his own ass."

Brent shifted his feet. "Let's not get carried away there. I don't think for a minute that will happen. For one, Georgia knows Eleanor's locked up here for life. I don't think the state's attorney back in Georgia will spend a dime on extraditing Eleanor there. They'll budget the money to go toward locking Delbert up for Orinda Salazar's murder. Cost considerations aside, that's the way the system works, whether we like it or not. But the bluff was a good idea and effective. Holding that over her head might be the only thing that keeps her off your radar...at least for a while."

Since everyone had arrived and settled in, Brent decided he might as well build up to why they were here. "The lab confirmed that Eleanor did hold on to the murder weapon. It's the same gun used to kill Orinda Salazar. And just for peace of mind, I talked to Flynn McCready again about Eleanor's accusation that he was the one who killed Layne and Brooke."

Cooper gripped Eastlyn's hand in his. "And?"

"For the second time, Flynn not only denied it was true, but he confirmed that Douglas and Eleanor had been carrying on an affair for years."

Caleb flinched at the thought. "So that's one thing she came clean about. I'm beginning to wonder if there's a man left alive in Pelican Pointe who didn't sleep with her."

Hannah poked him in the ribs. "At least you're getting more of the story, which is what you wanted." She studied the chief's face. "Is that why you asked us here?"

Brent smiled widely. "I figured while we have everyone under one roof, I'd go over how Micah Lambert became Andy DeMarco."

Hannah sat up straighter in her chair. "You know how he was kidnapped? Should we go get Andy? Is it for real?"

"I wouldn't include Andy just now. At least not yet. I thought it best to go over what I learned step by step. Before we drag Andy into this mess, I need everyone to understand how this all went down. We managed to solve a twenty-year-old double murder, Hannah's parents. That alone is extraordinary. But when you include the murder of a baby, that's exceptional. That doesn't happen every day. I feel good about the way we accomplished this and so should all of you. As it turns out, the guy who held most of the answers to this was Flynn McCready. All the rumors in town kept pointing me to the man who knew Bradford better than anyone else did."

Quentin spoke up. "I take it that wasn't Jack Prescott."

"Not even close. I'm not sure anyone knew the dark side to Bradford except for the handful of old-timers in town who knew what he was up to. Douglas liked to party and he was involved with a lot of women."

"And to think my mother died thinking her brother was gay," Quentin said, shaking his head. "Not to mention Jack professing allegiance to the man he thought he knew."

"We'll see about that," Brent began. "More like the secret was his addiction to a swinging lifestyle. Flynn shortened the investigative process considerably. He held the key to how Douglas hooked up with a woman named Felicia Atherton. That relationship started everything spiraling downward."

"Wait a minute," Hannah said. "You said Atherton? You're sure that's the name of the woman? Maybe this Flynn got it wrong."

"Nope," Brent said. "Felicia Atherton is her name."

Hannah exchanged looks with Caleb. "It can't be a coincidence that my mother's maiden name was Atherton. Laura Atherton Lambert."

Kinsey looked over at Quentin. "That explains the odd line in Mr. Bradford's will. He mentioned Felicia Atherton by name. He specifically spelled it out that she was not to get a dime from his estate. His exact words were 'absolutely nothing' even if she fights to get it. While we were working on the wording, Mr. Bradford became very emotional during that part. Otherwise, it was a straightforward document, simple even. After probate, I paid the final expenses, paid for his funeral and burial, and got in touch with his one surviving relative. I waited for this Atherton woman to show up to contest that part of the will. But she never did. Instead, Quentin came to town and I did all the paperwork to turn that old canning factory over to Quentin. And I've never given another thought to the name until right this minute."

Quentin fidgeted in his chair. "To be honest, it bugged me that he didn't leave the house to me."

Kinsey leaned back in her chair, at ease with a theory. "After doing some rethinking about that day, something occurred to me. I don't think Mr. Bradford wanted to burden you with the house. Thinking back to the day we drew up the will, I don't think Mr. Bradford wanted you near the house because of what was buried in the yard. Hindsight, as they say. If he left it to you, you might want to renovate it, which is exactly what you did. Revamp the ugly yard. Digging up that yard is what revealed his ugly past. The only reason Logan snapped it up at all was because he thought the location would make a great place for a library. If you hadn't come along, who knows how long it would've sat there without anyone unearthing those bones."

No longer able to sit still, Hannah stood up and started to pace back and forth. "I've been working on locating Micah for years. And I've researched the family tree on both sides of my family in detail. I don't remember a Felicia among them. Maybe she isn't a relative at all."

Brent slipped his hands in his pockets. "I wish it were that simple. I do. But Felicia changed her name when she left home to strike out for Hollywood, hoping for a modeling career." He took out a photograph from his file folder and handed it off to Hannah. "This is what Felicia looked like back then. The police report that day mentions her description as the social worker who took custody of Micah, claiming she was headed to the hospital. You can see the resemblance."

Hannah stared at the picture. "She looks like my mother."

Caleb peered over her shoulder. "You look a lot like her, same hair coloring, same eyes."

"Let's hope I don't have her whacked out mentality."

Brent held up his file folder. "There's more, a lot more in here. I stayed up until three this morning writing a report, trying to hit every detail. Felicia's birth name was Aurora Frances Atherton, your mother's older sister by five years."

Caleb's eyes settled on Brent. "So, Hannah's own aunt, this Felicia, killed her sister and brother-in-law for the sole purpose of getting a baby?"

"Aurora had problems early on, as early as sixteen. She wanted out of Turlock. She didn't much like her name so she changed it once she got to Los Angeles. There are a few neighbors left on the street where Laura and Aurora grew up. I talked to them and they all said the same thing. Aurora was always jealous of her little sister, jealous of Laura's marriage, the fact she had children, and what Aurora deemed was a stable relationship."

"But…I still…don't understand why my aunt would do such a thing," Hannah bemoaned. "Why did she have to kill them? What could she possibly have wanted with Micah?"

Brent repeated Flynn's account of what happened between Douglas and Felicia. "I'm afraid everything Flynn said checked out. Stanislaus County sheriff's deputies got a full confession from Felicia. Using Flynn's backstory, it all came together. It seems your mother's sister had done all she could to trap Douglas into marriage. She thought it was her one shot at the big time, marrying the mayor."

Brent lifted a shoulder. "I'm not sure how Felicia came by that notion, but she did spend quite a while on the ploy, almost a year. That included getting pregnant. The only deviation in what Flynn told me was about how the baby died. Felicia claimed to investigators not three days ago that once she brought the child home from the hospital there was something wrong with it and it stopped breathing on its own."

"And what did Flynn say happened?"

"That Douglas thought she deliberately did something to the baby once it came home from the hospital. The autopsy backs that statement up."

"Did Felicia ever refer to the baby as anything other than *it*," Hannah asked. "Because you've used that several times. The repeated use of the word shows a callous disconnect."

"I think that's an accurate assessment. Even after all these years Felicia appeared to show no special grief that she'd lost her little girl so soon after giving birth, at least outwardly. Hannah Justine was the name listed on the birth certificate."

Hannah's hand flew to her mouth. "She named the baby after me? Why on earth would she do that?"

"According to the psychologist I spoke with, it showed Felicia's mindset at the time. She had to be thinking about her sister and her sister's family even as she picked out a name. Once the child died, it seems Felicia and Douglas buried the baby in the front yard for no other purpose than to get rid of it. Discreetly, making sure it disappeared without anyone suspecting the child had ever existed. My cop radar goes on alert anytime someone gets rid of a child without a proper burial."

"Didn't anyone miss the baby? What about all those old-timers around here?" Caleb asked. "Someone had to know Felicia had been pregnant. Flynn knew."

"Those are all excellent points," Brent said. "My gut tells me Flynn wasn't the only one in town who knew about the baby's birth. If they didn't report the child missing that's on them and they'll have to live with that for the rest of their days."

"Do you think Felicia did it alone?" Hannah wanted to know.

"They both had a hand in the death. I'm convinced of that. Coroner confirmed there were several broken bones to the arms, a fracture to the skull. That indicates abuse right from the start. The death meant Douglas could get rid of Felicia, get his carefree lifestyle back."

"Oh, my God," Hannah stated, beginning to fully understand.

"Unfortunately for Hannah and her family, Felicia had other ideas. She decided she needed a substitute for Justine and she needed it quick. The only baby she knew anything about was her nephew, Micah. That day, she knew exactly where to find him. She got in the car, drove to Turlock and demanded your mother hand over Micah. Your mother resisted, of course. But Felicia wasn't there to take no for an answer. She took out a gun, the 9-millimeter registered to Douglas, and shot your parents with it. The neighbors called the cops before she could get Micah out of his crib and…"

Hannah couldn't believe what she was hearing. "It's just like you said. Felicia ran out of the house without Micah when the first cruiser pulled up. But she came back for him by pretending to be the social worker and the police just handed him over."

"I'm sorry," Brent said. "But during her interrogation, Felicia readily admitted to all of it. She led the detectives through how she killed your mother and father, shot them point blank, and then devised the plan to come back for Micah. She did all of it because she believed the only way Douglas would ever marry her was if she had a child. The psychologist was certain she'd probably suffered from some type of psychosis after giving birth that made her act so irrationally and so violently."

Quentin wasn't buying it. "Let's not bandy that word around like it excuses this woman for quite a bit of preparation and planning. I doubt psychosis played a part in the ploy to get pregnant in the first place."

"For what it's worth, I agree with you," Brent stated.

"But Douglas and Felicia don't even keep Micah," Hannah pointed out. "It's all for nothing. My parents died for nothing."

"I'm sorry," Brent repeated. "When Felicia showed up with another baby, that was the last straw for Douglas. He sent her packing. In truth, to a mental health facility in the Central Valley. Fortunately for him, he knew of a couple who'd been trying to have a baby or adopt without success right here at home."

Hannah let out a sigh. "The DeMarcos."

"You got it. They took Micah in after Douglas made a show of 'performing' an official adoption."

"That was a nice trick and totally illegal," Hannah grumbled, glancing at Quentin. She folded her arms across her chest. "I don't think I like your uncle very much."

"I'm beginning to feel the same way. Please tell me this Felicia is sitting in jail right about now?"

Brent stuffed his hands in his pockets. "I was standing there when they slapped the cuffs on her and loaded her up in the van."

"Will the authorities at least change the murder/suicide angle and let my dad off the hook now?" Hannah asked.

"Absolutely," Brent promised. "Felicia wouldn't be in jail if they hadn't done that already."

"No one contacted me. I guess the victims' family is the last one to know anything. Well, I don't know what to do," Hannah admitted, throwing her arms out wide. "How do I tell Andy about this whole mess, about his real family? How much they loved and cared for him? I just listened to this insane explanation of why it all happened and I'm still not sure I understand why. If I don't understand it, how will he feel about all of it?"

"We have to help you," Sydney offered. "That's the only solution. We have to bring Andy along slowly and plant the idea—"

"I disagree about the slow part," Caleb stated. "I say, rip off the Band-Aid and just be honest with him. He's a man, not a kid. You're underestimating the guy. For two years, he's taken care of his little sister like a parent, done what had to be done to see she didn't get carted off to foster care. He deserves to know the truth. If he finds out that practically the entire town was in on deceiving him, he won't be happy about it."

"I agree with Caleb," Cooper said. "And not just because he's my brother but because he's making sense. Honesty should be expected out of family members. Tip-toeing around the truth won't change what happened."

Even Quentin weighed in. "After getting to know Andy, he's not a kid. This man carries around the responsibility of taking care of his kid sister unlike anyone I've ever seen. You're doing him an injustice if you don't level with him about how he came to be Andy."

"Okay, then. It's settled. We go with the truth. Now, the question is, who goes through with the lengthy explanation?"

Thirty

Of course, the likely candidate had to be Hannah. The dirty job fell to her because that's what big sisters did—they took care of little brothers even if the chore proved difficult. The only problem that she could see with that idea was the fact Andy wasn't used to having an older sibling. He *was* the older sibling, had been all his life as a DeMarco. Where Faye was concerned, Andy had become the consummate big brother, protector, champion.

But that didn't mean Hannah could shirk what she now viewed as her obligation.

Hannah dragged her feet about approaching Andy until the DNA came back. But the Friday afternoon Eastlyn showed up at her front door with the piece of paper showing proof, there was no more stalling.

"Did you ask him to dog sit Molly like you planned?"

Hannah cut her eyes to the dog. "Yep. I feel guilty using an innocent animal as a ruse, but it set the whole thing in motion. He's due here in a couple of minutes. I feel like chewing off my nails."

"Don't. It's a bad habit and one that's hard to break. Ask me. I know. Stop pacing," Eastlyn decreed when she saw Hannah nervously walking back and forth into the kitchen.

"Maybe I should've done this at Caleb's place. I wish he'd get here. I texted him a couple of times to remind him that Andy's due any minute. Caleb was supposed to be here with me when I made the big reveal. I'll have to tell Andy I don't really need dog sitting services today. That it was just an excuse to get him here."

She blew out a nervous breath. "Who am I kidding? I can't do this. Maybe I'll just send him an email and explain the whole sordid mess."

"Buck up, soldier," Eastlyn ordered as she saw a shadow outside cross in front of the window. "Here he comes. Oh. Sorry, looks like it's only Caleb."

"Gee, thanks. I like you, too," Caleb said as he strode in carrying a six-pack of beer and a bottle of whiskey. "I wasn't sure what kind of liquid courage you preferred. Beer's always good for a nice sociable chat while the bourbon might dull the sensory overload."

He took one look at a nervous Hannah and yanked her to his chest, pressing his lips to hers in a long, much-needed kiss. "There. Better?"

"Yes. No. I don't know anymore."

"I'm outta here," Eastlyn stated.

"No. Stay. Please," Hannah pleaded.

"Sorry, you're on your own. I'll be…outside…sitting in my car with the report Brent wrote up if you should need backup, though. That's the best I can do."

As Eastlyn sailed out the front door, Andy appeared in the doorway.

"What's going on?" Andy asked. "Ryder told me I should knock off work early and come over to your house, said you had a dog sitting emergency. I don't even know what that means."

"Me either," Hannah said with a grin.

"Quentin and Sydney even offered to watch Faye for the rest of the evening. So why am I here?"

Hannah took a deep breath and held it for a long second and then let it out. She steadied herself and reached for Caleb's hand for support. "We need…I need to talk to you about…why I'm here in town…why I moved here four months ago."

"Are you getting ready to take Faye away from me or something? Does this have anything to do with that social worker? Because I have a lawyer on speed dial now."

His fierce determination and loyalty to Faye made Hannah smile. "No. No. It's nothing like that. Faye's fine. Call her if you want, if it'll make you feel better."

"Then I don't understand why I'm standing in your living room. I saw you at Quentin's place the other day, but I don't really know you. Other than Faye mentioning you might need someone to watch your dog." Andy studied Hannah's grip on Caleb's hand and then he looked over at Molly. The dog seemed to understand there was a problem and came over to lick the fingers on his hand. "But this isn't about the dog, is it?"

"No. It's about you and me. It's about the fact that I'm really your sister. Hannah Lambert from Turlock. We were born there to a couple named Robert and Laura Lambert."

Once she got started, the words came pouring out like water overflowing a dam, rushing out so fast like a flash flood shooting down a dry canyon. Nothing could stop the momentum.

Andy's face began to take on an understanding. "So that's the reason Ryder asked me all those questions on Saturday?"

"Yes. Sorry. I needed to know if you had any inkling you were adopted."

"Some. A few hints over the years. There were a lot of hushed conversations whenever I'd come into the room. I just thought it was…you know…adults acting secretive, keeping things from the kids. Now and then, though, there'd be something that came up with my birth certificate and the issue always made things stressful between my parents. They'd argue for a while and then run around like crazy to solve the problem. But the strangest thing I guess was the fact that my mother never went into a detailed account about the day I was born. She'd describe the day Faye came into the world, point by point, what her labor was like, how long it lasted, how much Faye weighed, that sort of thing. But with me, not a word. She didn't even try to make up a story. I found that odd." He lifted a shoulder. "You know, little things like that, things that never seemed to add up like they did with Faye. I just assumed Faye was their favorite."

Hannah went over and picked up a frame that held a picture of their parents. "Here's a photograph of our mom and dad the day they were married. Look close. You have the same eyes, the same nose, the same chin as our father."

Andy studied the image from so long ago. The color had started to fade. But the resemblance was unmistakable. It was like looking at himself in a mirror. He plopped down onto the little love seat.

Before he could dispute the photograph, Hannah shoved another one into his hands. This one was of her at six, sitting on Santa's lap holding a baby wearing a red stocking cap. "This is you and me, kid, taken at Christmastime at the mall."

Andy glanced back and forth from one photo to the other. "I see the similarities. It's amazing. You're actually, for real, no joke, my sister?"

"No joke," Hannah stated as she handed him the piece of paper Eastlyn had brought. "This is from the lab. It's a DNA analysis. I put mine in the system a long time ago, hoping this day would eventually get here. Yours came from a soda can Ryder pilfered out of the trash after you left work the other day. We're brother and sister, and science agrees."

"You've been looking for me?"

"Oh, honey, I've been looking for you so long I can't believe we're here in the same room talking to each other like this, having this conversation. I want so much to hug you. But I don't want you to freak out."

"Do I get to meet my parents? Have they been looking for me, too?"

Hannah bit her lip to keep from crying and shook her head. "I'm afraid that's another story in itself. The day they died, the person that… There's no easy way to say this. You were abducted, stolen by a crazy woman who wanted a baby. Not Carla DeMarco, not the lady who raised you but another woman, our aunt. They say now she was mentally unstable. I don't know about that. Brent says she's sitting in jail right now charged with killing our parents. They just arrested her the other day. Like I said, it's a long story. Brent's a phone call away if you need corroboration that I'm not making this stuff up. And Eastlyn's willing to provide you with several documents that say the same thing. I wouldn't blame you if you don't believe a word I'm saying."

"Wow. But your name is Summers, not Lambert?"

"I was adopted by a great couple named Summers when I was nine. I lived in the foster care system for three years before I went to live with them."

"Wow," Andy repeated. "My real name's Micah Andrew Lambert?"

"Andy. I'm fine with calling you Andy. You don't have to be Micah unless you want to be."

"It's just that…I don't know. All this…"

"I didn't want to overwhelm you. I had ideas about approaching this situation slowly, building up to it. But several others, Caleb, Cooper, and Quentin, to name a few, figured that you'd prefer knowing now, right away, rather than making a case over time. They thought it would be much less deceptive this way. They were convinced that you could handle the truth up front, rather than trying to convince you over several months that I'd make a fantastic big sister."

Andy grinned. "You've already proved that because you never stopped looking for me."

"I would've searched for you until they had to roll me around in a wheelchair. Ask Caleb. Ask anybody."

"I believe you. Tell me something about my parents."

Hannah breathed a sigh of relief and sat down next to him on the sofa. "Mom used to bundle you up and take you to Donnelly Park where we'd feed the ducks. You were too young, of course, but I'd go down to the pond and chase the ducks your way. I'd point out all the hummingbirds and woodpeckers to you that flew by. I probably got half of them wrong. But you didn't seem to mind. When you'd take your naps, Mom would let me put you down in your crib. All that time I spent in foster care, I missed you. I missed our house and the way you used to giggle. I missed the way you used to smile at me."

She stopped long enough to swipe away the tears streaming down her cheeks. "Dad liked to fish. He talked about waiting for you to get big enough to go with him. He'd take you out to the Tuolumne River to catch trout for supper. And never let it be said that Robert Lambert didn't sometimes have a temper. But his mad never lasted for long before he'd be all apologetic and try to make up for it by doing something sweet, like swinging Mom into an impromptu dance. He'd stop at the Dairy Queen and bring me a chocolate shake, or if he didn't have time to make a stop, he'd get a Hershey bar out of the machine at work and hand it to me as a reward for being good. Whether I'd been good or not, it didn't matter to him. He loved tamales and he had this favorite street vendor he always went to if he was in the mood for Mexican food. We didn't have much money but he always saw to it we had what we needed. He did his best to make things better for us. Always."

Fat tears moved down Hannah's cheeks at the memories, memories she'd buried. Before she could go on, she noticed Andy had water misting from his eyes, too.

"What kind of person kills a mother and father and takes a baby away from his parents?"

"A monster, pure and simple. But you have me now and I have you. You'll always have me," Hannah offered. "You have family now, Andy. I hope you can find a place in your life for a big sister."

Andy reached out and circled his arms around Hannah's shoulders. "I'd be a fool to turn that down."

Thirty-One

That night, a winter moon hung in the night sky as an overflow crowd gathered inside Caleb's house for food and drink.

Andy—still six months away from being old enough to legally indulge in alcohol—sipped on a virgin margarita Hannah had blended especially for him. But after taking a taste, Faye and Beckham decided they wanted the lemonade, lime-aid concoction that was basically nothing more than sweet, frothy citrus juice.

"Don't go getting any ideas about adding tequila to that," Caleb cautioned. "At least not for another nine or ten years. Everybody knows it stunts your growth and kills brain cells."

Faye giggled at the warning. "Hannah already told us the same thing. I can't believe she's Andy's real sister. That makes her my half-sister."

It didn't really—certainly not by bloodlines—but Caleb didn't have the heart to throw water on the girl's willingness to accept the change in Andy or her own enthusiasm at the prospect.

Hannah slung an arm over the teen's shoulder, placed a kiss on her temple. "Any sister of Andy's belongs to my tribe…automatic."

Faye bounced on her toes. "Beckham has his, now I have mine."

"Exactly. You've got your own clan now, sista." Hannah gave the girl a fist bump explosion. "I even have a stepsister I want you to meet. Her name's Cassie."

Faye gigged with glee and threw her arms around Hannah's neck. "You are too cool."

Quentin overheard the declaration and came over to the island where Hannah and Caleb stood near the buffet. "Sydney and I've been talking. We've decided that after all the crappy things Douglas Bradford did to this town, it's time to reverse some of the damage. We're going with Logan's original idea and turning the house into a library but with one caveat. We need a middle school and a high school here. There are enough rooms upstairs alone to use for whatever classrooms we'll need. And the downstairs will make an excellent public library."

"That leaves plenty of room for computer and tech training," Logan added, slapping Quentin on the back. "Kinsey and I are returning half the money to Quentin. Together our families will officially donate the property to the town."

"We plan to get rid of the Bradford House name on the shingle immediately. That goes away first thing tomorrow morning as soon as Logan and I pick up a screwdriver and take down the sign."

Logan leaned in with a laugh. "That'll be me. Our only doctor shouldn't be handling tools he knows nothing about using."

Quentin looked downright insulted. "Hey, I own a set of socket wrenches. I know the difference between a Phillips and a flathead."

"Good for you," Logan returned. "Bring your tool belt with you and I'll bring my black doctor's bag."

"Fine. You take care of the shingle. I'll stand by and wait for you to ram a nail in your thumb and then we'll see who finishes what job."

"It'll take me all of five minutes to remove the sign," Logan predicted.

Caleb held up his hands for peace. "Guys, good-natured ribbing aside, the point is we're getting a library and school out of the deal, something that gets the middle schoolers and high school kids off that damn bus heading to San Sebastian nine months out of the year. It doesn't matter who does what. And it's all due to you guys coming through for the town."

Quentin smiled and nodded. "We'll formally get everyone together so we can dedicate the building with a ceremony calling it..." He glanced at Logan to let him make the big announcement.

"Ocean Street Academy."

"So, something good came out of this, after all," Hannah said. "It makes me glad I've found my permanent home here."

Andy came up next to Hannah. "I'm glad to hear that. I'd hate to get to know you and then see you pack up and leave."

"Nope. I'm staying put."

Andy lifted his glass. "Here's to Hannah Lambert, who always believed we'd be together again no matter how the odds were stacked against it happening."

Hannah's head rested on Andy's shoulder. "The odds were made considerably better by..." She looked around the room and whispered in her brother's ear, "Ever heard of a man named Scott Phillips?"

"The dead guy who walks around town as a ghost? Sure. Who hasn't? He came for a visit about two months after my parents...my adopted parents...died in that car accident. I was really down."

"No kidding. He's the reason I'm here. Scott brought me here to find you. What did he say when you saw him? Was it about me? Did he at least indicate someone was searching for you?"

Andy smiled broadly at all the questions and looked over at Caleb. "Unfortunately, nothing about that, which would have been a huge help."

Caleb scratched his jaw. "Scott seems to pop in and pop out at the best of times. But do you notice he never explains a damn thing?"

Hannah let out a laugh. "I don't know about that. Maybe it was supposed to play out like this. During it all, Caleb even found that murdered infant, which turned everything upside down and got us to this point. I'm curious about how Scott managed to appear to each of us without really tipping his hand. It's as if we were pieces on his giant chessboard to be maneuvered into place." She stared at Andy. "Under what circumstances did he appear to you?"

"I was up late one night worrying about Carla Vargas taking Faye away from me. I'd fallen asleep on the couch. I woke up about three in morning, half asleep, and there he was. I recognized the guy sitting on the arm of the recliner. But it still scared the crap out of me."

"Yeah. He does that," Caleb noted. "Infuriating."

"Anyway, he looked at me and said, 'Everything's gonna be okay. I promise. You'll see. Don't worry so much.' I thought I was losing it for sure. And then things weren't okay. I broke my arm working construction on the elementary school. It set Faye and me back months financially. Every time I had to take a low-paying job just to put food on the table I resented Scott telling me that, knowing how hard things were."

"Understandable. But I don't think Scott works within time constraints. Resolutions to kidnapping and murder take time. Oh, don't get me wrong. I was plenty impatient with him when he stopped coming around. Just ask Caleb. I knew Scott was obviously avoiding me so I wouldn't ask any more questions like, 'Where's Micah? Tell me where I can find Micah.' I kept bugging him about it. But when things turn out like this, it's hard to complain about Scott's 'big picture' not coming together exactly like we wanted it or fast enough. I discovered four months ago he's a difficult man to say no to, especially when he dangles what you want just within reach and then walks away."

"I guess you could say, he's a ghost with a plan, but doesn't feel the need to share the details with anyone," Andy surmised.

"That's Scott."

The celebration went on until people started to clear out.

After everyone left, Caleb and Hannah began to clean up the kitchen until finally he snatched her hand in his and grabbed a flashlight out of one of the cabinet drawers. He led her out the back door to the deck and down the steps into what could only be described as a pitch-black hole with just the flashlight to guide their way.

"Where are we going?"

"You looked like you could use a walk. I know just the place."

"It's after midnight, Caleb. And it's been a very emotional day for me. What am I saying? Ever since I set foot in Pelican Pointe it's been like a rollercoaster ride, so many ups and downs..."

"That's true, a lot of twists and turns for both of us," Caleb supplied. "We've been so slammed dealing with the past, on both fronts, that we haven't had a lot of time to touch on the future."

"The future for me includes my brother. I love saying those two words, 'my brother.' Wherever my parents are tonight, they must be dancing. They have to be wrapped up in each other moving to Nat King Cole, with a silly smile on their faces, knowing their babies found each other again after all this time."

"And that right there is the reason I love you, Hannah Summers," Caleb blurted out.

"I love you, too."

"I love your devotion to family, the way you endured those years alone in the system at such a young age. Through all the rough times, you never gave up."

They reached the tall, swaying beach grass and Caleb shined the beam of the flashlight into the field. "There's something I've wanted to show you for weeks now."

"For weeks? Really?"

"It's important."

When she noticed he was taking her farther into the darkness where the rolling meadow ended near the canal, her nerves jangled up her spine. "Caleb, is it safe out here? What if we run into a—"

He didn't let her finish. "Can't you feel the freedom? I can. There are no ghosts here tonight, Hannah. No super stalkers sent by Eleanor to derail our lives. No more putting up with her interference, her craziness."

He shined the light into the blackness, illuminating the field of fertile grasses behind the house where the rolling hills were like a miniature valley, so green and lush. "The first time I set eyes on this place, I thought about trying to grow grapes here."

"You never told me that."

"I didn't think you'd believe me. It was your dream. You're the one who voiced it first. I kept my mouth shut because the idea scared me silly, always has. Starting a vineyard, having my own winery was a daunting task. But not anymore. The thing is, I love living where I live. Right here. I don't want to move to the city. I don't want to live in a big house. I don't want to drive a fancy car."

"I'm hearing a lot of don'ts in there. What *do* you want?"

"I want my life here…with you." He held out his arms wide encompassing the expanse of land and what would one day, hopefully, be their vineyard. "I want to grow grapes here with you, Hannah. This place could be the best winery along the coast. We could cultivate the finest table grapes here because I've tested the soil. It'll grow just about anything we put in the ground. Imagine corking the first bottle of fruity chardonnay for sale, or a bottle of our own vibrant merlot, right here. We could do it together."

She hurled her arms around his neck. "I love you, Caleb. I believe we can pretty much do anything we set our minds to. We've proved that over these past months. We're so much better and stronger together. Our past is done and over with. We'll make a new beginning, a home here, a life, rich with family and friends. I can still manage the co-op while we work toward the winery, put every dime aside for our success. I want to put down roots that run deep and last long after I'm gone."

"We'll dance in the moonlight under the stars."

"Promise me it'll be every night that isn't raining."

"What's the matter with a little rain?"

She laughed and turned a circle in the beach grass that tickled her legs. "You're right. Why not make it every night? Let's dance and celebrate because I think these roots are taking shape even now."

He grabbed her around the waist. "You bet they are. Our roots...stronger...beneath winter sand."

Epilogue

Six weeks later
Pelican Pointe, California

Clusters of bright green spring clover covered the hillside near the lighthouse as Hannah breathed in the fragrant white flowers that attracted the bees. The new section of butter lettuce she'd tested out had already sprouted new patches from the seeds she'd planted, no doubt due to the generous March rains.

She walked the grounds, making her way through the rows of early bean sprouts, pleased the shoots were, so far, insect-free. Same could be said for the tomatoes that budded out in little green orbs all up and down the vines. Given enough warm sunshine, the fruit would ripen in a few weeks yielding bushels of tasty heirlooms.

The new stalks of celery poking up through the ground were a delight to her. So were the asparagus spikes that seemed to have grown an inch overnight.

She glanced over at Andy and Faye hard at work hoeing the ground. The two showed up like clockwork every Saturday morning, rain or shine, to help with the weeding. Andy insisted on paying back the co-op for all the times it had kept the wolf from the door during so many months he'd struggled to put food on the table.

It warmed Hannah's heart to see him so happy, standing there, hoe in hand, back bent over the crop of thriving strawberries as he destroyed the root of a stubborn chickweed while Molly looked on.

After running around earlier, the dog had exhausted her energy supply and seemed to be contemplating a nap.

Molly had fully recovered, and now, went everywhere Hannah went. Maybe that's what made working at the co-op such a pleasure. The freedom she felt, allowed her to fully appreciate having Molly in her life. They spent so much time outside together that the bond between the two had grown into something solid in a short amount of time.

Or maybe she was just happier all-around than she'd ever been before having Caleb in her life.

Whatever it was, every time Hannah looked at her brother she realized what a miracle it was that they were even within yelling distance of each other. She'd had to get used to the fact that Andy looked so much like her father it was eerie. Each time she was around him, it gave her a jolt of nostalgia. She'd get used to it over time, she supposed. But now, she simply enjoyed Andy's company and his wry sense of humor. The man, who'd had such a rough two years taking care of Faye, could relate a funny story with a wicked wit that had a crowd laughing. Hannah often teased him about becoming a stand-up comedian.

She went over to where he worked and pretended to inspect the dirt. "You and Faye are making great progress today. You'll be done by noon."

"Beckham wanted to help us this morning, but he's grounded," Andy said, swiping at the sweat on his forehead. "Apparently, he caused a major uproar in science class the other day by making one of his experiments explode all over the teacher's desk."

"Ah. That's never a good thing. No wonder Faye looks a little lost today."

"About that. Do you think her relationship with Beckham is getting a little too serious?"

"Uh-oh, I see that protective father-figure rear its head. I think they're fine. They're good kids. Does Faye miss curfew? Does she defy the rules you've set down?"

"No. Not yet."

"Then I think you're fine. Until she gives you a reason to worry, don't go looking to pick apart her only friend. She'll resent you for it."

"I guess you're right. I just don't want to blow this. The teen years are a lot of responsibility. I'm not sure I'm cut out for this role."

"You're doing a great job with her, Andy. Just remember, you also deserve a life. Don't forget that."

"My life right now consists of putting in ten-hour days so I don't have to worry about paying bills."

"Did you ever want to go to college?"

"Nah. My grades weren't that good in high school. I like working construction, building something with my hands. Ryder keeps reminding all of us what a remarkable thing we're doing by working on getting the hospital ready for its grand opening after Easter. It's a vital addition to the town."

"I know Quentin and Sydney are so excited they can hardly wait. They'll probably get lost in that huge space and need a map to find their way versus that tiny, overcrowded clinic."

Faye ran over to Hannah carrying her straw hat in her hand. "It smells so wonderful out here with all this stuff growing and coming to life. It'll be Easter soon. Do you have enough eggs for the overflow from Phillips Park? The kids will be upset if they get here and find out there are no eggs to hunt. Beckham and I already talked about volunteering to hide them from the little ones this year."

It had become a town tradition that the Saturday before Easter, the kids would head to the lighthouse after the town's official Easter Egg Hunt. After scooping up all the eggs the park had to offer there, the kids and parents would move on to the hilltop where the Easter Bunny would make his second grand appearance of the day.

This year, Barton Pearson had agreed to wear the full costume, complete with bunny head and giant ears, and the big rabbit feet. Word around town said Barton couldn't wait to strut around in his purple frock coat, the one designed by Cora Bigelow, hoping the outfit would add extra depth to the character.

"Thanks for the reminder. I'll have to order a lot more of those pastel plastic eggs that come apart. You know, the ones you can put candy inside or dump in those little tacky prizes. What I could use are two eager helpers willing to stuff them and get them ready to hide," Hannah said, testing the water for a volunteer.

"Beckham and I will do that, too."

"Super. Do you think Beckham will be out of trouble by then? I heard he's grounded."

"Sure. Sydney and Quentin weren't all that mad. Not really. They just needed to make a statement that said next time Beckham shouldn't blow anything up in chemistry lab near Mr. Proctor's desk."

"That sounds like good advice to me. I guess I'll head over to the keeper's cottage and order those bags of eggs, and just to be on the safe side, the chocolate candy to go inside."

Hannah called for Molly and took off for the office, which by Memorial Day would act as the general store where the co-op could sell additional goods, like preserves, jams, and jellies, to the tourists.

But as soon as she opened the door to the cottage, she heard arguing. She found Landon deep in dispute with Caleb. The two men immediately went silent when they spotted her standing in the doorway. "What's up, guys?"

"Nothing."

"You guys weren't arguing over nothing. What gives?"

Landon sighed and took a step back so she could see what was on the desk. "You might as well tell her. In fact, show her."

"Show me what?"

Caleb grunted and shook his head. "We don't know where it came from at least not specifically."

"Where what came from? What are you guys talking about?"

Caleb held out a small burlap sack with a brown branch sticking out of the opening.

"What is that?"

Caleb exchanged sheepish looks with Landon. "That's what I've been trying to figure out. The nearest I can tell is it's a rare grapevine root that hasn't been seen in Napa Valley since the Casa de Havilland Vineyard burned to the ground in 1939."

"You're kidding? How's that even possible? Where'd you get it?"

"I found it in a shipment of roses from one of our largest vendors out of Fairmont. It was in a special growing container about two feet long. This card was attached and addressed to you." Caleb handed her the cream-colored envelope with her name scrawled on the front. "I thought the vendor had made a mistake until I saw the card. I almost sent the canister back. I did call and the guy who handles all our orders and he basically questioned my sanity."

"He didn't send it?"

"Nope. He doesn't even know how it ended up on the truck. He accused me of making the whole thing up."

"Weird. Why would anyone send me a vine in a shipment of roses to The Plant Habitat?"

She ripped open the paper and took out the card, which had a picture of the vineyard on the cover before it had been destroyed. "Look at this. What a charming old photograph. How wonderful. Look at the sign in front of the winery. It says it was established in 1909 by the de Havilland family."

She flipped open the card but didn't recognize the handwriting.

"What does it say?" Caleb prompted. "I've been dying to find out who sent it."

This grape cutting is a descendant from the de Havilland family vineyard that specialized in merlot, a personal favorite of mine. It hasn't been seen in California since before the war. If you plan to start a vineyard of your own, you couldn't go wrong with this classic grape. It'll probably take three years for this seedling to produce its first fruit and another two to make enough for your first bottle. You have nothing but time to become the winemaker you want to be, to create that perfect blend of vino that pleases the palate. Enjoy every aspect of the process. Don't rush the grape.

I ask but a small favor. Your first bottle must be shared with Nick and his lovely wife, Jordan. It must take place overlooking the cliffs at Promise Cove, where my grandmother first told me the story about how her family started their vineyard when she was just a little girl. With any luck, she'll be looking down on that spot, at that moment in time, watching as a long-lost tradition is brought back to life, thanks to you, and to Caleb, and the dream you two share.

Our paths are unknown to us. But if you follow your heart and are true to yourself and the ones you love, your journey will always be a happy one. Remember that as you walk through life.

Hannah looked from Landon to Caleb. "It's signed by Scott. How could he possibly have written this?"

Caleb looked at the note. "Yep. That looks like something he'd write. I've seen several of these before."

He reached over to Hannah and tenderly wiped away a single tear that trickled down her cheek. "Good to know we're following our hearts then."

"It is. But I don't know how he does it—Scott always manages to get in the last word."

Dear Reader:

If you enjoyed *Beneath Winter Sand*, please take the time to leave a review.
A review shows others how you feel about my work.
By recommending it to your friends and family it helps spread the word.
If you have the time let me know via Facebook or my website.
I'd love to hear from you!

For a complete list of my other books visit my website.
www.vickiemckeehan.com

Want to connect with me to leave a comment?
Go to Facebook
www.facebook.com/VickieMcKeehan

Don't miss these other exciting titles by bestselling author

Vickie McKeehan

The Pelican Pointe Series
PROMISE COVE
HIDDEN MOON BAY
DANCING TIDES
LIGHTHOUSE REEF
STARLIGHT DUNES
LAST CHANCE HARBOR
SEA GLASS COTTAGE
LAVENDER BEACH
SANDCASTLES UNDER THE CHRISTMAS MOON
BENEATH WINTER SAND
KEEPING CAPE SUMMER (2018)

The Evil Secrets Trilogy
JUST EVIL Book One
DEEPER EVIL Book Two
ENDING EVIL Book Three
EVIL SECRETS TRILOGY BOXED SET

The Skye Cree Novels
THE BONES OF OTHERS
THE BONES WILL TELL
THE BOX OF BONES
HIS GARDEN OF BONES
TRUTH IN THE BONES
SEA OF BONES (2018)

The Indigo Brothers Trilogy
INDIGO FIRE
INDIGO HEAT
INDIGO JUSTICE
INDIGO BROTHERS TRILOGY BOXED SET

Coyote Wells Mysteries
MYSTIC FALLS
SHADOW CANYON
SPIRIT LAKE (2018)

ABOUT THE AUTHOR

Vickie McKeehan's novels have consistently appeared on Amazon's Top 100 lists in Contemporary Romance, Romantic Suspense and Mystery / Thriller. She writes what she loves to read—heartwarming romance laced with suspense, heart-pounding thrillers, and riveting mysteries. Vickie loves to write about compelling and down-to-earth characters in settings that stay with her readers long after they've finished her books. She makes her home in Southern California.

Find Vickie online at
https://www.facebook.com/VickieMcKeehan
http://www.vickiemckeehan.com/
https://vickiemckeehan.wordpress.com

CPSIA information can be obtained
at www.ICGtesting.com
Printed in the USA
FSHW021143211218
54621FS